this time FOREVER

OTHER BOOKS AND BOOKS ON CASSETTE
BY RACHEL ANN NUNES:

Ariana: The Making of a Queen

Ariana: A Gift Most Precious

Ariana: A New Beginning

Ariana: A Glimpse of Eternity

Love to the Highest Bidder

Framed for Love

Love on the Run

To Love and to Promise

Tomorrow and Always

this time FOREVER

a novel

Rachel Ann Nunes

Covenant Communications, Inc.

Published by Covenant Communications, Inc.
American Fork, Utah

Printed in the United States of America
First Printing: January 2001

08 07 06 05 04 03 02 01   10 9 8 7 6 5 4 3 2 1

ISBN 1-57734-787-0

*Dedicated to Susan Eyring Jones for sharing experiences
that helped me gain the necessary insight to write* This Time Forever.
*While this is not Susan's actual story, I feel the novel was
greatly enhanced by her recounting of real-life challenges.
Thank you, Susan! I pray that you and Mike receive
all the happiness you both deserve.*

CHAPTER 1

Sometimes Mickelle Hansen wished she had never married. Eternity was a long time to spend with someone she often didn't like very much. Of course, she didn't tell anyone her deepest thought; in fact, only recently had she begun to admit it to herself. And then only on days like this, when everything—absolutely every-thing—seemed to go wrong. Feeling this way about her marriage went against all she had ever been taught, and against all her dreams. Deep down, she loved Riley—she did. But when she had exchanged vows with him in the Provo Temple, she had never expected their life together to be so difficult.

She stared at the pile of dirty laundry filling a corner of the unfin-ished basement where the washer and dryer stood like mismatched sentinels, witnesses to her newest dilemma. For two weeks the washing machine had refused to work, and she had been cleaning the most necessary items in the bathtub. Her neighbor, who had already fixed the washer twice as a favor, had told her this time that it wasn't worth fixing again. "You need a new one," he had declared, shaking his graying head.

She had hoped Riley would do something about finding a machine, but wasn't surprised when he didn't. Instead, his solution was for her to go to the Laundromat. Indefinitely.

Dutifully, Mickelle piled clothes in several large baskets and took them to the ancient Ford station wagon that gleamed a dull gold in her driveway. Secretly she called it the Snail, but she never said it aloud the way she once would have. It was too real to joke about.

Outside, the late April weather was warm and filled with sunshine. A beautiful, perfect day. There were a few clouds to the east that would probably bring showers that night or the next day, but Mickelle didn't mind the rain. Her peas, planted early last month, needed the moisture.

She drove to the Laundromat in downtown American Fork near her home. While the place wasn't overly dirty, there was a certain air of depression and despair about it. She could have endured that, as she had so many other things, but balked when she considered the cost of washing her family's clothes each week. They only had two children, but Riley was a large man, if not tall, and the dirty clothes he generated took up half the space in each load. Then there were Jeremy's sheets, still wet several nights of the week. In the long run, buying a machine would save time and money. She had suggested as much to Riley last week, but his mind was made up.

Moving past the dryers, she caught sight of a faint reflection in the glass. A slender woman with smooth, honey-blonde hair, blue eyes, and a pinched face stared back at her. Could that weary-looking woman really be her? Rebellion welled up inside her heart. Why did Riley have to be so stubborn?

She left the Laundromat and took the clothes instead to her older sister's house in Provo, feeling like an idiot and glad that her two sons were in school and couldn't witness the lies or half-truths she might be forced to tell.

"Mickelle! What happened?" Talia looked with surprise at the laundry Mickelle carried.

"My washing machine broke. I was going to the Laundromat, but couldn't bear the thought of hanging out there. Do you mind terribly if I use yours? I brought soap."

"Of course you can!" Talia took the basket out of her hands. "You shouldn't have even thought about going to the Laundromat. What are sisters for? You can use my machine—and my soap, for that matter—whenever you want."

"Well, it's only for today. I'm sure Riley will get me a new one very soon." Mickelle nearly choked on the lie, but Talia didn't seem to notice. "I'd better get the rest."

She headed back to the car, wishing she could toss off the sadness that seemed to eat at her heart. Why couldn't she face her trials with a better outlook? Why was she so weak?

Inside the house, she found Talia sorting the laundry into piles with her quick hands. Mickelle joined her, feeling her burden lighten.

"You know," Talia said casually, "last night I saw some ads in the paper for washing machines. I haven't thrown it out yet. Want to look?" At Mickelle's nod, she disappeared from the laundry room.

Mickelle finished the sorting, put in a load of whites, and started the machine. The room had ample space for the appliances, as well as an extra refrigerator and a long counter that held seven large baskets—one for each member of the family. She knew even Talia's six-year-old folded and put away her own clothing. Mickelle thought she might try something similar at her own house. Riley, of course, wouldn't have the time or inclination to do his, but the boys would. A pity she didn't have a nice room like this. Mickelle stopped the thought there, unwilling to let envy enter her heart. Talia was a wonderful person, and Mickelle was glad that she and Joe could afford such a nice house.

"Here they are." Talia came into the room with the same newspaper Mickelle had noticed at the Laundromat. "At Sears. Look at this—only three hundred dollars, and it's a super capacity. A bare-bones model, but still super capacity. You'll need that for Jeremy's sheets. Looks like a good deal to me."

"A lot cheaper than going to the Laundromat forever," Mickelle agreed.

Talia threw back her blonde head and laughed. "You're so funny. What a waste—who would do that? Besides, you deserve a new machine. Aren't you still using the old one Mom gave you when you got married?"

Mickelle smiled weakly. "You know me, frugal to a fault."

"Well, come on, let's go have a snack while we're waiting."

"Maybe I should zip down to Sears and see about a machine."

"Why don't you let Riley worry about that?"

Mickelle swallowed hard. "Well, he's been busy. Working overtime, you know." She didn't mention how much they needed the money.

"That's really great of him, working more so you don't have to."

Mickelle wondered what her sister would say if she told her that even though Riley worked a lot, she hadn't yet seen any of the extra income. Mostly it went to pay for the new stereo system he'd installed in his truck. "I wish he could get a better job," she said instead. "Although they've promised him a promotion. The pay just isn't that great until you get into upper management."

"Well, department stores aren't known for their high-paying jobs."

How well Mickelle knew that! Years ago, she had urged Riley to go back to school so he could find a better job, but he had refused.

"If you want to go down to Sears, I'll wash your clothes for you," Talia offered.

Mickelle knew she should look into possibly buying a used machine, but she didn't have enough cash. Buying it on credit seemed the only way. And suddenly, more than anything, she wanted to buy a washer. A new one. One that had never washed anyone else's clothing. Something that was all hers.

"Mickelle, did you hear me?" Talia said. "I'll wash your clothes if you want to run to Sears."

"Would you? You don't have to dry them. My dryer still works."

Talia laughed. "Yeah, right. I can just see you taking home baskets full of wet clothes. Very funny. I wish you'd come over more often. You make me laugh."

"Well, my toaster isn't working so well," Mickelle replied dryly. "How about if I come over every morning for breakfast?" Talia broke into laughter once again. Mickelle remembered a time when she had made everyone laugh, but she hadn't found much to joke about in the past few years.

Chuckling herself, she drove straight to Sears, where she found the least expensive washing machine and put it on her credit card. The salesman promised to have it delivered the next day. Mickelle felt good, even excited, as she drove back to her sister's house. She told herself Riley would understand.

He didn't. "You shouldn't have gone against me," he said that evening, his face turning so red that Mickelle thought he closely resembled a tomato with a rotten brown stem for hair.

She had waited until the two boys were in bed before telling him about her purchase. She had almost not mentioned it at all, but decided that even Riley would notice when a new machine turned up in the basement.

"It's going to save us money in the long run," she pointed out.

"That doesn't matter." His tongue wet his lips, and he flexed his large hands. "I can't believe you went against what I told you to do. I am the head of our family, aren't I?"

At that, her anger flared. "Well, *you* go to the Laundromat every week. I don't have the time! I can't believe you'd want me to do that, anyway!" *Joe would never expect it of Talia.* Tears of hurt filled her eyes, and she quickly ran to the bathroom, hoping the children were asleep and couldn't hear their fight.

Riley didn't speak to her for three days, except to ask what was for dinner. At least his silence meant that he didn't comment again about the washing machine or her insubordination. She noticed that while he might not have approved of buying the machine, he wore the clothes she washed in it.

The third night of the silent treatment, Mickelle felt close to a nervous breakdown. She wished there was someone she could talk to, but she had kept up the facade of a happy marriage for so long that she didn't know how to confess her problems. Especially to her parents or sisters.

After dinner, the family sat in front of the television in the living room. Mickelle lounged on the sofa with the boys, and Riley settled into his easy chair. Next to him was a mound of newspapers that would grow until Mickelle could no longer stand it and would haul them to the recycling bin herself.

In the corner, her curio cabinet nearly reached the ceiling. She and Riley had been married fourteen years, and it was the only piece of furniture they had that wasn't a hand-me-down from her mother or sisters or a cheap piece made of particle board. She had bought it on sale eight years ago, the month after Jeremy was born. In it she collected roses made of metal, crystal, porcelain, wood, or even clay. The ones she had purchased herself were inexpensive, found either at yard sales or on clearance at the department store where Riley worked. Many had been gifts from family and friends—even the boys had made her clay roses in school. All were treasured and brought her much joy. Her favorites were the crystal rose she had picked out for the top of her wedding cake and the hand-painted porcelain Capodimonte long-stemmed red rose Riley had given her for their first anniversary. Mickelle had always loved roses, but the real things were so expensive and died so quickly. In her collection, she could have them forever.

Contemplating the curio cabinet and its contents usually gave her satisfaction, but not tonight. She sighed, her heart heavy with melancholy. Jeremy noticed her depression and put his thin arms around her neck. Even at eight he was very sensitive to her moods. "I love you, Mommy," he whispered. Her arms tightened around him, and she touched her head against his blonde locks. How glad she was that he was hers!

Twelve-year-old Bryan looked up briefly from his Game Boy, a small, handheld game computer. "Everything okay, Mom?" he asked.

"Sure. Did you finish your homework?"

He didn't answer but gave a disgusted sigh, his brown eyes returning to the game. Riley didn't look away from the TV.

"Well, did you?" Mickelle pressed.

"Leave the boy alone," Riley snapped, throwing a glare her way. "He's old enough to take care of himself."

Mickelle swallowed hard, biting back sharp words as she so often did. Tears stung her eyes. Obviously he was still mad about the washing machine, and he wasn't going to let her forget it any time soon.

Bryan's Game Boy dropped to his lap. He looked back and forth between Riley and Mickelle, his long blonde bangs falling into his eyes. "I'll do it now, Mom," he said in a low voice. He left the room and didn't return.

An hour later, when Mickelle went to check on Bryan after tucking Jeremy into bed, his light was off and she assumed he was asleep. Tiptoeing softly into the room, she saw him lying half under the covers, one arm dangling off the bed. She tucked the blanket around him, kissing him softly on the forehead. "I love you," she murmured. Then she went to her room, lay down on the bed, and sobbed.

When Riley came in, he watched her in silence for a while. Finally he spoke. "I'm sorry."

She recognized the tone and knew what was coming next. Everything would be all right now. For a time. She stopped crying, though her heart was still heavy.

He stared at her with sincere brown eyes so much like Bryan's—the beautiful, sensitive brown eyes she had fallen in love with. "Do you want a divorce?" He always asked that after he had made her unhappy. She supposed it was his way of asking for forgiveness.

She pushed herself wearily up on one elbow. "No. Of course not. I love you." She wiped the tears from her cheeks.

He sat on the bed and ran his finger along her arm. Then he pulled her close and kissed her. She didn't resist, although she had no real desire to be near him. If she drew away, he would become sullen and angry, and she would have to face more days of loneliness and isolation.

Later, while he was dressing for bed, she went into the kitchen and ate a glazed donut she had saved from the day before. She ate it quickly and eagerly, licking the sugar from her lips and enjoying the peace of the quiet house. How wonderful it was to eat something alone, without having to share with the children or clean up after them! Though she loved them deeply, their demands were difficult to keep up with—and she only had two. She didn't know how her sisters, Talia and Brionney, each kept up with their five, and Lauren her six. Even her brother, who lived in France, had four boys.

The indulgence of eating the donut made her feel better, though she wasn't prone to binging. Her own eating was the one thing she could control in her life. She wasn't as slim as when she was first married, and certain places could use a little toning, but she still fit into her clothes. On good days, she knew she looked attractive.

"What are you doing?"

Mickelle started. She looked up to see Riley, dressed in striped pajamas, staring at her from the door. "Just having a snack," she said quickly. "I didn't eat much at dinner."

He approached and eyed the empty donut box. "Well, you don't want to get fat."

She stood and put her arms around his thick chest. She was tall for a woman, like her grandmother, and he was on the short side for a man, so she looked straight into his eyes. "Don't worry, I won't. And I'll buy you some more donuts tomorrow." Of course, that was the real reason for his comment. She massaged his back with her hands.

"Ahhh, that's nice." He put his face against her neck, and his hot breath sent warm shivers up her spine. For this moment, at least, she forgot about wanting to escape her marriage. They had problems, to be sure, but they could work it out. Love lingered in her soul like a seed ready to sprout and bloom.

"Want to watch a little TV before we turn in?"

Though it was already past ten, Mickelle nodded and went with him into the living room. She thought fleetingly how she wished the basement were finished, or at least partially, so they could have a family room. *No,* she corrected herself mentally. *I should be grateful we have three bedrooms upstairs so the boys don't have to share.*

She sat on the couch, and Riley settled in front of her on the floor. She continued to rub his shoulders while he picked up the remote and found a late-night show on one of the local channels. Though she was tired, she quickly became caught up in the movie.

Abruptly, Riley's shoulders jerked out from under her hands. His body began to twitch violently. A seizure! He hadn't had one of those for years.

Mickelle dropped to her knees and tried to hold him so he wouldn't injure himself. His arms and legs thrashed like the tail of a beached fish, and his eyes rolled in helpless terror. The jerking motions seemed to last forever, but Mickelle held him until the seizure finally ended.

"Are you all right?" she asked, her voice trembling.

"I think so."

But she could tell he was shaken. "I'll call the doctor." She started to her feet.

He grabbed her hand. "It can wait until tomorrow."

Mickelle hesitated. As a child, Riley had been hit by a car while riding his bike, and in the wake of his injuries his brain had developed scar tissue that had caused seizures throughout his life. They had been controlled by medication, but three years earlier the doctors had been able to remove the scar tissue, and the seizures stopped. He had continued the medication in decreasing dosages for another year, but he had been medication-free for the past two. The doctor had told them he would most likely never suffer another seizure in his lifetime.

So why had he?

"Come on. Let's go to bed." Riley lurched heavily to his feet. "I'm okay, really."

Mickelle tried to take his arm in the narrow hall, but he shrugged her off. He slumped onto their bed, and she watched him for a moment to make sure he was all right. Then she went into the bathroom to brush her teeth. Afterward, she checked the boys to make sure they were safe in their rooms. When she returned, Riley was snoring softly.

She touched the back of his head tenderly before kneeling to pray. *Please help him,* she pleaded.

Riley had changed since the seizures had stopped three years ago. Before, he had been sullen, hesitant, and shy. Now, while still reserved around others and at times very sullen, he was more outgoing and confident. He also seemed more self-centered and quick to anger. Though all the changes weren't positive, Mickelle believed he was progressing emotionally in ways he hadn't been able to as a child and young adult, when the constant fear of having a seizure loomed over him. Sometimes she wondered if he was reliving the youth he'd never been able to enjoy—perhaps that was the reason for his truck and the new stereo system. This could simply be a phase in his delayed development. He might actually be growing into the man she thought she'd married.

As she slipped between the covers, an uneasy feeling crept into bed with her. Riley appeared all right now, but what if he wasn't? Would the seizures return again? She knew that would break his heart.

Mickelle fell asleep wondering what the next day would bring.

CHAPTER 2

Rebekka Massoni was bored with life. At twenty-four, she had already accomplished many of her life goals. She had served a successful mission to her native France, she was an accomplished pianist, she had college degrees in French and English, and she now worked as a translator for the American Embassy in Paris. She was thinking about going back to school for a doctorate in English.

Many friends and family envied her achievements, but the goals closest to her heart had gone unrealized. The modern Rebekka didn't dare share her sentiments with anyone, except lately with Brionney, her American friend who was far enough away that Rebekka didn't feel embarrassed by confiding her deepest emotions. Besides, Brionney understood very well why Rebekka felt as she did. After all, she had once loved the same man who now filled Rebekka's dreams.

Rebekka sighed and closed the latest mystery novel by Mary Higgins Clark, her favorite American author. In four strides, she was through the French doors and on the balcony that ran the length of her mother's kitchen, looking down eight stories to the ground below. People walked along the cobblestone sidewalks, mostly carrying groceries from the market, occasionally holding a child's small hand. Grizzled old men sat on wooden benches in front of the café, talking and enjoying the warm day. Though Rebekka was too far up to see, she knew that many would be smoking cigarettes or eating pastries from the café as they watched the passersby and talked about the good old days.

She smiled to herself and leaned over the balcony to catch the slight breeze. Her long auburn hair—so dark it was almost brown—

fell over her shoulders. "Hmm," she said with a sigh. The smell of fresh bread permeated the Saturday morning air, reminding her that she had not yet eaten. Still she lingered, watching the old men below.

The "good old days" were in her mind much more than she would like to admit. Back then, she had still believed that Marc would wake up one day and realize how much he loved her—not as a friend or sister, but as a woman, as someone who would love him for eternity. He would take her in his arms and ask her to marry him and kiss her lips, her eyes, her face . . .

It had happened only in her dreams. She had loved Marc Perrault since he had come into her life when she was five years old. At first she had idolized him—probably because he had saved her mother's life when she had been caught in the terrorist bombing on a train in Paris. In the blast, he had sustained damage to both his kidneys that had later resulted in a transplant to save his life. The romance of his sacrifice had impressed her even at such a young age. Over the past nineteen years, her love had matured from the idolization of a schoolgirl to the love of a woman for a man. Yet Marc still treated her like a little sister.

She began to pace from one end of the balcony to the other in frustration, her right fist punching halfheartedly into the palm of her left hand. Why couldn't she make him see her as a woman?

"Rebekka, are you here?" Danielle called from the kitchen in a voice as soft as velvet.

"Coming, Mother." Rebekka went through the French doors and into the kitchen, shutting them behind her. Her mother came toward her, dressed in a gray robe that exactly matched her eyes. She had long, dark-auburn hair, high cheekbones, and a slender figure. People often said how much Rebekka and Danielle looked and sounded alike, more like sisters than mother and daughter. Rebekka found that hard to believe. She had always thought her mother was the most beautiful woman in the world. Even nearing fifty, she possessed a childlike innocence that Rebekka knew wasn't a pretense.

"Ah, there you are," Danielle said. She kissed Rebekka on both cheeks. "Marc rang below just now. He's coming up."

"He didn't need to. I could meet him downstairs."

Her mother smiled. "A gentleman always picks a lady up at her door."

Rebekka snorted. "Oh, Mother, this isn't a date. We're going to sing in the street with the missionaries and hand out flyers. Marc's like a brother, you know that. Could you ever imagine my own darling brother Raoul coming up to get me?"

Danielle's gray eyes grew melancholy. "It's a shame you feel that way. I know Marc's ten years older than you, but he'd make a good husband."

Rebekka turned from her mother to grab her Mary Higgins Clark book from the table—anything to hide her pain. "Yeah," she agreed softly. "A shame."

Her mother didn't notice her emotions. She never did; she took people at face value, accepting them for the front they presented. It would never occur to Danielle that Rebekka was in love with Marc unless she said so.

"Speaking of Raoul, where is he?" Danielle opened a cupboard and took out a mug for her morning milk.

"He had to work. He and André are finishing the designs for that new road the firm's building. Marc should be working as well, but he had promised the missionaries that he . . ."

Rebekka let her words trail off as her father entered the kitchen. He went to Danielle and drew her into his arms, kissing her deeply. "Why didn't you wake me up?"

Danielle put her arms around her husband. "With the hours you've been working, you've needed your sleep."

"I can't sleep without you next to me." Philippe kissed her tenderly again before releasing her. He turned to greet Rebekka with the customary kisses on her cheeks. "Good morning, daughter. And where are you off to today?"

"Marc's coming, and we're going to the marketplace."

Her father frowned, and the look in his blue eyes was intense. "With the missionaries again? I wish you wouldn't."

"I promised." Rebekka knew her father didn't approve of his wife and children's decision to join the Mormon Church, but she was grateful that he'd become tolerant enough to allow the membership. There had been a time when he wouldn't have permitted any of his family to set foot in a Mormon chapel, but over the years, Danielle had even convinced him to come to special Church activities occasionally. He doted on her, and she continued to love him with complete and blind abandon, despite his pagan ways. Though her father wasn't a member and Danielle couldn't have the temple marriage she craved, Rebekka envied their relationship. It was better than her imaginary one with Marc.

The door buzzer saved her from further discussion. "I'll get it." As Rebekka flew to the door, her heart beat rapidly in anticipation of seeing Marc. Involuntarily, she ran through ideas on how to get him to notice her. She had tried everything from subtle hints to purposely trying to make him jealous—nothing had worked. After her mission, she had even kissed him once on the mouth one night when he had taken her to the movies, but he had thought she was teasing.

Some joke.

The only joke here was that she was hopelessly in love with a handsome, dark-haired older man who didn't return her affections. A part of her thought that if he had married, she could have overcome her obsession. But another part vowed that she would never be whole without him.

"Marc, hi." She greeted him by kissing him on each cheek, enjoying the feel of his skin and the smell of his cologne. With the force of long habit, she stifled the urge to throw herself into his arms. "I'm ready. It's not cold, is it?"

"You could probably use a sweater." He gave her an indulgent smile, and his deep brown eyes twinkled.

Rebekka would almost swear that he wanted to ruffle her hair as he had done when she was a child. Swallowing with difficulty, she said, "It'll just take me a second."

But Marc was already heading for the kitchen, where Philippe and Danielle could be seen as they prepared breakfast together. "I'll just say hi to your parents. We have time."

Rebekka looked in the hall closet before remembering that she had left her good sweater in her bedroom. When she returned to the kitchen, Marc was sitting at the table, sipping a cup of hot chocolate. He sat across from Danielle, who cupped a warm mug of plain milk in her long, graceful hands. Between them was a plate of croissants. Philippe stood by the counter, pouring himself a cup of steaming coffee.

"So I don't know how much good standing there and giving out flyers is going to do," Philippe was saying.

You're just embarrassed because your colleagues might recognize me, Rebekka wanted to say. But she didn't, because one simply didn't say such things to her father.

"We're just doing our part." Marc spoke to Philippe, but his eyes were on Danielle. Rebekka knew every curve of his beloved face; in her dreams she had caressed the closely shaven cheeks, run her hands through the hair that he now wore long on top, and entwined herself in his arms.

Rebekka stopped walking toward them suddenly. She stared at Marc. He still watched Danielle, and on his face was the same expression her father wore when he looked at her mother.

No!

Her mind rejected the thought immediately. *He's mine! He may not know it yet, but he is mine. I've waited so long . . .*

But she couldn't deny the truth staring at her. She had just discovered the biggest irony of all. No wonder Marc had never married—he was in love with her mother!

The aroma of her father's coffee pervaded the kitchen. For years, she had linked the smell to her father and security, but all at once it had turned into something devastating.

Now that she knew the dreadful truth, she saw that Marc's feelings had been obvious all along. He had always made excuses to be near Danielle. He was the first to volunteer to go to the store for Danielle or to drive her to a doctor's appointment. Anything she wished, Marc had been willing to do. When Rebekka had been little, he had often taken her roller blading or to the park, and he had always been the one to help her with her homework. He had even taken her to get her driver's license, and to nearly every church or school activity. Rebekka had believed he had done those things because he liked her, but now she understood that he had done it all to be close to Danielle. Rebekka was nothing to him but a pest—a name she had heard him use more than once when he wasn't aware she could hear. She had thought he said it tenderly, but now she wasn't so sure.

Memory after memory assaulted her—occasions when Marc had arranged to be close to Danielle. Most vividly, Rebekka remembered the many times during the past year when she had thought about moving out on her own, only to be urged by Marc to stay with her parents. Of course! Without her in the apartment, what reason would he have to visit?

Was even their friendship a farce?

This thought cut Rebekka to the very core. She might be able to stand not having Marc return her love, but she couldn't take not being his friend. His friendship had been a mainstay in her life since she had been five years old. At this dreadful thought, her stomach heaved and acid stung her throat.

"Rebekka, what's wrong, honey?" Danielle asked in her soft voice. "You look pale."

"I don't feel too well," Rebekka managed. "I—Marc, you're going to have to go without me. I think—I'm going to be sick." She ran from the kitchen to the bathroom, locking the door behind her. With one hand she braced herself against the sink, and with the other turned on the cold water. She splashed her face repeatedly until the nausea subsided.

"Rebekka?" Her mother's voice came from the other side of the door.

Rebekka looked in the mirror at her face, red now with cold. Her gray eyes stared back at her, large and haunted. She clenched her teeth and lifted her firm jaw, the only physical endowment she had received from her father. "I'm okay, Mother. I'm going to take a bath and lie down. Tell Marc I'm not going. I'm sorry."

But she wasn't sorry. She wanted to rip his eyes out and throw them off the balcony. And then throw her mother off after him! *How could I have been so blind all this time? How could I not see that Marc loved you instead of me?*

Rebekka didn't cry. She was through wasting time crying for Marc. She was through being used. Sinking to the floor, she sat with her chin on her knees, holding her misery firmly inside until the urge to weep ceased.

Now, what to do.

Numbness settled over her heart. Marc was forever out of her reach, and she couldn't stay where she would see him so often. Even once a week at church would be too painful. No, she had to get over him once and for all.

America.

The thought was unexpected, but not unwelcome. Yes. Others had gone to America and found their dreams. Josette, Marc's twin, and his other sister, Marie-Thérèse, had done so. Both were now back in Paris, happily married and enjoying their children. Why couldn't she find her own dream in America? She might never have to face Marc again.

She rose resolutely to her feet, slipped off her shoes, and opened the bathroom door slowly. When she was assured her mother wasn't waiting outside, she crept soundlessly down the hall to her own room. Making sure the door was locked, she went to the phone by the bed and dialed the number in Anchorage, Alaska, where Brionney was temporarily living with her husband and five children.

"Hello?" Brionney's voice sounded groggy, and Rebekka belatedly remembered the time difference. With a twinge of guilt, she realized that for Brionney it was the middle of the night.

"Oh, I'm sorry, Brionney," Rebekka said in French. "It's me, Rebekka. I forgot about the time difference. It's morning here."

"It's okay," Brionney answered in French. "I was up with Forest anyway. In fact, I was singing him a French lullaby. Or actually, all the French songs I know. They seem to calm him. Or maybe they're calming me. Anyway, as soon as I get him back to sleep, it'll be Gabriel's turn to wake up and eat, though he'll go back to bed a lot more quickly."

"It must be difficult having twins." Rebekka tried to keep the envy from her voice.

"Yeah, but Jesse helps a lot. I'm still nursing, but they've been taking bottles for the past four months. I can't keep up with their demand. Some mothers of twins can, but not me." There was a cry in the background, and Brionney sighed. "Especially Forest's demands. Good thing he's so cute." She paused before asking, "So what's up?"

"I've been thinking . . ." Now that she was talking to Brionney, Rebekka was having second thoughts. Leaving France was a big step, and she would miss many things. What about her family and her job? Maybe leaving wasn't the answer. Then she remembered the way Marc had watched her mother. Why couldn't he look at her like that? New pain surged through her body. "I—I'm feeling a little trapped here. I was wondering if there was any way I could . . . I mean, it's just until I sort things out."

"You want to come and stay with me for a while?" In her excitement, Brionney forgot to speak in French. "But that would be too wonderful! I would absolutely *love* to have you come. It'd give me someone to practice French with—you can tell mine's getting rusty. Right now, I can't remember a word! That happens when I get excited."

"Just lack of practice," Rebekka said in English. "I speak English a lot at work, and at church we have the American missionaries."

"And Zack." Brionney sounded sad. Her brother had married Josette and moved to France. Rebekka had seen him more times in the past year than Brionney would for the rest of her life. Yet despite the distance, Rebekka knew Zack had stayed close to his favorite sister.

"You miss him."

"Yes, but he's with Josette and their children where he's supposed to be. And he comes home at least once a year. But I missed his visit last year because I was here."

"When are you leaving Alaska?"

"Soon. Jesse and our friend Damon have decided to go into business together. They're going to customize Jesse's hospital program and market it all over America. Damon seems to think it'll go big. He's already a multimillionaire—everything he touches turns to gold. Jesse's really excited, and I am too, because it means we can go back to Utah now. I miss my family."

As she said it, Rebekka suddenly missed her own family. But her parents and Raoul would be able to get along without her for a while. At least she wouldn't have to face Marc. *He loves my mother!* Her chest tightened until she wanted to scream, and she had to fight to listen to Brionney's words.

"So when will you be coming to visit?"

Rebekka's grip on the receiver was so tight that her hand ached. "As soon as you return to Utah. Let me know once you have a date."

"I can't wait, Rebekka," Brionney crowed enthusiastically. "Wait till you see how big the kids are! But what about a visa? Won't that take time?"

"I work for the embassy, remember? I can pull some strings."

"Oh, that's right."

There was a brief silence. "Thanks, Brionney," Rebekka said quietly. "You don't know what this means to me."

"Does this have something to do with Marc?"

Rebekka took a breath. "Yeah."

"Did you talk to him?" Brionney had been urging Rebekka to tell him how she felt.

"No. Not exactly." What would Brionney say if she knew Marc was in love with Danielle? "I—I just think it's time I moved on. I can't wait forever. He's already thirty-four. I don't think he's ever going to change."

"I'm sorry," Brionney said quietly. "I really am. Believe me, I know what it's like to have to leave him. But maybe your leaving will help him realize what's important."

Rebekka wanted to believe that Marc would come to his senses, that he would recognize how much she meant to him and come after her. But she knew he wouldn't. Once Brionney had loved him, and when she had returned to America, he hadn't gone after her. Their relationship had simply been over. "It didn't help you," she observed.

"What I felt for Marc was friendship," Brionney insisted. "There was never anything else. We both wanted it to be something else, but he . . . never mind. What's important is that I found my happiness. It wouldn't have been fair to either Marc or myself if we had tried to make things work. I'm supposed to be with Jesse. I know that. I love him, and he loves me. Someday you'll find the man you're supposed to be with—I know you will."

"I guess." The problem was that Rebekka felt Marc was supposed to be hers. She had believed it for so long that she didn't know how to go about thinking anything else. But her whole life had changed since that morning. Knowing what she did, she couldn't wait for Marc anymore. She still loved him, but maybe love wasn't everything. Maybe love wasn't enough.

Maybe there was even someone else out there for her.

"Our plans should be finalized soon," Brionney said. "I've already packed everything but the essentials. There was a brief pause. "Oh no, Gabriel's awake. I have to go now. I'll call you in a week or so."

Rebekka thanked her again and hung up the phone. She felt good about her decision and Brionney's response, but there was a little knot of fear in her stomach as well.

She slipped to her knees at the side of the bed. "Father," she whispered, "I've made a decision, as I've always been taught to do before asking You for confirmation. Oh, I know I made it a little hastily—Mother would say that's Dad's influence, You know, depending on my own knowledge and desires instead of Yours. I'm sorry. But I do feel it's the right thing for me. I just can't bear to look at Marc. I can't stand it anymore that he doesn't love me like I love him. Please let me know I have Your blessing in this decision. Is this the right thing for me?"

After her prayer, Rebekka continued to feel positive about going to America. The only thing she regretted was not going months earlier; she had already wasted so much time. She came to her feet, moved to a desk in the corner, and began a list of the things she would need to do before she left. The first hurdle was her job, but it shouldn't be too difficult to take a leave of absence—perhaps a permanent one. Who knew what adventures awaited her in America?

She wouldn't tell her family until her plans were set, and then she would swear them to secrecy. The vindictive part of her hoped Marc would be a little hurt and angry when he finally heard that she was gone.

"I'll get over you yet," she promised. Another wave of pain battered her bruised heart, but Rebekka refused to give in to tears.

"America," she said, "like the pilgrims of old, here I come."

CHAPTER 3

Damon Wolfe yawned as he looked in on his sleeping children. By choice, Tanner slept in the far end of the house near the spacious game room and the hot tub. He was fifteen and beginning to show his independence.

Isabelle—or Belle—just five years old, slept in the room next to Damon's. If the truth were told, the little girl more often than not ended up in her father's bed. He didn't mind; there was plenty of room, as there had been even in the years before his wife's death. Charlotte had stayed in a room by herself as she fought to survive the cancer that so viciously consumed her frail body. Her nurse and constant companion had often found it necessary to sleep in the same room to care for her, especially as Charlotte's condition deteriorated. At home, Damon had grown used to being alone or having only the children for company.

Belle was curled around a large brown teddy bear that Damon had brought home for her when she was three—just before Charlotte died. She loved that bear and slept with it every night.

"You're home, Daddy!" Belle opened her eyes sleepily, and her little arms reached out for him. "I tried to wait up, but Marina said I had to sleep. She said you might not be home tonight."

"She was right. You must listen to your nanny when I'm not here." Damon sat on the bed and pulled her warm body into his arms. "Ah, but I missed you, ma Belle," he said. He'd taken French in college and learned that *ma belle* meant "my beauty." He thought the name had fit Belle from the moment of her birth. She had soft brown hair that fell to her neck in gentle curls, a round face, and rosy cheeks—each feature an endowment from her mother. The only legacy from him were the large brown eyes that held a hint of amber.

"I missed you too, Daddy." She pulled away and regarded him soberly. "Is it true we're going to leave Anchorage? Tanner said we were, but I didn't believe him."

"I've been thinking about it very seriously. And, yes, I think we're going to move to Utah."

"Is it because of Kar? I mean, Karissa?"

Damon held his breath, then let it out slowly. "Partly," he admitted. His heart still hurt when he thought about how much he cared for Karissa. He should have known better than to allow himself to care for a married woman. There had never really been anything between them, of course, except the deep feelings in his heart.

"Is her baby okay now?"

"I think so. Remember that doctor I found for Kar? Well, he did a great job on baby Steph's surgery."

"Then Karissa doesn't need you anymore. Is that why we're going?"

Karissa certainly didn't need him anymore. She and her husband were working out their problems. Damon believed they would be happy. Still, knowing this didn't alleviate the longing in his heart to be whole again. While falling in love with Karissa, he had finally stopped missing Charlotte.

"We're going because I think it'll be good for Daddy's and Jesse's business, and for the hospitals we want to help. That's where I was today—talking to some hospitals."

"But why can't we stay here?"

"Because there are a lot of people who want to work for us in Utah. A lot of students. And because Jesse's wife has family there. She misses them."

"I know. She told me." Belle's face grew sad. "I'm going to miss my friends, too."

Damon smiled. "Oh, but that's the best part. Rosalie will be there, remember? All of Jess and Bri's children will be there. You like them, don't you?"

"Yes." Her voice was still subdued.

"And I'll be home more."

At this she smiled. "Promise?"

"I do." He hugged her tightly. "And it may take some time, but I promise you're going to love it."

"Can I have a horse there?" Belle asked. Horses were her latest craze.

"We'll see. Maybe."

"I love you, Daddy."

"I love you, too, ma Belle." He settled back on her pillow and pulled the blankets over them both.

Belle lifted her head suddenly. "Will Marina come with us?"

Damon had hoped she wouldn't ask that, at least not tonight. Marina was a retired nurse who had looked after the children for the past two years. Other nannies had come and gone during Charlotte's long illness, but since Charlotte's death Marina had been a much-needed constant in Belle's life. They had grown very close. "I don't think she will be able to move with us," he said gently. "Her family is here, you know—her children and grandchildren. As much as she loves you and Tanner, I don't think she'll come."

"Then who's going to watch us?" Her voice wavered.

"Jess's wife says—"

"You mean Brionney," Belle interrupted. "You keep calling her Jesse's wife. Her name is Brionney. Well, I guess you call them Jess and Bri."

Damon smiled in the dark at his precocious daughter, who well knew his penchant for nicknames. "Bri says she has a friend in France who's planning to come to America for a while. She might agree to come and stay with us. And I bet you'll like her a lot if she's Bri's friend."

"What's her name?"

"Rebekka, I think. I'm not sure."

"But what if she doesn't wanna?"

Damon felt the pressure behind his eyes that signaled the beginning of a headache. He took one hand from around Belle and rubbed his left temple, then his right. "Doesn't want to what?"

"Come and stay with us?"

"Then we'll find someone else. Don't worry about it. That's my job. And haven't I always found you the best nannies? And the funnest?"

"Yes."

He wiped a tear from the lower eyelashes of her left eye. "Don't be sad. It's going to be all right. Better than all right. You'll see."

She nodded and laid her cheek trustingly against his chest. By the soft glow of the nightlight, he could see her eyes droop and close. He held her until her regular breathing told him she was asleep. Tucking her carefully under the covers, he kissed her porcelain cheek, then shuffled sleepily to his own room.

CHAPTER 4

"Will you knock it off?" Riley shouted. It was Monday evening, and he had just returned from work. "The doctor said it was just a fluke occurrence. I'm not going have another seizure. Gee, you're just as whiny and insistent as the kids."

"I'm just worried about you, that's all." *You don't have to be mean.* Hurt filled Mickelle's heart, as it so often did where Riley was concerned. To hide her feelings, she began to gather the dinner dishes.

"Well, I'm fine."

She filled the sink with sudsy water and piled in the dishes. "But shouldn't you take someone with you on Saturday, just in case?" Riley had announced his intention to go fishing the next Saturday—alone. Upon hearing the plans, Bryan and Jeremy had begged to go, but Riley refused all their pleas. Mickelle didn't like the idea of Riley going by himself. "At least take Bryan."

"Look, I just need some time away. To think. I don't want to have to look after anyone."

"You don't have to look after me!" Bryan yelled. His face had gone an angry red, and the veins in his neck stood out. With his solid physique, he was a miniature version of Riley. "I don't even want to go with you. Who wants to kill a bunch of fish, anyway?"

"Good," Riley retorted, his face equally red, "'cause you're not going!" He raised his fist threateningly, and although he had never hit either of the children, Mickelle's heart constricted with fear. "And don't back-talk me, or you're going to get it."

Bryan stalked out of the kitchen, and a few seconds later Mickelle heard the door to his bedroom slam. So much for her plans for a nice family night. Neither Bryan nor Riley would cooperate now.

"I want to go fishing," Jeremy said in a small voice.

Mickelle put her hand on his shoulder. "Jeremy, why don't you go outside and check on the dog? I'm sure she needs a walk."

Jeremy's blue eyes opened wide. "Can I take her all by myself?"

"Yes, but just around the block, and don't—"

"Talk to strangers. I know!" Jeremy was out the door at a run, calling for Sasha, their yellow Labrador.

Mickelle turned to her husband. "Riley," she began.

"I'm all right."

"No, it's Bryan. He wants to be with you. Can't you—"

"Kids get too much of what they want these days. Not going on Saturday will just make him appreciate the next time he goes. Besides, he always scares the fish away. I want to catch something for a change."

"What if he doesn't want to go with you the next time?"

Riley looked at her as if she had horns sprouting from her head. "He always wants to go," he said contemptuously.

"I mean when he's older. If you don't have a relationship now—"

"You don't know what you're talking about. Kids are selfish, and we have to teach them differently."

"But . . ." Mickelle gave up and stopped talking. Why did she bother? Riley always had an answer. If Bryan and Jeremy weren't so important to her, she wouldn't try at all.

Tears filled her eyes and spilled down her cheeks. She tried to turn away before Riley saw them, but was too late. "Why on earth are you crying?" he demanded.

"You hurt my feelings," she muttered. Silently she added, *Why can't you be nicer to me? Why do I always feel like such a nothing around you?*

His annoyance turned to indulgence. "I'm sorry," he said, putting his arms around her. "What did I say?"

You said I was whiny and insistent, she thought. *You treated me like my opinion means nothing.*

"Huh?" he asked.

She didn't reply.

"Do you want a divorce?" A smile tugged at his lips.

"No." Her voice was low.

"Then everything's okay. But I'm still not taking anyone next Saturday."

Maybe you'll have a seizure and die. But Mickelle immediately repented of the thought. Whatever the problems between them, Riley didn't deserve that.

* * * * *

Late Tuesday afternoon, while the boys played soccer in the backyard, Mickelle worked on finishing her household chores. As she cleaned, she listened to Oprah on TV. She had the program on mostly for company, but suddenly the discussion penetrated her thoughts. She dropped her broom on the kitchen floor and went into the living room.

Oprah was talking with an author who had written a book on mental and emotional spousal abuse. Several of the guests were talking about their home lives, and how their relationships had improved after reading the book. One woman's husband sounded remarkably like Riley. "I finally realized that he only had the power to hurt me because I gave it to him," the woman said. "Once I stopped giving him that power, our relationship had to change."

Mickelle sank to the couch, sitting on Bryan's Game Boy. Without taking her eyes from the TV, she tossed it to the other side. She had recognized for a long time that Riley didn't treat her right, but she had believed that if she just loved him enough, he would change. Yet since his surgery, things had only become worse. Was she facilitating his abuse by not standing up to him? Did the solution to their problem ultimately lie with her?

Methodically, she wrote down the name of the book. "I'll zip on over to the library right now," she said aloud. "That way, I can return the books I already have before they're overdue." She would have liked to take Sasha and walk to the library, but if she did she wouldn't have time to get dinner for Riley and the boys before she went to the church for the women's midweek activity.

She called out the back window for Bryan to keep an eye on Jeremy for a few minutes. "I've just got to drop off some books at the library." The boys waved to her and continued their game.

Fortunately, the book she had seen on television was in at the library. Mickelle also picked out a stack of novels. She adored reading; sometimes it was the only highlight in her day. At the checkout counter, she noticed a stack of pamphlets that told about continuing education for adults. She took one, interested to see what courses were being offered. Of course, she couldn't afford to take any classes now, but perhaps after she paid off the washer, she could save a little here and there—enough to pay for a class. Or maybe Riley would get his promotion.

The elderly librarian smiled at her. "We just received this book yesterday," she said, tapping the book on abuse.

Mickelle's heart quickened with embarrassment, but she willed her face not to flush. "How lucky for me," she said, pulling it toward her and stacking the novels on top.

The librarian's white head bobbed with pleasure. "We have plenty more on that subject if you'd like me to show you . . ."

"Not today, thanks. I'm in a hurry." Mickelle flashed her a stiff smile and headed quickly for the door. Safely outside, she paused and took a breath of the fresh spring air. She shut her eyes, willing her heart to slow to normal. Why did it bother her so much to admit— even to herself—that she and Riley had serious problems?

She got into the Snail and dumped the books onto the passenger seat. The abuse book fell on top. She again covered it with the novels. *If Riley sees this . . .*

When she arrived home, the boys were still playing soccer and the phone was ringing. She answered it.

"Where have you been?" a gruff voice demanded. It was Riley, calling from work.

"The library."

"Why?"

"I had some books that were due, that's all."

"I've been calling for a long time."

"The boys are outside playing, or they would have picked up. I was only gone for half an hour."

"I think it was longer."

Mickelle knew better than to argue. Riley hated for her to go anywhere without telling him about it beforehand. Was that why she had stopped visiting her sisters? Her parents? Her friends? Her heart started beating oddly again, and she had to force herself to focus on what her husband was saying.

". . . dumb jerk gave it to Greg, can you believe it? When I think of all the favors and all the bootlicking . . . and then he gives the promotion to Greg. I'm so angry I could—I could kill him! Maybe I should quit! Then they'd all see how much they need me!"

Panic rose in Mickelle's heart. Money was tight enough without him thinking about such a drastic move. "There'll be another promotion," she soothed. "Probably a better one."

"But I wanted to go to the new store in California. It would have been fun. No more snow and cold. Warm beaches. Ooh, I wish I dared do something . . . Now I'm going to be shoveling snow for another winter."

Mickelle felt a sudden absurd desire to laugh. Riley almost never shoveled snow; that task usually fell to her and the boys. Occasionally he'd do the front walk, but mostly he was at work, trying to make ends meet.

"Maybe I'll take a second job. Stop working overtime here."

Mickelle breathed easier. "You'll think of something. Everything'll be fine."

"I'll be home in an hour," Riley said. "I'm not staying late tonight. What are you going to do now?"

"Make dinner."

"Good. Well, I've got to go."

"I love you."

"You too." He hung up.

As Mickelle replaced the receiver, her eyes fell on the books she'd spread across the small bar where they normally ate their meals. She quickly gathered the books and carried them to her room, where she added them to the small stack beneath her dilapidated bed. For the millionth time, she couldn't help wishing they could afford better furniture—or, failing that, at least a nightstand.

She thought of her parents' house, of the elegant and tasteful furniture that was the result of a lifetime of good planning and thrift. She wondered if she and Riley would ever reach that point. Well, at least she had her curio cabinet. And material possessions were not among her primary goals in life.

She left the books and returned to the kitchen, stopping for a moment to check on the boys in the backyard. They were wrestling now, but Bryan was obviously not using his full strength. Mickelle smiled, and a lump formed in her throat. How lucky she was to have them! She had wanted more children, especially a daughter, but after Jeremy arrived, Riley had wanted her to "do something permanent about it." A tear escaped her eye as she remembered.

"No, I can't," she had said, fighting the panic inside her heart. She had been raised to believe that the ability to procreate was a gift from the Lord, and she wasn't ready to terminate it so quickly. That was a decision to be made only after much prayer and discussion.

"Why not?" he demanded, the telltale red rising into his square face.

"Because I want more children. I want a daughter."

"I don't. Children are too expensive."

"Then you do the surgery, because I won't." Mickelle had stood her ground, but even now felt queasy when she remembered his anger. She had thought he would hit her, even wished he would. At least then she might fight back. Instead, he had not spoken to her for a week, except to make comments meant to hurt her feelings.

In the end, neither of them had undergone surgery, and since Riley refused to take other precautions, Mickelle had hoped she would have another child. Riley would have been furious, of course, but he would have been forced to live with it.

Years passed, and a child never came. Mickelle had nearly given up hope.

She put a dinner of rice and meat on the stove to cook, then went to her bedroom to change into something nice for her church meeting. The air in the small room was stifling, so she opened the window before pulling on a pair of newer jeans and a short-sleeved sweater. Then she applied makeup and brushed her blonde hair that seemed to grow darker with each passing year. She smiled at herself in the mirror, her spirits revived. *Amazing what a little blush and lipstick can do.*

She checked on dinner and the boys again before returning to the room to pick up a book without looking at the title. *Just for a few moments,* she told herself. The book in her hand was the one about abuse. She put it down. *I don't need this. It was silly to get it. I'll just take it back.* She read a chapter of a novel instead, losing herself in other people's problems that kept her own at bay.

When Riley arrived, Mickelle greeted him with a hug and kiss, then called the boys in for dinner. They sat around the small bar on stools instead of using the square table by the stairs to the basement. Mickelle found it easier to clean up this way, and they had fallen into the habit of only using the table for birthdays and holidays.

Riley appeared to be in a sullen mood, and he said little as the boys chattered about their day. As usual, Bryan and Jeremy finished eating quickly. They didn't seem to notice their father's silence.

"I only have two Pokémon left to catch, Mom," Bryan told her, his face lighting with enthusiasm. Pokémon was the latest Game Boy cartridge their grandparents had given them, one version for each boy. "Then I'll have them all. Have you seen my Game Boy?"

"On the couch," Mickelle said. "You might want to think about keeping it in your room. I accidentally sat on it today. After spending so much money for your birthday, Grandma and Grandpa wouldn't be happy if something happened to it." Bryan headed for the living room. Jeremy followed, but returned shortly with a piece of blank drawing paper. "I'm going to draw Pikachu," he announced.

"Is he your favorite Pokémon?" Mickelle asked him indulgently. She glanced at Riley, who continued to eat without looking up.

Jeremy nodded. "He's the cutest, but I like Charmander, too. I wish I had them both. A kid at school says you can get them for three bucks at Shopko. They come with a Poké Ball and everything. You can carry them at your waist, just like in the cartoons."

"What's a Poké Ball?"

Jeremy looked at her incredulously. "That's what you put the Pokémon in. Didn't I tell you?"

"I don't think so. Maybe," Mickelle laughed.

Riley continued to eat in silence. Mickelle knew he was brooding about the lost promotion, but there was nothing either of them could do about it. Secretly, she was relieved that they wouldn't have to move, sandy beaches or no.

Jeremy moved to the drawer in the bar where they kept the markers. He tried to pull it open, but Riley's body blocked part of the way. Jeremy tried again.

All at once, Riley seemed to explode. He slammed the drawer shut, barely missing Jeremy's fingers. "Can't you see I'm eating? Just because you're finished doesn't mean the rest of us are! Darned kids are so selfish. All they ever think about is themselves!"

The light in Jeremy's blue eyes disappeared. For a moment he stood completely still, then his chin quivered and he looked as though he would cry. "I just wanted to draw," he said in a barely audible whisper.

"You can wait!" Riley thundered, not looking up from his plate. He loaded another forkful of rice into his mouth.

Jeremy blinked hard and stared at Riley. Mickelle could bear it no longer. She jumped to her feet and hustled Jeremy from the room. "Why don't you watch your brother play for a while? You can draw later."

Jeremy glanced toward the kitchen. "Why is he so mean?"

She put her arms around him. "He's had a hard day, that's all. He wanted a new job at work, and someone else got it."

"He could have said it nicely."

Mickelle's heart wanted to break at the pain in her little boy's voice. "Yes, he could have. But even dads make mistakes. It doesn't mean that he doesn't love you."

"I know, but he's still mean." Jeremy turned from her and went to the couch, where Bryan was engrossed in his game. Mickelle was relieved that neither child had homework and she didn't have to make them do it. She returned to the kitchen where Riley was finishing his food.

"Riley, I . . ." Most things Mickelle could let slide, but Jeremy was too important.

"They have to learn," Riley said. "And we have to teach them."

"I know, but if you said it in a different way . . ."

"I'm tired. I've had a bad day."

"Jeremy doesn't know that. He shouldn't have to pay for your bad days. He deserves to be treated nicely." Mickelle left the kitchen quickly, before Riley could say something hurtful. If she gave him time to think, sometimes the whole cycle of hurt and honeymoon could be avoided.

In her room, she read another chapter of her novel before realizing that she was already late for her meeting. She flew to the living room, wanting to make sure the boys were all right before she left. She stopped suddenly in her tracks at the scene before her.

Riley sat between the boys on the couch, Bryan's turquoise Game Boy in his hands. "No, Dad," Bryan was saying. "You can't fight with Charmander again until you go to the Pokémon Center and heal him. He's fainted."

"Well, show me where that is," Riley said.

"Go up. Keep going. Now over. No, the other way." Both boys giggled. Jeremy's head lay on Riley's shoulder.

Mickelle found her spirits restored. "Okay, gang, I'm off."

They looked up. "Where are you going?" Riley asked.

"Church. Enrichment meeting."

"It's tonight?"

"Yeah."

Riley frowned. "Why don't you stay home? We'll miss you, right guys?"

"Mom doesn't like to play Pokémon," Jeremy said matter-of-factly.

"That's right," Mickelle said. Riley still looked reluctant to let her go, but Bryan was urging him to heal his Pokémon. She made her escape the second Riley looked back at the game. Why was he always so possessive of her time? The truth was, Mickelle needed a break from all of them—especially Riley. Sometimes it was good just to hang out with the sisters in her ward.

When she arrived home a few hours later, she saw that the dinner dishes had been washed and were drying in their rack. The counters weren't very clean and the floor wasn't swept, but Mickelle was grateful for the effort Riley and the boys had made.

She found Riley in the living room watching TV. "Have fun?" he asked.

"It was all right." She was careful not to respond too enthusiastically, because he might take it wrong. "I needed a break from the kids."

"I just sent them to bed."

"Good." Mickelle went to their rooms to kiss them good night. Jeremy put his arms around her neck as she bent to kiss his forehead. "Did you have fun with dad?" she asked.

"Yeah, a lot."

"Good. Did he say anything about changing his mind and taking you and Bryan fishing?"

"No. But that's okay. Sometimes he's mean, but I love him."

"He hasn't had an easy life, you know," she said. "And he loves you very much."

"I know. Don't tell him, but I kinda feel sorry for him."

"He'll be all right. Things are getting better every day." Mickelle meant it. "I love you, honey. Have a good sleep."

"I love you too, Mom."

Mickelle was on her way back to the living room when the phone rang in the kitchen. It was for Riley, and she brought the portable to him.

He talked for a few moments, then hung up the phone. "Oh, brother," he said. "They're calling to remind me about that long, boring ward teacher development meeting tomorrow night. I wouldn't go at all if I hadn't missed the last two. Those meetings are stupid. Like I don't know how to teach already. I hate them telling me how to do my job. If I'm not doing well enough, they should just get rid of me. Heaven knows I've been teaching those kids in Primary long enough—two years! Humph! And they think they can teach me how to teach! I wish I didn't have to teach at all. It takes so long to prepare. And it's about time I got to go to priesthood meeting, don't you think? For once, I'd like to be with the men."

Mickelle knew that, and suspected everyone else did as well. Outside the home, Riley wasn't overly loud, but since the surgery, he did manage to make his opinions known. As for teaching, she suspected that he'd get more out of it if he didn't prepare the lessons during sacrament meeting.

The rest of the week went well for Mickelle. She felt happier than she had in a long time. The new washer ran like a charm and lightened her work load considerably. Buying it had certainly been the right thing to do, whatever Riley's reaction.

On Friday, Riley came home with the announcement that he had been given a raise. Mickelle hoped that this would alleviate his anger and hurt at not being given the promotion.

"Maybe we should celebrate," he told the boys. "Let's go out for dinner."

"We could go fishing with you tomorrow instead," Jeremy suggested eagerly.

Riley regarded him for a long, silent moment. "Yeah, maybe you could."

Mickelle felt so happy she could burst. Things were working out better than she could have hoped. Maybe Riley was finally growing up.

* * * * *

Mickelle's sense of peace shattered Saturday when she returned from an early morning shopping spree with her sisters, Talia and Lauren. Mickelle hadn't actually bought anything except a card for Riley, but she had enjoyed being with her sisters. On the way home, she even told them about Riley and the drawer scene. Now that things were on the mend, she wanted to pave the way so that someday she could tell her sisters everything.

"A lot of men have trouble talking with kids," Lauren said from the back. She held her compact in one hand and reapplied her lipstick with the other. "They seem to think they should act all grown up already. Eventually, they learn that children are children, not adults in small bodies."

"Some just take longer than others," Talia said. She was driving the van, looking somewhat odd wearing a pair of newly purchased cat-eye sunglasses.

"You can say that again," Mickelle said from her comfortable passenger-side seat. "Like molasses uphill. Or like my station wagon, the Snail." Her sisters laughed.

"You seriously call it the Snail?" Lauren rolled her eyes. "That's *too* funny. You know, thinking about it, it kinda looks like a golden Snail." They laughed again.

"Good thing I love him," Mickelle said. "My husband, I mean, not the car." More laughter. With regret, Mickelle noticed they had already arrived at her street. "This is wonderful, being with you guys," she said with a sigh. "Too bad Brionney's still in Alaska."

"She's coming home soon, I think," Talia answered. "Jesse and a friend of his are going to do some business here."

"You think they'll have a job for Riley?" Mickelle wondered aloud.

"Probably." Talia turned into their driveway. "Hey, it looks like Riley and the boys are home."

"Mom! Mom! I caught a fish!" Jeremy ran up with something in his hands. "Bryan did, too. It was so fun!"

Riley came from in front of his truck, still dressed in his fishing gear. He nodded cordially at Lauren and Talia. "Hi, need some fish? We caught plenty."

Lauren shuddered. "The only way I want fish is in a restaurant."

"I'll take some," Talia said. "Joe loves fresh fish. So do the kids."

Mickelle hurried into the house to find something for Talia to take the fish home in. After her sisters drove away, she turned to talk to Riley and found his expression changed.

"Where have you been?" he demanded.

"Shopping. Or looking, mostly."

"You didn't tell me you were going with them."

Mickelle was confused, though the confusion was accompanied by a desperate sense of déjà vu. "I didn't know. They called me after you and the boys left. Riley, why are you upset?"

"You seem to have had a good time with them."

"What's wrong with that?"

He shrugged and bent over the bucket of remaining fish.

"Didn't you have fun today?" Mickelle asked, wanting desperately to reclaim the joy she had felt minutes before. "Aren't you glad the boys went? They loved being with you."

"I guess." Riley would say nothing more, and Mickelle was glad the boys weren't around to hear his unenthusiastic reply.

A tear slipped down Mickelle's cheek. Why was joy so fleeting?

CHAPTER 5

Sunday morning before their ten o'clock meetings, Riley was called in to meet with one of the bishop's counselors. Since he was in a sullen mood, Mickelle was relieved to see him go. She put a CD of church music into their battered old player, hoping to create a spirit that even Riley couldn't destroy.

She dressed for church, recalling the enjoyable time she'd had with her sisters the day before. As though responding to her thoughts, the phone rang, and Mickelle went to the living room to find the portable. Brionney was on the line.

"You're calling me from Alaska?" Mickelle asked, sinking to the couch. "Oh, it's so good to hear your voice!"

"You too. Talia called and told me what a fun time you guys all had shopping yesterday. I was so jealous! That's why I'm calling to tell you that we're coming home soon. I don't know the exact date yet, but when I get there, we'll all go out."

"That's great, Brionney." Mickelle said. "It's just not the same with you in Alaska and Zack in France. And those little twins of yours—we can't wait to see them."

"They are a handful, but so cute. Forest is rather loud, though. Jesse keeps threatening to buy us earplugs and him a muzzle."

Mickelle giggled. "Sounds just like Jesse. But I'll bet he's a big help."

"Except with the diapers! Do you believe that I can get him to wash all the dishes—by hand, mind you—and make all the beds if I agree to let him out of just one diaper change? It's really funny."

"At least you get a lot of chores done."

"That's right. I've only done the dinner dishes twice since the babies came." Brionney's laughter showed that she realized who had the best of the bargain.

"You'll have to call the minute you know what day you'll be here," Mickelle told her. "We'll have a big dinner at Mom and Dad's."

"Sounds good. In fact, if I know Mom, she's already planned the menu."

"What about a place to live?"

"I asked Dad last week to find us a house. And one for Jesse's partner as well."

"So what's holding you up? From coming back to Utah, I mean."

"Jesse just has a one more contract to fill, and then we're done. Some friends of ours were having some trouble with their baby, and we felt we should—well, never mind. Everything's okay now. We're coming home for sure. And Jesse's very excited about this new business he and our friend are setting up. They've already got most of the program written, and five hospitals have agreed to test it out. Imagine that!"

"Sounds promising." Mickelle felt a twinge of envy, but remembered that her sister had experienced her share of trials. Her first marriage had failed miserably, then she and Jesse had gone through financial difficulties and a miscarriage that had severely tested their faith and their relationship. "I'm glad for you. I really am. You deserve the best. I know it hasn't been easy."

"Well, it'll only mean more in the end," Brionney answered. "Look, I'd better get going. Forest is screaming again in the other room, and the girls need me to fix their hair for church. You take care now."

"Give my love to Jesse and the kids."

"I will."

Mickelle hung up and placed the phone on the couch cushion. She started at a sound from the doorway. "Riley! How long have you been there?"

He leaned his sturdy frame slightly forward, his hands thrust deep into his pockets. "Who was on the phone?"

"Brionney."

He grunted.

"What's that supposed to mean?"

"I hope you didn't talk a lot. It's long distance to Alaska."

"Don't worry," Mickelle replied dryly. "*She* called me. We won't have to pay."

Riley didn't reply. He slumped onto his favorite chair.

"So what happened in your interview?" Though the bishop's counselor was a nice and caring man, she knew he wasn't one of Riley's favorite people.

"I got released."

Mickelle smiled. "Hey, that's great! You kept saying you didn't want that teaching position anyway. So did they give you another calling?"

"Yeah. I'm going to do something with the men's sports, I guess." He gave a disgusted snort. "Can you imagine me and sports? And with all the hours I work. Sometimes I just don't get it."

"It'll be fun," Mickelle said. "You wanted to be with the men, and now you are. Big time." *And maybe it'll help you lose weight,* she added silently. He had begun to complain that his clothes were getting too tight.

Riley continued to act morose, almost as though he had been demoted. Mickelle wanted to tell him to snap out of his bad attitude, but knew from experience that he would retaliate until she was brought to tears. She opted to ignore him, and went about helping the boys find their ties and matching socks, though neither Bryan nor Jeremy had the least qualm about wearing one blue and one black sock.

At church, Riley seemed to relax, and even made a comment about this being the last time he had to read a lesson during sacrament meeting. Mickelle smiled, thinking that the Lord had blessed them with this new calling. Perhaps what Riley needed was a break, where he could learn from the speakers and feel the Spirit.

After sacrament meeting, Mickelle went to the nursery, where she had been serving for the past two years. She loved being with the little children. Their eyes were so innocent, so trusting, and she loved them with her whole heart. Today she had a new reason for enjoying her calling: her cycle was late, and she could, if only for one day, dream that next year at this time she would be holding her own little daughter.

* * * * *

The next day, Mickelle paused in her housework to read a bit. But she didn't devour her novel as she normally did. Instead, she picked up the book on abuse and began to thumb through it, reading snatches here and there that interested her. Some of the questions on a "risk chart" amazed her. *Does your partner act possessive of your time? Does your partner question your every move when you are away? Do you feel the need to ask permission to do things? Are outside friendships discouraged? Does your partner control your access to money? Are you afraid to speak your mind for fear of offending your partner and starting a fight? Does your partner call you names or yell at you? Do you make excuses for your partner's behavior?*

She felt uncomfortable reading the list, seeing too much of herself and Riley. She caressed her bloated stomach, wondering if it now held the daughter she had craved, or if her cycle was late because of stress. What if she was pregnant? How would she tell Riley? Why should she have to worry about telling him?

"We have to get help." She whispered the words aloud, feeling their truthfulness. There was no longer any room to deny what was happening in her life. She needed to feel the peace and happiness she believed she and Riley were capable of creating.

I can do it, she thought. *I can take control of my life.* As she thought it, she felt immense relief that deep down Riley was a good man and he loved her. He might do a lot of things wrong, but he did a lot of good things, too. She doubted that he had any inkling of his abuse at all. Mickelle shuddered and said a silent prayer on behalf of the women in the world who were in a much worse position. She didn't think she would be strong enough to face their trials.

But I am strong enough to face this, or the Lord would not have given it to me. This Mickelle firmly believed. She knelt at her bed and said a prayer, asking the Lord to help her reach into the essence of who she was—His daughter—and find the courage it would take to lead her family to happiness.

A strange elation settled over her. She sang as she completed her housework, surprised that it went so quickly. Then she took Sasha for a walk, noting the beauty of the late morning. This was the last day of

April, and already the May flowers were out in abundance. She drove to the store and bought a flat of pansies to plant in the yard near her rosebushes, whistling as she did. When the boys arrived home, she had fresh chocolate chip cookies waiting. "Great, Mom!" they shouted.

She watched them devour the cookies, their lips framed with milk moustaches and chocolate smudges. Like a scene from a movie—how easy everything had gone today. And with so much time to spare! She felt as though she had awakened from a deep sleep, a depression that had saturated her life until each day had been a trial and a thing to be endured, rather than a celebration, a gift from God.

She helped the boys with their homework and then went outside to play soccer with them in the backyard. Sasha barked happily as she ran after them on the grass. Mickelle laughed, lifting her face to the sun. Dinner tonight would have to be frozen corn dogs, because she wasn't going to let this precious opportunity with her sons go to waste.

They were still playing when Riley arrived home. With a little encouragement, he joined in their game. Giggles and mock screams filled the backyard. At last Mickelle fell to the ground, exhausted but content. "Well, that was an impromptu family night if I ever saw one. What do you say we heat some corn dogs in the microwave and make some caramel popcorn to finish out the night?"

"Yay!" the boys shouted.

Bryan added, "We can play Monopoly!"

"Okay, but only until bedtime," she warned.

Riley helped her up from the grass. Mickelle hugged him, and his familiar scent filled her nose. She felt a twinge of nervousness, knowing that she would eventually have to talk to him about seeing a marriage counselor, but she banished the thought from her mind. *I'll cross that bridge when I come to it.*

When the boys were in bed, Mickelle changed into her nightshirt. She found Riley in the living room with the television on, but he wasn't watching the movie. "What's this?" he asked, holding up a college brochure.

A knot formed in her stomach, but she forced herself to reply honestly. "Oh, I picked it up at the library last week. At first it was just an idea, but I've been thinking about it and I'd really like to start taking classes. You know, one at a time. Utah Valley State College has a branch here in American Fork, up by the temple. It's only a few minutes away."

Riley's face was devoid of all expression. "Isn't that expensive?"

"Yes, but I may be able to get a scholarship. Of course then I'd have to take more classes. I don't know. I thought that with your raise, maybe we could afford two or three hundred dollars every four months. We could budget for it."

"Why do you have to go back to school?"

The knot in her stomach grew heavy, and her hands involuntarily clenched into fists. She took a deep breath. "The kids are getting older. Soon they'll be gone. I need to do something with my life."

"You are doing something. You're a mother and a wife, for heaven's sake."

"But I can do this, too." She took a few steps toward him. "There are a lot of hours in the day."

Riley's bottom lip jutted out, and now Mickelle recognized the expression: he was jealous. "Are you sure you aren't going so you can meet guys?" His voice was light, but she knew he was completely serious.

She fought rising panic and fury. Why did she feel so helpless? "Oh, Riley, don't be ridiculous! I'd be going for an education."

"Well, we don't have the money, so there's really no point in talking about it."

She touched her abdomen, remembering the daughter of her dreams. "But I want to go."

Mickelle saw his surprise. Ordinarily, she would have backed off by now. No, she wouldn't have even brought it up. She would have deflected his first question by throwing the college brochure away.

"You don't need to go," he insisted. "You could work on the house or yard if you need something to do. Heck," he smirked, "you could make a real dinner instead of corn dogs."

She knew what he was really saying—that she wasn't worth the added expense; that she wasn't trustworthy, so he needed to keep track of her whereabouts; that she was a failure at being a wife and homemaker. Deep feelings of hurt began in her heart, but at the last minute Mickelle remembered that *she* had control of her emotions, and that no matter what he said or did to her, *she* chose whether or not she would be happy.

She counted for a full five seconds, then forced a little chuckle. Remarkably, the hurt went away. She even felt sorry for him. "Oh, Riley. That's funny. I would much rather play soccer with the boys than make dinner. And in case you hadn't noticed, our yard looks great. Didn't you see the flowers I planted today? And the peas in the garden have already grown more than a foot. I love taking care of our home and you and the boys. But please listen to what I'm saying. I want to go to school. I want to learn."

His lips pursed as though tasting something sour. "Well, I don't have the money to give you."

"Then maybe I should get a job in the mornings while the boys are at school."

"No!" he roared.

Mickelle knew it wasn't her suggestion that inflamed him, but the fact that she was holding her ground. She was taking control of her life instead of allowing him to control her.

Without another word, she turned and left the room. She climbed into bed and lay there without sleeping. Misery was close by, but she refused to let it settle over her in its customary place. Today had been wonderful, and already she could see that happiness was attainable. It wasn't as easy as it had seemed this morning, but she wasn't going to give up. She would fight for every moment of happiness—if not for herself, then for the children.

She loved Riley very much. This was a fact that she admitted freely to herself. When it was good between them, it was very good; when it wasn't, she wanted to run away and hide. But this time she would fight to find and keep the very best of what their life had to offer.

She was beginning to feel sleepy when Riley entered the room. He came to her side of the bed and sat down. "Are you awake?" he asked.

"Yes." She sat up.

His face was barely discernible by the light coming from the streetlamp outside their bedroom window. "I'm sorry," he said in a cajoling voice. "I've been thinking about it, and maybe I do understand why you want to go to school."

Mickelle waited for more. He peered at her, but it was obvious that his eyes hadn't yet adjusted to the dim light of the room. If they had, he would see that she wasn't hurt by his earlier comments.

"Can you forgive me?" he asked.

Still, she held her peace. She wanted him to think about what he was saying.

He added forlornly, "You don't want a divorce, do you?"

Fury overcame her. As usual, he was using the words to evoke her pity, her sense of duty, her approval. And perhaps even as a threat. This time she wasn't going to let him get away with it. "Yes, I do," she answered tightly. Her heart raced at her audacity. "If you don't start treating me better, then, yes, I want a divorce."

She heard a swift intake of air as he gasped in surprise. She couldn't see clearly in the dark, but she knew his square features would be turning a dark crimson. His mouth contorted, and for a moment she thought he was going to lose control and lash out physically. Fear swept through her, swift and paralyzing. Then he swallowed noisily. "You really want a divorce?" he asked with difficulty after a few moments. "Am I that bad?" In the dark he looked pasty white, as though the color had suddenly fled from his face.

Mickelle shook her head. She gazed at him earnestly, willing him to hear and understand as he had never done before. "I love you, Riley. Very, very much. And I want to stay with you. But I've realized in the past few weeks that love isn't enough. I can't let you abuse me anymore. I won't let you control my life. I deserve the same respect and care I give to you."

"I respect you."

"No, you don't. And we need to find someone to help us. I would like to see a marriage counselor."

"Is this all because you want to go to school?"

"No!" Mickelle said, leaning toward him. "This is about us! This is about being partners for eternity!"

The muscles in his cheek rippled as his jaw clenched. "You're trying to make me let you go to school."

Mickelle nearly laughed at his observation. "Make you let me go? Oh, no, Riley; I'm going to school, period. I would like your approval, but I don't need to ask your permission. I'm not a child. If you don't like it, you can . . ." She didn't know exactly how to finish the sentence. All she wanted was to attend one little class, to get out of the house for a while. She might not even want to continue, but she needed a chance to find out. She needed a chance to grow without Riley constantly looking over her shoulder, threatening her.

Emitting a feral growl from the back of his throat, Riley whirled on his heel and left the room. In a moment, Mickelle heard the door to the house slam shut behind him, and seconds later the motor of his truck roared to life.

A long time passed as she lay in bed, contemplating what she would do the next day. According to the brochure, new classes began tomorrow, so she might still have time to register. But where would she come up with the tuition? Maybe it would be better to wait until June, when another session would begin. That way Riley would have time to adjust to the idea, and she would have a chance to find the money.

Mickelle fell asleep, her dilemma unresolved. She awoke once in the night when Riley returned, but he didn't come into the bedroom. Normally she would have gone to him and tried to get him to talk about it, but this time she let him alone. *He'll have to work it out himself,* she thought. *As for me, I'm going to begin to celebrate life.*

* * * * *

The next morning, Riley was sullen and wouldn't speak to her. She purposely talked to him as though nothing had happened, but she didn't try to draw him out of his shell or ask him to talk about his feelings. As she made pancakes and helped the boys gather their school books, she whistled or sang. After a while, she didn't have to force her enthusiasm; she really was happy. She was in control of her own emotions. What a wonderful feeling!

After Riley and the children left, she changed Jeremy's wet sheets and finished cleaning the kitchen. Looking around with satisfaction, she thought fleetingly of the novels under her bed, but decided to read them later. Right now she still had a lot to do. She made a few calls to the college and found that she could register, but there was still the problem of money. Of course, she could just show up and sit in on a class, but that really wouldn't be the same thing. She wanted to prove to herself that she could go back and earn good grades.

Only a little deflated, she decided to drive to her mother's home in Provo. In the car, she sang the Primary songs she had been teaching the children in the nursery. The joy of the gospel swelled in her heart. *What a beautiful day,* she thought.

When she arrived at her parents' home, her mother wasn't there, so she used the key her mother had given her years ago. The rooms were spotless, and everything looked so elegant that for a moment, she couldn't help comparing it to her own shabby existence.

Then she spied the piano in the living room. She had taken lessons for three years as a child, but the only one in their family who played well was Zack. Growing up, everyone had always considered the piano to be his. She still did, although he had a new one in his home in France.

Mickelle did a few scales, and then, almost of their own volition, her hands began to play "The Entertainer." It had been the most difficult piece she had ever learned, and the only one she could remember completely. Her fingers were stiff, but gradually they loosened and played fewer wrong notes. At last, she played it once through without making one error.

There was clapping behind her. Mickelle arose, startled. "Mom!" she exclaimed.

Irene smiled and walked over to the piano, giving her daughter a hug. Mickelle breathed in the perfumed scent of her short, carefully styled hair that was as white as a cloud against a deep blue sky. "That was wonderful, Mickelle. This poor old piano hasn't had anyone playing it in a long time." She sighed. "I remember when you and Zack used to play."

Mickelle laughed. "Zack played. I banged."

"No, you played. You were just impatient. Zack was more content to let a few wrong notes go by. But you wanted it perfect."

"Yeah, I was a regular little Mozart," she returned dryly, and was rewarded by Irene's laugh.

"You always were my funny girl." She squeezed Mickelle's waist. "So, what brings you here this morning?" With a final embrace, Irene began walking toward the kitchen. Mickelle followed.

"Oh, I just dropped by."

"Well, you're just in time to help me unload the groceries."

They went to the garage, where Irene's car was crammed with plastic sacks. Mickelle groaned. "Don't tell me you've already been shopping for Brionney's homecoming."

Irene met her gaze sheepishly. "Well, yes." Her laughter tinkled like bells reverberating from the sides of the garage. "She'll be here before we know it. I just want to be prepared."

"All of this could feed an army." Mickelle hefted two plastic bags full of frozen meat. "Of course, in retrospect, we are getting to be rather an army."

Irene picked up several more bags, her willowy figure stooping with the weight. "Let's see. With Talia's five, Lauren's six, your two, and Brionney's five, that makes eighteen grandchildren. Not bad at all. Of course, it would be more if Zack and his family were here."

Mickelle grimaced with exertion as she set her bags on the counter. Zack's wife was expecting baby number five—probably another boy. They seemed to run in the family. Only Brionney had more than one daughter. Mickelle stared at the meat in the sacks, remembering her own secret hope. She wished she had the money to splurge on a pregnancy test, but she had already purchased too many over the years, only to be disappointed. This time she would wait a few weeks.

"Uh, Mom, I've been thinking about going back to school."

Irene paused in the doorway. "Really? What made you decide to do that?"

"I don't know. I guess I'm bored. I'm looking for something more. If we had more children, maybe it'd be—" Mickelle stopped. Suddenly she was crying.

Irene rushed to her side. "What happened? Are you all right?"

"Yes. No. Actually, Riley and I are having some trouble. His attitude since the surgery has been . . . well, he says things to me that he shouldn't."

"Riley?" Irene looked puzzled. "But you always tell me how great you're doing."

"Oh, Mother!" Mickelle began to sob loudly. Words tumbled out over each other as she told her mother the truth.

Irene kept shaking her head in disbelief, unshed tears glimmering in her eyes. "Why didn't I see? How could I not know?"

"I didn't even realize it myself," Mickelle sniffled. "I—I'd forgotten what it's like to be myself." She looked at her mother pleadingly. "It's one of the reasons I've got to go to school. I have to learn who I am. I've been Riley's wife for so long that sometimes I don't know how I used to feel. I don't know what it is to be *me*."

Irene held Mickelle, stroking her hair as she had often done when she had been very young. "I think it's a good idea," she said. "And I'll support you. Whether it's money you need, or watching the kids, I'm here for you." The tears spilled out and over her cheeks. "Oh, Mickelle, I feel so stupid. How could I not have noticed?"

"Don't blame yourself, Mom. I'm the one who let things get out of hand. I'm the one who chose to make excuses instead of standing up for what I believed." After years of not understanding, it all seemed so clear to Mickelle now.

Irene dabbed at her face. "I wish you had told me before."

Mickelle laid her cheek against her mother's. "Me too. But I couldn't. Now I can."

"You'll get through this," Irene whispered. "And I want to help."

"I know. Thank you."

A little self-consciously, they dried their tears and brought in the rest of the groceries. As they did, they discussed Mickelle's options. "I want to see if the college offers financial aid or scholarships or something," Mickelle said. "Riley . . . well, he doesn't really want me to go, and we don't have the money for it."

Irene grabbed her hand. "I meant what I said about helping."

"I know, Mom. I just want to try it my way first. If I need to, I'll ask for help. Maybe I could even work part time at Dad's office. You know, like Brionney did before she married Jesse."

"The most important thing is to get Riley to go to counseling."

"I know. That's why I don't want to rush everything else." Mickelle looked at her mother earnestly. "I believe Riley's a good man. He just has his own issues to deal with. It might take a while, but we're going to be all right."

"That's the spirit." Irene smiled with pride, but the sorrow in her expression was still evident. Mickelle wondered how she would feel if their positions were reversed, if Irene had been living with a man like Riley. Mickelle found she didn't relish the idea. Her mother deserved to be cherished as she had been all these years by her father.

So do I, she thought.

Mickelle left her mother's home feeling decidedly happier. How good it was to have things in the open, and a confidante to share both the good and the bad. Things would work out—somehow.

* * * * *

Riley Hansen drove to work feeling very unsettled. He almost didn't go to work at all, but then that would mean seeing Mickelle's cheerful face all day. How could she be so happy when his world was falling apart?

Everything was slipping out of his control. He had experienced another seizure last night in the truck, his wife wanted who knew what, and his job sucked. His lips twisted in a wry grin. Mickelle hated it when he said something sucked.

Not that he didn't want her to be happy; it was just that things were changing too fast. He needed to get a handle on his life. But how? Turning up the radio, he tried to tune out his thoughts.

Come to think of it, *he* hated the word suck—especially when the children used it. But it made him feel better now . . . a little rebellious.

Mickelle was so beautiful, so loving and caring. He often wondered why she had married him in the first place. Over the years, he had sometimes worried that she would leave. And now she had finally come right out and admitted she would seek a divorce if he didn't treat her better. But what was he doing wrong?

Riley's heart beat rapidly, and it was suddenly difficult to breathe. He took in a ragged gasp of air. He couldn't lose Mickelle! Sometimes he thought she was the only reason he continued to live.

She said she loved him. Was it true? It had to be.

I'll do better, he vowed silently. *I'll do whatever she wants.*

There was a part of him that rebelled at this admission, but his love and need for his wife gradually overcame his darker thoughts. Mickelle seemed to believe there was hope for their relationship, and he had to at least try, though he didn't understand her problem.

The positive thoughts erased much of his unhappiness. He had been at work for an hour when he decided to call Mickelle to tell her he loved her. She didn't answer the phone. Where had she gone? Was she outside or somewhere else? What was she doing? *She should be there,* he thought with gritted teeth. His breath came more rapidly. Fighting his anger, he returned to work.

When he called her again after lunch, she finally answered. "I tried to call earlier," he said. He knew his voice was accusing, but he couldn't help it. Now she would be hurt, and that meant he would have to comfort her. Maybe not a bad thing after all.

But he was wrong. "I'm sorry I missed your call," she answered cheerfully. "I've been at my mother's, then at the college, looking into financial aid. So is something up? Why did you call?"

Riley was astonished. Why wasn't she resentful of his checking up on her? Just what had she been doing at that college, anyway?

He couldn't lose her.

"I just called to say I love you," he managed.

"How sweet! I love you too, Riley." There was unfeigned happiness in her voice, and Riley's terror diminished. "Hey, I was just thinking about going grocery shopping," she added. "Is there anything special you'd like?"

"No. Nothing." He told her good-bye and hung up. Instead of being content at her words, he began to worry about who she might see at the grocery store. Would she leave him? Why was she acting so strangely?

Riley put his head in his hands to fight a sudden onslaught of dizziness. Was he having another seizure? The thought scared him senseless.

"You okay, Hansen?" It was his boss, Monte Williams.

Dumb jerk. This is all your fault. If you'd given me the promotion instead of Greg, my life would be so much better. I detest you! He stood up, grateful that he was able to do so. "Yeah, I'm okay. Just a little tired."

"Good, because your department is looking shabby. Better get it straightened. And there are two customers by the weed-whackers who need your help."

Riley wished he could tell the man where to go. "I'll get right on it," he said, making sure his voice held none of the venom that was in his heart.

What a terrible day!

CHAPTER 6

Rebekka had mentally packed her suitcases a million times over the week as she waited for Brionney to call. Everything was settled at work. She hadn't talked with her family yet, but she would as soon as Brionney called.

She hadn't seen Marc since that fateful day when she had realized that he would never love her as she loved him. He had called the apartment and had even come over a few times, but she had either pretended to be out or indisposed. Her mother couldn't understand her attitude, but accepted it at face value, as she did everything else.

Rebekka went through the motions of living, sometimes feeling numb and other times enduring such agony of heart that she didn't know if she would survive another day. Her dreams had vanished, and all she wanted to do was to run and hide, to lick her wounds until she was ready to face the world again.

The world, but not Marc. She thought she might never be able to look into his eyes again. And if she couldn't do that, then what was the use of living at all?

The only person who had an inkling of her plight was her brother Raoul, who was twenty-six and two years her senior, her only sibling. The week after Rebekka had made her horrendous discovery, Raoul answered the phone in the living room when Marc called. She refused to talk with him. "What do you want me to tell him?" Raoul questioned.

"I don't care," Rebekka replied bleakly, "but I'm not talking to him."

Raoul made an excuse and hung up. He gazed at her sympathetically as she sat on the couch, clutching the *Liahona*. "So you know about Marc and Mom."

Rebekka stared at him for a few seconds. Raoul had her father's broad shoulders and lean face, and her mother's auburn hair—though a bit lighter—and also her gray eyes. The kindness in those eyes made a lump come to her throat. She nodded miserably. "Mom doesn't know."

Raoul shrugged, coming to sit beside her. "Mom's a perfect innocent. Nothing can touch her. I think she had to be that way to love Dad."

She knew what he meant. Despite the religion and values that separated them, Danielle loved their father deeply and totally. Over the years, he had learned to return that devotion. But he hadn't always been so doting.

Raoul touched her shoulder tentatively. "I'm really sorry. I know you like Marc."

She forced lightness into her voice. "Just a childish crush." She turned her face away from him and added, "I'm not a child anymore." To her disgust, her voice shook slightly. She hoped he wouldn't notice.

"The guy's a fool," Raoul replied. "Thirty-four years, and he hasn't made any progress in his personal life. He should have moved on a long time ago." He paused, and what he said next showed Rebekka that Raoul had not only heard but understood the tremor in her voice. "Like you are doing."

She turned back toward him in surprise. "It's so hard."

"I know." He hugged her like he had when they were little and she had cried because she couldn't tie her shoe. If only that were her problem now. Raoul gave her a final squeeze and stood. "I hope you know that I'm here if you need me."

"Thanks." Rebekka did want to talk further, but she dared not put too much trust in her brother. He worked with Marc every day at their engineering firm; something might slip accidentally. And she couldn't bear for Marc to understand her true feelings now, when it was too late.

"Are you going out with Desirée tonight?" she asked, noticing that he was dressed in his Sunday best.

Raoul grinned sheepishly. "Yeah."

"She's a nice girl." In fact, the only flaw Rebekka saw in the girl was that she wasn't a member of the Church. But that could change; she was very sweet and seemed serious about searching out truth.

"I know." His face grew serious. "I don't plan to let her get away."

"Good."

Rebekka watched him go with tears in her eyes. How she wished it could be her and Marc.

But no! She couldn't think that way. Somewhere there had to be someone who would love her for herself. Someone who wouldn't pat her on the head and call her a pest.

The phone rang, and she let the answering machine pick up, fearing that it was Marc again. She sat stiffly, waiting to see if the person on the other end would leave a message.

"Hello, this is Brionney Hergarter. I'm calling to talk to—"

Rebekka snatched the portable receiver from the charging unit. "Hi, Bri, I'm here."

"Good. How are you?"

"All right."

"You don't sound all right."

"I'm just stressed. Do you have any news?"

"Yes. We don't have an exact date yet, but you can leave anytime. I would have called sooner, but we have some friends here whose baby has been terribly sick, and we've been holding off because of them, but I think she's nearly out of danger now. As soon as she is, we'll leave. Meanwhile, my mother said you could stay at her house until I get to Utah. She's actually excited about having you. I had to remind her that you were *my* guest—but that was before something else came up."

"What do you mean? She can't have me stay?"

"No, no, not that. It's just that I was wondering if you could help out a friend of ours—Damon, Jesse's partner. He asked me last week . . . no, it's been longer than that. Anyway, he's also moving to Utah, but his nanny doesn't want to leave her family here in Anchorage. Little Belle, that's Damon's five-year-old daughter, is upset because this nanny has been with them since Belle's mother died two years ago. Damon's looked around for another nanny, but so far he can't find anyone suitable. So I—now, don't hate me—I suggested you. Not for anything permanent, mind you; just temporarily until he can find someone in Utah that he can trust with his kids. There's so much going on right now that he doesn't have much time to find a good nanny. He promised Belle one she'd like, and he doesn't want to let her down. Do you think you'd be willing? I mean, I know it's not what you expected, but after they find someone else, you can come stay with me and teach French or something at the . . ."

As Brionney talked, Rebekka considered. She imagined what it would be like to be needed by someone—anyone. Maybe taking care of these children was just what *she* needed. She wouldn't have Marc, but in a way she would have a family of her own, something to keep her busy until she found another means of supporting herself.

"Sure," she said. "I'd be glad to help out until they find someone permanent."

"That's wonderful! I don't think you'll regret it, although *I* probably will. I was so looking forward to having you stay with me. But we can get together during the day. Tanner—that's the older boy—will be in school during May, and you'll only have Belle. And you'll have evenings off after Damon gets home. But, oh, you are just going to fall in love with little Isabelle. She's very petite and beautiful. She can be a bit of a stinker sometimes, but she's so cute, you have to forgive her."

Rebekka was imagining the little girl already. How she would enjoy dressing her up and taking her places! Of course, she really didn't know much about children, but surely it couldn't be any harder than double majoring in college.

Or being rejected by Marc.

She sighed inwardly and tried to listen to Brionney.

"So, if you'll tell me your flight number, I'll have someone meet you at the airport in Salt Lake—probably my parents. You can stay with them until—"

"Couldn't I come to Alaska and help you?" Rebekka interrupted. "I mean, flying to Utah with five kids won't be easy."

"What a wonderful idea! Of course, there'll be seven children, actually, since Damon and his two are flying with us. Which is perfect, because then you can meet them. And I can use an extra hand with the twins—even with Jesse along." She paused. "Oh, but that's a much longer flight for you, and it'll be more expensive—"

Rebekka shrugged. "Money's not a problem. Besides, I've always wanted to see Alaska."

"Well, Damon's already volunteered to pay for your flight. And money's no concern with him, either. Like I've told you before, that guy is loaded. And he's really sweet."

"I'm sure he is," Rebekka said dryly, understanding the hint. "So when do you want me to come?"

"As soon as you can."

"What about Saturday? I already know what I'm taking, and I've given notice at the embassy." Since it was Wednesday now, that would mean she wouldn't have to elude Marc again at church on Sunday.

"Sounds perfect! I'm so excited."

Rebekka laughed with delight at Brionney's exuberance. "Me too." And she was.

"Look, Damon has a service he uses to book flights. Since they're doing our flights, I'll call them up and let them worry about getting you on the same ones we'll be using. They'll let you know about your ticket, and I'll be at the airport to pick you up."

"Good." Rebekka paused. In the background, she could hear one of Brionney's twins babbling something at the top of his baby voice. "Thanks, Bri," she said. "I owe you one."

Brionney laughed. "Just wait till we're on that airplane with the kids. Then we'll see who owes who!"

Rebekka hung up, smiling. What would she do without a friend to help her through this time? Tears pricked at her eyes, but she didn't let them fall. She would not cry for Marc.

CHAPTER 7

Wednesday and Thursday passed by like a dream. Mickelle could hardly believe the change in her life now that she no longer gave Riley—or anyone else—the power to control or hurt her. At times, when Riley would do some small spiteful thing, she felt herself slipping back into the crevasse of fear and hurt, but each time she prayed hard and schooled herself not to show Riley her true feelings. Before long, her contentedness was unfeigned. Then it was with some amusement that she watched him flounder with questions, accusations, and finally with apologies. He never again asked her if she wanted a divorce, already knowing the answer. And between his episodes of suspicion, he treated her well.

Riley had even agreed to attend counseling, although he insisted that he didn't need it. "*I* need it," she told him, "and that should be reason enough." He hadn't agreed on a date to start the sessions, and he complained about the money they would spend, but Mickelle was content with the baby steps they had taken.

The boys seemed to notice the difference in their father, and had adopted the same attitude as Mickelle. If their father yelled at them or said something hurtful, they didn't cry or rebel, but left him alone to calm down. Riley didn't seem to know what to do about the change, but Mickelle felt as though a load had been lifted from her shoulders.

Thursday night, they once again played soccer as a family and had a wonderful time. Only Riley's determination to win marred the evening, but not enough to spoil the game. Mickelle scored the winning goal for her team, consisting of her and Bryan, and in frustration and anger, Riley kicked the ball over the yard's ancient wood fence. Jeremy happily retrieved the ball, and everyone pretended nothing had happened. Mickelle busied herself eating one of the ice cream sandwiches Bryan had brought from the freezer, giving Riley time to deal with his emotions.

He apologized to her later when they were alone. Then he added, "Maybe we really should make an appointment to see a counselor."

"When?"

He smiled. "Soon. I need to think about it some more."

Mickelle suspected he had ulterior motives for bringing this up, but she felt so happy with the progress he was making that she didn't argue. Instead, she put her arms around him and let him kiss her.

* * * * *

On Friday morning, Mickelle hugged and kissed Riley, who was more subdued than usual. After he left for work, she helped the boys off to school, then showered quickly and hurried outside to the Snail, anxious to keep her appointment with a financial counselor at Utah Valley State College. The May morning was warm, and the scent of flowers wafted in the air. Mickelle didn't even mind driving the Snail or the pitying looks she garnered from the young students in the parking lot. Life was good, and the car she drove had no bearing on who she was or would become.

After waiting half an hour, she was ushered into an office cubicle by a dark-haired girl almost young enough to be her daughter. The girl flashed her a smile. "I'm sorry I kept you waiting," she said, "but I have good news. I think we'll be able to get you some funding. You will have to maintain a certain number of credits, though."

When Mickelle left, she carried in her hands a short stack of financial aid forms that she needed to fill out and submit. Now she wouldn't need Riley's money to get her through college. She still craved his support, but felt confident that he would eventually come around. With a smile, she thought of the soccer game. Maybe one day her husband would even learn to be a gracious loser.

She decided to stop by the store and pick up pork chops to make Riley's favorite meal. Perhaps she would tell him tonight about the possibility of a new baby. She was only a week late, and while that was not an unusual occurrence, this time she felt hopeful. *Thank you, Father,* she prayed. *I am so grateful for all my blessings.*

She went to Macey's and decided to eat an early lunch at their snack bar. It wasn't often she treated herself to even such an inexpensive meal. By the time she had finished her hoagie sandwich and diet 7-Up and completed her shopping, it was nearly noon.

She could see nothing unusual about her house when she pulled into the driveway—not a single thing to warn her that her life would soon change forever. The kitchen door was unlocked, however, and at once uneasiness sprang to her heart.

"Hello?" she called. "Is anyone there?" She took a few tentative steps into the kitchen. "Riley? Bryan? Jeremy?"

No answer.

Mickelle lowered her single bag of groceries onto the small table. There was nothing out of place. "I must have forgotten to lock the door," she said aloud to dispel her sudden fear. "Good thing we live in a decent area."

Humming to herself, she put away the groceries. Then she did the breakfast dishes and swept the floor. "Now for a little gardening." She left the kitchen and started down the narrow hallway toward her room, where she planned to change her clothes. But something, glimpsed from the corner of her eye, caught her attention. Turning, she spied the crystal rose that had once graced her wedding cake. It lay on the tan shag carpet just outside the living room, smashed into pieces.

She gasped. "What? Who?"

Fear seized her heart and held her in its icy grip. Instinctively, her hand went to her abdomen, as though to protect her unborn daughter.

It's just an accident, she told herself calmly. *One of the boys got it out and dropped it. I just didn't notice it before.* But they had been warned countless time not to touch her collection.

She walked slowly to the living room, her heart pounding as she listened for intruders. Bending down, she began to gather the scattered pieces of her precious crystal rose. Another step brought her in full view of the living room, and when she saw the destruction there, she nearly stopped breathing. "Oh, my . . ." She stood frozen with horror, staring helplessly.

Her curio cabinet had been tipped over onto the television, which in turn had fallen onto the floor, crushed into ruin. Pieces of glass from the cabinet and the TV were scattered across the room, and Mickelle's carefully collected roses lay in a broken jumble inside the damaged cabinet. A few were spread out on the floor, including the red porcelain Capodimonte rose Riley had given her for their first anniversary. Unlike many of the others that had escaped damage or were broken only in one or two places, this rose looked as though someone had crushed it under the heel of a sturdy shoe and ground it into the carpet.

With a hand to her mouth, Mickelle gave a stifled cry of outrage. What had happened here? Fury filled her and she left the room, searching for a culprit, unmindful of any possible danger to herself. But the house was empty. Even the basement revealed no sign of intrusion.

Who would do such a terrible thing? A suspicion formed in her heart, but she didn't give voice to it. Instead, she searched sorrowfully through the remains of her rose collection to find something that could be saved. When she had removed all of the pieces from the cabinet, she struggled to right it. Tears rolled down her cheeks when she saw that not only was the glass shattered, but one of the solid wood side panels had cracked and been severely gouged from its fall onto the television set.

It was someone I know, she thought. *Someone with a key.* This realization made the destruction more disturbing.

There were about fifteen salvageable roses, made of stronger material than the rest. These she gathered onto the couch before finding a box and placing the other pieces inside. Thoughts of revenge filled her mind, blocking out the feelings of betrayal in her heart.

The one material thing I cherish! How dare he! She didn't name the "he," not yet. It was still possible that she was mistaken. *Oh, please let me be wrong!*

She nearly jumped when the phone rang. It was Monte Williams, Riley's boss. "Is Riley sick?" he asked.

Mickelle felt her spirits sink even further. "No," she said, her throat suddenly dry, her voice croaking. "He's not here. He left for work on time this morning." She drew in a quick breath. "I hope there hasn't been an accident."

But she almost hoped there had been. A man in a car accident couldn't be responsible for the wanton destruction of her roses.

"Nobody's seen him here," Monte said. "And his time card hasn't been punched."

"Well, thank you for calling. I'll look for him."

"If you find him, tell him to get in here or he'll be looking for another job."

Mickelle hung up on the man without further comment. No wonder Riley hated the guy!

She stared at the living room without seeing anything. *I must call the hospitals. Maybe the police.* Then another, more chilling idea came to her. She searched the house again, beginning in her room. Uncertain what she was looking for, she examined everything thoroughly. In the clothes closet she shared with Riley, she found it.

The metal box was empty, gaping as though the opening was a mouth laughing at her, mocking her. Normally it was locked by a key Riley carried with him always, to prevent the boys from getting to what was inside.

Mickelle gulped. She bit her quivering lip. *Why would Riley need a gun?*

She remembered a comment he had made when Monte had given Greg the California promotion: "I'm so angry I could—I could kill him!"

Had Riley taken leave of his senses? He had apparently returned to the house for the gun, but would he use it? Fear crept through Mickelle, permeating every part of her body. She began to tremble.

What if Riley's target wasn't his boss?

"You're overreacting," she told herself.

She paced, not knowing what to do. *Please, God,* she prayed over and over, not daring to voice her fears. When the doorbell rang, Mickelle jumped as she had at the sound of the telephone.

Two police officers stood on her cement steps. Mickelle stared at them, wide-eyed. She noticed little things: one of the officers, the one in back, had a hand on the black iron railing along the porch; the same officer had a black mole on his left cheek, beneath hazel eyes. The other officer twitched his nose as though he needed to sneeze. "Mrs. Hansen?" he said.

"Yes. May I help you?" Her voice was remarkably calm, but inside she was screaming, telling them about the missing gun. About her fear that had a name, but not one she was capable of voicing.

"I'm afraid we have some bad news for you," said the officer in front. He had bright blue eyes like Jeremy, but dark hair like Riley.

"My children—"

"It's not your children."

Mickelle's fist went to her mouth in utter relief. *So tell me!* she shouted silently.

"May we come in?"

She hesitated. "What's this about?"

"Your husband."

Wordlessly she backed away from the door, allowing them to enter. She led them from the tiny, narrow entryway into the living room. Their eyes went from the ruined cabinet to the smashed television.

"I just got home," she explained lamely. "The cabinet must have fallen over."

The policemen glanced briefly at each other. "I think you'd better sit down," the blue-eyed officer said.

Mickelle shook her head. "Tell me." The words weren't a scream like in her head, but whispered and filled with trepidation.

"Your husband's been killed."

She sank to the chair that Riley had always used. "No," she mumbled. "It can't be." She looked at them pleadingly.

"I'm afraid it's true," the same officer continued. "We found his truck up the canyon. Apparently . . . witnesses say he drove off a cliff."

"But the gun . . ."

"What do you know about a gun?" the second officer asked.

Mickelle's gaze shifted to him, but she could barely see him through the haze of tears filling her eyes. "My husband's gun is missing. I noticed just before you came."

The officer with blue eyes squatted near her seat. "There was a gun found with the body. We believe he intended to kill himself with it. Witnesses say he sat in the truck for a long time before he drove over the edge."

Mickelle couldn't believe it. "He just drove over?" she asked, the numbness spreading through her body. Her face was wet and she was crying, but she didn't feel the tears or the sobs.

"Is there anyone we can call?" the second officer said.

Mickelle stared at him without seeing.

"Please," the officer with the blue eyes said. "Do you have any family?"

"Sisters. My parents." Mickelle made no move for the phone. Riley had committed suicide. She didn't doubt the officers for a minute. He had left her. Now she understood about the curio cabinet and Riley's destruction of her collection. It was his last attempt at hurting her. He wanted to make her pay for his pain, to make her suffer for not letting him control her. *Misery loves company,* she thought. *He would be happy to see me now.*

Riley had completely and totally removed himself from her reach—from everyone's reach. His last stab. His final rebellion. His final triumph.

What a waste.

The blue-eyed officer had the phone in his hand, using the preprogrammed numbers in her portable phone. Mickelle put her head in her hands and sobbed.

Things had been going so well between them. There had been such improvement in the last week. She had actually begun to have hope for their relationship. Even he had seemed happier.

So what had brought him to that point? Had he seen her dressed up that morning for the interview with the financial counselor and become jealous? Had her words to him about divorce last Monday driven him to despair?

Mickelle had no concept of how long she sat in Riley's chair and cried while the officers tried to console her. Then her mother was there and her sisters, and shortly afterwards, her father. Mickelle was wrapped in the cocoon of her family's love. Eventually her tears abated, and the numbness took over.

"The boys . . ." she began once.

"Your dad went to get them," Irene told her. "Don't worry about anything. We're here to help."

Mickelle watched, detached, as her family went to work. Talia and Lauren went to arrange things at the funeral home, while Irene called Mickelle's church leaders, answered the ensuing phone calls, and fielded people who appeared at the door. In between, she cleaned up the broken glass in the living room.

When the boys arrived, Mickelle saw immediately that her father hadn't told them what had happened. Jeremy ran to hug her and Bryan stood uncertainly by her chair, his hands clenched together tightly.

Jeremy's eyes were huge. "What's wrong, Mom? Grandpa wouldn't tell us. But he's—why's everyone acting so strange?"

"I thought you would want to be with them when they heard," Terrell explained.

"Thanks, Dad." Mickelle closed her eyes, feeling new tears escape from beneath the lids. "It's your father," she said softly. "He's dead."

Jeremy started crying, but Bryan stared at her, shaking his head. "No," he said.

"Yes, he is." She held her hand out to him, at the same time wrapping an arm around Jeremy. For a moment Bryan hesitated, as though he might run from the room. "Come here," Mickelle beckoned, and Bryan came into her arms, sobbing loudly.

Mickelle held her boys, and they all cried together.

CHAPTER 8

Rebekka's family didn't take the idea of her leaving easily, but in the end they had to agree. "It seems you've already made your decision," Philippe said, seeing the firm set of her jaw, "and I guess it's up to you. You're not a child anymore."

She smiled. "Thanks for noticing, Father."

"I wish you weren't leaving so soon." Danielle's eyes watered with unshed tears.

"Brionney needs me now," Rebekka answered, knowing that she stretched the truth. "And I need a change, Mother. I really do. It's not like I'll be gone forever. I just want to experience America."

"If that's what you need to do, we'll support you," Danielle answered, hugging her.

Philippe nodded, although Rebekka suspected that he would veto her decision if he thought it might make her stay. But her mind was made up, and she was too much like him in her determination.

Raoul was both the unhappiest and the most supportive about her leaving. "Would you like me to take you to the airport?" he asked with a sad face.

She shook her head. "No. But thank you. I'd rather say good-bye here, and take a taxi. It'll be easier for me that way."

Her father nodded. Rebekka knew that he agreed with her decision not to make a public display of her departure. Danielle was more reluctant, but she honored Rebekka's wishes.

Saturday morning finally arrived, and Rebekka bid farewell to her family. She didn't say good-bye to anyone else, although she gave Raoul a letter to pass on to Marc. She knew her brother planned to go with Marc and André to inspect their new bridge site again that morning. "Don't give it to him until I'm well in the air," she instructed.

Raoul hugged her tight. "I won't."

Rebekka clung to him for a moment, squeezing her eyes shut so hard they hurt. A tear slipped out of the corner. She pulled back and searched her brother's tanned features. His obvious reluctance to let her go mirrored her own reluctance to leave him. Over the years they had occasionally fought, but they had always been friends.

Her father and brother took her suitcases down to the waiting taxi. "If you need anything—money, whatever—let me know," Philippe said. He hugged her briefly, then Danielle flung her arms around her and sobbed as she had when Rebekka had left for her mission.

Rebekka gently extracted herself from her mother's embrace. She ducked into the taxi, pulling the door shut, and waved as the driver started away from the curb. *I love you,* she mouthed.

She had expected to cry for the first half of the taxi ride, then use the remaining time to compose herself before she arrived at the airport and embarked on her new life. But as soon as her family was out of sight, thoughts of Marc filled her mind. And then she couldn't cry because she wouldn't give him the satisfaction—even if he would never know.

She watched the familiar sights of Paris stream past the taxi. So many places reminded her of Marc. What would he say about her impulsive move? Would he miss her at all? Would he find some other excuse to visit her mother, or would he worship her from afar until he died a lonely, ignominious death?

Rebekka swallowed the bitterness in her mouth and lifted her jaw firmly. She would not think about him.

* * * * *

Marc picked up his younger brother, André, outside his apartment. On the first-floor balcony, André's wife and two little girls waved good-bye. "I'll be home for lunch," André called to Claire.

The tiny, dark-haired woman smiled. "I won't hold you to that, dear. But try to be home before dinner."

As André blew her a kiss, Marc felt a twinge of envy rise in his chest. Thoughts of Danielle came to him, as they always did when he saw couples in love. Of course, Danielle wasn't aware of his feelings and never would be.

"Is Raoul coming?" André asked.

"Yes, we'll pick him up last."

"I hope he's awake," André said. "Ever since he met Desirée, he's been a little distracted."

"A little!" Marc snorted. "The other day when we went out to lunch, I caught him just about ready to cut his steak with a pen. And he tipped over his water twice!"

André threw back his head and laughed. "Yep, that sounds like Raoul. I'll bet he marries her."

Marc sobered instantly. "I hope he does," he said quietly.

André regarded him for a moment without speaking. "So, have you seen Rebekka lately?"

Marc shook his head, glad for the change of subject. "No. I think she must be mad at me, though I can't think what I did to her."

"Maybe she's got a boyfriend."

It was an idea Marc hadn't considered. "I guess that could be it. But I think she would have told me, don't you?"

"Well, she's my friend too, and she hasn't told me anything."

"Maybe you could call her." Marc tapped the steering wheel with his fingers. "That way you could find out what's going on."

"I don't think Claire would appreciate it. I mean, she knows I used to have a crush on Rebekka."

Marc raised his eyebrows. "You did? I never knew that."

"It's true."

"But she's so young. You're what, seven years older than she is?"

"It wasn't the age," André said. "Seven years, ten years—it doesn't matter. But she never looked twice at me."

"Maybe you never let her know how you felt." For some reason he couldn't define, Marc was beginning to find this conversation uncomfortable.

"Well, she was always too tied up with . . . and then I met Claire. Oh, never mind. Let's just ask Raoul what's wrong with her. But I'll bet she's got a boyfriend. It's bound to happen to everyone sometime."

"It can't be a boyfriend."

André's voice took on a teasing note. "You're just jealous because she decided not to wait for you anymore."

"Oh, right." Marc rolled his eyes. "Rebekka hasn't had a crush on me since she was fourteen. She grew out of it a long time ago. We're just friends."

André smirked. "That's what you think."

Marc made a rude, smacking noise with his lips. "Oh, you're just upset that you weren't her idol."

"You got me there," André said with a laugh. "Thank heavens Claire loves me. And the girls. I haven't got what it takes to have an unrequited love."

Marc frowned at the sudden pain the words brought to his heart. "No one has what it takes for that."

André peered at him. "Well, thank heavens that's not your problem, either. Think of it this way: now that Rebekka isn't taking up so much of your time, you can find a wife. You're not getting any younger."

André's words were light, but Marc grimaced. "Don't you start with me. I hear enough of that from Josette. She's constantly on my case."

"Older sisters are like that."

"She's only a few minutes older. That hardly qualifies her as—"

"Look, there's Raoul outside waiting for us," André interrupted when they turned onto the next street. "No, he's going back inside. His parents are with him. Didn't you tell him we were coming? Honk so he'll see us."

"He knows we're coming." But Marc gave a short blast on his horn, just in case. With the ease of long habit, his eyes went to Danielle, drinking in her beauty. He wished he could talk to her, even if it was only about the weather.

Raoul turned and held up a finger, signaling them to wait. He briefly conversed with his parents, kissed them on their cheeks three times, and sprinted toward Marc's car. He slid into the backseat. "I didn't realize it was time for you guys to pick me up. So are they expecting us? Do we need to stop at the office first?"

"I don't." Marc noticed that Raoul didn't explain why he had been outside so early. *Well, a man's business is his own.* He was dying to ask about Rebekka, but didn't want to appear too anxious. Maybe André would bring it up.

But André and Raoul were talking about Desirée, Raoul's new girlfriend. "She's taking the missionary lessons," Raoul was saying. "I've never prayed so hard in my life. I don't know what I'll do if she doesn't join. I'm crazy about her."

"What if she doesn't?" André asked.

Raoul's brows drew together. "She has to. I'm not giving up on her."

Marc stopped at a red light. "Like your mother has never given up on your father." Until the others looked at him, Marc hadn't realized that he had spoken aloud. The light turned green, and in relief he busied himself with driving.

"Yeah," Raoul said. "She's a pretty neat person, my mother."

Marc felt his friend's eyes boring into the back of his head, and he wondered if Raoul had possibly guessed his secret. The only one to whom he had ever confided his love for Danielle had been Brionney Fields, now Brionney Hergarter, and he had confessed to her only because she had already figured it out. No one in his family knew; he was almost certain of it. He had learned to be careful over the years. He had even almost become engaged to a woman once who had served in the mission field with him. But in the end, he had let her go because he couldn't love her as she deserved to be loved.

Only one woman had come close to breaking his obsession with Danielle, and that was Brionney. He still regretted letting her return to America. Over time, he was certain his love for her would have grown and overcome his passion for Danielle. He should have gone after her.

Marc pushed the thoughts aside, unwilling to relive the memories they evoked. "So what's up with Rebekka? Why won't she return my calls? She's not still sick, is she?"

From the corner of his eye, he saw Raoul shake his head. "Rebekka's fine," he replied tersely. "So, has the cement arrived?"

Marc blinked twice at the quick change of subject. What was his friend hiding? Being one of the senior partners in the engineering firm had taught him a lot about people, and he sensed now that there was something Raoul was not telling him.

"Well, I'm a little concerned about her. Does she," Marc took a deep breath, "have a new boyfriend or something?"

"No-o-o." Raoul elongated the word as though to give himself time to think.

André swiveled in his seat. "Then speak up, man. Why is Rebekka mad at Marc?"

"She's not . . .well, not exactly."

Marc felt an odd panic swell in his breast. "You can't deny that she's been avoiding me," he said tightly, stopping at another red light.

"Well, no. I mean, yes . . . I don't know." Raoul looked miserable.

Marc held his breath and slowly let it out as he turned onto the freeway. "Look, Raoul, what's going on? Rebekka and I have been friends since she was five and I was fifteen. If she's in some kind of trouble, I'd like to help."

Raoul glanced nervously at his watch. "Well, I guess it's okay to tell you now. I mean, she had to be there at eight-thirty, and it's after that now."

"She had to be where?" Marc was feeling angrier and more confused by the moment.

"At the airport. She's going to Utah—well, actually, Alaska first and then to Utah."

Marc swallowed hard. "She's taking a trip? Why didn't she tell me?"

"Not a trip, exactly. She's going to *live* there. For a time, anyway. She's going to be a nanny until she can start teaching French or something."

Marc's jaw dropped. He wondered if he was hearing right. Why would Rebekka leave France without telling him? Why would she leave France at all? She had never said anything about wanting a change.

André glanced at Marc and then back to Raoul. "She left without saying good-bye?"

Raoul brightened. "She left a letter for Marc." He made a face. "Nothing for you, André. Sorry."

"Story of my life," André mumbled good-naturedly.

Marc ignored his brother. "Let me see it," he demanded. Raoul thrust the letter under his nose. Eagerly, Marc ripped it open.

"Careful of that car!" André's voice rose to a squeak as Marc braked to avoid hitting the car in front of them. "Do you have to read it now?"

Marc didn't bother to reply. There was no place to pull over, so he scanned the letter as he drove.

Dear Marc,

I'm sorry for leaving without telling you. It's just that Brionney's come up with an offer I can't refuse. I'm not content with my life as it is, so I have to go and find what it is I am missing. I'm sure you'll agree that I must follow my dreams. I'm going to Anchorage, Alaska, first, and then on to Utah. I don't know where I'll be staying yet, but I'll send you an e-mail soon.

Take care,
Rebekka

"Marc, watch out for that—" André sighed with relief when Marc switched lanes just in time.

Marc dropped the letter in disgust. It told him nothing of why she was going, nothing of what he had done to provoke her mistrust. There had been a time when Rebekka had shared everything with him. What had gone wrong?

André retrieved the note and read it quickly. "Well, good for her," he commented.

Marc's jaw tightened. "How long have you known?" he questioned Raoul.

"Wednesday, I think it was. But she first talked to Brionney a week or two ago. It was that day you went to the street meeting with the missionaries."

That had been the last time Marc had seen Rebekka. He felt numb at the unbelievable fact of her departure. They were friends— no, closer than friends. She was like a little sister to him. In fact, she had taken the place in his life that had been vacated by his real-life sisters: Pauline, who had been ripped from him by death, and his twin Josette, who had deserted him by marriage.

He thought hard to see if she had given a clue to the reason for her departure, but wrack his brain as he might, he couldn't think of a single thing. Her words and actions up until the day of the street meeting had been normal, though he did admit that Rebekka's actions had often remained a mystery to him. Was that why he so enjoyed her company?

The more he thought about it, the angrier he became. She owed their longstanding friendship more than a flimsy little note. "What time does her plane leave?" he asked abruptly.

"What?"

"You said eight-thirty, but was that the time she had to be there, or the time the plane took off?"

"What's the difference?"

Marc forced his voice to sound patient. "For foreign flights, you have to check in at least an hour early. Maybe two."

"I don't know."

Marc took his eyes from the road and glanced briefly at his friend. "What time did she leave your apartment?" He held his breath as Raoul answered.

"About fifteen minutes before you came. She went by taxi. I offered to take her, but she didn't want to make a scene at the airport."

Marc smiled grimly. There was still time! They were going in the right direction; perhaps he could make it to the airport before her flight. She might think she could get away with a brush-off, but he would prove her wrong. He deserved an answer. He jerked the wheel, taking them to the next exit.

"Where are you going?" André asked.

"The airport."

Raoul leaned forward, and Marc caught a glimpse of his pale face. "You can't do that! I promised her I wouldn't tell you until she was in the air."

Marc felt like cursing, but managed to hold back his emotions. "Why'd you do a dumb thing like that?"

André cleared his throat. "I'm sure she had a good reason for not saying good-bye in person." Then he added, somewhat mockingly, "It's not as if you're her boyfriend or anything."

"No, but . . . ," Marc sputtered. He felt angrier and more upset than he had in years, and he didn't know who to blame. Rebekka?

Yes, she was at fault. They were friends, but she was treating him like a casual acquaintance. He wished her well—he really did—but he needed some sort of an explanation.

Ignoring the others, he sped toward his destination, hoping he was in time. When he arrived outside the airport, he tossed the keys to André and bolted from the car, heedless that he had stopped in a no-parking zone. André would take care of the car.

"Wait!" Raoul shouted after him. "She's going to land first in a place called Cincinnati, Ohio. Or something."

Marc put the information in his mind and kept running. He only knew that he *had* to get to Rebekka before her flight left. His eyes searched up and down the ticket counters and around the lobby, but she was nowhere to be seen. He searched for a TV monitor and found a flight leaving for Cincinnati at ten-fifteen. That must be the one! But when he tried to pass through to the gate, they wouldn't let him. "This is the way to the foreign gates," said a security guard. "Only ticketed passengers beyond this point." Marc explained the situation briefly, but the man still refused to let him through.

"But couldn't you at least let me . . . look, I'll leave you my identification."

"I'm sorry, but it's against the rules."

Marc was beginning to feel desperate. "Please! There's got to be some way!"

"I could page her."

"Okay."

While the man spoke on the phone, Marc paced. Time was racing by, and soon Rebekka would be gone. He glanced at the ticket counter. Perhaps he could buy a ticket to Cincinnati. But no, his passport was at home, and he didn't have any of the visas that might be necessary. He had submitted his visa application papers so he could attend an engineering convention in New York at the end of October, but that did him little good now.

Then he saw Rebekka, and his heart seemed to drop to his stomach. She was coming from the ladies' rest room just outside the security gate, carrying her purse and a small flight bag. She wore a black suit dress that fit her curves perfectly and set off her dark auburn locks. For a moment he watched her, not knowing what to say now that he had found her. He had planned to demand an answer for her unusual behavior, perhaps try to get her to listen to reason. But now he realized that André was right: as much as he didn't agree with it, he had no say in her decision.

"Rebekka," he called.

She looked up, and her white face paled further. She glanced once toward the security guards that blocked the way to the foreign gates, as though she might escape behind them. Marc was utterly confused. Why would she run away from him?

"Weren't you even going to say good-bye?" He tried to keep the hurt from his voice, but feared it came through anyway.

She didn't meet his steady gaze, but stared at his left ear. "There wasn't time," she said a bit breathlessly. "I've been busy. I was going to write."

"Why are you going?"

Now her gray eyes met his fleetingly, looking large in her oval face, and Marc felt an odd sense of déjà vu. Where had he seen those eyes before? They were Rebekka's, of course, and yet . . .

"I *have* to go, Marc."

"Why?" he pressed. "If it's some guy, just tell me."

She looked relieved. "Yes, it's a guy. I have to get away."

"Do you need me to talk to him? I can make sure he doesn't bother you."

"Playing the big brother again?" Her laugh sounded strained. "I have Raoul, remember." She stared down at her black square-heeled leather pumps. "But no, I don't need you to talk to him. It won't do any good."

He knew her well enough to see that her mind was made up, and he had no choice but to let her go. "I'm going to miss you."

"I'm going to miss you, too."

He hugged her, but her flight bag fell between them, making the contact unsatisfactory. The fragrance of her thick auburn hair filled his nose, arousing unfamiliar sensations within him. When he drew away, there were tears on her pale, fine-boned cheeks, and the sight made him want to hug her again.

He tried to smile. "Be happy."

"Good-bye, Marc," she whispered, her voice like silk.

She left, and Marc stared after her, feeling a great loss as she disappeared from sight. He pounded a fist into his other hand.

"There he is!" Marc heard André's voice behind him and turned slowly.

"You just missed her," Marc said. "You were right, André. She left because of a man. I wish I could pound some sense into that guy."

Raoul studied his face for a moment, then mumbled something about eyes and blindness that Marc didn't understand and was too distraught to analyze.

"She'll be okay," André said, slapping him gently on the back. "She's a survivor."

Marc nodded, trying to cast off the feeling of gloom that had settled heavily over his shoulders. He remembered feeling this way once before—when Brionney had left for America so many years ago. He hated losing another friend, hated change.

"Hey," Raoul said, intruding on Marc's dour thoughts, "my mom wanted to ask if you'd teach Rebekka's Sunday School class tomorrow. She has the lesson manual at home. Rebekka left so quickly that she wasn't able to make arrangements. One of us would do it, but we have our own classes to teach." He laughed. "And since you're the Sunday School president, we decided to ask you."

Marc brightened. "Sure. I'll get the book when we drop you off." At least he would be able to see Danielle, to talk to her and hear her velvet voice.

Yet for once, the anticipation of seeing his beloved was small comfort.

CHAPTER 9

Rebekka walked away from Marc on trembling legs, feeling her stomach do somersaults, which left her nauseous. In the instant she had looked up to see Marc staring at her, hope had leapt to life in her breast. Had he realized that she was the woman of his dreams? Had he finally understood that he couldn't find happiness without her?

Her disappointment at the ensuing conversation had been deep and bitter. She had simultaneously wanted to throw herself into his arms and slap his face. She also felt a sliver of satisfaction that her departure had upset him. That meant something, didn't it?

But what?

He was still in love with her mother—and probably had been for as long as Rebekka had loved him. The thought made her stomach more uneasy.

She spent the next hour before her departure trying not to cry. When she finally boarded the plane, she had her emotions under control but was exhausted from the effort.

A man sat next to her on the plane. He wore casual pants and a button-down shirt, much as Marc had been wearing at the airport. Also like Marc, he had lightly tanned skin as though he had spent some time outdoors. There the resemblance ended. Marc had a slightly rugged look, with dark hair, expressive brown eyes, and broad shoulders tapering to a narrow waist. This man's hair was a sandy blonde, and his eyes were green. He was also taller than Marc by a good six inches, and very lean. He was handsome, and his confident demeanor made him appear as though he had just stepped out of the pages of *Fortune Magazine*.

"Hello," he said in English, noticing her gaze. His voice was deeper than Marc's and full of life.

Rebekka smiled. "Hi," she replied easily.

"Good, you speak English." He grinned and held out his hand. "I'm Samuel Bjornenburg, and I was just thinking what an awfully long trip this was going to be since I don't speak French."

"Well, practically everyone speaks English these days."

"You're French?"

"Yes."

"Most of the French people I've met speak with English accents. Yours is decidedly American." He had an endearing way of cocking his head to one side as he spoke. Marc didn't do that. No, Marc would just look at her deeply, as though he could see into her soul. Of course, he hadn't seen her soul or the feeling there. Not even close.

"I have a lot of American friends," she answered.

"And your name is . . .?"

"Rebekka with two Ks. Rebekka Massoni."

"That's a German derivative, isn't it?" She nodded, and he continued. "Ah, I thought so. I do know a little German."

"So what are you doing in Paris if you don't speak French?"

"Business. I own a software company, Corban International. I usually send someone else, but sometimes there are things that only I can take care of. I have a company rep in Paris who does all the necessary translating."

"I'm a translator, too." Rebekka didn't think as she spoke. "In fact, I used to work for the American Embassy."

His eyebrows rose, and she noticed they were the same sandy color as his hair. "Oh? Are you looking for a new job?"

"Not really," she said. "I'm going to America to stay with a friend—well, actually, I'm going to help a friend of hers out with his children until he can find someone . . . it's a long story."

His smile was encouraging. "Good thing it's a long flight."

Samuel was good company, and Rebekka gradually felt her tension ease. She briefly shared with him her decision to find a new life in America, leaving out any mention of Marc. But even though she didn't speak of the man she loved, she couldn't help comparing him to this tall, good-looking stranger.

When the plane landed in Cincinnati, Samuel invited her to have something to eat with him in an airport restaurant while she waited for her next flight. She politely refused, explaining that her plane would be leaving too soon. The real truth was that the last thing she wanted was to encourage his attentions. Not when her mind was so filled with Marc.

"Well, thanks anyway for the great conversation," he said graciously. "This has been the most pleasant flight I've had in a long time." He paused, looking at her for a few seconds without speaking. "You're quite a woman, Rebekka with two Ks—intelligent, witty, *and* beautiful. I don't know what you're running from in France, but if you're ever ready to stop running, or if you need a job, give me a call." He handed her an off-white business card embossed with gold foil lettering.

"Thank you." She shook his hand briefly. *How observant he is, and how like Marc—except where my feelings for him are concerned. Marc never saw how much I loved him . . . I wonder if Marc thinks I'm beautiful . . . Oh, stop it, Rebekka. Marc is gone.*

She turned resolutely and began making her way to the next gate. There were other men out there, and somewhere she would find one who would make her forget Marc. As she turned the corner, she saw that Samuel, the youthful CEO of Corban International, still watched her with his lively green eyes.

She didn't have to change flights again, though her plane stopped once to exchange a few passengers and take on more fuel. When she finally arrived in Anchorage on Saturday night at ten o'clock local time, she was glad to get off the plane and stretch her legs. She had read two entire novels during the last flight, and her eyes ached despite the nap she had worked in between books. A glance at her watch told her that it was morning in Paris, and nearly time for her to wake up and get ready for church. She wondered who her mother had found to teach her class, and if Marc missed her yet as terribly as she missed him.

"Rebekka!" Brionney waved enthusiastically from where she stood in a crowd of others who were awaiting loved ones. Her chin-length blonde hair was almost white, her eyes a bright sky-blue. Two girls stood next to her, looking up shyly. "You look positively wonderful!"

Rebekka hugged her and kissed her cheeks. "You're looking well yourself." The last time Brionney had visited her brother in Paris, she had complained of her weight, but Rebekka saw that she had little to complain of now.

"It's all the exercise I get with the twins," Brionney confessed. "They run me ragged. And they still like to nurse more than they like bottles, so I can't eat enough to put on too much weight. It's a nice change for me."

"You were always beautiful."

Brionney hugged her again. "Keep saying things like that, and I won't let you move in with Damon for any amount of time!"

Rebekka laughed, then turned her attention to the girls. "You must be Savannah and Camille." The girls nodded vigorously.

"We left Rosalie and the twins at home with Daddy," Savannah reported. She looked just like her mother with her white-blonde hair and startling blue eyes. Camille also had blue eyes, but hers were darkened with an intriguing mixture of brown.

"You've grown a lot since your last picture."

Savannah's cheeks dimpled when she smiled. "I'm eight and a half now. Camille just turned six last week. We had a party."

"You did? Was it fun?" At Rebekka's question, Camille nodded soberly.

Savannah continued, "And Rosalie's four and the babies are zero—well, seven months, but that doesn't really count."

"It does so," Camille interjected.

Brionney sighed. "I can't tell you how many times we've had *that* conversation." She paused. "Well, I guess we'd better get your luggage."

Savannah tugged on her mother's hand. "Mom, you didn't tell her." Sorrow creased Brionney's face, and tears rose in her eyes.

"What's wrong?" Rebekka asked.

"It's my brother-in-law. He died yesterday. They're delaying the funeral until Tuesday so we can be there. We'll have to leave on Monday."

"On Monday," Rebekka repeated. She had expected at least a week in Anchorage. "I'm so sorry. How's your sister holding up?"

Brionney began walking. "I don't know, really. I've just talked to her once since it happened. Of all my sisters, she's the one who kept mostly to herself, though I think I'm beginning to understand that it was more because of her husband than anyone else. Turns out he was kind of possessive."

"How'd he die?"

Brionney glanced at the girls, who had run ahead. "He committed suicide. Ran right off a cliff in his car. My mom says he had planned to shoot himself, but he must have chickened out at the last moment. I still can't believe it. My dad says he's had a lot of mental problems because of the seizures he used to have and the medication he took for so many years. I don't know. I feel like I shouldn't blame him, but I do. I've never heard my sister sound so lost. She really loved him."

"I'm sorry." Rebekka put a comforting arm around Brionney as they continued walking. "That's tough."

"Well, I suppose we'll get over it eventually. Mickelle, too. But I can't imagine living without Jesse. Mickelle has to be hurting really bad."

Rebekka could imagine it—at least somewhat. Marc was dead to her now. Tears burned behind her eyes, but she clamped her jaw tightly shut until the emotion faded. It wasn't the same thing, not really. Marc still lived out there somewhere, even if he was not a part of her life.

"At any rate," Brionney continued, "I don't expect you to fly with us on Monday. Damon can't leave until Friday at the earliest, so I thought you could just stay with him and the kids until then. They have a part-time cook, and a housekeeper, so you won't be alone with them. The housekeeper is actually going with them to Utah until they can find a replacement, but she's not very good with the children."

"Probably because they're making the messes." A picture popped into Rebekka's mind of a mean-looking woman following the children around to prevent them from dirtying anything. She nearly laughed.

"Something like that," Brionney said.

"I can still go with you. I don't mind flying again so soon."

"But you wanted to see Alaska. It's not doing you any good to stay just a day." She gave a long sigh. "And to think that the other choice in flights was to change planes in Salt Lake City. You could have just stayed there."

"It's okay, Brionney. Don't worry about it. I'm here now, and I'll do whatever you want."

Brionney grinned. "I was hoping you'd say that. With us having to leave so quickly, there's a whole list of things I haven't been able to do yet. I was hoping you'd stay and make sure they get done."

"Okay," Rebekka said, laughing. "I'm at your disposal."

"You're a life-saver. I'm so glad you're here."

* * * * *

On Monday morning, after Brionney's friend Damon had driven the Hergarters to the airport, Rebekka took Brionney's short list of things to do and began her duties. First she packed the rest of the toys and books in the children's bedrooms and stacked the boxes with the others in the living room, then she began to work on the kitchen items. She was kneeling on the floor, elbows deep in pots and pans, when she heard a sound and looked up to see a man watching her.

He was in his late thirties, she decided, and his short hair was a yellow blonde. His angular face was full of sharp planes, from his slightly hooked nose to his strong chin. He wore the beginnings of a moustache over well-molded lips, but his best feature by far was his amber-brown eyes, framed by thick, feathery brows. While he wasn't the type Rebekka would normally consider handsome, he had a magnetism that somehow compelled her to return his gaze.

"Hello," she managed, sitting back on her feet. "You must be Damon." She recognized him vaguely as the shadowy figure who had helped Jesse load the Hergarters' luggage into a borrowed van that morning when she was still half asleep.

He smiled, and she caught a glimpse of something gold in his mouth as he spoke. "Yes, Damon Wolfe. And you must be Rebekka." He moved toward her with an outstretched arm.

She came to her feet, her own hand extended. "Nice to meet you. I mean, I kind of saw you this morning when you were piling suitcases into a van." She grinned. "At least I think it was you, and I'm pretty sure it was a van. I must still have jet lag."

He laughed, a warm, full sound, but the unique amber eyes held a sadness that made her wonder if he still mourned his dead wife. "It was a van. But I took it back to its owner." He perused her work. "Can I help you?"

"Well, actually, this is pretty much the last room," she told him. "I've packed the rest of the children's things, and Brionney had her room already done. There are a lot of boxes. I guess it's a good thing the furniture's staying."

"What about the books in the living room?"

Rebekka grimaced. "I didn't see those."

Damon bent over to pick up a stack of dishes Rebekka had wrapped in paper. "Well, good thing you're here. The movers are coming at noon. I thought I was going to have to do this all myself." He put his load gingerly into a box.

Rebekka started laughing. The idea of this multimillionaire packing someone else's boxes was just too funny.

"What?" he asked.

"Nothing." His genuine puzzlement made her laugh harder. She collapsed onto a wooden chair.

His mouth twisted into a wry smile. "I know exactly what you're thinking."

Rebekka sobered enough to gaze at him innocently. "What?" Another giggle burst through, and she covered her mouth with her hands.

His lips pursed. "You're thinking a man doesn't know how to pack dishes."

She shook her head, enveloped by another giggle. "It's not that."

"Then what?"

"It's just the idea of you packing at all," she finally managed. "I mean, are you doing *your* packing?"

"No, I'm hiring a company. Oh, I see—you have a problem with me packing because I have a lot of money."

She nodded and began laughing again. "It's funny." A tear escaped and rolled down her cheeks.

"It's not *that* funny," he said, his lips twitching beneath the moustache.

"No," she agreed. Yet she didn't stop laughing. After all the agony with Marc, she needed a good laugh.

Damon began to chuckle. He sat down on the chair next to her and let out a loud laugh, which made Rebekka laugh even harder.

How long they laughed, Rebekka didn't know; but she felt the anger and sadness in her soul evaporate. The melancholy in his eyes also seemed to disappear, and a kinship sprang up between them. Finally they settled down, though a stray laugh still emerged occasionally.

Damon jumped to his feet. "I think I like you, Bekka!—I can call you Bekka, can't I?—and I think my children are going to like you, too. What do you say we go get them and grab a late breakfast?"

"But the movers . . ."

"We'll be back before they get here—with plenty of time to finish the packing. Have you ever known movers to be on time?"

"You're right." She stood and followed him from the room, noticing how broad his shoulders seemed. There was a lot to be said for a man who could laugh at himself and let others do the same without taking offense. It showed his self-confidence.

He led her outside to a dark-blue Mercedes and opened the passenger door. They drove ten minutes to Damon's house, a mansion really—especially to Rebekka, who had lived all her life inside an apartment building. She had always considered her parents wealthy, but this was way beyond her idea of rich. There were boxes everywhere, but no workers in sight. And she understood that this was just the beginning; the expensive furniture she saw everywhere would be going to Utah, as well.

"Tan! Belle!" Damon called. No answer.

He gave her a knowing smile. "Watch this." He made his voice louder. "I'm going out for some food. Wanna come?" Almost immediately, Rebekka heard movement among the boxes. A teenaged boy with brown hair and eyes materialized in front of them. He was as tall as Rebekka, but looked as though he might grow again at any second.

"This famished young person is my son, Tanner," Damon said. "Tan for short. Tan, this is Bekka."

"Nice to meet you," Tanner said politely. "And actually, Dad's the only one who calls me Tan. Everyone else says Tanner." The lower half of his hair was close-cropped, but the top hung to one length about an inch above his ears.

"I'm glad to meet you, Tanner. I had no idea you were so grown up. I'll bet you're going to be taller than your dad one day."

The tips of Tanner's exposed ears reddened. "Maybe," he said. Rebekka saw Damon flash her an amused glance over the boy's head.

Tanner looked at his dad. "Where we gonna eat?"

"Where would you like to go?"

"Anywhere."

"That's a first. You usually have an idea. What happened—cat got your tongue?"

Tanner shrugged, but his adoring glance at Rebekka spoke volumes.

Damon seemed to know when to back off. "Have you seen Belle?"

"She's hiding," Tanner said in a loud whisper. "She says she's not going to Utah."

"I am not hiding," proclaimed a small voice from nearby. Rebekka looked around but couldn't find the speaker.

"She's mad," Tanner continued.

"Am not!"

Damon put a quieting hand on his son's shoulder. "I guess Belle isn't here," he said. "I think we'd just better go out to eat without her. But that's okay, because she doesn't like McDonald's that much."

"It's really her favorite," Tanner whispered to Rebekka.

To Rebekka's right, a box rose partially and two little feet appeared. Damon helped lift the box off his daughter. She looked up at them through brown eyes tinted with amber like her father's, her tiny hands clutching a stuffed brown bear that was half as tall as she was. She lifted her chin. "I wanna go, too."

"Okay, but first I want you to meet Rebekka."

"I thought her name was Bekka."

"That's for short—like Belle, for Isabelle."

Belle's eyebrows drew tightly together. "I like Rebekka better."

Rebekka bent down to face the little girl. "You can call me Rebekka."

Belle regarded her quietly for a moment. "You talk kind of funny."

"Belle," Tanner groaned.

"She's from France, remember?" Damon said.

"Oh, yeah. Then you know what my name is."

"Yes, it means beauty." Rebekka touched the bear. "And who's this?"

Belle held him tight. "Bear."

"Just Bear?"

She nodded solemnly.

"Is Bear going to eat with us?"

Belle nodded.

"Well, I hope he doesn't eat too much." Rebekka was gratified to see a brief smile. She straightened and looked at Damon in triumph.

But Belle wasn't finished. "I don't like you, and I want you to go back to France!"

Having made her announcement, Belle turned and disappeared into the maze of boxes. Damon started after her. "Don't worry," he called over his shoulder to Rebekka. "She likes to shake people up."

Tanner looked at her sympathetically. "She'll come around."

Rebekka realized that her mouth was hanging open in shock. She smiled at Tanner and was gratified to see him flush. At least one of the children had taken to her. Still, maybe this job wouldn't be as easy as she'd expected.

Before long, Damon had rounded up Belle and they were on their way to McDonald's. Once there, he took care of everything, including making a trip to the rest room with Belle. Rebekka was amazed at the wealth of kindness and patience in the man.

It was then she realized that since Damon had walked into Brionney's kitchen, she hadn't once thought of Marc.

CHAPTER 10

Tuesday dawned—the morning of Riley's funeral. Mickelle was so numb and exhausted that she didn't think she could cry any more tears. But when she saw Riley's bulk in the casket, his bruised and battered face forever molded into an expression of peace that he had rarely displayed in life, she began to sob again.

It's not my fault, she told herself.

But she felt that it was. She kissed his cold, tranquil face before allowing them to close the casket one final time. Her heart ached.

The service was beautiful and comforting to Mickelle. She listened as her father talked about Riley's good qualities and the challenges he had faced because of his seizures. And she began to forgive him for leaving her.

I cannot condemn him for this, she thought. *The Lord will be the judge. Only He knows what desperation and confusion could have led Riley to commit such an act.*

If only she could forgive herself so easily.

Another thought, less charitable than the first, came as she glanced around at those who had come to the funeral. *Riley would love all this attention. He would be glad to see my tears.*

Brionney and Jesse had flown in from Anchorage the day before, and Mickelle was glad she had delayed Riley's funeral so they could be present. However, she wished the reunion with her little sister could have taken place under better circumstances. With everything going on, they had only moments to exchange a few words.

Brionney's three daughters were cute and well behaved, and the twins noisy—at least one of them—though they were so cute that no one seemed to mind. As the youngest children in the family, with the exception of Zack's children in France, they had no end of older cousins who were wannabe baby-sitters.

After the burial at the cemetery and a luncheon at the church, Mickelle went home. Her parents and sisters stayed until the evening meal was cleared away and the dishes washed. Then they went home to their waiting families. Irene and Terrell were the last to leave.

"Are you sure you don't want me to stay a few more nights?" Irene asked. "I really don't mind. Or if you'd like, you can all come home with us."

"No, thank you, Mom. You've done enough." Mickelle and the boys hadn't been alone in the house since Riley had died. And she wanted to be. She wasn't worried about being alone; in fact, she couldn't feel much of anything. Except the guilt, and she would have to live with that.

Her parents left, carrying the few remaining boxes of Riley's things that she was sending to Deseret Industries. How thankful she was that her mother had helped her with that; going through his clothing was something she hadn't been able to face alone.

Mickelle snuggled into her bed with the boys. In the past week, neither of them had wanted to be far from her at bedtime, so she had let them fall asleep with her. She always had to move Jeremy back to his own room before too long, because he invariably wet the bed. His problem had grown worse since the accident, but Mickelle understood why and tried not to be angry.

She stayed with her sons until she heard their regular breathing. Then she arose and walked through the house, which had seemed small before, but now felt large without Riley. Her steps took her to the living room, where the only sign of the violence that had occurred there were the scars on the curio cabinet and its missing glass. The remaining roses from her collection had been placed carefully inside the cabinet, despite its damage, and even the television had been replaced with an old one belonging to her parents. At a casual glance, the room appeared unchanged.

She sat on the couch in the dark, staring at nothing. *Why did you do it, Riley?* She wished she could talk to him. *Do you regret it? What's it like being dead? Do you miss me?* Suddenly she wanted his arms around her, craved desperately to smell him and run her hands through his thick hair, to feel his warm body pressed against hers. But all that was denied her now . . . perhaps denied her forever.

Devastation struck deeply through the protective veil of numbness that had been her constant friend and companion since the police had arrived on her doorstep. Mickelle fell face-downward onto the couch, pounding it with her fists and wailing out her frustration in sobs muted against the cushions. *I hate you!* she screamed silently. But she didn't. She loved him, and she wanted him back.

When she was too weak to cry more tears, she lay on the couch, letting the desolation and misery continue silently in her mind. Eventually she felt sleep tug on her consciousness, and her eyelids drooped.

Then she saw it—a warm and full vision of hope that pierced her black despair. A little girl sat on a mother's lap, her eyes full of laughter and mischief. The mother gently brushed the girl's brown, loosely curled hair. The two shared a hug, so full of love that it brought a sweet ache to Mickelle's broken heart. Glancing up, she looked into the mother's face, startled to see that it was her. She glanced back down at the little girl, but the scene faded before she could see the child again clearly.

Abruptly, Mickelle was wide awake. Her hand went to her stomach, which was even more bloated than before. She had lost so much this past week, but inside she had something that was hers alone. Riley couldn't take it away or mar it with his bitterness—or even his death.

My daughter, she thought with the first smile she could remember in days. *Where the Lord takes away, He also gives.*

Slowly, she stood and made her way back to her room and the sleeping boys. She carried Jeremy to his bed, then snuggled next to Bryan and let herself drift off to sleep.

CHAPTER 11

On a Saturday two weeks after Riley's death, Mickelle was cleaning out the small shed in the backyard. Sasha watched her eagerly from a corner, wagging her tail each time Mickelle looked her way.

Actually, she hadn't planned on cleaning the shed, but had come looking for a screwdriver to fix the loose toilet paper holder in the bathroom. She had begun to clean because she couldn't find anything in the cluttered mess. More than a month earlier she had asked Riley to take care of the holder, but he had never gotten around to it. Now he never would.

At last, Mickelle spied a screwdriver small enough for the job. She picked it out of the cardboard box where it lay amid a jumble of screws, bolts, and other tools.

"There you are," Brionney greeted her as she emerged from the shed.

"Hi, Brionney."

Brionney's eyes took in her sister's old black jeans and black T-shirt. "I dropped the kids off at Talia's to play and escaped. Since we don't close on our new house until next Friday, I really had nothing to do. You know, it's weird staying with Mom; she's got everything so organized. I never thought I'd miss grocery shopping or sweeping the floor. Anyway, I thought I'd come see how you're doing. You don't mind, do you?"

"Not at all." Mickelle accepted the explanation at face value, though she thought it might be an excuse. At least one of her sisters or her parents stopped by each day. Mostly, she was grateful for the company.

She grimaced and held up the screwdriver. "I'm going to take a shot at fixing something. Want to watch?"

Brionney must have thought the idea amusing, because she burst into a grin. "Sure."

Mickelle led the way into the house. Brionney stopped for a minute to talk to the boys, who were on their way out to play soccer in the backyard. Mickelle took advantage of the moment to wet a piece of tissue and wipe off the dirty fingerprints on the bathroom wall. Once she would have been appalled at that type of cleaning, but now she realized it was necessary for her survival.

Mickelle attempted to tighten the screw, but despite her efforts, it remained loose. Now what? Impotent fury rose in her chest, and she had to fight the urge to throw the screwdriver into the toilet. What was the use? She'd only have to fish it out.

"It's stripped, huh?" Brionney had come into the small bathroom, and now watched her with interest.

"Yeah." Mickelle felt miserable. For one moment she had felt power and confidence, but in an instant it had been transformed into frustration and anger.

"Is it going into the two-by-four behind the plasterboard, or just the plasterboard?" Brionney asked.

"The two-by-four. But the hole is too big." Her frustration must have shown in her face, because Brionney gently removed the screwdriver from her grasp. "Good—that it's got the wood behind it, I mean. If you'll just show me where your Elmer's Glue is, and find me a few matches, we can fix it in a jiffy."

Mickelle found the items and watched as Brionney broke off the red match tips and discarded them. Then she squeezed glue inside the hole and inserted the matchsticks, using the handle of the screwdriver as a hammer. "There," she said, returning the screwdriver. "Now just wait until it dries, then put the screw back in."

Mickelle shook her head in wonder. "Where'd you learn that trick?"

"Well, I just sort of made it up once in Anchorage when I needed to hang something—I don't even remember what. Jesse was gone a lot, and he's not that handy at fixing things around the house anyway. I mean, give him a computer and a problem and he's a genius, and

he's great playing with the kids and helping them with their homework, but he's not real hip on screwdrivers and baby diapers. So I
made do with what I had." Brionney laughed. "It's amazing what you
can do when you have to."

Mickelle was quickly finding that out. She had thought Riley
contributed little to the household, but she discovered there were
things he had done. Like helping the boys with their math, filling the
cars with gas, and fixing holes in the walls.

They went into the kitchen and sat at the counter. "I can't stay
long," Brionney said. "The twins are a handful, even for Talia."

"Are they still nursing?"

"Oh yes, but they'll take bottles, too. They just don't like it as
well." Brionney leaned forward suddenly, her blue eyes earnest,
searching. "Mickelle, how are you doing, really?"

Mickelle met her gaze. "It's hard, but it's okay. The boys are
sleeping in their own beds now, and I'm getting by."

"I just can't understand." Brionney shook her head. "Why do you
think Riley did it?"

The boys had asked her the same question many times in the past
weeks, and Mickelle had developed an answer that had satisfied them.
"I think life just fell in on him all at once. He didn't get his promotion, I wanted to go back to school, he was released from his church
job, he had another seizure." She looked down at the yellow-
patterned counter, tracing a scratch in the Formica with her finger.
Her voice lowered as she added something she had not shared with
the boys. "I—I told him I wanted a divorce if he didn't start treating
me better." Mickelle began to cry, and at once Brionney left her stool
and put her arms around her.

"It's not your fault."

Mickelle clung to her sister. "I know that in my mind, but my
heart doesn't feel the same way."

"But it will someday." Brionney tightened her hug. "I'm so very
sorry this happened."

"I know. And you've all been so good to us. In fact, Dad's been
spending so much time with the boys, talking and doing things, that
they seem to be adjusting to Riley's absence better than I am. I mean,
Jeremy's cried a few times, and he's wetting the bed every night, but

the plain truth is—no matter how I don't want to admit it—they weren't that close to Riley."

"It's natural that you would miss him more. You loved him."

Mickelle detected a slight question in the statement. "I did love him," she confirmed. "Enough to want him to change. I wanted to be with him forever." Her tears began to fall again. "During the good times, it was really, really good. But I guess there were just too many problems for him to face."

"What can I do to help you?" Brionney's voice was agonized.

Mickelle straightened, trying to find her courage. "It's not all bad."

"What do you mean?" Brionney stepped back to look at her curiously.

"I mean Riley's dead, but there's a part of him that lives on."

"In the boys," supplied Brionney. "And you'll see him again in heaven."

"No, not just that." Mickelle smiled through her tears, glad to have something to share that wouldn't bring sorrow. "I'm pregnant. I mean, I haven't taken a test yet, but I'm almost three weeks late. I know I'm pregnant. I must be." She hesitated before adding, "It's the silver lining in this cloud, don't you see?"

Brionney's smile lit up her face. "Oh, that's wonderful! I know how much this means to you after so many years of not being able to get pregnant. Have you told the boys? Mom? Dad?"

"No one—except you." Mickelle felt the sadness drain from her heart and the hope return. It was the next high on the roller coaster of her emotions. "I wanted to be sure. And I wanted to keep it to myself for a time."

"I understand." Brionney hugged her again, this time in joy. "I won't tell anyone until you're ready. Not even Jesse, in case he might let it slip. But you need to take a test."

"I've scheduled an appointment on Monday with one of the nurse midwives at Mount Timpanogos Women's Health Care."

"I heard they were really good—and sympathetic."

Mickelle smiled. "That's why I'm going to them. I'm older this time, and I know it's going to be harder on me, but with a little female support I'll be ready for it. They wanted me to watch a video and stuff for my first visit, but I really wanted to talk to a real person, one on one. They said that was okay. Besides, I didn't want to wait clear until Friday, when they have the film." She lifted her shoulders and let them drop again. "I'll probably complain the whole nine months."

"Complain as much as you want. We'll all be here for you."

Their conversation was cut short when the boys ran into the kitchen, their cheeks bright with exertion from their game. "Grandma's here!" Bryan yelled. "And Grandpa and Uncle Jesse, too! They've got a surprise!"

"Come see!" Jeremy danced from foot to foot, tugging at her hand.

"What?" Mickelle glanced at Brionney, who only smiled enigmatically.

Mickelle was practically dragged out of the house by the boys. Her eyes widened when she saw her dad's truck in her driveway, loaded with her mother's piano. Jesse and Terrell were removing protective cording and blankets.

"You knew about this!" Mickelle accused her sister.

Brionney laughed. "Oh, yes. In fact, I was sent ahead to make sure you were home and that you didn't leave."

Mickelle hugged her mother. "But it's your piano, Mom. Or Zack's. He's the one who can really play."

Irene smiled warmly. "Zack isn't moving back to America any time soon; I think we all know that. And your father and I don't play. What do we need a piano for? I meant to give it to you a long time ago." Her face clouded, and the wrinkles under her eyes became more pronounced. "Actually, two years ago I did mention it to Riley, but he refused. Said he'd get you one himself, if you wanted it. He said you weren't interested in playing."

Mickelle's breath caught in her throat. "He—he never told me."

"I thought as much." Irene shook her head sadly. "I should have seen through him. I should have talked to you."

Mickelle recognized that denying her the piano had been one more way for Riley to control her. Why had he felt such a need?

They rounded up a few of the neighbor men to help carry the piano into Mickelle's living room. She had to push Riley's easy chair over by the couch to make it fit, but it looked wonderful.

"Thank you so much!" Mickelle ran her fingers over the white keys.

"It'll need tuning in four weeks or so when it settles," Irene said. "And you'll need this." She pulled out a book from the bench. "It's an adult all-in-one course. You teach yourself."

Mickelle didn't know what to say.

"Can I take lessons, Mom?" Jeremy asked eagerly.

Bryan played a few notes. "Me too."

"I think so. We might be able to swing it." Mickelle thought that with the life insurance money and the social security she would be getting, it might just be possible to afford a few extras.

Her heart swelling with thankfulness, she began to play "The Entertainer."

* * * * *

On Sunday, Mickelle took the boys to Church for the first time since Riley died. Everyone greeted them with kindness and love, and more than a few stopped to ask how they were doing. "I wish they'd quit asking," Bryan muttered. Jeremy nodded in agreement, but Mickelle was gratified to know that people cared.

During sacrament meeting everything appeared eerily normal—as though life had not changed in the least. Sister Sunberg, who normally sat in the middle row across from Mickelle, still jiggled her colicky newborn daughter constantly during the service. In front of her was Brother Chatham, whose head jerked as he began to doze soon after the sacrament was passed. Near the front on the left were the six Reeves boys, who poked at each other and made faces behind their parents' back. Jeremy and Bryan sat on Mickelle's left, as they always did. The only difference was that Riley's space on her right was empty.

The first speaker gave an interesting talk and bore strong testimony. A few people nodded in agreement or had tears in their eyes. The congregation sang a familiar hymn with feeling.

Sister Sunberg passed the baby to her husband, who continued to bounce the infant. To pause even for a moment would bring a wailing cry. Brother Chatham gave a snort and jerked himself awake, to the delight of the other Sunberg children. The older Reeves boy pulled the hair of the girl in the row in front of him, while the youngest gawked at a newlywed couple in the seat behind, who stared deeply into each other's eyes, ignoring the service completely.

The vacant space next to Mickelle seemed to scream for attention.

She joined in a congregational hymn, then listened to the second speaker talk about how to become part of an eternal family. She held Jeremy's hand.

Up and down went the Sunberg baby.

Mickelle's eyes were drawn again to the seat beside her. A tear slid down her cheek, and she quickly wiped it away.

* * * * *

Monday morning, after Mickelle got the boys off to school and changed the sheets on Jeremy's bed, she showered and readied herself for her appointment at Mount Timpanogos Women's Health Care. The sky was overcast, and she fought a feeling of impending doom.

"It's just depression," she told herself as she looked out the window. Her voice sounded loud in the quiet of the kitchen. She had been reading books about dealing with suicide and depression, and recognizing her emotions for what they were helped her deal with them, but today she was finding life particularly difficult.

Her appointment was at eleven, so she had plenty of time to put the house in order and read the mail. One of the letters quickly drew her attention. It was from the company who carried Riley's life insurance policy. She eagerly tore it open, hoping it was a check. Funds had been very tight during the past weeks, and without contributions from her family and neighbors, she wouldn't have been able to pay her bills at all.

There was no check, just a letter saying something about a "suicide clause." Mickelle felt her pulse race in her ears. She remembered something about that now. Did the fact that Riley had killed himself preclude her from receiving the money? Tears came so fast that she couldn't read the rest of the letter. Instead, she called her father at his real estate office.

"Calm down," he said gently. "Tell me more slowly."

She explained about the letter. "It seems like I won't get the money." She had already lost the money invested in Riley's truck since it had not been fully insured, and who knew how long it would be before the first social security check would arrive? What would she do?

"Look, don't do anything now," her father said. "I seem to remember that there's usually a time limit on the suicide clause. Let me check into it, okay? I'll be free to come over in about an hour."

"I won't be home. I have an appointment." Mickelle wasn't ready to tell him where, and he must have sensed her reluctance because he didn't ask.

"Just leave your policy and the letter on the table, and I'll look at it. I still have the key you gave me."

"Thanks, Dad."

"And, Mickelle . . ."

"What?"

"Don't worry. No matter what, you are not in this alone."

That meant more to her than anything. "I know that," she whispered.

When Mickelle hung up the phone she was shaking, but in control of her emotions. She set aside the letter and went out to her garden. The peas she had planted in March were beginning to ripen, and she pulled a few pods off the vine, opened them, and ate the firm peas with relish. Then she chewed on a pod, enjoying the sweet juices before burying the rest in the soil. The day was still overcast and gloomy, but she felt better.

As she drove to her appointment a short time later, a queasy feeling began in her stomach—not surprising given her condition, but unsettling nonetheless. She walked into the building feeling a little out of place among the younger women in the waiting room. Most looked pregnant with a first or second child.

They took a urine sample, then asked her to return to the waiting room. Instead of chafing at the delay, Mickelle thought of her daughter and began trying out names. She also imagined the expression on the boys' faces when she told them her surprise. They would be so excited!

She was soon called in to see a midwife. The slightly plump woman had short brown hair and was of average height. Her kind face encouraged trust. Mickelle felt content with her choice to come to the midwives for her care.

Then she was given the results of her test.

Negative.

Mickelle couldn't believe it. She was three weeks late!

In her exam, the midwife could find no sign of pregnancy. "Perhaps you're simply not as far along as you think," she suggested. "We could do a blood test. Or wait a few more weeks and do another test."

A sinking feeling began in Mickelle's chest, but she fought her despair. "Isn't there any way to know right now? For sure?" She felt that her life would end at that moment if she didn't know. She couldn't wait another day, hoping against hope. "I'm thirty-six years old, and my husband just died a little over two weeks ago. I can't go home not knowing. Please!"

The midwife was visibly touched by her desperate plea. "We could tell by an ultrasound, but I don't know if they have any free time." Her hand rested sympathetically on Mickelle's shoulder. "I'll be right back."

Mickelle waited, feeling her life hanging in the balance.

The midwife returned, smiling. "Someone hasn't shown up yet for their ultrasound, so they'll work you in."

The negative outcome was shortly verified. The midwife offered comforting words and suggested a checkup if her period didn't begin soon, but Mickelle barely heard her. She stumbled from the office, using every bit of strength she could muster to avoid falling into an abject heap on the floor. Once in the car, she drove to the far side of the parking lot where there were no cars. Crossing her arms over the steering wheel and resting her head against them, she allowed the deep sobs in her breast to break free.

There was no daughter.

There was nothing.

No hope at all.

Time passed, and her grief refused to be quenched. She wondered if she would cry forever. *This is all your fault, Riley!* It felt good to blame someone.

A knock on her window startled her. She looked up to see Brionney's concerned face. Mickelle unlocked the door, and her sister slid inside the over-warm car.

"What happened?"

"How did you find me?" Mickelle said through her tears.

"I waited at your house to hear how the appointment went, but you never came back. I decided to come see if you were still here. So what's wrong?"

Mickelle drew a shuddering breath. "I'm not pregnant. I'm just late or something. Maybe the stress . . ."

"Oh, Mickelle!" Brionney hugged her tightly. "I'm so sorry!"

Tears made her vision dim. "But I saw her! The night of Riley's funeral. I saw my daughter! She even had Riley's dark hair. Now there's no chance at all."

"I'm so very sorry, Mickelle," Brionney repeated. Mickelle could tell by her sister's voice that she felt helpless to assuage her pain.

"Everything is wrong. Everything!" Mickelle couldn't bear the agony any longer. First Riley had chickened out of their relationship by killing himself, then the life insurance had fallen through, and now her dearest dream had evaporated. All were gone.

Mickelle felt more devastated than the day she had learned of her husband's death. Riley had killed not only himself that day, but also her hope for their daughter.

CHAPTER 12

Rebekka liked almost everything about Utah. The peaceful house in Alpine was exceptionally large and beautiful, surrounded by lofty birch and black walnut trees and wide expanses of grass and flowers. The summer weather was perfect, and she was continually amazed at the sight of the clear blue sky unfettered by tall apartment buildings. Brionney was only fifteen minutes away in her new home in American Fork, and they saw each other often. Rebekka also savored the rare occasions she spent with Damon. Most of all, she was glad to have put some distance between herself and Marc.

One of the negatives of living with the Wolfe family for nearly four months was that Tanner's crush on her had become almost annoying. He turned moony-eyed the minute Rebekka walked into the room, and he monopolized every second of her attention until she wanted to scream for privacy. She longed for school to start next week, the last part of August, so she would have room to breathe.

"Go play with your friends," she constantly urged her ubiquitous shadow. But he chose to stay with her. His friends didn't seem to mind coming to the house instead, and they occupied themselves at the tennis court or in one of the two swimming pools.

There's something for being rich, she thought. At least his father's wealth made Tanner happy. He could keep his friends busy and still maintain his crush on her with minimal effort.

Belle was a different story. She spent her days trying to avoid Rebekka, and seemed bent on chasing her out of the country and especially away from her father. The little girl thwarted her authority at every turn and refused to allow Rebekka into her heart.

"I don't know what I did to make her hate me so much," Rebekka confided to Brionney the Thursday before the children's school started. Damon had come home at the agreed-upon hour of six-thirty, leaving Rebekka free for the rest of the evening. She would have liked to stay with him and talk, but Belle had somehow arranged to have him read to her alone in her bedroom. "It's like she doesn't want me around at all."

"She'll get used to you." Brionney picked up one of the twins, who was babbling loudly. "She's probably still having a hard time adjusting."

Rebekka grimaced. "It's been four months. And frankly, I think it's time I look for another job. I mean, as soon as Damon finds someone else for the children. Once I'm not her nanny, maybe Belle will start to like me."

"Oh." Brionney smiled noticeably. "Does that mean you're interested in Damon?"

Rebekka felt color rise to her face. "He's nice. I really like him. But you know, I've lived with them for almost four months now, and I hardly see him. He leaves at an indecent hour, like at four in the morning or something, and when he comes home, he's mostly alone with the kids. I couldn't tell you if we were actually compatible. We only exchange a few words now and then."

"Tell me about it!" Brionney said, rolling her eyes. "Jesse leaves early too, and when he comes home, I can tell his mind is still at work."

"Well, I wouldn't know about that. When Damon comes home, Belle makes sure I don't stick around. She gets whatever she wants. Now she's decided she wants a horse, and Damon is looking into buying the pasture next to the house. How can a child that young be so manipulating?"

Brionney smiled. "They manage." She tickled the baby in her arms. "This one here knows all about that. Don't you, Forest? Don't you?"

The eleven-month-old gave them an open-mouthed giggle. His twin, Gabriel, looked up from across the room, then returned to playing blocks with his sister Rosalie.

"So even if I liked Damon, there are still his kids to consider. I mean, I never thought dealing with children would be so hard. Maybe I'm just not cut out to be a mom."

That sent Brionney into a fit of laughter. "I tell you, it's different with your own kids. You get them one at time as babies"—she glanced at the twins—"well, mostly one at a time, and you sort of grow together."

"I hope so. All I know is that Belle hates me, and she doesn't want me anywhere near her father. And Tanner follows me just about everywhere. I'm afraid one of these days he's going to try to kiss me."

Brionney's eyes twinkled. "Well, there's less of an age gap between you and him than there is between you and Damon."

"That's a totally different thing! He's just a kid."

"I know, but it is kind of funny."

"I guess," Rebekka said glumly.

"Anyway, Jesse says the end is coming. I mean the end of the push and the overtime. They're going to contract with another software company to handle the foreign end of the business. That means they're going to tailor Jesse's program for hospitals in France and a few other countries. It's supposed to make a lot of money."

Rebekka frowned. "Well, there has to be a point where it's not worth it anymore. I mean, you can't sacrifice your family for money." Not even her father had done that.

"Exactly." Brionney kissed Forest and set him on the floor. He immediately crawled over to his siblings and knocked down their blocks. Over a chorus of indignant wails, Brionney continued, "Jesse and I have talked about this a million times. He has a tendency to work too long and too hard, but he's controlled it quite well. We've actually had him quite a lot the past few years, so for these few months we can sacrifice some time. By next month, he says he'll be home by five every day. And by next year, we'll have enough money for him to be able to take off just about whenever he likes. I can live with that."

"Yeah, but Damon already has so much money. Why does he need more?"

"He doesn't. But he likes business." Brionney's voice lowered. "To tell you the truth, I think he's lonely."

Rebekka grimaced. She knew all about that.

"I think he needs a wife even more than those kids need a mom. I guess that's why I asked if you like Damon. I mean, if you do, then I won't try to set him up with my sister."

"Your sister?" Despite her resolve not to force herself on Damon, Rebekka felt a twinge of jealousy. "How's she doing?"

Brionney gave a long sigh and tucked her chin-length blonde hair behind her ear. "Honestly, I don't know. To talk with her she seems all right, but every time I see her she's wearing black like she's in mourning. She's also been having anxiety attacks that haven't gone away like the doctor promised. She only goes to church occasionally, and she asked to be released from her nursery calling. I think it just hurt too much for her to see those little kids, knowing she wasn't going to have another baby. As for her boys, Bryan seems to be angry all the time, and Jeremy's problem of bed-wetting a few times a week has turned into an every night thing. I know Mickelle is over-whelmed, but she won't admit it. I think she's just stopped living."

"That's so sad. Is there anything we can do?" Suddenly, Rebekka's own problems came into perspective.

Brionney shook her head. "I don't think so."

"Well, try to set her up with Damon if you think it'll do any good. Not that he'll agree if her name isn't Belle or Work. You'll have to hit him over the head with it. You know, sometimes he reminds me of Marc." At the mention of the name, Rebekka's heart tightened and tears pricked behind her eyes. She took a deep breath.

"That's it, isn't it?" Brionney said softly. "Marc's the real reason you aren't going after Damon. You still miss him."

Clenching her jaw, Rebekka nodded slowly. "Terribly. He e-mails me all the time, but I haven't talked to him in person. It hurts too much." She looked pleadingly at Brionney. "Why do I have to love him? Why did I fall for a man who sees me as a child?"

"I don't know. I wish I did. But at least you're doing something about it. There are other fish in the sea."

Rebekka snorted. "First Marc, and now Damon."

"What?" Brionney leaned forward.

Rebekka stood. "Nothing. I guess I'll be getting back. I always receive an e-mail from my brother on Thursdays. I think he'll have some news for me. He's been ready to propose to his girlfriend for months, but her parents are upset because he wants her to join the Church first."

"Sounds like a mess."

"It is." *But at least they're both in love.*

Brionney walked with her to the door. "You want to do something on Saturday? Jesse promised me he'd spend some time with the kids so I could get out."

"Well, I'm not working. A neighbor girl watches Belle on Saturdays if Damon has to work. But I don't know. I'll give you a call."

She left Brionney and drove back to Damon's in the bronze four-door Nissan Altima GLE she had purchased upon arriving in Utah. The lights were out in Belle's room, though it was only eight, and Damon and Tanner were nowhere in sight. The house felt too large and empty.

Rebekka went to her room, where she had set up her laptop on a new desk Damon had purchased for her. She checked her e-mail, and found one from her brother and three more from other friends. None from Marc.

She read the e-mail from Raoul.

Dear Rebekka,

I miss you. I wish you were here to share with me this wonderful, incredible, unequalled night of all nights to be remembered forever. Desirée has agreed to marry me! My feet hardly touch the ground, I'm so happy. So ecstatically and completely happy. There has never been a man more happy than I on the whole entire earth!

She can't be baptized until she's away from her parents, so I'm not pushing it. But she promises she will go into the waters of baptism after we are wed. I'm willing to wait if that is what it takes.

You will come for my wedding, won't you? It won't be until the spring. I hate the idea of a long engagement, but will endure it if doing so makes my future in-laws happy.

I await your e-mail. I know that you will be happy for me. I only wish that you also could find someone who is worthy of your affections.

Your loving brother,
Raoul

Rebekka felt a mixture of gladness and melancholy. She typed a quick response.

Dear Raoul:

I am so happy for you. I hope that all your dreams come true. I will most certainly come for the wedding. I would not give up hope of her being baptized first, however. It could be more difficult for you and for her later.

Here, things are the same. The little minx still hates me and her brother the opposite. I haven't seen much of the father, though I am working myself up to asking him to dinner or something. I am attracted to him quite a bit.

I'm going to look for another job, I think. I don't know if I'm cut out for this. I miss translating. Or perhaps I'll teach.

I love you,
Rebekka

She clicked on the send and receive button, knowing her brother would get the e-mail when he awoke, since it was the middle of the night for him. To her surprise, another e-mail came in, this one from Marc. What was he doing writing to her when he should be asleep?

Her heart began the familiar pounding. Rebekka had two separate impulses, as she always did when seeing his name in her e-mail inbox. She wanted to delete it immediately to spare herself further pain, and she wanted to devour it with her eyes while she imagined his face and his touch. Each communication with him was bittersweet.

Sighing, she clicked on the message.

Hi Rebekka,

So how are you? Are you ready to come home yet? Everything is pretty much the same here. The bridge is nearly finished and we're on to another project.

For some reason I couldn't sleep, so I decided to write to you. You're probably not home but out having fun. Raoul told me you date a lot. I haven't been dating, but that's nothing new. I guess I'm tired of trying to find someone who lives up to my ideals.

You mean someone who lives up to your vision of my mother, she thought uncharitably. She was grateful Raoul had told him she was dating, even though it wasn't true.

Anyway, I feel at a strange point in my life. I wish you were here to talk to about it. I don't know what direction to go. It's like I'm lost, you know? I feel stupid saying this to you, because you have always known what you want and haven't let anything stand in your way. I've always admired that in you. I don't like to admit it, but sometimes I feel like I go with the flow too much. That I let other people determine my destiny, so to speak.

I guess that's because I don't know what I want. My problem is nothing so serious as doubting the truthfulness of the gospel—I know the Church is true—but it's more a doubting that I've done any good in the universe. My company designs and builds safe bridges, roads, and even buildings, but does anyone really care? Someone else could build them just as well. I make a lot of money, but I have no one to spend it on.

I would laugh at myself and these notions if you were here. Think of how we used to go roller blading down by the river—could you imagine us doing it now? People would stare at us, two adults acting like children. But you wouldn't care, and neither would I if we did it together.

When are you coming home? At least you're not going to marry some American and stay there forever. We've agreed how hard that's been for Zack and Josette. You've got your head on straight—which is more than I can say for myself. Rebekka, what should I be when I grow up?

Don't laugh too much at me when you read this, though I know it's funny. Sometimes I feel closer to you when I can write this way. But I still wish you were here.

> *Take care,*
> *Marc*

Rebekka didn't know what to say to this. Apparently, Marc was doing some soul-searching. It was what she had always wanted. But wasn't it too late for them?

Yes, of course it was too late. Because no matter how he changed, he still loved her mother.

At once, uncontrollable hurt and anger consumed her. She typed a response, wanting to hurt him as his blindness had hurt her.

Hello Marc,

I, too, am at a changing point in my life, so I understand what you are going through to some extent. I've discovered that Americans aren't half bad. My boss is very nice. Very nice, if you get the idea. I think I wouldn't mind staying here forever.

Then guilt at her deception provoked a sliver of compassion.

I think you need to decide what you want in life, Marc, and go for it with your whole heart. Only you can make things happen. At the end of your life, you don't want to look back with regrets. Time shouldn't be wasted.
                                    Love,
                                    Rebekka

She didn't send the message, not wanting to seem eager. She could do that later tonight, or when she checked her mail in the morning. *He can wait. Like I've been doing for nineteen years.*

Feeling restless, Rebekka made her way down the sweeping front staircase that led into the two-story entryway outside the sitting room. Adjoining the sitting room was the music room, where a full-sized concert grand piano stood like a silent friend. Neither Damon nor his children played the piano, and in her first weeks with the family, she had wondered at their owning such an exquisite piece. She had quickly overcome her awe, and now practiced daily as she had on her baby grand at home.

She ran her fingers lightly over the keys. The piano was a hand-made Steinway, with dark wood and intricate inlays, and a sound so rich and pure that tears came to her eyes each time she played. She thought that if she had owned such a fine piece while growing up, she might never have studied anything other than music.

Compelled, she propped opened the large lid and sat on the padded mahogany bench. She began to play from memory, using the soft pedal to be sure she didn't awaken anyone. First she played a little Bach, then Mozart, and then something more personal—a simple melody that she had composed for Marc six years ago, meant for their wedding day. It didn't have words, but her heart soared as she played, feeling her love as she had on the day she had first written it.

He had never heard it. He never would.

She stopped playing abruptly, hitting a stray key that sounded awkward and discordant in comparison to the rest of the music.

"Don't stop," a gentle voice protested.

Rebekka's head jerked around. "Damon!"

"I'm sorry. I didn't think you'd notice my being here. I didn't want to interrupt. It was beautiful."

"Did I wake you?" she returned anxiously. "I didn't mean to."

He approached, smiling. "Oh, no. Not at all. I hadn't gone to bed yet, and besides, you were playing so softly that I wouldn't have been able to hear in my room. How do you do that, anyway?"

"This pedal." Rebekka showed him.

"Ah. The mystery solved."

She wondered that he could know so little of the piano. "Do you play at all?" she asked.

"No." But he sat on the bench beside her. "Actually, I can play 'Chopsticks.'" He played the notes slowly, missing occasionally, then stopped and looked at her sheepishly.

She laughed, feeling comfortable and more than a little tingly at his closeness. "There's more, you know." She played it for him, adding several variations to make it more interesting, and glancing up occasionally to see his expression. His eyes were wide with surprise, and the yellow light from the overhead chandelier made them look more amber than usual.

"I didn't know 'Chopsticks' could sound like that," he said when she finished. "You have quite a talent."

"A hobby," she corrected. "What I'm really good at is languages."

"I can believe that." He clicked his tongue. "What I can't believe is that with so much talent you agreed to stay with my children."

"Well, I needed to get away. You pay well. And your children are basically very good."

The rugged, angular lines of his face increased as he grimaced slightly. "I'm sorry about how Belle's been acting. I don't know what's gotten into her."

She sighed, still keenly aware of his closeness. "I see her attitude toward me hasn't escaped you."

"I guess I'm pretty observant when it comes to my children—usually, anyway. But don't feel too bad. I think she'll come out of it."

"Have you had any luck finding a replacement for me?" She felt odd saying it, and hurried to add, "I mean, I'm not anxious to leave or anything. I really do like it here. But I won't be able to stay forever."

He gave her an apologetic grin. "To tell you the truth, I haven't even begun looking. I meant to take out an ad or something, but I've been intent on finding another software company to help us do business in other countries. We thought we might try it ourselves, but if I could buy or make a deal with another company who already has a foot in the door, it might be easier and we could grow . . . But you don't want to hear about that."

"It's interesting," Rebekka said eagerly. She turned slightly on the bench, and her knee accidentally brushed his. He didn't move away.

"Well, now we need to find just the right company. One that has a strong background and reputation so there's a measure of trust." Damon spread his fingers, moving his hands over the piano keys as though searching. "That takes time."

"I see what you—" Rebekka abruptly remembered the plane trip from France. She snapped her fingers. "Hey, I may know someone who can help you. I met him on the plane on the way over. Samuel something. I have his card in my room. He owns a software company and does business overseas. He practically offered me a job in translating."

Damon's brow creased. "Hey, you're not bailing out on me, are you?" By the way he said it, she knew he was joking.

She laughed. "Yes, eventually. So you'd better find a replacement. But don't worry, I'll stay as long as I'm needed." *Even if Belle hates me.*

Damon stood. "Well, I'd love to talk to this guy. If he made an impression on you, he must be something."

Rebekka flushed as she gazed up at him. "I'll take that as a compliment."

"It was meant as one."

She studied his face, trying to see if there was something behind the words, but she saw only honesty and friendship. *As though I'm his little sister,* she thought. She knew the look only too well. *What's wrong with me, that the men I'm attracted to can't see me as a woman?*

She ran her hands once more over the piano keys before she shut the keyboard lid and rose from the bench.

"My wife used to do that before she would leave the piano," he said suddenly, staring at the piano as though someone still sat there.

"She played?" Rebekka asked as she lowered the top lid to keep the dust out of the piano's interior. The wood was heavy, and she thought he might help her, but he was lost in his reverie. "I mean, I wondered if . . . since none of the rest of you seemed to play . . ."

He made a strangled sound that bit into Rebekka's heart. "I guess it must seem funny, us having a grand piano when nobody plays." He continued to stare at the Steinway. "But it's not too odd. Many people I know have them for looks, or for guests."

A rather expensive knickknack, Rebekka thought.

"But Charlotte did play." His voice had taken on a rough note that conveyed a deep tenderness. "We had another piano, though. I bought her this one right before she became pregnant with Belle. Charlotte had been diagnosed with cancer—that was the first time she was diagnosed with it. I wanted to cheer her up. It's one of only a hundred made—of this style—and even back then it cost over a hundred thousand. She loved it so much. She went into remission shortly after. I sometimes wonder if the piano didn't help with her recovery."

"It brings good memories, then."

He met her eyes for the first time since he had started talking about his wife. "Yes, it really does. And hearing you play does, too. Thank you."

"You're welcome." Growing uncomfortable under his continuing gaze, she added, "I can get you that man's card, if you like."

He followed her up the main staircase to her room and waited in the doorway while she rummaged through her purse. "Here it is." She crossed the room and handed the rumpled card to him. His hand felt warm against hers, but for some reason she shivered. Damon looked at the card and stuck it in the pocket of his pale green button-down shirt.

Rebekka could feel his closeness, and her need for companionship seemed more intense than she could bear. The words from Marc's e-mail came back to her: ". . . you have always known what you want and haven't let anything stand in your way." Without thinking, she moved closer to Damon and fixed her eyes on his.

"I'd like to get to know you better," she said confidently, then held her breath for his reaction.

His face wore a puzzled expression that quickly turned into acute embarrassment. Rebekka felt herself cringe inside, as she always did when Marc hadn't responded to her hints.

"I—I didn't know . . . I always thought of you as so much y—. . . I mean, I'm flattered. Really." He stopped talking and searched her face for a long moment before continuing. "You're very beautiful, Rebekka, but I'm so much older."

Rebekka took an even breath. "I'm not a child, Damon. And I still mean what I said."

His face showed amazement and disbelief as Rebekka closed the final step between them. She could smell his aftershave, and even the trace of detergent in his shirt. His eyes didn't leave hers. Watching him carefully, she kissed him.

She had meant it to be a brief kiss, something that perhaps two friends—she and Marc?—might exchange, but she wasn't prepared for the celerity and fervency of his response. His lips pressed hard against hers, filled with thinly disguised passion . . . searching . . . searching . . .

She pulled away, her eyes wide. There was a need in his face, a need she felt strongly echoed in her own heart. "You . . ." She wanted to say that she understood about losing a loved one, about wanting to be with another person who cared about you. But how could her feelings compare to the loneliness he must feel at having lost his wife, the beloved mother of his children?

Damon leaned against the doorframe, watching her with half-veiled eyes. "Rebekka." His voice was warm. "I am still flattered. And I am surprised, mostly at myself. You see, there is this woman in Anchorage—on Kodiak Island, actually—and I love her. She's the first woman I've ever cared about since Char—Charlotte—died. But she loves her husband, and I want them to be happy. She's the real reason I left Alaska." He chuckled in self-deprecation. "I was prepared to be the martyr, you know, the sufferer of an unrequited love. And I guess I even reveled in the whole idea a bit. But you have shown me something tonight." He took her hand, smiling. "You have shown me that the world is a beautiful place with wonderful surprises. Thank you."

He pulled her forward a few inches and kissed her chastely on the lips, a kiss that held none of the vibrancy of their first encounter, but

This Time Forever 115

was much more appropriate given their level of involvement. His blonde moustache tickled her skin. "I would enjoy getting to know you better, too, Rebekka."

She smiled, trying to digest all the information he had given her. He was a man with a twice-broken heart, but he wasn't afraid to accept an opportunity to search for love again. *If only Marc—*

"Good." She winked at him. "I'll let you take me to dinner tomorrow."

His grin grew wider. "It's a deal. But it'll have to be next Friday, because I promised Belle I'd take her to the movies tomorrow."

"Okay, agreed. Next Friday, then."

"Do you want to choose the place, or shall I?" His eyes seemed to sparkle with enjoyment.

She accepted the unvoiced challenge. "I'll choose."

He released his grip on her hand, and Rebekka took a few steps into her room. Damon flashed her another grin. "Until tomorrow."

She watched him walk down the hall, headed toward the far wing of the house where he and Belle had their rooms. The silence without him was almost deafening, although she was accustomed to being alone at night. Tanner slept in the basement, where the new cook and the maid had their quarters. Damon had refused to let him stay in the empty room near Rebekka, for which she had been very thankful.

Why, then, did she feel so alone now?

She brought a hand to her lips, recalling their first kiss and wondering at the intensity of it. "I need to tell Brionney not to set him up with her sister," she murmured aloud.

Rebekka closed the door and went to the desk where her laptop sat. She pushed the button to bring it to life, then rapidly added an extra line to her e-mail to Marc before sending it.

P.S. Tonight Damon kissed me.

What would he make of that? Would he feel as devastated as she had when he was dating that returned sister missionary?

No, of course not.

As she lay in bed, sleep wouldn't come. Her mind went over the events of the day in a continuous cycle. Despite her pleasant time with Damon, it was Marc's letter that stood at the heart of her sleep-lessness.

He was right when he said I knew what I wanted in life. And I have always achieved every goal—except to marry him.

Her only failure. The thing that meant the most to her. What did all her achievements mean without a soul mate to share them with?

"I will not cry for him." Her voice was a tortured whisper in the darkness of her room.

She forced her thoughts to Damon. Tonight he had kissed her. She didn't fool herself that his passion had been for her, but at least he had begun to see her as a woman. Damon had been in love and had lost, but he was ready to move on—a point of maturity that Marc had never reached.

She, too, was ready to move on.

CHAPTER 13

Weeks stretched into months for Mickelle, and she hardly realized their passing. More and more, she found it difficult to get out of bed. The boys took care of themselves quite well, and didn't need her except for the occasional dinner. They spent most of their time playing with cousins or friends. Their grandmother and aunts took care of Jeremy's ninth birthday in August, buying him everything on his list except the motorcycle he'd seen in a magazine. Brionney even made him a cake and took him roller skating.

Mickelle didn't register for college as she had planned, using her lack of money as an excuse. It was true that she didn't have funds, but she could have received financial aid—if she could have brought herself to fill out the papers.

The lack of money was a constant source of pressure. Riley's life insurance company had continued to refuse payment of the hundred thousand dollars she had expected. The suicide clause was in effect for two years after purchase of the policy, and Riley had died three weeks too soon.

At times when she was feeling perverse, Mickelle laughed at the irony of the situation. Three weeks more, and she and the kids would have been taken care of. *It's just like him. A responsible husband would have waited three weeks before killing himself.* Then she would cry. She cried a lot. Sometimes she wondered where all the tears came from.

An ocean of tears.

A universe of tears.

All her dreams gone.

Donations from family, friends, and neighbors had buried Riley and paid immediate bills. Now she lived off a slim social security check. She knew she needed a job to make life good for the boys, but she simply couldn't find it in herself to do anything.

Her house was a mess—four months' worth of mess. Each morning she awoke to Jeremy's wet bed, new mounds of dirty clothes, and trash that needed to be taken outside. Books, toys, and games were on counters, floors, beds, and even the couch. She had learned to overlook it all. Who cared about any of it? Not her. She did nothing about the housework, except for the flecks of burnt toast the boys had scraped off when they forgot and left it too long in the broken toaster. The black flecks stuck to the wet parts of the sink, covered the light-yellow countertops, and speckled the floor. She exerted herself enough to wipe them up, but silently berated the boys for not cleaning up after themselves, and herself for not making them.

It was easier to stay in bed.

"Mom! Mom!" A voice penetrated Mickelle's sleepy brain. Jeremy rushed into her room. "Are you going to take me to school, or should I walk? Bryan says I gotta walk, but I'm nervous. Will you go with me?"

Mickelle blinked at him. What was he talking about?

He put his hands on her shoulders and looked directly into her eyes. "It's school," he explained patiently. "Today's the first day."

"What? Oh, yeah."

Mickelle swung her feet out of bed. "I'll take you both. Are you ready?"

"Yes, I took a bath like you said." He grimaced, and Mickelle felt guilty. She wished there was some way she could help him to overcome his problem of wetting the bed. "And I'm wearing the new clothes Grandma bought me."

Mickelle hadn't known her mother had bought him clothes, but seeing his cheerful face, she was glad someone had. "Did you eat?" she managed.

"Uh-huh. Cereal. Can we go now?"

She glanced at the clock. "You have almost two hours. You don't have to be there till nine-thirty. But you can come with me while I take Bryan. Let me get dressed, and I'll be right out." Five minutes passed while she hunted in a pile of black clothing for a pair of relatively clean black jeans and a black shirt with tiny white buttons. In the bathroom, she dragged a comb through her limp hair.

Bryan eyed her with relief when she emerged from the bedroom. "I thought Jeremy would have to go alone."

"I know the way," Jeremy said.

"Yeah, but you're too little to go by yourself."

Jeremy threw his brother a scathing look. "Don't worry about me."

"I just meant you should go with Mom or your friends."

"I'm big enough!"

"Are not!"

"Mom! Bryan's being mean!"

"I wasn't trying to be mean, stupid." Bryan banged his open hand on the counter. "Ooh! You make me so mad!"

Wouldn't they ever be quiet? All they did was chatter constantly, whether fighting or playing, leaving her no room to think her own thoughts. Their young voices had never bothered her before, but since Riley. . .

"Bryan's right, Jeremy," Mickelle interjected, forcing her thoughts away from her husband. "If you walk, you have to walk with somebody. You remember that from last year. But I can take you in the Snail."

"The Snail?" Jeremy asked, puzzled.

Bryan laughed. "The station wagon. Mom, that's too funny! It does drive like a snail."

"I get it," said Jeremy, grinning.

"Don't you have to be to school by eight?" Mickelle asked Bryan.

"Ten after, I think." He glanced at the door. "Mom, I want to ride the bus with my friends. We planned to go together."

The first day of junior high school. Mickelle understood. "That's fine. But behave yourself."

Bryan took a step toward the door, then paused and looked at her carefully. "You gonna be okay, Mom? I mean, you're not depressed, are you?"

He looked so much like Riley at that moment that she had to force a smile. Not Riley during the bad times, but Riley when things were good between them, when his love had shone through his insecurities. "I'm fine. Don't worry about me. Now get going." She kissed his cheek and he ran out the door, a new dark blue backpack over his shoulder. Another present from her parents, most likely.

"I don't want to walk." Jeremy began to organize his school supplies.

"But you told Bryan you did."

"No, I said I knew the way. I just don't like him acting like I'm a baby. I'm not five or six . . . or seven."

"He's just worried about you."

Jeremy's eyes stared into hers. "Can't you go with me today, Mom? I mean to school. Can't you stay there?"

"No." Mickelle took a bowl from one of the old dark cupboards that were caked with grime so thick she could scrape it off with her fingernail. In fact, scraping was the only way to remove the thirty years of buildup; washing the cupboards simply wasn't enough. She had always planned to replace them, but how could she now?

"But what if you miss me?"

"Then I'll come see you."

"You're not going anywhere, are you?"

Mickelle finally perceived his worry. School was their first extended separation since Riley had died. One parent had left and never returned, and he was afraid of losing her, just as Bryan was. She sat on a kitchen chair and drew his thin figure into her arms. "Oh, Jeremy. I'm not ever going to leave you. Not if I have anything to say about it. And you're going to have so much fun in the fourth grade that you'll hardly know how the day went so fast."

His face brightened. "Okay. Then you'll pick me up?"

"Yes, but only today. We're close enough for you to walk with your friends."

He hugged her. "Can we go?"

She certainly admired his exuberance. Once, she had felt that way about going back to college.

"Mom, what's wrong?" Jeremy's voice was tense, and Mickelle forced her face to relax.

She smoothed his hair. "Nothing. I was just thinking that I should go to school, too."

"You should. It's fun. So can we go now?"

She groaned. "Not for another hour and a half at least. You're too early."

Jeremy got another bowl out of the cupboard. "In that case, I'll eat some more cereal."

At ten minutes after nine, Mickelle drove Jeremy to Forbes Elementary. She walked him to his fourth grade class, where he was immediately swept up into his circle of friends. To be sure he was going to be all right, she waited and watched, but he seemed to have forgotten she was there.

In the car, loneliness and despair settled once more on her shoulders. She didn't return to the house, but drove aimlessly. Somehow, she found herself on the freeway driving twenty miles over the speed limit. Dangerous thoughts popped into her head, insidious whisperings promising immediate relief. How easy it would be to end it all by driving the car off an overpass, or to turn around and drive into oncoming traffic. If she was lucky, she might die before she felt any pain. All her suffering would be over in an instant.

No! What am I thinking! Horror seeped into every pore of her body.

Was this how desperate Riley felt?

Never. I am not a coward. I have not yet lost sight of reality.

Aloud she said, "I'm sorry, Bryan, Jeremy. I'm sorry for even thinking it." But she admitted to herself that it wasn't the first time since Riley's death that she had thought of joining him and leaving her too-painful existence behind.

Mickelle took the next off-ramp and turned the car around. Using the Alpine Highway, she drove methodically back to American Fork.

The sound of a siren abruptly broke her concentration. With surprise, she saw a police car behind her, its lights whirling. Her heart started pounding as she glanced at the speedometer. No, she wasn't going too fast. Why was he pulling her over?

Her pulse increased again, and she fought against the panic rising in her chest. The world around her began to spin. Her chest constricted and she couldn't breathe. Her vision dimmed. The terrible thumping of her heart in her ears continued loudly. She tried to swallow, but couldn't.

A panic attack. She had been suffering them since the day she had learned she was not pregnant. Sometimes they were severe, but usually she could ease them by avoiding stressful situations. Knowing the cause of her symptoms was comforting, but how could she get rid of them altogether before she became completely agoraphobic? Wasn't she reluctant enough to leave her home already?

Another thought came, even more disturbing. How could she possibly pay for a traffic ticket and the resulting insurance hike?

The officer still sat in his car behind her. She knew he was calling in her license plate and checking her record. Thank heavens it was clean, and the delay gave her time to recover enough to speak.

Finally the police officer emerged from his car, carrying a pad. He motioned for her to roll down the window.

"Was I speeding?" she asked timidly. "I didn't think I was."

"No." He peered at her carefully. "You were just driving rather slowly, and I wanted to make sure you were all right."

Mickelle understood what he was not saying: he had suspected she was drunk. She remembered learning once in a health class that drunk drivers often compensated for their impaired senses by driving more slowly than usual. "Are you going to give me a ticket?" She knew desperation colored her voice.

"No, I . . . hey, I know you." He thought a moment. "Oh, you're the lady whose husband . . ." He trailed off, looking apologetic.

Mickelle put aside her fear enough to recognize him as one of the young officers who had come to her house with the news of Riley's suicide—the one with blue eyes and brown hair. She nodded. "I remember you now," she said, peering at his name tag, "Officer Lowder." He had been kind—very kind—and she had never thanked him. "You were nice that day. Thank you."

He put the pad in his pocket. "Are you all right?"

"Yes. I just drove my son to school, and I was being careful because I didn't want to get into an accident. My boys need . . ." Without warning, her eyes filled and tears spilled onto her cheeks.

"Look, is there something I can do?" His gaze was earnest, his voice rich with compassion.

She wiped her face with both hands. "No, really. Thank you. Just don't give me a ticket." She tried to grin.

His answering smile sent a ray of sunshine into her heart. "I won't. But you go home now, okay? And be careful."

"Thank you."

Officer Lowder stepped back and watched as she put the station wagon into gear and drove away. She glanced in the mirror and saw that he was still staring after her. *Nice man.*

Back at home, she changed the sheets on Jeremy's bed before reading the obituaries in the *Daily Herald* that arrived on her porch each morning. It was a free gift subscription someone had given her anonymously. She suspected it was a subtle hint from Brionney to find a job in the "Help Wanted" section, but she never got past the obituaries. Usually most of the dead were older, but today there was a thirty-year-old mother of four who had died of cancer and a toddler who had been fished out of a canal. Mickelle wondered about the loved ones left behind, and if their lives had changed as much as hers.

Sighing, she tossed the paper on the pile near Riley's chair and went into the bathroom to pick up Jeremy's wet pajamas. He had left the water undrained as usual, and the ring in the tub was dark. She should clean it, but she couldn't make the effort. Why did everything demand her attention? All she wanted to do was go back to bed and pull the covers over her head. No more demands. No feelings.

Abruptly, the dimming of her vision and the rapid beating of her heart signaled another panic attack. She sank to the floor, dropping her head to her knees until the feelings subsided. At that moment, she wished more than anything that she didn't have to pick Jeremy up that afternoon, that she could stay in the house forever.

Leaving the bathroom, she went to her room and collapsed on her bed. The curtain was drawn, and only a small amount of light filtered through. Mickelle had never realized how comforting the dark could be. She let herself drift to where she could feel no pain.

A persistent ringing sound jolted her awake. The doorbell. She glanced at the clock. It was already after noon. "Go away," she muttered, turning over.

The ringing continued. At last it stopped, but she heard someone in the hall. "Mickelle? Are you here? Mickelle, it's Brionney. I've brought you some bulbs to plant for next year. Daffodils, and they had a clearance on roses. I bought red, white, and pink. They were out of yellow—that's why I got the daffodils. I have no idea if this is an okay time to plant roses or bulbs, but I thought you might know. Mickelle?"

Mickelle groaned and swung her feet out of bed for the second time that day. Why couldn't people just let her sleep?

"Mickelle!" Brionney had reached the door to her room. "Are you sick?" She eyed Mickelle's black clothing with a grimace, but didn't comment on it.

"No. I'm just tired."

Brionney sighed and sat next to her on the bed. "I hear you. The twins both had something last night, and Jesse had to pull an all-nighter at work, so I was alone." She jumped up. "Oh, that reminds me—Rosalie and the boys are still in the van. I have the alarm on, but I shouldn't leave them there too long. Come and help me unload the plants, will you? There's a lot of them!"

Mickelle let herself be urged along by her sister's enthusiasm. Outside, they let the children into the backyard to play before returning to the van for the plants.

"Don't you need any?" Mickelle asked.

"Oh, I already dropped a whole bunch off at home on my way from the store. Damon has offered me the use of his gardener for a few days, so he's planting them for me. Apparently Damon pays him a salary, and he didn't have anything to do at his place this week." Brionney lowered two rose bushes to the sidewalk next to the flower bed. "He's a really nice man, Damon is."

Mickelle vaguely remembered that Damon was Jesse's partner. "How's the company doing?" She asked from habit, though some remote part of her knew that once she would have actually cared about the response.

Brionney looked up from her squatting position. "Good. Today they're meeting with a guy from another company to see about getting their programs into foreign countries. And the money is finally coming in. Jesse's even taking a week off sometime soon. We can't go anywhere since the kids are in school, but I'm excited anyway."

Mickelle sat down on the sidewalk, running her hands through the rich, moist soil, wondering who had watered it for her. If she could find enough energy, she might even thank them. The smell of the earth filled her nose and she breathed it in, relishing the aroma and the memories of her childhood that the smell brought to her mind. The gritty feel of the dirt was somehow clean and refreshing.

There was a long silence, and Mickelle searched her mind for something to say. "So is the partner taking a week off, too?" Not that she cared in the slightest.

Brionney brushed her hands against her jeans. "Not a chance. He doesn't have much interest in taking a vacation. His children are in school and he's not married. I mean, he's a widower. You know what? I think you should go out with him. He's really nice."

"So you said." Mickelle was irritated at the suggestion.

"Well, he is nice," Brionney insisted. "And it wouldn't hurt you to at least meet him. Someday you may want to get married again."

"I'll never marry again," she said flatly.

"Why?"

She lifted her eyes to Brionney's. "That's what I want to know. Why should I cook for another man or wash his clothes, or go see a movie I don't want to see? I'm through being a slave to someone else."

Brionney's eyes opened wide in shock. "What are you saying? That's not what marriage is about! Sure, there's the cleaning and the service, but there's so much more. There's the lying in bed at night, discussing the day or the future or the kids. There's the support when something goes wrong. There's the intimacy—"

"When you're really too tired or upset for it." Anger burst to life from the apathy in Mickelle's heart. "And the insinuation that if you don't respond, it means you don't love him."

"But not all men are like that. Sure they have different hormones, but a good and loving man will come to the realization that sex isn't love, and that intimacy and feelings of love come from simply being together, watching TV, working together, being a family. So much of marriage is compromise. You can't throw away the whole institution because Riley couldn't see past his own desires."

Mickelle looked away, her heart aching at the sincerity in her sister's voice. She had no doubt that Jesse was a good marriage partner to her sister. But that still didn't mean that Mickelle wanted another relationship. "Well, I don't want to worry about what someone else is thinking at every minute, worrying that I might say or do something wrong."

Brionney's hand crept to Mickelle's, tears glistening in her eyes. "I know what that's like. Derek was that way. But Jesse's not. We've faced challenges, but if you love the other person and God more than yourself, things can be worked out."

"Then Riley didn't love me." Mickelle knew it was true. He had wanted her, he had feelings toward her, but he hadn't truly loved her. "He couldn't and still treat me that way."

"Riley had a lot of problems." Brionney's eyes were sad. "I wish I had been around to help you more."

"I'm fine now." Mickelle rubbed her hands together to remove the dirt.

"Are you?"

"I'm lonely sometimes." Mickelle met her sister's searching gaze. "For what it's worth, I love Riley. And I would give anything to have him back. I think if he'd been able to bear the pressure for just a little longer, we could have made our marriage work. It was heading in the right direction. And maybe there will still be a chance for us in the next life."

Brionney nodded. "None of us knows what the future holds. But there's still that dream or vision you had about your daughter. What about that?"

Mickelle gave a long sigh. "It was just a dream."

"But what if it wasn't? What if there's someone else out there for you? And what if you're supposed to have another child?"

Mickelle smiled weakly through the growing pain in her chest. "Then her father will have to enter my life with a bang, because I'm not going looking for him."

Brionney shook her head and sighed. She stayed to help plant the roses, keeping up a steady conversation about less volatile subjects. Then she washed her hands and piled her children into the van. "Do you want me to pick up Jeremy at school?" she asked. "I was going to let my kids walk, but I have to pick up Damon's little girl today and drive her home."

"No. I'll get him. I promised him. Besides, you don't have enough seat belts in your van if that girl and Jeremy go with you. But thanks for coming. I really appreciate it."

Mickelle watched her go, feeling grateful that her sister had taken time from her day to lighten her sadness. The rose bushes, as bare of blooms as they were, brought her a feeling of warmth and happiness. Next spring they would flower, and life would go on.

As would she.

With a feeling of renewal, she went inside and looked through a stack of mail. There were two bills that were due, and she had enough time to write out checks before leaving to pick up Jeremy at school. "I can mail them first if I hurry," she said aloud.

Bryan walked up as she was opening the door to the Snail. From his contented expression, Mickelle assumed that his first day at junior high had gone well.

"Sorry I'm late. We walked home instead of taking the bus. I didn't think you'd mind. Do you?"

"Not as long as you're careful and come straight home." Mickelle hadn't even realized he was late. "What time do you get out, anyway?"

"Two-thirty."

It was almost three-thirty now.

As though reading her mind, he added, "But we didn't leave till almost three. We were talking to some kids in the hall."

"I'm going to get Jeremy. Want to come?"

For an answer, he slid into the passenger seat. Mickelle knew that meant he wanted to talk. Otherwise, he would have gone inside to find his Game Boy.

She started the engine. "So how'd school go?"

"Cool. I like it. I got classes with all my friends, and I like the teachers except the music one. He's kind of weird. But the guys like him, so maybe I just don't know him yet. They say he's unusual, and that the kids . . ."

Bryan rattled on and Mickelle listened, amazed that she did not feel drowned in the flow of words as she had so often of late. She drove west on 100 North, toward the post office. At the 100 East intersection the light was red, so she slowed to a stop. Across from her sat an old model Volkswagen Bug with a shiny new red paint job. Mickelle craned her neck to see if the light for the other direction was near changing. She didn't want to be late to pick up Jeremy after his first day of school, and she still had to make it to the post office. The light was yellow. There, red now. She moved forward a few inches, anticipating her green light.

Suddenly a truck with oversized tires roared through the red light. Mickelle slammed on her brakes, and the Snail died.

"Did ya see that guy?" Bryan yelled. "Nice truck, but what a jerk! He went right through the red light! Where's a cop when ya need one?"

Mickelle's light was green now, and she shakily restarted the engine and pushed on the gas, holding one hand to her thumping heart. She glanced at Bryan and then back to the road. She had only a second to notice the shiny red Bug as it tried to turn left—directly into the path of her car. Again Mickelle punched the brake, hearing the screeching tires, the sickening grind of metal as the two cars collided.

Was Bryan even wearing a seat belt?

Only yesterday, she had read in the newspaper about a young boy who had died in a low-speed crash at an intersection.

Dear Lord, she prayed. *Let my son be all right.*

CHAPTER 14

Damon left before his children awoke on Tuesday morning, confident that Rebekka would get them off to their first day of school without him. He had given Belle a father's blessing the night before to help her adjust to being in school all day. She had attended preschool during the summer so she would be ready for kindergarten, and at the teacher's repeated suggestion, he had reluctantly agreed to have Belle tested to determine her grade level. The school psychologist had concluded after several visits and numerous tests that Belle actually read above a third grade level and had social skills far advanced for her age. Apparently, her nanny in Anchorage had taught her many things over the past two years.

"Usually I see kids who are borderline above their peers," the psychologist said. "If they are moved up, it's because their parents insist, not because they are actually advanced. Quite frankly, I don't think most of them should be moved up, and I try to talk their parents out of it. But Belle is one of the few children I believe would benefit if given more challenge. I recommend that she go into the first grade. Actually, she could do the second or third grade work just fine, but I think that would be pushing the social aspect. She's still very young."

Damon worried over the decision, making it a matter of deep thought and prayer, but Rebekka had seemed pleased. "Don't worry so much," she said. "I graduated early, and so did my brother, and we turned out just fine. Belle will do great." She grinned at him. "Imagine you, the epitome of a Type A personality, worried because a child excels. Aren't you supposed to expect that in your children?"

"But she's my baby. I don't want to mess this up."

Rebekka grinned. "You won't. Believe me. She'll be happy later to graduate a year early. I was."

But Damon wondered if Rebekka was simply grateful that Belle would be in school for most of the day. He had to admit there was good reason for her to want to be away from the child. No matter how Rebekka tried, and he knew she tried hard, Belle continued to want nothing to do with her. At first Damon had been amused at the situation, knowing that he had to find a new nanny soon anyway. But since last Thursday night when he had kissed Rebekka, he was beginning to worry about her relationship with Belle. He couldn't let himself fall in love with a woman Belle hated.

"We don't really need a nanny anymore," Belle had told him last night after he had given her the blessing. "Now that I'm in school, she'll have nothing to do."

"But you still get home way before I do."

"I could watch myself." Belle poked her lip out in a pout.

"Who would drive you to school?"

Even though they lived in Alpine and not in American Fork, Belle had insisted on attending Forbes with the Hergarter children. It meant more driving for Rebekka, but both she and Damon had thought it a good idea to give Belle what she wanted for her first school experience. When the school had placed Belle in the first grade with Camille, the Hergarters' second daughter, Damon believed the whole arrangement had been inspired.

Damon had been at work two hours when Jesse tapped on his office door. "Juliet can't come to work today. Apparently she's sick." Jesse sighed in exasperation.

Damon turned from his computer. "Maybe it's time to hire a new secretary."

"Actually, I think once she gets married, she'll be fine." Jesse gave a wry laugh. "It's all these late nights with her fiancé that put her out of order."

"So in the meantime, who's going to do her work?"

"Don't know. We've got that meeting at one, and Juliet was supposed to pick up Samuel Bjornenburg from the airport at that time. It won't look good if we invite the guy to discuss marketing our product overseas and then don't even show up at the airport to collect him."

As he always did when thinking deeply, Damon began to twist the ends of his moustache before he reminded himself that he was trying to break himself of the habit. Instead, he rubbed his jaw. "What about Terry or John?"

"Nope. Terry's out talking with those doctors, and John's in San Diego, remember?"

"Oh, yeah."

"And McCall, Brody, and Nick have to be in our meeting."

"Well, that's all of us." Damon thought a minute, then reached for the phone. "Rebekka. She can pick him up. She'll even know what he looks like. I should have thought of it before."

Jesse leaned against the edge of the desk. "Brionney can pick up Belle from school in case Rebekka doesn't get back in time."

Damon rubbed his jaw again. "That could work. I'm sure Rebekka won't mind."

"Come to think of it, maybe Rebekka should attend the meeting too—that is, if you're still thinking of asking her to be in on the translating. There's nothing like a native to get a good job done. We'll still need a medical person to . . ."

At that point, Damon stopped listening. He would like Rebekka to work for him at Hospital's Choice, Inc., but what about his children? They still needed a nanny.

No, they needed a mother. Would Rebekka get along any better with Belle if she married him? Whoa, he was really jumping the gun! His Type A personality again. This was the second time in one day that he had thought about Rebekka and Belle together with respect to the future.

Damon sighed. He noticed that Jesse had stopped talking and was staring at him, waiting for him to say something. Without thinking, Damon asked, "Jess, do you think Bekka's too young for me?"

Jesse smiled. "You mean Rebekka? What is it with you and nicknames? But, no, I don't think you're too old for her at all. I mean you're old, but not *that* old. And you look good for your age." Jesse's brown eyes gleamed with mirth. "Your yellow hair hides the gray. Not like me. I'm getting a few white hairs here above my ears—see? At least all your gray doesn't show."

"Thanks—I think," Damon said dryly.

"So are you going out with her?"

Damon replaced the phone without making the call. "Not yet. We're going somewhere on Friday. She's picking the place."

Jesse slapped him on the shoulder. "Way to go! Brionney will be pleased. I think she'd just about given up on getting you two together. She's been talking about setting you up with her sister."

Damon held up his hand. "Hey, one at a time! I have enough going on as it is."

Jesse picked up the phone and handed it to him again. "You'd better call Rebekka before she leaves to take Tanner or Belle to school."

* * * * *

Tanner watched Rebekka as she picked up the phone. She seemed to glow as she spoke. "Sure, I'll do it. I'll call Brionney to arrange things for Belle." Suddenly she flushed and giggled. "No, I haven't forgotten. I know exactly where I'm going to take you." Pause. "Yes, fax the directions. I don't want to get lost."

As she hung up the phone, Tanner continued to stare. She was so beautiful. All his friends thought so and were envious that she lived in his house. Having her there had definitely added to his prestige.

Most importantly, since Rebekka had come, he hardly ever dreamed about his mother anymore—the dark dreams of sickness, of her lying on the bed, withering away until she finally died. He had cried for days after her death. He didn't miss her exactly, not the way she had been, but he often dreamed of what she would have been like had she never become sick. She would have been like the mothers of his friends, able to take him places, to play ball with him, or even scold him. He wouldn't have minded.

"Tanner . . . Hello, Tanner."

He blinked. Rebekka was talking to him. "What?"

"If you want me to take you to school, we'd better get going or you'll be late. But you'll have to take the bus home this afternoon. I have to go to Salt Lake to pick someone up at the airport, and then I have to attend a business meeting with your father."

Belle glared murderously at Rebekka, but both Tanner and Rebekka ignored her.

"I'm ready now." Tanner grabbed his backpack. He didn't really need a ride to school, but going with Rebekka was much better than taking the bus. "Can I drive?" he asked with a grin.

Rebekka tossed the car keys into the air and caught them. "Not until you get your license."

"Aw, I'll be sixteen in a few months. I know how to drive."

"Talk to your father."

Tanner already knew what he would say. Damon had taken him driving a few times on some remote roads, and had even paid for an old VW Bug that Tanner had rebuilt over the summer and had painted a glittering red. Everything was ready for his debut into the driving world—except his license.

"Well, I'd rather go with you, anyway," Tanner said, following Rebekka into the four-car garage. He smiled, enjoying the way she shook her head at his comment, her perfectly shaped eyebrows drawing together in concern.

"I don't want to go!" announced Belle.

"Sorry. You have to come." Rebekka leaned over to open the door to the Altima, and her long hair fell in auburn disarray around her shoulders. Tanner loved it when it that happened. She looked like one of the sexy movie stars on the posters he had pasted up in his room.

"Belle," he said in warning, "you'd better behave. You know what Dad will say."

"Tattletale!" She stuck her tongue out at him, but she moved toward Rebekka's car. Tanner stopped for a second to run a hand over the smooth finish of his Bug. *Someday soon,* he told it. *Maybe Dad'll take me out driving tonight.* He hurried to the Altima and slid into the front leather seat.

"Now, when the Hergarters bring Belle home, I need you to keep an eye on her. Okay?" Rebekka said as she backed out of the drive. "I don't know how long that meeting will last."

"Sure," Tanner agreed, not really hearing her. She had said something about Belle, and whatever it was would be okay. Belle was no problem and usually entertained herself. Rebekka's being gone was more of a worry. "But hurry back."

Rebekka's beautiful gray eyes rested on him momentarily. "I'll try." Her voice sounded kind of odd, strangled, or maybe like she was holding back a laugh. He searched her face thoroughly, but her expression showed no mirth. Good. Maybe she was starting to really like him.

* * * * *

Tanner rode the bus home, hefting a backpack full of books. It had been an awesome day, completely awesome. His teachers were cool, his friends all had similar schedules, and Amanda, a girl who was almost as beautiful as Rebekka, shared not one, but two of his classes. She was thin and short with long blonde hair and bright emerald eyes. Of course, she didn't have Rebekka's soft voice or French accent. Or Rebekka's maturity. That made all the difference in the world.

He began looking for Rebekka the minute he walked in the house, before remembering that she was at his dad's office. Why was she there, anyway? He vaguely remembered something about a meeting and the way she had flushed when she was talking to his father. What did that mean? He wasn't sure he wanted to know the answer.

He went into the kitchen for a snack, taking it into the game room. Almost immediately, Mrs. Mertz, the housekeeper, appeared carrying a cloth and window spray. She had short, gray-streaked blonde hair and was tall and chubby, but very agile. He had seen her climb a ladder to clean the lights, and lean over the stair railing to wipe up a stray spot of dirt. "Don't be getting crumbs all over," she told him. "I just vacuumed in here."

"Okay," he said, though it didn't make sense—her cleaning and then expecting him not to get it dirty. If he kept it clean, then she'd be out of a job, wouldn't she?

She gave him a bland smile before shuffling past the pool table to the double sliding glass doors, which she began cleaning inside and out. Tanner, having nothing better to do, watched. As she left, he put his plate on the end table by the lamp and reached for his latest *Star Wars* book. Crumbs fell from his lap onto the marbled carpet. Oops. He looked at them guiltily before remembering that he was actually helping Mrs. Mertz by giving her job security. Obviously she needed the job, since she had decided not to return to Alaska as she originally planned.

He heard his name being called, and looked up to see his friends Randy and Eric peering through the glass doors, their hands and noses spoiling the freshly cleaned surface. Mrs. Mertz would have a fit about that, he knew, despite the addition to her job security.

"What's up?" he asked as he let the guys in.

Randy sprawled his thin, gangly form over a padded easy chair. He had small hazel eyes and thick bleached hair that hung straight in a blunt cut an inch or two below his ears. "Nothing. You?"

"Same. I was just waiting for Rebekka to get home."

"Ah, Rebekka," Randy said, his eyes glinting.

"Rebekka," Eric repeated in a reverent whisper, his short-cropped red curls bobbing as he nodded knowingly. He was about average height, an inch or two shorter than Tanner, and his face was covered with freckles. His large blue eyes were framed by thick, curly lashes that were the envy of his two older sisters.

"You got homework?" Tanner asked them.

"Nope." Eric picked up a cue and walked over to the pool table. "Never get any the first day."

Randy picked up another cue and chalked the end. "So where's Rebekka?"

"I don't know. Some meeting with my dad."

Eric took a shot at the balls, but missed. He set aside his stick. "Want to swim?"

The indoor and outdoor pools were both filled, but they were locked. Rebekka had the key, and Tanner and Belle had to have her permission and supervision to swim. Tanner knew better than to jump the gate; they would find out somehow. Besides, he'd promised. "Maybe when Rebekka comes back."

Eric frowned and reclaimed his cue. "I have a class with Amanda."

Tanner smirked. "I have two classes with her."

"No way." Eric botched the shot again.

Randy sent a ball into the pocket. "Cool."

Tanner stood up to join them. When he played, he always won. He'd been practicing since he was Belle's age.

Belle's age. Where was Belle?

He froze. "What time is it?"

"Three. Why?" Eric took another shot and sent Randy's ball into the pocket. "Dang it!"

Tanner relaxed. "I was supposed to watch Belle, but she doesn't get out of school until three-thirty or so."

"Who's picking her up?" Randy asked. "I mean, if Rebekka ain't here."

Tanner thought back to the conversation that morning. What had Rebekka said? Did she say anything about who would get Belle? What if nobody did? "Rebekka probably asked someone," he said.

Randy leaned on his cue. "Sometimes they forget. Once when I was in kindergarten, my mom forgot me. She went shopping and just forgot. They had to call my dad at work. Boy, was he mad."

"Rebekka wouldn't forget." But suddenly Tanner wasn't sure. "I'll just call my dad and find out." He crossed to the phone lying on the end table next to his discarded plate and dialed his father's cell phone number. Instead of his dad, the answering service picked up. "No, I don't want to leave a message." Tanner hung up and called the office number. Again he got the answering service. Not even the secretary appeared to be in. "Dad must be in a meeting." A vision of Belle in tears at her school filled Tanner's mind. "I know, I'll call Brionney."

"Who?"

"A friend of my dad's. She's got a kid that goes to school with Belle."

The Hergarters didn't answer their phone either, and Tanner's worry increased. Belle was a pain much of the time, but she was his sister and his responsibility.

"You could go get her." Randy's small eyes glinted.

"I can't walk that far. She's going to school in American Fork."

Randy grinned. "I know."

Eric laughed and slapped Tanner on the back. "Randy means your car, man. Use your car. It's an emergency. You can't leave Belle alone at school."

Tanner stared as his two friends chuckled and nudged each other. The idea made sense. He had to make sure that Belle was all right. "Okay, let's go. But just to the school. I know the way, I think."

"I know the way." Randy threw his stick on the pool table. "It's by Albertson's."

"Got any money?" Eric asked, leading the way to the garage. "We could stop for some stuff."

"I don't know." Tanner was beginning to feel uncomfortable about his decision.

Randy pushed back the blonde locks that fell in his eyes. "I got some money, and so does Tanner, don't ya? But what time does your sister get out? Smith's is only a little farther, and if we stop there we could get a video. My sister works there, and she has a membership."

"Good idea!" Eric bounded into the backseat of the Bug. "Cool. This is so cool. I wish I had one of these."

Randy took the passenger seat. "Yeah, show us how it works, Tanner buddy."

Tanner swaggered a little as he walked around the car and opened the door with an exaggerated motion. Being behind the wheel felt great.

"You do know how to drive, don't you?" quipped Randy.

"Just watch." Tanner backed out of the long drive quickly and smoothly, purposely screeching the tires when he came to an abrupt stop.

His friends hooted with joy. "Go!" they shouted.

A sense of elation flooded Tanner's body. He was free and going strong. What's more, he was helping Belle. Even his father would see the reason in that.

"Let's drive by Amanda's house," Eric suggested. "I know where she lives." Tanner wanted to know too, so he agreed.

They found Amanda and her brother Mitch outside in their front yard. "We're going to the store," Eric shouted. "Want to come?" They laughed and hooted when the two came running.

"I didn't know you had a car," Amanda said to Tanner.

"Like it?"

"Yeah." Amanda slid in the back with Eric and her brother. Tanner could feel her looking at him.

By the time they left Smith's, Tanner was feeling confident. Driving was easy and his friends were having fun. He especially enjoyed being with Amanda. She was one good-looking girl! The way she acted, she liked him, too.

They were nearing the intersection by Albertson's when the light turned red. Tanner stopped reluctantly, glancing at the clock on the dash. It was after three-thirty. Did Belle get out at three-thirty or three forty-five? He couldn't remember, but he'd better hurry. He put on his left blinker. Across the intersection, an old gold station wagon sat waiting for the green light, noticeably vibrating as though it might fall apart at any moment. Tanner could make out a lady and a boy in the car. He was glad he didn't have to drive in that embarrassing piece of junk.

Randy was fiddling with the radio. The music was up loud and the beat flowed through Tanner, making him want to move his feet. He began to sing with the music and tap his hand against the steering wheel. He had never felt so great.

"Change the channel!" shouted Eric. He leaned up and stretched an arm over the seat, trying to reach the buttons. "There's a better station—"

"Leave it alone!" Randy grabbed Eric's arm.

The light turned green, but as it did, a truck barreled through the intersection. The lady in the station wagon seemed frozen, as though she was too afraid to move. Tanner revved the engine.

"Just go," Randy urged, still struggling with Eric over the radio. "She's in shock or something."

Tanner started forward, sure he could turn left before the lady in the station wagon awoke from whatever dream she was in. He glanced back at Amanda, saw her watching him. She winked. Her eyes were the color of emeralds.

When he looked back at the road, he saw the station wagon coming much too quickly toward him. He had read the situation completely wrong. He tried to stop to let the gold car pass, but accidentally pushed on the gas instead. Helplessly, he slammed into the other car. The music was so loud that the rending sounds of the crash seemed to be playing a weak accompaniment. He caught a brief glimpse of the right front side of his Bug buckling as the impact threw his head back against the seat.

The music still blared. He looked around at his friends. Their eyes were wide and they looked scared, but they seemed to be all right. But he was in big trouble. BIG TROUBLE. A sick feeling formed in his stomach. Now what?

CHAPTER 15

Rebekka drove to the airport in Salt Lake, following the detailed instructions Damon had faxed to his office at the house. Finding the airport was considerably easier than driving anywhere in Paris.

As she waited for the flight to come in, she thought about Marc. She hadn't received any e-mail from him since she had told him Damon had kissed her. That had been Thursday, and today was Tuesday. It had seemed much longer than five days.

She pictured Marc's handsome face, the way his brown eyes seemed to twinkle and jump out at her when he laughed. The way his eyelids drooped enticingly when he teased. Oh, how that had always made her ache inside! To be so close, and yet so far away, had been a delicious torture.

Moisture gathered in her eyes, but Rebekka blinked it away. She didn't need tears—or Marc.

"I'm sure hoping you're here to pick me up," a voice said.

Rebekka was startled to see the figure of a lean, blonde-haired man standing in front of her. "Samuel!" He was just as tall and handsome as she remembered.

"Hello, Rebekka with two Ks. You were hundreds of miles away." He chuckled. "Let me guess—France?"

She smiled. "Yes. My brother became engaged recently. But I'll be going back for the wedding next spring."

"Maybe I'll arrange to be in France at the same time. You could show me around." He sounded so hopeful and friendly that Rebekka laughed and nodded. "Sure, but I don't know if I really want to go to the Eiffel Tower again."

"Been there—three times, actually. So I think I'd settle for the Louvre, a cathedral, and maybe a palace or two."

"Now that I could arrange." She stood, noticing how tall he was. When she looked at him straight on, her eyes were level with the top of his broad chest. To return his gaze, she had to tilt her head back and go past the firm mouth to the green eyes.

He was watching her intently, a half-smile on his lips, and Rebekka felt herself flush. What was wrong with her? One moment she was pining over Marc, and the next flushing at the stare of another man. Not to mention checking him out.

The drive to Damon's company, Hospital's Choice Incorporated, in Orem, was comfortable. Besides being handsome and nice, Samuel was knowledgeable about the world and current events, and they carried on an interesting and lively conversation that made the trip seem short and pleasant. By they time they arrived at their destination, they were chatting like old friends.

Hospital's Choice Incorporated consisted of a small suite of offices in a large building filled with other small companies. The space was rented for the time being, but Rebekka was aware of plans to build at a later date.

Damon and Jesse had barely finished their previous meeting with the administrators of several hospitals, and they came to meet Samuel with outstretched hands and sincere smiles. "We're so glad you could make it," Damon said.

"I was intrigued by the offer." Samuel glanced at Rebekka. "It was the first time that my giving a business card to a beautiful woman on a plane led to any business opportunities. Frankly, I was just trying to steal Rebekka away from whomever she works for now." He grinned. "That's you guys, I guess."

"Actually, Bekka's been kind enough to help me out with my children." Damon indicated a chair for Samuel and sat on another. Rebekka sat next to Samuel. "But now that they're back in school, we've been hoping she'd agree to work on the foreign side of our Hospital's Choice program. It isn't every day that you find someone so skilled in two languages."

"That's what I thought when I first met her." Samuel was looking at her again, and Rebekka pretended to cough into her hand to break the hold he seemed to have on her eyes. She knew without a doubt that he was flirting, and her heart raced at the thought of being the pursued instead of the one doing the pursuing. It was definitely a nice change. If only Marc could see her now.

* * * * *

Mickelle's heart was hammering so hard that she almost couldn't breathe. Her vision dimmed, and she felt blood rushing from her head. A panic attack. But she couldn't give in to it now. She had to make sure Bryan was all right. She turned toward him, willing her eyes to see.

"Bryan." Her voice sounded anxious in the sudden stillness.

"I'm okay, Mom."

She heard the click of the seat belt and then felt his hand on hers. The fogginess in her vision cleared, and his face came into view. "Are you hurt?" he asked.

She shook her head. "He just came at me. We had the right of way."

"We're blocking the intersection," he said, surveying the situation. "Look, they're backing the Bug over to the side. Does our car still work?"

Mickelle tried to start the engine, afraid someone would ram into them again. On the third try the engine managed to stay running. She put the car into gear and inched forward carefully. A horrible grinding noise filled the air as the station wagon lurched across the intersection and to the side of the road in front of Hopper's Footwear.

When she tried to get out of the car, her door wouldn't open. She had to bring her feet up and push hard on the door before it finally gave way with a screech and grinding of metal.

Bryan exited his door and ran around to her side. "Look, Mom. The metal's pushed up against the tire," he observed excitedly. "That's what was making the noise when you drove."

The whole metal panel around the tire had also shifted, which was why she hadn't been able to open the door. Mickelle tugged on the metal touching the tire with her hand, but it didn't budge. At this rate, she was not going to be able to drive home, and she certainly couldn't pay for a tow truck.

When she gave up, Bryan tried without success.

Trying to breathe evenly to stave off another panic attack, Mickelle glanced at the Bug, where a crowd of teenagers were gathered, surveying the damage. One disappeared inside the car.

An employee hurried out of Hopper's, his face and eyes bright with suppressed excitement. "I've called the police," he said. "They should be here soon. But I'd keep an eye on those kids. They look like they're going to take off."

Bryan started toward the teens, his fists clenched and his face growing red with anger. Mickelle caught up to him. "Easy, Bryan. You catch more flies with honey than with vinegar." She was relieved to see him nod. His temper since Riley's death had been quick and volatile, but lately she had noticed a reduction in its intensity. He was trying to maintain control as he dealt with his father's death, and he had in large measure succeeded.

"Are you all right?" she asked the teens, who watched her warily. There were five in all, four boys and a thin girl with long blonde hair and pretty green eyes. Mickelle thought they all looked about sixteen.

"Yeah," was the mumbled response.

"Well, that's the important thing—that everyone is okay." She paused a minute and asked, "Who was driving?" The kids pointed to a tall brown-haired boy of average build who stared sadly at his crushed red Bug. The entire front end on the passenger side had buckled like an aluminium can stepped on by a heavy man wearing hiking boots. Mickelle glanced back at her gold station wagon. On the driver's side, the front had been pushed in, but not crunched. For all its cosmetic drawbacks, the Snail was rather sturdy.

The boy touched the smooth paint above the ruined metal on his car. His eyes were wide, and he looked as if he wanted to cry. A sudden wave of pity rose in Mickelle's heart. He was just a child, really. And he needed someone to give him support.

Mickelle approached. "That's a lot of damage," she ventured.

He nodded, his jaw tightening. "Just got her painted. I fixed her all up inside, too. My dad helped me—when he could." He glanced at his friends and swallowed hard. The blonde girl touched his arm, but he didn't seem to notice.

A police car pulled up at the scene, and two policemen emerged. Mickelle recognized one of them as the young officer who had pulled her over that morning. "You again?" she asked.

He permitted himself a small grin. "It's a relatively small town." His voice lowered. "Are you all right?"

"Yes. Thank you."

"Look, here's a sheet to fill out about the accident. You start in on it while we talk to the kid."

Mickelle nodded. For some reason, seeing someone she knew, even as remotely as Officer Lowder, made her relax. She also became acutely aware of her old jeans and rumpled shirt. The black must make her look even more washed out than usual.

She was nearly finished with the sheet when Bryan appeared at her elbow. "Mom, that kid doesn't have insurance. I heard the cop say so. He doesn't even have a driver's license. He's only fifteen."

Mickelle tensed. Immediately, she walked over to where Officer Lowder was questioning the boy.

"I was just going to get my sister from school," the boy was saying. "Nobody else was home. The nanny, my dad . . . there was a meeting."

"What about your mother?" Mickelle asked.

The boy's gaze flicked to her. "My mom is dead."

She felt stunned. This boy had apparently already suffered a great deal. The urge to comfort him again welled up inside of her. "I'm sorry," she murmured.

He turned his face away and stared dejectedly at his car.

"So you thought you could just drive on down with no license and no insurance." Officer Lowder clicked his tongue. "And then you just went through the intersection when it wasn't your turn. Why did you do that?"

The boy shook his head. "I don't know. The music was loud. The guys were fighting . . ."

Officer Lowder looked at the other teens. "What happened?" he asked.

A tall, gangly boy with small hazel eyes said, "The light was green, and she wasn't going. She just sat there. So we went. And then she crashed into us."

"Write it down." Officer Lowder handed him a sheet of paper. "Anybody else?"

"I saw the same thing," said a boy with curly red hair and freckles. "She crashed into us."

In disbelief, Mickelle looked into the boy's large blue eyes, noticing the long, curly red eyelashes. "I crashed into you? *I* had the right of way."

"Yep, she did," said the employee from Hopper's. "I saw the whole thing."

The red-haired boy shrugged. "I was messing with the music," he muttered. "That was what I saw."

"The music was loud," offered the blonde girl.

Officer Lowder gave them all sheets to fill out. He took Mickelle's paper and exchanged it for one the boy had filled out. "Just wait at your car for a moment, okay? I'll be there in a minute. We're going to impound the boy's car and try to find someone to come and get him."

Mickelle glanced worriedly at her watch. "I have to get my son from school in about five minutes. He'll wonder what's keeping me. I can't really drive the car . . ."

Officer Lowder consulted briefly with his partner, then walked back with Mickelle to her station wagon. After studying the damage, he went to the police car and removed a crowbar from the trunk. He put the edge between the metal and the tire and pushed. It took him four tries before the metal moved away from the tire.

"There, that ought to get you home at least."

Mickelle looked at him gratefully. "Thank you."

He appeared about to say something, but his partner called to him. "I have to go," he said to Mickelle. "Look, this boy's in big trouble, but you're going to have to contact his father to see how he's going to pay for this. And sometimes getting these jerks to pay is tough. With all you've been through . . . anyway, I'm really sorry."

"Thank you," Mickelle repeated. "Uh, are you going to give him a ticket?"

"Not for the accident. In this city, we don't give tickets in an accident. But he will be cited for not having a license or insurance."

"I see." It didn't make sense to her. The boy had caused the accident and should have received a ticket.

Officer Lowder walked away, and Mickelle tried to open her door. It refused to move. She pulled harder. The door handle broke. "Oh, great." Tears stung her eyes. Blinking them firmly away, she went around to the passenger side and climbed in, sliding over to the driver's seat.

Bryan followed her inside. "Sorry, Mom."

She smiled at him weakly. "I didn't think the Snail could get any worse."

"It could have blown up," he offered. They both laughed.

"You're right," Mickelle conceded. "We're both okay, and that's a big blessing." She took a deep breath. "Well, here goes nothing." But the engine started on the first try, and Mickelle drove slowly past the scene of the accident, once again noticing the young driver of the other car. His expression of sadness continued to tug at her heart. She turned right on the next street and then right again, driving toward the school. They were just in time to pick up Jeremy. Once again, Mickelle had to use her feet to open the door, but it was easier this time.

Jeremy met them at the front entrance of the school, full of excitement about his day. Before he could say anything, Bryan launched into an enthusiastic account of the accident.

Back at the car, Mickelle felt the curious eyes of other parents as she entered from the passenger side and scooted over. On the drive home, she discovered that the screeching noise of metal against the tire sounded again each time she turned left. She wondered how much it would cost to repair the vehicle. The boy didn't have insurance, but would his father pay? Could she make him?

She felt her heart start to race, signaling the onslaught of another panic attack. *Don't think about it.* She slowed the car to a crawl and let the attack roll through her as she clutched the steering wheel. "You guys have homework?" she asked almost desperately. Focusing on something else helped, and her panic subsided.

The boys did have homework, but once they were home it took only a few moments to complete. "What's for dinner, Mom?" Bryan asked when they had finished. "Can we eat now?"

Mickelle sighed. What she really wanted was to go to bed.

"Yeah, I'm starved," said Jeremy.

She pulled a box from the cupboard. "How about cereal?"

"Cereal for dinner *again*?" Jeremy said. "Aw, Mom, I'm sick of cereal. Can I walk to Aunt Brionney's? I bet she's having a real dinner."

"Shut up," Bryan said sharply, looking at Mickelle's face. "Cereal's good enough."

"Mom, Bryan told me to shut up!"

Mickelle leaned against the counter, stifling an urge to run into the bedroom and bury her head under the pillow.

"Mom! Did you hear me?"

She took a few steps toward the hall, still contemplating escape.

"Mom, where are you going?" Jeremy's plea reminded her of the way he had worried about her disappearing while he was at school.

But hadn't she already left the boys by sinking into depression? By spending most of her time in the dark bedroom under the covers? What was she waiting for? Her knight in shining armor was dead, and he wasn't coming back. He had never really been much of a knight anyway. Besides, wasn't it her responsibility to take control of her life? She had thought so before Riley had stolen everything out from under her. Maybe it was still true.

She drew herself up to her full height. "Why don't we order a pizza?" They hadn't bought pizza since Riley had died. People had brought them pizza, and once they'd eaten it at Brionney's, but Mickelle had been either too concerned about money or too depressed to order it herself.

"Do we have the money?" asked Bryan, as though reading her mind.

"I have a coupon for Papa Murphy's. For a large combo, it'll only cost ten bucks." Papa Murphy's was her boys' favorite pizza place because of the large size of the pizzas. It was her favorite because it was a take-and-bake place, meaning that the pizza was never cold when they got around to eating it.

The boys cheered, but Mickelle held up a finger. "On one condition. I want you to clean your rooms—including on top of the dressers, under the bed, and in the closets."

"In the closet, too?" Bryan moaned.

Mickelle had seen the four months' worth of clutter in his room and took pity on him. "Okay, not in the closet, but everywhere else. And don't throw it all in your closets, either, because this weekend you are both going to clean them out." She hoped she wouldn't be too depressed to follow through.

She went to the phone to call in the order. "You can stay here and clean while I go pick up the pizza. And remember," she warned, "I'll still have to cook it, and I won't do it if I can't see the floors in your rooms. I can always stick it in the freezer."

"Can I turn on the oven?" asked Jeremy, nearly jumping with enthusiasm.

"Not until I'm sure we're going to eat the pizza tonight."

She made sure the boys began working before she left to pick up the pizza at the drive-through window. By the time she arrived home, she could actually see the color of the tan carpet in their rooms. Feeling a sense of satisfaction that had long escaped her, she let Jeremy preheat the oven and slide the pizza in.

Later, at the table, Bryan stared at the cooked pizza and wrinkled his nose. "Mom, they put mushrooms on it," he whined. "We don't like mushrooms."

"Yeah." Jeremy removed a mushroom from his slice. "Only Dad liked mushrooms."

Mickelle took an unsteady breath. It was true. Riley had always insisted on having mushrooms on his pizza, and she had always ordered them, despite the fact that everyone else in the family picked them off. Why would she still order the mushrooms when Riley was no longer here to complain or insist?

Mickelle fought tears and bitterness. This was one more problem added to her terrible day, but she had to be strong for the boys. She had already let them down so much in the past months. For a moment, she hated both Riley and every one of the two-thousand-plus varieties of mushrooms in the world.

No one said anything for a long time, and then Bryan picked up his pizza and took a bite. "Hmm, not bad," he said, keeping his eyes on her face. "I think I like mushrooms after all."

Jeremy stared. Then he nodded solemnly and replaced the mushroom he had taken from his pizza. He took a big bite. "It is good," he agreed. "I can't even taste the mushrooms."

Bryan took another bite, then another. Shortly, he was reaching for another slice. Mickelle took a bite of her own pizza. Then she started to laugh, nearly choking.

The boys joined in, making her laugh harder, until a tear rolled down her cheek. Here they were, eating mushrooms they hated, and enjoying every minute because it reminded them of Riley. Of the good times, and even the bad.

"I think we should always have mushrooms," Jeremy said.

Bryan reached for his third slice. "Me too."

* * * * *

Rebekka was mostly silent as the meeting progressed. She could tell the men liked each other and shared similar business ideals, and she suspected that soon Jesse's hospital programs would be marketed abroad by Samuel's company. She wondered what religion Samuel believed in. It would be too much to hope that he was a member of her church. Well, at least Damon was.

She looked at Damon at the same time he glanced her way. He smiled. She remembered their plans for Friday and her promise to take him somewhere interesting. But where? If they were in France, she would know exactly where to go. She would take him to that little restaurant near the Seine where she and Marc—

Damon winked at her, and Rebekka swallowed hard.

"Well, I guess that's about the extent of our plans," Damon said to Samuel. "Do you feel your company would be interested?"

"Actually, yes." Samuel put down the pen he had been using to take notes. "The more I learn, the more I am intrigued with the possibilities." He smiled at Rebekka pointedly. "In fact, I'm finding everything about Utah more interesting than I had expected. I think you have a potential vein of gold here, and I would like to be a part of mining it. However, before I commit my company, I'd like to stick around a few days, take a look at the program itself. Maybe see it at work in a hospital. I'm not a programmer by a long shot, but I have had some programming experience, and I know quality when I see it."

"I'll be glad to walk you through the program," Jesse volunteered.

Damon leaned back in his chair. "Are you free to stay now, or do you need to come back at another time?"

"I could stay now. I'll have to make a few phone calls, but I have good people who can cover for me. I'd appreciate it if you could direct me to a nice hotel."

"I could do that," Damon said, "or you could stay with me. We have a lot of space in the wing where Rebekka's room is—and a cook who makes really tasty Cincinnati-style five-way chili."

"Five-way chili? Well, then I'll *have* to accept your hospitality." Once again Samuel smiled at Rebekka, and somehow she was sure she was the real reason he agreed to stay at Damon's. She wasn't sure how that made her feel, but she couldn't stop smiling. This certainly beat baby-sitting the cranky Belle and the besotted Tanner.

"What's five-way chili?" she ventured.

"That's chili served on a mound of spaghetti with chopped raw onions and red kidney beans on top, all smothered in a very thick layer of shredded cheddar." Samuel ran his tongue over his lips. "There's nothing like it."

Rebekka didn't think the dish sounded good at all, but she was willing to try almost anything once. "Sounds like an adventure."

"You'll love it." Samuel continued to hold her gaze, smiling.

Damon frowned, seeming to notice Samuel's interest in her for the first time. He was about to speak again when one of the employees poked his head in the door. "Sorry for the interruption . . . I just checked the answering service, and you have a pretty important message. It's about your son." He glanced at Samuel, as though not wanting to say more.

"Thank you, Brody." Damon rose to his feet. "If you'll excuse me, Samuel, I'll leave you in Jesse and Rebekka's capable hands."

Samuel nodded, and they shook hands. "That will be just fine."

* * * * *

Damon drove to the American Fork police station in his dark-blue Mercedes. At first he had been shocked and concerned at the news of Tanner's accident, but now he was more angry than anything else. He admitted to himself that part of his anger had been caused by Samuel's apparent interest in Rebekka, though aside from his jealousy, he liked the man and felt a great deal of professional admiration for him. Rebekka was a beautiful woman. Why wouldn't Samuel be interested? She was more his age, anyway.

He gave a protracted sigh. Tanner was really going to get it. *If I've told him once, I've told him a thousand times that he couldn't drive until he had his license. I'm going to wallop him until he's too sore to sit down!*

But when he picked Tanner up at the police station, his son's face seemed to bear the weight of the world. All the angry words and recriminations on the tip of Damon's tongue evaporated, and he said a silent prayer of thanks for the distance between American Fork and Orem, which had allowed him to calm down before facing Tanner. Without saying a word, he hugged his son.

Tanner started to cry. "I thought I was doing good," he said. "But I wasn't. I—I crashed . . . the car—my car . . . I'm so sorry, Dad."

Over his son's shoulder, Damon met the interested stare of the woman behind the long front desk. He whispered to Tanner, "Come on. Let's go home. We'll talk about it there."

They drove away from the police station in silence, with Tanner staring mournfully out the window as though his best friend had died. Damon prayerfully thought about what he should say to his son. From the policeman's description of the accident, the event was Tanner's fault. But what had really happened?

Suddenly, Tanner turned toward his father. "Belle. Where's Belle?"

"She's at the Hergarters's. Bekka arranged for Bri to pick her up after school. They tried to take her to our house, apparently, but you weren't home to baby-sit, so they took her back home with them. We need to pick her up now." Damon knew he was stalling for time; he didn't know what to say to his son.

Tanner leaned back against the seat in relief. "Good. I was worried about her."

Damon pondered that. He appreciated the fact that Tanner had acted to help his sister, but he was a firm believer that the end did not justify the means. That motto had served him well in business over the years, and he didn't believe in coincidence.

Damon used his cell phone to call Rebekka and let her know they were picking up Belle. After collecting her at the Hergarters', they drove straight home. He motioned Tanner into his office and closed the door.

The boy slumped into one of two padded chairs next to the extra computer. "You know you are not allowed to drive," Damon began, sitting in the other chair. "I bought you that car and allowed you to fix it up because I knew it would not only be a good experience, but also because you would need transportation. Now you've betrayed my trust, Tanner. I'm not sure what to do about that."

Tanner sat up stiffly in his chair. "It was her fault, Dad! Really. Eric and Randy'll tell you. She wasn't moving, so I just went, and she hit me." His voice held a note of belligerence.

"You were turning," Damon stressed. "She had the right of way."

"But she just sat there! Honest."

"For how long?"

"At least five minutes. Okay, maybe a little less, but it was a long time, Dad. And I was worried about the light changing and about getting Belle. It would have been okay, if she just would have went." The belligerence disappeared as Tanner's eyes filled with tears. "I just wanted to help Belle."

"You should have known we would take care of Belle."

"I know that now," Tanner agonized, "but it seemed so . . . Randy said once his mother forgot, and Rebekka was gone . . ." He laid his head on the computer desk, and his tears wet the wood surface.

Damon could feel his son's sorrow, and his heart was heavy with the boy's pain. "Okay, look, the bottom line is that your car is damaged and has been impounded. That's going to add up to a lot of money." He allowed his voice to soften. "But I do feel you have learned a lesson, so I'll help you out. Of course, we'll still have to go to juvenile court. They can't overlook the fact that you were driving without a license or insurance."

"Court?" Tanner's brown eyes grew wide.

"Yes. You've broken the law."

"What will they do to me?" he asked.

"I'm not sure." He leaned over and put his arm around his son. "But I'll be right there beside you."

"What about that lady? I mean her car had hardly a dent, but I think she wants me to pay."

Damon set his jaw firmly, already disliking the woman who had caused the accident. "If she contacts us, I'll deal with her. No one is going to push my son around."

CHAPTER 16

It was Wednesday night, and Marc Perrault didn't feel well. He stretched out on his bed in his quiet apartment and stared at the ceiling. He wasn't sick exactly, as the doctor had assured him today; he just wasn't himself.

Everyone in the family had noticed his disquiet, and at the family dinner on Monday, two days earlier, they had all been full of advice. His twin, Josette, teased him about having a mid-life crisis. Ridiculous. He was only thirty-four. Zack, Josette's husband, suggested that Marc write in his journal—as if that sage piece of advice was the answer to the problems of the world. His brother André told him he was bored and needed new challenges, which he could begin immediately by watching André's two daughters for an entire weekend. Right. His other sister, Marie-Thérèse, said bluntly that he needed to find a wife. Her husband Mathieu proposed a vacation.

Even his grandfather and two grandmothers had suggestions, like doing more work for the Church, eating more vegetables, and getting more exercise. It was enough to make him crazy.

After his father, Jean-Marc, had advised him to search his soul, Marc found himself grateful that his younger brother, Louis-Géralde, was serving his mandatory time in the French army and couldn't add his counsel to the growing din. *Of course, it would be just my luck that Louis-Géralde is probably the one person who has the answer,* Marc thought ironically.

Besides the absent Louis-Géralde, his mother was the only family member who hadn't offered advice of any kind. Ariana had simply regarded him mutely from her seat across the table. When he had slipped away to the living room to ponder his problem in private, she had quietly followed and sat with him on the couch.

"I just feel strange," he told her. She touched his hand, held it as she had when he was little. Marc leaned against her, enjoying the comfort.

"You feel normal to me," she said softly. There was no amusement in her voice, but a small smile played on her lips. Marc grinned in spite of himself.

She hugged him. "That's better."

In the dim lamplight, Marc noticed that she was a beautiful woman. Her figure wasn't as thin as it had been in her youth, but she was active and supple. Her thick, dark brown hair was cut short and showed no signs of gray. He wondered if she dyed it, and thought she probably did, since his father's hair now had generous streaks of gray. Ariana's real beauty was in her face. Each curve, each line showed years of laughter, sorrow, and great joy. Real character. She was a woman who had lived and loved and served. Remembering the trials she had overcome in her life always gave Marc a sense of wonder. And also a hunger to have achieved such a triumph himself.

To be sure, he had experienced trials, but nothing severe since his kidney transplant at age fifteen. Sometimes he felt that his life had ended there, that he hadn't moved on or really lived since.

"Maybe I'm sick," he suggested to his mother in the quiet of the living room. Perhaps this dark feeling looming over him was related to his transplant. The kidney had already lasted nearly twenty of the thirty years the doctor had predicted in a best-case scenario. There might be something wrong.

Ariana's dark eyes showed concern. "Maybe you'd better make an appointment with your doctor."

Marc leapt to his feet and began pacing, glad they were alone. "I'll do it tomorrow." He could hear the others in the kitchen playing a board game. Usually he would have been with them, probably winning, except for Monopoly, which Mathieu seemed to win every time. The man loved buying hotels and property, even if he had to go into debt on his older holdings to do it. He joked that it was the only borrowing his wife permitted.

Marc stared out the window into the dark night. Five stories below, he could see a few pedestrians walking along the street. "It's quiet out there," he said to lighten the silence.

Ariana followed his gaze. "It usually is on Monday night. Not much going on, even in the pubs."

A burst of laughter came from the other room.

"It even seems a little quieter in there," Ariana said. "I liked it when Rebekka and Raoul would join us for our family dinners. Especially Rebekka. I miss her."

Marc suddenly wanted to cry. He didn't know why it affected him so deeply that his mother missed Rebekka. He would have to write Rebekka another e-mail and tell her. Maybe then she would stop this foolishness about her employer, and return to France where she belonged.

But didn't she belong with a man who loved her?

Now, Marc sat up and sighed, pushing away the memories of Monday night. He was surprised to find tears on his cheeks. *Drat!* He had to get to the bottom of this malady now and get on with his life.

Let's see . . . There wasn't too much wrong with him. He couldn't eat, he couldn't sleep, and his mind wandered at work—but those things were nothing new. He had experienced all of these emotions before, when he had first realized that he was in love with Danielle and that she was out of his reach forever.

Danielle. Usually, when he thought of her, he could stave off any depression. Even though he could only love her from afar, just seeing her was enough; even hearing her velvet voice was enough. But he had just come from Raoul's, and Danielle had been there. They had talked for exactly one hour. Why hadn't that satisfied him?

With another long sigh, he rose to his feet and walked down the hall and into the bathroom. He splashed water on his face, obliterating the tears. Then he stared at himself. *You're thirty-four years old,* he thought, *and what do you have to show for it?* His engineering firm didn't matter; he had realized that. So what did?

His reflection showed a brown-eyed, dark-haired man who could pass for much younger. Not many lines—none of the rich experience that had given his mother's face such character.

I've had a few trials, he thought in his own defense. He had served a faithful mission, which had taught him many things. He had watched his little sister die when she was only sixteen, and had learned even more. What else? What else had he lived through or done that meant anything? Oh, yes: even before any of the other experiences, he had saved Danielle's life and fallen in love with her.

Why did everything always come back to that?

He walked back down the hall like a man in a dream, pausing at the door to his office. The computer stared blankly back at him. He could write to Rebekka. Maybe talking to her would help.

But she might write back and tell him she had kissed her boss again, or that she was engaged.

He sat at the computer and put his head in his hands, fighting the impulse to sob out his frustrations. He just had to think it out, decide what was wrong and fix it. He closed his eyes. There had to be a way . . .

Marc heard a voice. A voice like soft velvet, caressing his body, running over him like warm water in the shower. For a moment, he was completely happy, reveling in the silky feel of the voice, of the love that surrounded his entire being.

The next thing he knew, his face hit the desk and he was wide awake. "Danielle," he whispered against the growing ache in his chest.

But it wasn't Danielle whose voice he had heard. The voice belonged to Rebekka.

CHAPTER 17

Mickelle was absolutely furious. She couldn't remember when she had been so completely angry. She gave the fender another push with her booted feet and slid out from under the car. If only she could get the fender to bend enough so the wheel wouldn't scrape when she turned left!

She had found out that her uninsured motorist coverage obligated her insurance company to pay for her repairs, since the driver of the other vehicle had been uninsured. At first this had relieved her, but then she had discovered that the repairs would cost six hundred dollars, and her deductible was five hundred. That meant Mickelle would have to come up with the first five hundred dollars by herself. It was money she didn't have. Money they needed for food and other necessities.

A panic attack came upon her so suddenly that she sank back to the cement near the tire, closing her eyes and trying to focus on her breathing. In. Out. In. Out. Her heart pounded in her breast, and she was afraid to open her eyes. Any stimulation would only make it worse. She heard an odd sound, an agonized whimpering, and realized it was coming from her own lips. Clamping them together, she breathed slowly until the symptoms began to ease.

When she had recovered enough, she glanced at her watch. Bryan would be home any minute now, and then Jeremy, who planned to walk home with the neighbor children. They were safe, she reminded herself, and that was the important thing. Her parents, or any of her siblings, would give her the money to fix the car if she asked.

But she knew she wouldn't ask. Not yet. Her pride was already wounded and beaten; somehow, she would find a way out of this herself. Perhaps then she could find some reason to drag herself out of bed each day.

She hurried inside and called the number on the sheet she had exchanged with Tanner Wolfe. The boy himself answered. "Is your father home?" she asked after identifying herself.

"No. He's gone. He's never home." The boy's voice was matter-of-fact.

Mickelle felt her anger dissipating. The poor, lonely child! "When can I get ahold of him?"

"Tonight maybe. He's working really hard."

"Look, you're a nice kid," Mickelle said, "and I know you didn't mean to cause the accident. But my car needs to be fixed."

"You'll have to talk with my dad."

"All right." She hesitated. "Are you home alone? I mean, is there anyone with you?"

"We have a nanny, but she's not home right now."

Mickelle wondered where the nanny had been the day before, when she was supposed to be taking care of him. "I'm sorry about your mom," she said. "I really am."

"That's okay."

"It must be hard."

"Yeah."

Mickelle wanted to say something else. She wanted to make everything all right, but she couldn't bring back his mom, and she still needed her car to be fixed. "I'll call later," she said.

The boy grunted.

"Uh, Tanner?" she said before he could hang up. "I want you to know that I understand. I know what it's like to lose someone you love. And I also know what it's like to cause an accident. It happened to me when I was young, and I thought it was the end of the world. But soon it'll be just a memory—once we get it all straightened out."

The boy was silent, and Mickelle felt like an idiot. Then he said, "Thanks." It was just one word, but she was listening so hard that it spoke volumes. Instinctively, she knew that he was grateful for her understanding.

All at once, she wanted to tell him that if he needed to go somewhere, to call her and she would drive him. That if his sister needed a ride home from school, she could help. But he was a stranger and a child, and her offer wasn't appropriate.

"Good-bye." The boy hung up before she could deliberate any longer.

Mickelle called the boy's house twice more that evening. Once no one answered, and once she talked again with Tanner. Thursday night she tried to call a fourth time, but the line was busy. On Friday evening, still no one answered. "I bet they have caller ID," Bryan volunteered. Mickelle gritted her teeth.

* * * * *

Rebekka was having fun. Working with Damon and Samuel for most of the day instead of baby-sitting was rewarding. No longer did she have to worry about what she said around Tanner, or try to elicit sullen responses from Belle.

Samuel was a large part of her enjoyment, and she realized she would miss him when he returned to Cincinnati. He wasn't a member of the Church, but she could tell he was a religious man. Whoever had raised him had done a very good job.

"My parents," he said when she asked on Friday afternoon. They sat alone in the meeting room, which doubled as a break room, eating a late lunch. "They just celebrated their fiftieth wedding anniversary."

"Are they religious?"

"Actually, yes. Active Catholics. Great people. They raised me with good values."

"Do you attend church?"

"When I can." His eyes met hers, and he added quietly, "I believe in the role of religion, if that's what you mean. What about your family?"

She told him about her parents and about Raoul, who hadn't e-mailed her since the night of his engagement.

"Aren't you leaving someone out?" His voice was gentle and understanding.

She met the green eyes that seemed to stare at her so compassionately. "There was a very dear friend of mine whom I've sort of had a crush on since I was five."

He whistled. "That's a long time to have a crush."

"Like I said, we were friends. It was hard to leave him."

"So why did you?"

She didn't reply right away, but he waited patiently. "Marc is a lot older than I am. I'm more like his sister than anything else." She thought of her mother. "Or perhaps he sees himself as my father. I don't know."

Samuel sat back in his chair, his eyes twinkling. "Ah, that explains it."

She gathered up the remains of her sandwich and stuffed them into the empty lunch container Damon's cook had given them. The sandwiches had been too dry, but at least they hadn't been that horrible five-way chili. After tasting it earlier in the week, she didn't see how anyone as nice as Samuel could stand the dish.

"Explains what?"

"Why you like Damon so much."

Rebekka bristled. "He's a nice man."

"I know he's a nice man." Samuel leaned forward and grabbed her hand unexpectedly. His warmth surged through her. "But he's old. I mean, you're so young and beautiful. So full of excitement. Damon's so much more conservative and . . . well, I admire his business sense . . . but—" A look of sheer frustration filled Samuel's face. "I guess the truth is, I'm jealous. There, now you know."

Rebekka didn't know what to say.

"Look," he continued, "I'm not saying that you don't like Damon for the great guy he is, but could it be that you see in him a lot of what you saw in your friend—Marc, wasn't it?"

She nodded dumbly. This possibility had crossed her mind more than a few times, and it bothered her more than she was willing to admit to anyone. "I'll think about it," she said.

Samuel rose, still holding her hand. "I have to fly back to Cincinnati tomorrow—I've already stayed longer than I was supposed to. Would you like to go out to dinner with me tonight?" For a moment, he didn't look like a tough CEO, but an eager young boy.

Rebekka wished she didn't have to let him down. "I can't. I really would like to, but I have plans already."

His grin vanished. "That's okay. I understand." He paused. "I'll be back next week, you know."

She knew he could easily send someone instead of making the trip himself. He would be coming to see her. "Then let's go out next week."

The grin on his face reemerged like the sun from behind a cloud. "Okay, Rebekka. We'll go out then."

Damon walked into the room. "Am I interrupting?" he asked, eyeing their linked hands. He rubbed his jaw with his fingers as he spoke.

Rebekka pulled her hand away from Samuel's. "No." She glanced at her watch, searching for an explanation. "Oh, look at the time! I have to pick up Belle at school. I'd better hurry."

"Mrs. Mertz said she'd watch Belle for us tonight," Damon said. "What time are we leaving for our dinner?"

Rebekka felt her face color slightly. She didn't dare glance at Samuel for fear he'd be watching her. Was she attracted to Damon because he reminded her of Marc? Samuel seemed to think so.

Nonsense. They didn't look anything alike.

She smiled at Damon, realizing that she still didn't know where she was going to take him. "Six-thirty. Now, if you gentlemen will excuse me?" She took a few steps toward the door.

"May I go with you to get Belle?" Samuel asked. "I'm finished here, and I'd like to come along for the ride. Besides, Belle likes me."

Rebekka could hear the grin in his voice, though he kept his face straight. "By all means." She motioned to the door. From the corner of her eye she saw Damon grimace, but there was nothing she could do to reassure him when she didn't know how she felt about Samuel. He was so tall and smart and good-looking. What would it be like to be kissed by him?

As if reading her thoughts, Samuel put an arm around her when they were out of Damon's sight, once again making her skin tingle. "I can't wait until next week."

* * * * *

They arrived five minutes before school let out. "So, do you do a lot of traveling?" Rebekka asked as they waited in the car for Belle.

"Actually, yes. I don't need to, really. I employ people I trust and who are very qualified, but I enjoy moving around and meeting new people. Besides, most of my top executives are married, and they don't like to be away from their families so much."

"So you go instead."

"Well, I have to make a lot of decisions anyway, and it's always easier for me if I can get a feel of things myself."

"Do you make a lot of business decisions because of your feelings?" Rebekka found that a fascinating concept. All the men in her life had displayed strong business acumen—her father, Marc, Damon, and now Samuel. She was curious as to how they worked inside, and what her fascination with them might say about her.

"It's more of a gut instinct." Samuel made a fist and held it to his stomach. "Perhaps like what you Mormons call inspiration."

Marc had told her many times of feeling inspired in his business dealings. She had figured it was the Holy Ghost prompting him, but how did Samuel feel it? And Damon hadn't been a member long, yet every business he touched—even before he joined the Church—had turned to gold. *Perhaps the Father isn't looking so much at the religion as He is the man.* Of course that didn't explain evil men who became rich every day. *We are all born with talents,* she reminded herself. *We are all children of God, even if we choose another path.* Like her father. Rebekka sighed.

"You haven't heard a word I've said," Samuel accused.

She looked at him sheepishly. "Sorry. I've been thinking."

"About our date next week, I hope."

"Are you sure you're coming back?"

"Well, to tell the truth, I was going to send someone else. But now, even two software mergers couldn't keep me away."

Rebekka laughed. "You're funny."

"I was being serious." He tried to look offended, but his eyes were laughing.

"What's keeping Belle?" Rebekka asked, grateful to change the subject.

"Should we go in and look for her?"

"We'd better."

They went into the school and down the hall to Belle's first grade classroom. The teacher looked up at them expectantly. "May I help you?"

"I'm here to pick up Belle," Rebekka said, thinking the woman must not remember her from the two times she had come into the classroom with her young charge.

"Yes, I recognize you. But Belle already left. Right when the bell rang. You didn't see her in the hall?"

"No. She was supposed to meet me outside."

The teacher looked worried. "I don't know what to tell you. Maybe she's down at the office."

Rebekka's heart thumped heavily in her breast. "I'll check the office," she told Samuel. "Would you mind going back to the car in case she goes there?"

Samuel nodded. "Don't worry. She's a smart little scamp. I'll bet she's fine. Yeah, she probably heard we were having five-way chili again for dinner and decided to hide out until the danger was past."

Rebekka gave him a brief smile of gratitude before turning away. Belle had hated the chili; it had been the first thing they had agreed on in a long time. But the cook wasn't making the chili tonight, so Belle had no reason to hide—unless she had been upset about Rebekka's pending date with Damon. Was this the child's way of rebelling? Anger nearly blotted out the worry in Rebekka's chest. Belle was all too capable of such a thing.

But Rebekka had also seen Belle when she had been helpless and crying—very much the child in need. Damon had been away on business the first of the summer, and Rebekka had left the intercom to Belle's room on, just to be sure she was all right. Around midnight, Belle had started to cry. Rebekka had gone to her room to offer comfort, but Belle had turned her face to her brown teddy bear and refused to look at her. Rebekka had stayed with her anyway, until the child was asleep. She had been so young and helpless, and Rebekka's heart had ached at not being able to help her.

"She does that sometimes," Damon said when she told him about the incident later. "Not very often. Usually when it happens she'll come into my bed, or I'll hear her and go in. I just hold her till she goes to sleep."

"She wouldn't let me touch her."

"I'm sorry. That must have been hard on you."

Rebekka swallowed the sudden lump in her throat. "No. She was the one suffering. I wish she'd let me help."

Now, Rebekka stored the memories away. This wasn't the middle of the night, and Damon wasn't away on business. Belle had to be pulling one of her tricks. *Please let it be one of her tricks.*

Belle wasn't in the office, and she wasn't anywhere on the school grounds. The principal contacted the police while Rebekka called Damon. In her emotional state she stumbled over her words, and her slight French accent was more pronounced.

"Have you called Bri?" Damon asked. "She went home with them before."

"Yes. She's not there."

He sighed. "I'm coming right now."

She hung up and waited for Samuel and several of the other teachers who were checking the bathrooms again. She prayed hard. What if someone had taken Belle?

* * * * *

Damon's throat felt dry. He wanted to break every speed limit to arrive at the school faster. Where could Belle be?

It was his fault, of course. He should have taken better care of her. But how?

He didn't know. He had stopped going out of town on business unless it couldn't possibly be avoided, and he spent quality time with Belle, reading stories and just plain talking. He supplied her with everything she wanted or needed—except a mother, which was hardly his fault. Charlotte had been dead only two years, although with her long illness, he had mourned her for longer than that. He couldn't help it that he hadn't found a new wife. It wasn't like he hadn't been trying.

"I'm going to spank her," he said aloud. It made him feel better to say the words, though he knew he wouldn't follow through. He hadn't spanked either of his children since they had been very small and just learning to obey.

At the school, he found a distraught Rebekka with the principal and a nearly frantic teacher. They were talking with two police officers. "You're sure you've searched everywhere?" one asked.

"Yes." Rebekka's voice was controlled, but her smoky gray eyes were worried. She spied Damon with obvious relief. "Here's her father now, thank heaven."

As he talked with the police, Samuel appeared from one of the halls. He nodded at Damon, his face grave. "I checked the playground again. Nothing."

Damon left his cell number with the officers and began driving the streets. He called his neighbors in Alpine as he drove, asking them to put out the word about Belle's disappearance. If Belle was all right, he wouldn't put it past her to be able to find her way home alone. All the same, a sick feeling developed in his gut, making him want to vomit. He had dealt with powerful men in his business ventures, had faced losing his wife, and had survived when Karissa had chosen to work things out with her husband. But he couldn't imagine life without his Belle. She had been his reason for going on when it had appeared easier to give up. Not even his precious son had given him that. He saw more of himself in the little girl than in Tanner, who seemed to take after Charlotte. A sob threatened to erupt from his throat, but he bit it down. He had to remain calm. Losing control would not bring Belle back to him.

He drove the streets slowly, searching for his daughter. He stopped to ask people if they had seen her. They shook their heads, pity showing in their eyes. Several of the fathers began to help him search, going door to door to talk with the neighbors. Damon gave them his cell number and prayed harder.

He called the police and the school, where Rebekka and Samuel waited, but they had no news. Next he drove to the Hergarters' to see if they had seen Belle. Jesse had already arrived home from the office, and he answered the door.

His brown eyes took in the situation at once. "Brionney just told me about Belle. You haven't found her yet?"

Damon shook his head, unable to speak past the lump in his throat. His stomach churned, and he tasted gall in the back of his throat.

Jesse put an arm around him. "Look, don't worry. We'll find her. She's probably just gone to some friend's house to play."

"The principal is calling her classmates now," Damon managed. His hands twisted the ends of his short moustache, as he was too stressed to care about his efforts to break the habit. "I thought I was a good father," he said with a groan. "I tried to be everything to her, but . . ." He stopped talking, knowing that one more word would bring an unending torrent of tears.

It wouldn't have mattered. Jesse's eyes had already filled with moisture. He turned and faced the entryway, where his two oldest daughters and Brionney waited anxiously. "We're not going to the drive-in tonight," he told them. "We need to help find Belle."

"Of course we do," Brionney agreed. "We can go to the movie any night."

The girls' faces showed disappointment, but also indecision, as though they were trying to be brave about their sacrifice. "What will you do when you find her?" Camille asked. "Are you going to spank her?"

Damon forced a slight grin for the child's benefit. "I might at that. She needs to learn to be obedient."

"Does this mean you're not going on your date?" Savannah asked, her blue eyes earnest.

Damon didn't hide his surprise. "How did you know about that?"

"Belle told us. She said you and Rebekka were going to go out without her," Camille said. "She hates Rebekka. I don't know why. Rebekka is so nice and pretty."

Brionney looked apologetically at Damon. "Girls, come on. Let's get the boys ready. We can walk around the neighborhood and look for Belle." She paused. "On second thought, I could probably call everyone a lot faster."

"You call, I'll walk," Jesse said, stepping onto the porch. "Divide and conquer." The girls and Brionney hovered in the doorway.

Damon turned and sprinted to his Mercedes. "Call me if you find anything." Belle was no closer to being found, but his friends' willingness to help made him feel inexplicably better.

* * * * *

Camille watched Damon drive slowly away. "He looks so sad," she said. Savannah nodded, glancing toward the hall that led to their bedrooms.

"Of course he's sad," their mother said. "If one of you were missing, I don't know what I'd do. Come on, let's go make some calls." She disappeared into the house.

Camille looked at the neighbor's house, where her daddy was already knocking at the door. All of this was Belle's fault. Bossy little Belle, who didn't seem to care for anybody but herself. Tears stung Camille's eyes. She looked at Savannah, who was unusually quiet. "Savvy," she began.

Savannah shook her head. "We promised," she whispered.

"But this isn't good."

"She's our friend."

"She's my friend mostly," Camille corrected. "She's in my class. And I think we should tell."

Savannah's expression was agonized. "Just a little longer?"

"Okay." But Camille didn't want to see the look on her parents' faces when they heard. They might not even get her the weeping fig she wanted for her room, and that would break her heart. She adored plants and someday wanted to have a greenhouse like her friend Karissa, who lived in Alaska. The only reason Camille had gone along with Belle's plan in the first place was because Belle had promised her a real yucca plant.

Camille felt someone watching her, and turned to see her mother in the doorway leading to the kitchen. Brionney stared thoughtfully at them until Camille squirmed under the look in her intense blue eyes.

"What if Belle found her way to the river?" Brionney asked. "She's very little, even if she is smart. She might get hurt."

"Oh, she won't," Savannah said quickly.

Camille regarded her mother's face solemnly. *She knows*, she thought. *But how?*

Brionney's lips pursed. "I thought so. Come on into the kitchen, girls. We're going to have a little chat."

Camille felt her sense of dread immediately fade. Her mother would know what to do. And Belle wouldn't be able to boss her mother; not even Dad did that.

* * * * *

Damon had been waiting for his phone to ring with such prayerful anxiety that when it did, he started. "Hello?" He carefully guided the car to the side of the road.

"Damon, it's Jesse. Look, it's about Belle."

"You found her?" Damon almost couldn't get out the words. The next few seconds could change his life forever.

Jesse's voice held a note of embarrassment. "We found her. She's safe. I'll let Brionney explain. She's the one who found her."

Tears of relief streamed down Damon's face. He barely heard Brionney's explanation. "When you first called and I told the girls about Belle, I thought they were acting sort of weird. I mean, they were so quiet—not at all concerned about Belle as I expected they would be. I thought at first it was because they were so excited about going to the drive-in, but then when you showed up and they began asking questions about your plans tonight, I put two and two together."

Brionney paused dramatically before continuing. "They planned this whole thing with Belle so you wouldn't go out with Rebekka. Can you believe that? This whole time, she's been hiding in Camille's room. They were even going to sneak her into the van and let her go to the movie with us! I'm so sorry, Damon. Believe me, they are going to be punished."

"I'll be right there. And thanks." Damon hung up the phone and bowed his head in a silent prayer of thanks. As the fear gave way to relief, he started to feel angry. He added a plea to the Lord that he would be wise in finding an appropriate punishment for his daughter. He suddenly wished he had an earthly partner with whom to share the overwhelming burden of parenthood. What would Charlotte have done? There was no way of knowing.

He called the school and talked to Rebekka. "I've found her," he said.

"Where?"

"At the Hergarters'. She was hiding in Camille's room."

"Why would she . . . ? Oh, I see. She didn't want us to go out."

Rebekka was certainly sharp. "That's right."

"I should have realized that," she said. "Well, it did cross my mind, actually, but I thought . . ."

"That she wouldn't resort to this." He managed a laugh. "Me too. But look, Bekka, do you mind if we cancel for tonight? I think Belle needs me."

"Are you sure that isn't playing right into her hands?" Rebekka didn't sound happy.

"Maybe. But I'm her father, and I see this as a plea for help. I have to be here for her."

"I understand."

"Thanks. We'll take a rain check, all right?"

She sighed. "Okay. The important thing is that Belle is safe."

"Call off the search there, will you? I'll let the police know." Damon hung up the phone feeling guilty, but at the same time relieved. He was attracted to Rebekka, far more than he cared to admit, but his relationship with Belle had to come first.

At the Hergarters', he found an unusually docile Belle waiting for him. Her face was pale and her eyes huge in her small face. Yet unlike Savannah and Camille, her eyes were dry and unreddened by tears. "Oh, ma Belle," he said, sweeping her into his arms. "You gave me such a scare."

Now she began to cry softly, burrowing her face into his shoulder. "You want to be with Rebekka more than me. Why? She's just going to leave, like all the other nannies. You shouldn't start to love her."

He held her more tightly. "I love you, ma Belle. That's who I love. And I'm always going to be here for you." He didn't bother to wipe the tears from his face as he made his way to the door. "Come on, Belle. Let's go home."

She was right, in a way. Rebekka was going to leave them. Unless he married her. But he didn't even know her well enough to imagine that, even though they lived in the same house. One thing was certain: Belle was afraid of loving and losing another friend. What could he do about that? Rebekka was so young and beautiful and unpredictable. No wonder Belle didn't feel she could be trusted.

As he drove home, Damon wondered what Rebekka was doing at that moment. Had she gone back to the house, or was she with Samuel? Should he even care? Why did he suddenly feel so alone?

Once again, he prayed. But this time his words weren't for Belle but for himself, for the utter loneliness burgeoning in his soul. If only he had someone to talk to, someone who loved Belle as much as he did. Someone he could hold and love. Could such a person even exist?

CHAPTER 18

Rebekka was happy that Damon had found Belle, but distressed that he had canceled the date she had anticipated with pleasure for the past week. The logical side of her knew that Belle was acting out to protect her place in her father's heart, but the feminine side of her felt rejected. Rejected again as Marc had rejected her.

As though feeling her unspoken pain, Samuel took over. He talked to the principal and then ushered her out to the Altima. Without asking permission, he took the keys from her and started the ignition. "Hey, since you're free tonight after all, do you suppose we could have that date now?"

She looked at him in surprise. "Well . . . I don't . . ."

"Why not? I'm sure old Damon won't mind." He grinned. "And I do mean old."

"He's not even forty," she protested.

"And you're twenty-four."

"So?"

"So let's go dancing."

She looked down at the suit she was wearing. "In this?"

"No. We'll stop by the house for a change."

A smile found its way to her lips despite her dour mood. "Okay. Let's go. But no chili."

Samuel laughed, and she laughed with him. "You look like the cat that swallowed the canary," she said.

"Not yet," he responded, making her feel warm inside. "But I might have gotten her away from the dog."

Rebekka rolled her eyes. "You are *so* funny."

"You ain't seen nothin' yet." Then his brow furrowed. "Uh, that is if you can tell me how to get back to Damon's."

At the house, Damon's car was in the drive but there was no sign of anyone. Rebekka and Samuel went up to their rooms, which were in the same wing. "I'll race you," he challenged.

Rebekka agreed, but she purposely took her time, dressing carefully in a clingy but modest black skirt that reached all the way to the floor and a black top that shimmered with crimson highlights to accentuate her dark auburn hair. Dressy enough for a nice place, and yet comfortable enough to go anywhere. For an added touch, she swept her hair into a pile on the crown of her head and freshened her makeup.

Samuel was waiting for her in the sitting room, playing a simple tune on the Steinway. As he sensed her presence he turned, his hands falling immediately idle. "You look . . ." He searched for the words. "Absolutely gorgeous." He bowed his head over her hand and kissed it as though in another time and place. Rebekka felt goose bumps ripple up her arm and tingle down her spine.

"Shall we?" she asked.

"Yes."

Rebekka saw no sign of Damon as they left, and she couldn't help wishing he could see her all dressed up. Not that it was the same thing she would wear if she were with him. No, she would have chosen something more sedate, more classic. This outfit was more like something she would have worn dancing with the fun-loving Marc.

The sharp feeling of longing came so unexpectedly that tears sprang to her eyes. Would her love for Marc ever dim? *I will not cry for him.* She had said the words so many times that they had an almost palliative effect on her. The tears stopped and the pain slipped away.

Being with Samuel was fun and incredibly exciting. Rebekka had never felt so utterly appreciated, even desired. They didn't talk about Damon, or Marc, or work, but about world events and politics, places they had visited, people they had met. When she was with him, she didn't think of the future, but only the present. Nothing life-altering, no tough decisions—just good, clean fun.

She did share experiences from her mission, and while he seemed interested in them, he showed no interest in learning more about her faith. By his own admission, he was not interested in any particular denomination, but in the values that he felt were universal to all religions. Rebekka was familiar with the idea, as her father had voiced the same thoughts to her many times. But it wasn't good enough for her. *It's a lucky thing Samuel and I are only friends. Unlike my mother, I couldn't spend my life with a nonmember.*

Samuel was a complete gentleman, and the more time they spent together, the more she liked him. While he was a great conversationalist, he was an even better dancer. She enjoyed the evening thoroughly. Thoughts of Damon were far from her mind, and only once or twice did she remember Marc.

When they returned to Alpine, Samuel walked her to her bedroom door. Her hand went out to the knob, but his hand closed over hers. "I had a wonderful time tonight," he said, his green eyes smouldering with feeling. He was so close that Rebekka imagined she could hear his heart beat. She thought he might kiss her, worried that he would. As pleasant as she believed the experience would be, she didn't want to lead him on. She still had to resolve her relationship with Damon, and besides, there was the matter of their differing faiths. She moved her head back slightly, and he released her hand, as though understanding her signal.

She spoke softly. "I had a good time, too."

"I'll be gone in the morning, but I'll call you from Cincinnati."

"Okay."

He shook his head, looking bemused. "Ah, Rebekka with two Ks, little did I know that when I got on that plane, I'd meet you."

She grinned. "You just needed a translator."

"Well, it looks like I found what I needed."

"Do you always get what you want?" She didn't know what made her ask.

"Always. At least so far." His eyes spoke more, but she opened her door, turning purposefully away before she could be tempted further by his nearness.

"Good night, Samuel."

He bent swiftly and kissed her cheek. "Good night, Rebekka." She watched him walk to the suite of rooms next to her own.

"You're back." The voice from the stairway took her by surprise.

"Hello, Damon." *How long had he been there?*

He approached slowly, taking in her appearance. "You look beautiful. Did you have fun?"

Rebekka suddenly felt guilty for enjoying herself when he had been dealing with the difficult Belle. "Yes. Samuel's very nice." She didn't offer an explanation as to where she had been, and he didn't ask. "How's Belle?"

"She's all right. I haven't decided on a punishment yet. I just don't even know where to start. But I learned something tonight. About why she's been giving you trouble." He leaned against the wall across from her. "She said something about you leaving. I think she's worried about saying good-bye and getting another nanny. Her entire life, she's had nannies—Char was too ill to care for her at all, since the cancer came back at the end of her pregnancy. And all the nannies eventually had to leave. Or we left them, like the last one."

A tender feeling entered Rebekka's heart. "I understand. And she's right. You are looking for another nanny."

He sighed. "What she needs is a mother." He straightened up suddenly, as though realizing what he had said. "Look, I am interested in pursuing our relationship, but I honestly don't know that it will work. I have to admit that I'm scared of Belle's reaction, and also of forcing a ready-made family on you."

She lifted her chin. "I make my own decisions."

"I just don't want you to feel obligated," he explained. "I mean, if someone comes along who sweeps you off your feet—"

What I want is for you to sweep me off my feet! But she couldn't admit that aloud. "You mean Samuel."

Damon glanced down the hall. "Him or someone else." He sighed. "I really don't know what I'm saying. Belle needs a mother, but I can't expect to race through a courtship because of that. I know it takes time. But meanwhile, with you living here in the same house . . ." He paused. "Maybe we should find an alternative. Maybe then Belle won't feel so threatened."

"I can stay with Brionney," she said, feeling relief at the suggestion. "But first we'll have to find someone to take my place here in the mornings and afternoons. Frankly, I can't see Mrs. Mertz filling in for that time."

Damon grimaced. "Me either. But I still haven't found anyone, though I've thought about it a lot—especially if you're going to keep working for the company."

"I'd like to. I'm really enjoying it."

"I know, I'll talk to Bri. She's good at arranging things." He smiled at her in the dim light, sending happiness winging through her body. "And I like the things she arranges."

Rebekka smiled, glad that she hadn't allowed Samuel to kiss her. "Then our date is still on?"

"Yeah," he said with obvious relief. "And maybe if Belle sees you as a friend instead of a nanny, she can start to loosen up a bit."

"I hope so."

Damon reached out and touched her hand softly. Then, like Samuel, he leaned over and kissed her on the cheek. For one clear instant, Rebekka recalled the passion and depth of their previous kiss and was tempted to repeat the experience. But she hesitated to evoke the fiery emotions that both frightened and thrilled her. Those emotions were meant for permanent partners, not for fleeting satisfaction. Regardless of what happened in the future between her and Damon, she wanted to maintain their respect and friendship.

She smiled at her thoughts. Maybe she was learning something in America after all.

Damon took her smile as his dismissal and retreated toward his wing of the house. Doubtless, he would check on Belle. She wished she could go herself, but didn't feel she had the right. She wasn't even the nanny any longer, not really. Besides, Belle would not welcome her presence.

Inside her room, she changed into a long silk nightgown the color of midnight and went to her laptop to check her e-mail. There was one from Raoul and another from Marc. Her heart started thumping the loud, uneven beat that signaled another onslaught of painful emotions.

She deliberately read the one from her brother first.

Dear Rebekka,

I am confused. Desirée has decided not to be baptized for the time being or to continue to see the missionaries. She still wants to marry me. I love her so desperately that I cannot stand to be without her. But I see the unhappiness that Mother has endured because of Father, and I do not want that for myself. Life once seemed so easy, but now I don't know what to do. At least you are there in Utah with many members to choose from. Do yourself a favor and don't put yourself in such a dilemma. Oh, that I had listened to André before I began to love her! But how can I gaze into her beautiful eyes and wish that? Eternity seems very far away at that moment, but then I look at Mother . . .

Sorry to be so depressing. I want to make the right decision, but I don't know what that is. Life without Desirée seems too bleak to consider. Yet Mother and Father love each other so much, but cannot share everything. Is that my future? Your advice would be greatly appreciated.

Love from your older but not wiser brother,
    Raoul

His words instantly spanned the miles between them. Her dear, dear brother. He was such a romantic and felt things so deeply. Rebekka couldn't bear to see him hurt. Yet she hesitated to give him advice. What if he made the wrong decision and lost a love that would sustain him throughout his entire life? She knew that at one time, she would have given anything to be with Marc, including her membership in the Church. The realization pained her, but she had to admit the truth to herself. She had loved Marc much more than God. Much more.

And now?

Rebekka sighed as she began to type. She was glad Raoul's choice was not hers.

Dearest Raoul,

I don't know how to answer you. I really don't. But I have just now asked myself whether or not the Lord comes first in my life, even before the man I love. Should it be so? Would being with him lead me to true happiness? Or by putting the man first, would I give up something even more precious than true love? The thought is enough to tear my heart in two, but perhaps it will help you. I am weak and cannot make such a decision, but you have always been stronger.

I should count myself lucky that I'm not in love—at least not with a man within my reach—but I confess I almost long for your dilemma.

My prayers are with you,
    Rebekka

She read Marc's e-mail next, longing too much for his news to care about the pain it would bring.

Rebekka,

The doctor told me two days ago that nothing's wrong with me, except a slightly lower red blood cell count. That could mean a decline in kidney function, but for now I'm okay. I think it was a temporary thing, due to a cold or whatever. I'll have more tests in a few months, but just as a precaution. Louis-Géralde has assured me that he will give me one of his kidneys should I ever need it, but I don't relish going through another surgery, or having my little brother suffer such a thing for me.

The real reason I'm writing is to say that at our last family dinner on Monday, my mother mentioned that she missed having you and Raoul over, particularly you. I thought you'd like to know.

I miss you too, but I'm sure you are much too busy there to miss or think about me. So are you engaged yet? Maybe I should come and meet him before things go any further.

Be good.

    Love, Marc

Acting the father again, Rebekka thought acidly. She wanted to write a scathing retort, but made herself count to ten before beginning. Perhaps a more subtle approach would serve her purposes better.

Hello Marc,

Tonight I went dancing. I love dancing and had a great time. Do you remember when we would go dancing? In fact, wasn't it you who taught me how? My date is taller than you, but we were good together anyhow. The music was divine. You would have enjoyed it.

As for coming to check out Damon, come on! We have enough room for you. If I get married, maybe you can be our best man.

I'm glad you're not sick. Thank you for telling me. Let your mom know that I miss her, too. Perhaps as much as my own mother.

    Big hugs,

    Rebekka

She sent the messages, then shut the computer down, feeling strangely unsatisfied. Falling to her knees, she said a prayer, remembering to include her brother. At the end she added, "And please help Belle to get what she needs."

Feeling considerably better, Rebekka snuggled under the covers, wondering if Marc would respond to her e-mail soon or wait another week as he had the last time. She wondered what he would feel when he read her words.

CHAPTER 19

Mickelle had no answer from the Wolfe residence all weekend. The lack of response was irritating, but she refused to lose hope that they would come through with the money to pay for her car. They *had* to pay.

On Sunday, she arose early and readied herself for church. Jeremy looked surprised. "You coming, Mom?"

"Of course I'm coming." She realized with guilt that she had only attended church four times since that fatal day in May. Examining her feelings, she decided that Sundays had become difficult because she couldn't hide from all the caring embraces and well-meaning smiles. While at first they had been comforting, now they reminded her acutely of Riley's death. She found it easier to stay at home.

But today she needed to take the sacrament. She needed to do something to rid herself of the smoldering anger in her heart since the car accident. Perhaps in a strange way, the anger was good. At least it wouldn't let her sink into her normal state of apathy.

The car continued to make the grinding noise, though it was considerably less noticeable since she had pried some of the metal loose with Riley's old crowbar, and she could open the door from the inside by shoving her shoulder against it instead of her feet. At least that was something.

"We could get Uncle Jesse to look at it," Jeremy said as they drove to the chapel. "I'll ask him when we go over to Grandma's for dinner today."

At church, nothing seemed to have changed. Across from Mickelle, the Sunbergs still bounced their baby, no longer a newborn, but as colicky as ever. Sister Sunberg's face was weary, but as she rocked and cuddled her daughter, Mickelle felt envious. She would give up all her nights of sleep and welcome aching arms if only . . . The painful thought was too hard to finish, even silently.

She tried instead to focus on Brother Chatham's nodding head as his eyes drooped. If he could sleep, so could she.

One of the Reeves boys threw a wad of paper. It sailed through the air and hit Brother Chatham on the top of his balding head. He snorted and opened his eyes, then smiled and waved at the boys, as though grateful they had awakened him in time for the passing of the sacrament.

Mickelle returned to watching the hypnotic up-and-down motion of the Sunberg baby. Her face held a beatific smile that vanished each time her parents stopped the bouncing. Mickelle continued to watch them with the baby and noticed that Sister Sunberg rocked out of habit, even when she wasn't holding the child.

The bishop stood and announced time for testimonies. "As usual, we invite the Primary children to come forward and start us off. We are so grateful to hear their faith and partake of their sweet spirits."

Primary children filed down the aisles in virtual streams. Jeremy jumped to his feet and started toward the front with the others. As Mickelle listened to their simple testimonies, she felt the anger drain from her heart and thankfulness take its place. She had lost so much—her husband, her financial security, and now her car. But she had her children, an extended family who loved her, and the gospel of Jesus Christ.

When the testimony time was turned over to the adults, Mickelle found her heart too full to deny the prompting within. She walked to the front of the congregation, her legs shaking and heart pounding—not with the usual panic attack, but with the simple nervousness she had always felt when bearing her testimony.

Hands gripping the edge of the podium, she stared out at her friends and neighbors, amazed at the love surging through her. She understood that the love came not only from them but from her God, her Father. And in that moment, she understood how He suffered with her. How He had carried her through the difficult summer.

Finally, she began. "Thank you so much for everything you have done for me in these past months." She took a deep, cleansing breath.

"Today I just needed to tell you that I know God lives! And I know He loves us."

Even as she spoke, she vowed that she would no longer let her life continue in shambles. She would make something of herself, of her children. She was a daughter of God! A beloved child! If she had been given this trial, it was because her Father knew she would rise to the occasion. And she would have help—His help. Why hadn't she remembered that before? Whatever else she did in her life, she could not fail the Lord's expectations. He knew her better than anyone. He knew that she had been hiding from life, and He had now given her a subtle reminder that it was time to change. She was worth that; she was His daughter.

With this renewed realization, Mickelle made a goal to begin again the scripture reading that she had so long neglected. She decided to study by topic, beginning with prayer. She had heard that prayer could work miracles, and she believed that to put her life back on the right path, a miracle was exactly what she needed.

* * * * *

The next morning, Mickelle went to UVSC to pick up the latest class schedule and financial aid forms. She felt self-conscious as she climbed into the passenger side of the Snail and slid over, but tried not to let it bother her. As yet, Mr. Wolfe had not returned her calls or made any move to settle her expenses.

She made a sudden decision. "I'll go over to that boy's house tonight and confront his father about the damage. I will make him pay for it! He should be responsible for his son."

That night they had an early dinner and family home evening. Bryan gave a lesson on donations to the Church. It occurred to Mickelle that the only one in their family who really needed this lesson wasn't around to hear it. Tithing had been a source of constant contention between her and Riley. He had never really believed in the concept.

After eating ice cream and cookies for dessert, the boys went with her in the Snail to search out the address on the sheet Officer Lowder had given her. As they drove toward Alpine, dark clouds gathered in the sky, making it appear much later than seven-thirty, and a heavy rain began suddenly, falling in sheets from the heavens. Mickelle could barely see the road, even with the wipers on high speed. The wiper blades were old and didn't do a decent job of cleaning the windshield. Mickelle had asked Riley to replace them, but he had never gotten around to it. Since then, she hadn't cared enough about anything to figure out how to change them herself.

She almost gave up and drove home, but knew she would only be putting off the inevitable. Eventually, she would have to deal with Mr. Wolfe. She pressed on, peering at the street signs through the dark and the rain.

It took them nearly half an hour to find their way to their destination. The Wolfe residence, situated regally at the end of a long, tree-lined driveway, took her by surprise. It was not a house, but a Victorian mansion, surrounded by bright flower beds, a very green lawn, and paper birch and black walnut trees that reached far into the darkening sky. There were large windows and a covered porch that wrapped around the right side of the house, giving it the circular feel of a castle. Another turret sprang from the top floor of the left side of the house, looking like the perfect place for a captive princess. So beautiful, yet the overall appearance was eerie and sinister in the darkness and rain. Mickelle blinked, too stunned to feel anything but amazement. This was where the people lived whose lives continued unaltered by the car accident, while each day she endured unimaginable turmoil.

"Wow! They must be rich." Bryan had his face pressed up against the passenger side window.

In the backseat, Jeremy shuddered. "Is that a witch house?"

"Of course not." But Mickelle felt disturbed by the question.

"It just looks that way 'cause of the dark," Bryan said. "And those towers."

"Turrets," Mickelle corrected, turning off the engine. "It's a beautiful house. Look, you guys stay here and wait for me. I don't know what kind of reception I'm going to get." Amid their protests, she raised her voice. "I mean it. I'll be right back."

She walked with determination up the flower-lined walk. Approaching the porch, she saw tiny climbing roses in many colors inching along the white-painted wooden railings. *So beautiful,* she thought with a little burst of envy and more than a little resentment. She couldn't help thinking that the roses would look beautiful climbing the metal railing on her own narrow cement porch, or even trailing over her old fence in the backyard.

The house was even larger up close, and a nervous knot formed in her stomach. The rain had lightened considerably, but it still came down strongly enough to make her feel like something dragged from a ditch. At least her hair, drawn back at the nape of her neck with a clip, couldn't be any worse for the pelting.

On the porch she was protected from the rain, though she still felt wet and chilled. She began to tremble, though whether with cold or nervousness she couldn't tell. *Maybe I should leave.* But she knew that if Mr. Wolfe was a Mormon, Monday night would be the best time to find him at home. Of course, that was presuming he believed in family night. Holding her breath, she rang the doorbell.

A series of low-pitched bongs sounded throughout the house. For a long time nothing happened, but then she heard footsteps approaching, followed by the turning of a series of locks. The door opened to reveal a yellow-haired man in his late thirties. He was a few inches taller than average height, and Mickelle had to look up to meet his eyes. Oh, those eyes! They were the most unusual color of amber she had ever seen, and framed by thick, feathery brows. His face was ruggedly handsome with sharp curves, angular jaws and cheeks, and a few deep lines in his cheeks and forehead that added individuality. He wore a short moustache, slightly darker than his yellow-blonde hair, combed neatly above a generous mouth. In all, he was a strong-looking man with undeniable magnetism.

This can't be Mr. Wolfe, she thought. If he was, he didn't look much like his son.

"May I help you?" he asked. As he spoke, she caught the glimmer of a gold tooth far back in his mouth. He smiled at her graciously, waiting.

Mickelle abruptly felt conscious of the black stretch pants and oversized black sweater she wore. With the added effect of the rain, she must look like a dark, wet blob. The mascara she had put on for her visit to the college was likely making black tracks down her face.

She wiped at her cheek; sure enough, her hand came away with traces of mascara. Why did it have to be raining? Why did he have to be so terribly good-looking? And why on earth was she even noticing?

"I'm here to see Mr. Wolfe," she announced, gathering the remains of her courage.

"You've found him." He said it quickly, with the air of a man who had nothing to hide.

Mickelle wanted to shout, "Aha, I caught you!" but refrained. "I'm Mickelle Hansen," she said. "Your son crashed into my car last week. I've been trying to call you to talk about what—"

"My son crashed into you?" His feathery eyebrows rose. "From what I heard, it was sort of a mutual thing."

Mickelle bristled. "*I* had the right of way! Your son turned right in front of me—into me!"

"The policeman didn't give him a ticket."

His matter-of-fact manner made her want to scream. "They don't give tickets for causing accidents in American Fork," she said through gritted teeth.

"I've never heard of that."

"Well, that's what the officer said." Mickelle was beginning to doubt that she had done the right thing in facing Mr. Wolfe alone. He was obviously accustomed to being in charge. Why hadn't she asked Brionney or Jesse to come along? Or even Talia?

"How much are the repairs on your car?" he asked. His fingers touched the ends of his short moustache briefly, then he rubbed his chin.

The tightness in her stomach eased. "Five hundred dollars. That's my deductible. My uninsured motorist coverage will pay the other hundred."

"That much, huh? My son said there was hardly any damage." He peered over her shoulder at the Snail, barely discernible in the increasing darkness. "On the other hand, the front end of my son's car was completely ruined."

She wanted to say, "Good!" but she didn't really rejoice in the boy's loss, not when he had been so devastated about it. At the same time, she needed her car repaired. She simply didn't have five hundred dollars—unless she borrowed it from her parents or siblings.

Fighting tears of frustration, she glared at him. "So are you going to pay or not?" She pushed back a stray piece of hair that had escaped from her comb. "He's responsible for the accident, and I won't give up until he takes care of the damage!"

For a long moment, Mr. Wolfe watched her. Mickelle felt uncomfortable under his stare—why was he looking at her so intently? Then, "Well, my son says that *you* hit *him*. The police didn't even give him a ticket. So it looks like it's his word against yours."

"He's fifteen years old! And driving without a license!"

"He had a reason."

Was that a smirk on his face? For a moment, he looked just like his namesake—a shaggy, yellow-eyed wolf who grinned at his prey before he attacked.

Fury raged through Mickelle's heart. How could a man be so black-hearted and so completely blind? "I don't know what your son told you," she said tightly, "but driving without a license is against the law. And no fifteen-year-old has the competence to drive without training. If he hadn't broken the law, there wouldn't have been an accident at all. And my car wouldn't have been damaged." Mickelle abruptly stopped her tirade, afraid that if she didn't, she would burst into tears in front of this pompous, arrogant idiot! *Good-looking pompous, arrogant idiot,* her mind corrected.

Before he could reply, she added, "If you won't take responsibility for your son's actions, I guess I'll see you in court." Without another word, she turned and marched down the porch and into the rain. She didn't look back for fear he'd see the tears and desperation in her eyes. The familiar symptoms of a panic attack washed over her, but she held her chin up, her shoulders straight as she walked, almost blindly, to the station wagon. Gratefully, she reached for the door handle, but remembered too late that the latch was broken. Feeling utterly humiliated, she went around to the passenger side and climbed over Bryan to get to her seat. She laid her head against the steering wheel, praying that her shaking would stop.

"How'd it go, Mom?" Bryan asked quietly, his voice worried.

The panic faded, and within the confines of the Snail she felt safe enough to glance up at the mansion. That awful man should be gone now, after having witnessed her complete humiliation with that mocking smirk on his face. To her surprise, he was still on the porch, staring in their direction.

In one motion, Mickelle started the Snail, thankful the rain had abated. She backed down the long drive a little faster than she would have ordinarily, barely missing their elaborate brick mailbox. *Serve them right if I knocked it down.* She was so angry that if she'd had a carton of eggs, she would have thrown them at the mansion's windows. *Stupid, dumb jerk of a man. I hope he falls down in a ditch and dies!*

She didn't really hope that, but thinking it made her feel better. Had she been alone in the car, she might have put her head in her hands and cried.

"Well, Mom?" Jeremy stared curiously at her from the backseat.

Mickelle let her intense frustration and anger seep out of her before she replied. Her children had enough to deal with, and she wasn't about to add to their problems.

And to think she had pitied Tanner Wolfe as a child practically abandoned! Ha! He was little more than a liar. His mother was probably alive and well, sitting in a hot tub somewhere with the members of her bridge club.

Calm down, she told herself. "Mr. Wolfe doesn't seem to think his son is at fault," she said evenly

Bryan's face grew angry. "So he's not going to pay?"

"He'll have to," she said with determination. "There has to be a way. I'll take him to court if I have to."

Jeremy's mouth rounded in an O, but he didn't say anything.

"You should have let me come with you," Bryan said. "I would have taught him a thing or two!"

Mickelle smiled at his endearing display of protectiveness. "I know you would. But everything's going to be all right. You'll see." Turning onto the main street, she picked up speed. "But now we have to get home and in bed. We need to be up early tomorrow."

For once, the boys didn't grumble. As they readied for bed, Mickelle put away the dishes she had washed after dinner. She felt so drained by her anger that it was almost too much effort to stack the plates in the cupboard. When the doorbell rang, she nearly dropped a dish onto the floor. Likely, it wouldn't have broken on the inexpensive vinyl tile, but the near miss made her feel shaky. *Please not a panic attack,* she thought.

"I'll get it!" Jeremy shouted at the top of his lungs. Mickelle followed him to the door, wondering who would come to visit on a Monday evening. She almost hoped it was her mother or one of her sisters. If she could talk it out, her course of action might become clear.

"Officer Lowder," she said in surprise, recognizing him even in civilian clothes.

"Hi." His blue eyes met hers briefly. "May I come in for a moment?"

"Sure." Mickelle took a few steps back so he could enter, her mind racing to understand why he had come. Could there be more bad news about Riley's death? But what could be worse than suicide?

"Boys, go on into your rooms," she said, wanting to protect them. "I'll be in to say prayers in just a little while." Jeremy looked as though he would protest, but Bryan caught his arm and pulled him down the hall.

Mickelle led Officer Lowder into the living room. She had rarely come in here in the past few months, and was embarrassed at the covering of dust on the TV and piano. Her eyes went instinctively to her curio cabinet, where the cracks and gouges still marred the surface of the wood. A heavy sadness filled her heart.

"I guess you're wondering why I'm here."

Mickelle tore her gaze away from the curio cabinet, having almost forgotten the officer's presence. "Is it . . .?" She couldn't bear to say her husband's name.

"It's personal."

That surprised her. "What do you mean, Officer Lowder?"

"Jim. Please call me Jim."

"Okay . . . Jim. And you can call me Mickelle. But what do you mean?"

"It's just that I . . . well . . ."

This was a whole new side of the self-assured young officer. Mickelle smiled at him gently, hoping to put him at ease.

"I wanted to know if you'd like to go out to dinner. With me."

Mickelle stared. Had she heard right? Did Officer Lowder—Jim—actually want her to go out with him? "Well, I don't know what to say."

"How about yes?"

"Well, I . . ." She could think of a hundred reasons to turn him down. She still felt married, she didn't want to date a police officer, he was at least five or six years too young for her, Riley wouldn't like it, she didn't want to date. The list went on. But she couldn't help remembering how ugly and awkward she had felt on Mr. Wolfe's porch. A wet, black blob. Yet here she was, looking exactly the same, minus a little of the mascara she had wiped off in the bathroom, and now she felt attractive and vitally alive. This young police officer wanted her—*her!*—to go out with him. She found herself wanting to say yes. *It wouldn't be like a real date,* she thought. *He's so young. We'll just be friends.* There was no chance of anything else. But then why was she even considering accepting his invitation?

"I'd love to," she said, wondering where the words had come from.

He looked immensely relieved. "How about on Friday?"

"Okay."

"Thanks," he said. "I'm looking forward to it."

"So am I." She walked with him to the door.

"See you Friday. About seven?"

She nodded her acceptance, then watched him drive away in a small, new-looking truck. Brionney would be proud of her. *If* Mickelle told her. This would be her first date since Riley's death. What a long way she had come in the week since she had told Brionney she had no interest in men!

Butterflies began in her stomach. Why on earth would Jim Lowder want to date her? Probably an overactive sense of duty. Still, there was nothing like having a cop on your side when you went to court. Smiling to herself, Mickelle thought of the infuriating Mr. Wolfe. She wished she could tell him about this ace up her sleeve. He would certainly treat her more respectfully! So what if he was handsome and rich? She had the law on her side, in more ways than just one.

In her mind, she began to plan what she would say to the judge, and what she would wear for the occasion. The next time Mr. Wolfe saw her, she wouldn't be a wet, black blob, but a confident woman determined to obtain justice!

And she would win.

* * * * *

Damon watched the ancient gold station wagon disappear into the rain. *Why did she get in the passenger side? Did someone drive her here? Is there a Mr. Hansen?* It was too dark to be certain. If there was a Mr. Hansen, Damon wasn't too impressed that he had allowed his wife to face him alone, though perhaps Mr. Hansen didn't agree with her efforts to elicit money from a mostly innocent child.

He recalled her face, with its anger and determination, as clearly as though she still stood before him. She had glared at him as though he was mocking her, which he wasn't. He had simply wanted to understand where she was coming from.

What was it about her that affected him so?

His hand brushed the doorknob. The children were waiting in the game room. He had promised them a quick indoor swim at the end of family night, as long as there was no lightning, and they would be anxious. Still, he didn't move, replaying the scene that had just occurred.

The woman had confronted him on the porch, her chin lifted slightly, looking oddly like she belonged there. She was dressed in black stretch pants that were neither too loose nor too tight, a classic sweater that reached nearly to her hips, and comfortable black loafers. It wasn't an elaborate outfit by any means, but she wore the clothes with dignity and ease, though he imagined such a feat was difficult, as the clothes were obviously damp from the rain.

What little makeup she wore was evidenced by the black trails down her cheeks, as though the rain had tried to uncover the real woman beneath. But he could see she hadn't worn much makeup to begin with, so there wasn't much for the rain to wash away. The slight streaks of black were like delicately colored tears that seemed to accentuate the large blue eyes as they stared at him, leaving him feeling unsettled and uncertain. Her honey-blonde hair, swept back from her finely boned cheeks, was held in place by some sort of a comb. She looked regal and at the same time very human, as though she would be at home living in a tent or a castle, waited upon by servants.

A classic beauty.

In all, she reminded him of something from a dream or a movie. Then she spoke, and the dream shattered. It wasn't her voice, but what she said. Her view of the accident utterly contradicted Tanner's, and Damon had to believe in his son.

Even as he defended Tanner, he was intrigued by her. A piece of loose hair danced along her forehead and into her eyes, and he had a sudden urge to tear out the comb and watch the rest of the hair fall around her face.

What was he thinking?

Fascinated, he watched her sweep the hair back into place. Her blue eyes seemed to capture his, delving for things he didn't want to reveal. In order to retrieve his train of thought, he had to remind himself that this woman was a cold, hard person who was deliberately trying to take advantage of his son.

Their conversation did not go very well, he admitted to himself as she left the porch. He didn't seem to have as much control over the situation as he would have liked. He should have been able to convince her that she was in the wrong, and it was useless to pursue him or Tanner for money to pay for her mistakes. His game was definitely off.

Damon sighed. The station wagon had long since disappeared, but he continued to stand on the porch, enjoying the quiet fall of the rain and the fresh, clean scent emanating from the lawns and trees.

I really love Utah, he thought. He was glad he had come. His heart had healed much more quickly than he had anticipated, the business was going well, and the air smelled clean. *What more can a man ask for?*

A lot more. He stared wistfully down the drive. Was her car really damaged, or was she using the accident for her own ends?

He finally gave up his deliberation and went inside. The children were waiting, and they wouldn't understand the delay—especially when he couldn't explain it himself.

Rebekka was descending the front staircase that curved in an artistic arc along one wall of the entryway. She moved with such grace that she appeared to be gliding. "I was just going to play your piano," she said with an enchanting smile.

Rebekka was gorgeous, as usual, but tonight Damon barely noticed. He thought, *She is so young.* Not like the furious Mrs.

Hansen, who had to be near his own age. "I'm going swimming," he said, shaking away the thoughts. "Want to come?"

"What about Belle?" Rebekka's beautifully shaped brows rose expressively.

He shrugged. "If we're going to date, she's going to have to get used to it sooner or later. Besides, it's family night, and at least for now you're part of the family, aren't you? I think it'll be okay."

But in the end, no one went swimming that night except Damon. Belle had fallen asleep, and Tanner was on the phone with a girl in one of his classes. "Can't we do it tomorrow?" he mouthed with one hand over the receiver.

"At least we got in the lesson part," Damon said with a laugh. He bent to pick up the sleeping Belle. In her arms she hugged not the brown teddy bear that often accompanied her around the house, but a plastic, cream-colored horse that resembled the real horse she wanted him to buy her. "I'd better get her to bed."

Rebekka touched Belle's cheek. "Good idea. I guess I'll go play the piano."

Damon tucked Belle into bed, who then awoke and demanded a story. By the time she was asleep and he had gone to bid Tanner good night, Rebekka had retired to her room. Damon found that while he was exhausted, he had no desire for sleep.

He went to the pool house, which was connected to the main house by a covered walkway. There, he changed into his suit and dove into the warm water. He began to swim laps. Swimming was one of his favorite pastimes and the primary way he stayed in shape. *Pretty good shape, too,* he thought, although he doubted that Mrs. Hansen had noticed.

Where did that come from?

What did he care what she thought? She was a greedy, no-good, lying— He stopped himself. No need to call her names.

Mrs. Hansen had said that she was going to take him to court. Many times in his life he had been faced with that possibility, and it certainly didn't bother him now. He had nothing to hide, nothing at all. And he would do whatever was necessary to protect his son.

It could be a spirited fight. There had been sparks in her eyes, he remembered. Sparks of anger, defiance, and indignation. Well, no matter, he had justice on his side . . . didn't he?

Taking a deep breath, he swam underwater to the far side of the pool. When he touched the wall, he did a half-somersault under the water to position himself to swim again to the other side. Without taking a breath, he continued on. This time he made it only halfway across the pool before he had to come up for air.

Abruptly, he wondered what it would be like to see Mrs. Hansen laugh.

CHAPTER 20

On Tuesday morning, Mickelle had planned to go outside and work in the garden. But by the time the boys were off to school and she had the kitchen straightened, she had replayed the confrontation with Mr. Wolfe in her head so many times that her fury and sense of helplessness had returned in full force. She wished she could simply forget it and move on, but she had to get her car fixed before the metal grinding against the rubber ruined her tire.

She picked up the phone and dialed quickly. Maybe if she shared her feelings with someone who loved her, she could get on with her life.

"Hello?" Brionney's voice was a welcome sound. How grateful she was that her sister and Jesse had settled in American Fork, so close by.

"It's me, Mickelle. Got a minute?"

"Sure. The kids just left for school, and the boys and Rosalie are playing in the toy room—peacefully for now. Forest hasn't found anything to scream about yet."

"I'm just frustrated," Mickelle blurted out. "And angry. It's eating me up inside."

"What happened?" Brionney sounded genuinely interested.

"Well, last night I went to see the father of that boy who crashed into me, and he didn't listen to anything I said. He's refused to take responsibility in the matter." Mickelle described the confrontation in detail, including the smirking. "I was completely humiliated, and so angry I couldn't see straight! I mean there he was, defending his son and practically calling me a liar! Who's the liar here, anyway—a boy who drives without a license and insurance, or a woman who just happens to be driving through an intersection? With the right of way, I might add."

"What a jerk!" Brionney exclaimed sympathetically. "I mean, I believe in defending my children, but this is utterly ridiculous! Can't the guy see what a mess his son has caused? How is he going to teach him a lesson if he doesn't allow him to suffer the consequences? Boy, this makes me so angry, I've half a mind to go out there myself!"

Mickelle felt vindicated at her sister's support. "It won't do any good. He'll just treat you the way he did me. He's so arrogant. And you know, I felt he didn't give a darn what happened to me, so long as he saved his precious son from any inconvenience. It's not like he couldn't afford to pay for my car repairs, from the looks of the mansion they live in."

"So what now?"

Mickelle sighed. "I just don't know. The car is terrible the way it is. Because of the damage, the handle wouldn't open and I broke it. Now I have to get in from the passenger side. I can still get out of the driver's side, but it's so embarrassing. That car was embarrassing anyway, but now it's worse."

"Why didn't you tell us yesterday at dinner?" Brionney's voice grew a little sharp. "Or sooner? The accident was a week ago. You've been driving like that for a whole week?"

"That's not the worst part. Whenever I turn left, the metal scrapes into the wheel and makes this terrible grinding noise. I've straightened it the best I can, but it really needs something more. I tell you, I've been driving myself crazy trying to figure out how to get everywhere without turning left."

"You should have told someone. We could have helped. That's what families are for."

Mickelle felt a tear trickle down her cheek. "I am telling you." She paused and took a deep breath. "What I want to do is tell Riley. I want him to deal with it. But he's not going to. Even if he were here, I don't know that he would deal with it unless it was his truck. He wouldn't even fix the wipers, for Pete's sake. I have to learn to do it all on my own. I have to. I need to. Don't you see? I can't be running to my family every minute."

"I know that." Brionney's tone was subdued. "I mean, I see it now. But we need you to rely on us occasionally . . . please?"

Mickelle wiped the tears from her face. "That's why I'm calling you. I was so angry I couldn't function. Now I'm feeling better."

"The guy is obviously an idiot."

Mickelle gave a short laugh. "You said that already."

"Well, he is. I can't believe he'd treat any woman that way—especially my sister!"

As though Brionney had taken some of her anger, Mickelle felt lighter. The compassion she had previously felt for the motherless child crept back into her heart. "Well, his wife died, and it's hard raising children on your own. Besides, he did look like a good boy. I wonder—"

"Don't want to hear it! I'm too mad! Besides, it could all be a lie. The mother could be very much alive. Maybe she's in Italy, picking out a new gold necklace or another diamond ring."

Mickelle laughed aloud, a real laugh this time, remembering her similar thought. "See? I knew calling you was the right thing to do. But don't get so upset."

"You have to take him to court!"

"I'll think about it."

They talked for a few more minutes until Forest started a fight with his brother and Brionney had to hang up. "Call me if you need me again."

"I will." It was comforting to know that help, should she need it, was only a phone call away.

Instead of going outside to the garden, Mickelle went to her room and found her scriptures. On Sunday after testimony meeting, she had decided to begin her study on prayer by looking up every scripture about the subject in the Bible's topical guide. She had looked up many scriptures, but still had many more to read. Certainly she needed the inspiration. She didn't want to go to court. Aside from the fee she knew they charged to file a claim and serve papers, the time and energy involved were too much to consider. Perhaps prayer could solve this problem better than her instinct for revenge.

She knelt near her bed, the scriptures opened in front of her. A light from the window fell on the Bible as though highlighting the words. She found her place in the topical guide and looked up the next scripture in Matthew. At once she recognized it: "But I say unto you, Love your enemies, bless them that curse you, do good to them that hate you, and pray for them which despitefully use you, and persecute you . . ."

Mickelle's heart rebelled, but the whisperings of the Spirit were too strong to deny. Before she had talked to Brionney, there was no way her anger would have allowed her to follow this strong prompting. No way at all. But now she remembered the boy looking wistfully at his ruined car, and the father staring after her from the porch like a lost soul.

Mickelle prayed. First she gave thanks for her blessings, then she prayed for herself and for her family, and finally she prayed for Mr. Wolfe, his son, and the unseen little girl Tanner had been going to pick up at the school.

The rest of the anger and frustration in her heart faded, and the lust for revenge dimmed. Somehow, everything would work out. It was in the Lord's hands now. She would focus on fixing her car and being happy.

It was the beginning of a miracle.

* * * * *

Damon was in Jesse's office, discussing the latest addition to their program, when Brionney strode into the room. Jesse looked up from the computer. "I'll be ready in just a second, hon. Do you mind waiting a minute?"

"Not at all. The twins and Rosalie are at my mother's, and she said to take as much time as we want for lunch." She smiled, but Damon thought her sky-blue eyes didn't shine with their usual good humor.

Jesse glanced at Damon. "Ah, a peaceful meal for a change."

Damon chuckled. With five small children under the age of nine, they certainly had their hands full. Maybe exhaustion explained the difference in Brionney's eyes.

"So, as I was saying," Jesse continued, "all they have to do is type in the patient's name, and . . ."

Damon listened, but couldn't help noticing how Brionney paced the room, as though she had too much energy and didn't know what to do with it. He had come to know her well enough to see that something was eating at her.

Jesse had stopped talking and also stared at his wife. "Bri, are you okay?"

She looked at them, surprised. "Yeah. Why wouldn't I be?"

"Well, you look kind of . . . well, mad."

She sighed and flopped into the stuffed chair against the wall. "I guess I am." Then she hurried to add, "But not at you. It's Mickelle." She jumped to her feet again and started pacing.

Jesse's brow rose. "You're mad at your sister?"

"Goodness, no." Brionney stopped pacing and faced them. "I talked to her this morning, and she was really upset about the accident. Last night she went to talk to the father of the boy who caused it."

"What happened?"

"The father just brushes her off. This dumb guy believes his son instead of *my* sister. It makes me want to kill him!" She made a fist and hit it forcefully into her other hand. "Can you believe that a father would excuse his son's driving without a license or insurance? And then make matters even worse by not taking care of the problems his son caused by breaking the law? He should be grateful for the opportunity to teach his son a lesson. I mean, this is a relatively minor incident. No drugs, no unwed pregnancy. We're talking minor stuff here, but big enough for a great teaching moment. But no, this guy bails his son out once again. And I bet he'll keep doing it until finally it's too big a problem to bail him out of. It's disgusting! How are children supposed to learn values when parents won't let them pay the consequences? Five hundred bucks would be nothing to this guy, if his house is any indication. But no, he won't take responsibility. My sister's already suffered so much, and now this. Ooh, I'm so angry!"

"It'll be okay, Brionney." Jesse stood up and went around the desk. He put his arms around his wife. "We'll help her. I'll fix her car myself."

"When are you going to have the time? Besides, she's determined to do everything herself. And meanwhile, she's having to drive around in that sorry excuse for a car." Brionney wiped tears from under her eyes. "It was bad enough before the accident, but now she has to get in from the passenger side because the other door won't open. People stare at her and laugh. And every time she turns left, the wheel scrapes against the metal. Can you even imagine what driving that thing must be like?"

"I'll go over there tonight," Jesse promised.

Damon listened to the exchange with growing remorse. Stories he had heard about Brionney's sister came back to his mind, and they made his guilt even heavier. "Uh, can I insert something here?"

The Hergarters looked at him, and Damon returned their gaze miserably. "Well, I—it seems . . . uh, Tan got in an accident the other day, and—"

"*You're* the insensitive jerk!" The anger in Brionney's eyes changed to sudden understanding. She put her hands on her hips. "Well, now you know the truth. My sister was *not* at fault, and she needs help. What are you going to do about it?"

He looked at her sheepishly. "Buy her a new car?"

To his relief, she smiled. "Well, you don't have to do that. But you could at least take care of the repairs."

"Give me her address and number," Damon said decisively. "I'll get right on it."

Looking satisfied, Brionney left for lunch with Jesse, and Damon decided to do the same. *But first I'm going to take a detour to the high school.* There was obviously more to the accident than Tanner had let on, and he was going to get to the bottom of it. Now.

He went to the school office, and was directed to Tanner's math class. "I need to speak with my son for a moment," he told the teacher.

Tanner came out into the hall quickly, his face pale with worry. "Is Belle . . .?"

"She's fine."

"Rebekka?"

Damon smiled. Tanner's crush on Rebekka was apparently stronger than ever. "Everyone is fine." He put his hand on Tanner's shoulder. "But I do want to discuss something with you."

"What?" Tanner's face was the picture of innocence.

"About the accident."

Tanner's smile vanished.

"I want to hear again what happened."

Tanner began talking. Damon stopped him when he got to the part about the music. "So your friends were fighting over the music. You really didn't see if the lady was moving or not."

"She wasn't! And then Randy said to go, and I looked at Amanda—"

"Who was in the backseat, I understand."

"And then I started to go—"

"Did Amanda do anything?"

"When?"

"When you looked at her."

"She smiled. She's really pretty when she smiles—"

"So you were looking at Amanda's smile when you crashed into the lady?"

"Well, I looked back to the road, and there she was, right in front of me. I couldn't stop!"

"You do know that she had the right of way—no matter how slow she was?"

Tanner looked at the floor. "No. I didn't."

A couple of students passed by them in the hall. Damon smiled at them and waited until they were out of earshot to continue. "You didn't know the person going straight ahead has the right of way?"

Tanner met his eyes. "Well, maybe I did. But I was worried about getting Belle on time."

"Oh, yes—the reason you took the car in the first place." Damon started to twist the ends of his moustache, but remembered to rub his chin instead. "Did you really think Rebekka and I would forget Belle?"

Tanner stared back down at the floor. "You could have."

"Well, we wouldn't. And even if we had, there were other options open to you. For instance, you could have called the school and told them to ask the teacher to watch out for Belle."

"I didn't know the number," Tanner muttered.

"Oh, come on. I raised you to be more intelligent than that! I've seen you look up your stocks on the Internet. Getting the number of the school would have been a piece of cake. The bottom line is that you knew there were other options, but you *wanted* to drive your car. Am I right?"

Tanner said nothing, but clenched his fist against his stomach as though it pained him.

"Well?"

"Yes," Tanner answered softly.

"Did you or did you not know that you were breaking the law?"

Tanner nodded.

"And did you or did you not go somewhere other than the school?"

"I did."

Damon's heart ached for the distress in his son's face, but he remembered Brionney's words about taking the opportunity to teach Tanner. He wanted his son to become a man the Lord could be proud of, a man who would be true to others and himself.

Damon squeezed Tanner's shoulder. "Thank you for admitting that, son. I know it's not easy. But you know what? Together we're going to make this right. And someday we're going to look back on this as a learning experience. To that end, I think we're going to have to restrict you from hanging out with Randy and Eric for a while. And you have to come up with a way to fix the lady's car."

Tanner met his gaze, and Damon was touched to see the tears shimmering in his eyes. "I want to help the lady," he said. "I really do. When I talked to her on the phone, she was nice. And I did start to feel guilty." He blinked hard. "I wish it hadn't happened. But it did— so maybe we can fix her car before mine. I'll even use my savings to pay for parts."

Pride filled Damon's heart. "That might mean your car won't be ready when the juvenile judge says you can get your license," he warned.

"That's okay, Dad." Tanner's mouth twisted into a grimace. "I don't know if I want to drive, anyway."

Damon blinked away his own tears. "You will one day." He glanced up and down the hall to make sure no one was watching, then he put his arm around his son's shoulders and gave him a quick hug. It lasted only a second—nothing that should embarrass Tanner. "I'm proud of you for wanting to make it right," he said. "Really proud. And I think the Lord is proud of you, too."

Tanner gave him a weak grin. "I sure feel a lot better."

"We'll go over there after work tonight and talk to the lady," Damon continued. "We'll get it all straightened out." He gave his son's shoulder a final pat, wishing Tanner were as young as Belle so that he could sweep him up into his arms and hold him close. But the time when he could insulate Tanner from everything was long past. Now he would have to teach by other methods—and do a lot of praying.

Damon took a few steps down the hall, then turned back toward his son. "Uh, aren't you going back into class?"

"Yeah. But I'm just going to wait a minute to make sure my eyes aren't red. Amanda's in there."

That explained everything. "You look great. But if anyone says anything, just tell them your dad needed your advice on how to help fix a car."

Tanner's smile was larger this time, and the tears all but gone. "I will."

Damon had taken a few more steps when Tanner's voice stopped him. "Uh, Dad."

Damon turned. "Yes?"

Tanner's brown eyes were once again luminous. "Thanks. I'm glad you came. This has really been bothering me, and I didn't know what to do."

Inside, Damon sang for joy. Tanner was a good boy; he had simply needed a strong guiding hand.

* * * * *

Belle insisted on accompanying them to the Hansens'. Damon really didn't mind, so he gave in. She had been grounded since pulling the disappearing act on Friday, and he thought she had learned her lesson. She was probably going crazy with nothing to do.

If he had known Belle's real reason for accompanying them, he wouldn't have let her come. "I don't want to be left at home with Rebekka," she explained in the car. "Besides, she's waiting for another phone call from Samuel." She leaned forward in her seat belt to eye her father's face. "He called earlier today, but she couldn't take the call. He said he'd call back tonight. I think she's in love with him."

"What gave you that idea?" Tanner asked quickly. "I mean, just because he likes her doesn't mean she's in love with him."

The irony of Tanner's words made Damon smile.

"You just want her to love you!" Belle taunted.

"Do not!"

"Kids!" Damon warned. "Bekka will love whomever she pleases. But remember, I'm the one she has agreed to go out with this Friday." He met Belle's glare briefly as he paused at a stoplight. "And no pulling a stunt like you did last Friday, young lady. I'll be watching you!"

"Maybe I should have stayed home with Rebekka!" Belle clamped her mouth shut, stuck her chin in the air, and stared out the window. She was quiet the rest of the fifteen-minute drive to the Hansen home in American Fork.

Damon felt nervous as he thought about the impending conversation. From Brionney's description, Mickelle Hansen hadn't been too impressed with their meeting the night before. Had he really been so stern and unfeeling as she had perceived? He remembered how beautiful she had looked in the rain, mascara smudges and all, and how he had wanted to free her hair from its clasp.

They drove up in front of the small house, and he immediately recognized the gold station wagon. "It's such a tiny house, Dad," Belle observed.

Tanner slid out of the car. "Yeah, that whole thing could fit into our living room and the piano room."

"It doesn't need to be big to be comfortable," Damon reminded them. The outside of the house was brick and clapboard, covered with peeling paint. The shingles on the roof were curling, and the cement walk was severely cracked. But even though the house had seen better days, the yard had obviously been cared for. There were no fancy cement borders around the yard, but flowers—mostly roses—lined the walkway and filled the flower beds. Much of the work looked recent, as though the occupants of the house had weeded and trimmed the flowers within the past week.

No one answered their knock, but Damon knew from Brionney that the Hansens had no other car. "They must be in the backyard," Tanner said. "I hear voices." The boy sounded nervous, but no more nervous than Damon. What was it about this woman? He had faced much stiffer business opponents before.

She's not an opponent, he reminded himself. Aloud he suggested, "Let's go around back."

Damon followed the children down the walk to the cement slab where the station wagon was parked. Stopping to look at the front fender on the driver's side, he saw where the complete front side panel of the fender had been shoved toward the tire. The paint was also peeling and cracking, but wasn't too noticeably different from the rest of the car. He bent for a closer look and noticed that the paint was completely peeled away where the door rubbed against the misplaced panel. Forcing it open had most likely caused the broken door handle.

He shook his head and sighed. The car wasn't really worth repairing, in his opinion, but if that was what she wanted . . .

"Dad, come on." Belle tugged on him, as impatient as ever. Damon let her pull him to the opening in the old wood fence that led to the backyard. Once there had been a gate, but now even the hinges were missing.

He saw her at once, sitting in the middle row of a garden that ran along nearly the entire length of the back part of the yard. In her black T-shirt, she nearly blended in with the rich color of the earth as she carefully dug around a vine-type plant with a gardening tool, stopping occasionally to pick out the uprooted weeds and throw them into a pile on the grass. Her shoulder-length hair was loose today, and the honey-blonde locks gently lifted and swirled in the slight breeze.

Suddenly a soccer ball hit her shoulder, and two boys came running toward the garden. "Sorry, Mom," they chorused.

"Oh, yeah?" she called, grabbing the ball. In an agile movement, she was on her feet and jumping over the rows to the grass. She set the ball on the ground. "Try and stop me!" She dribbled the ball along the grass as the two boys laughingly tried to steal it from her. She feinted with one foot and kicked with the other, causing the youngest boy to kick air instead of the ball. Back and forth she went, dodging and kicking, the boys and a yellow Labrador following her. Once the older boy succeeded in taking the ball, but a few seconds later she had it again. Finally, she kicked hard and the ball slammed against the wood fence.

"Goal!" she shouted, then collapsed in a heap. The boys piled on top of her, and all three began laughing and shouting and tickling one another. The dog ran in circles around them, barking wildly.

Damon found himself wanting to laugh and shout with them. At the same time, tears came to his eyes. This was the life he had wanted with Charlotte. Not that he and the children didn't have a good life now, but sometimes it was so hard forging on alone. And yet, wasn't that what this woman was doing?

Tanner and Belle were staring almost enviously at the scene. With a start, Damon realized that neither child had ever played that way with a woman. Charlotte had always been too ill, except when Tanner was very young, and the nannies had been more sedate types, except for Rebekka—and Damon couldn't imagine Tanner or Belle wrestling with her. Tanner was too much in love with her, and Belle was too angry.

Damon could have watched the Hansens forever, and had he an ounce of artistic ability, he would have wanted to paint them. But impatient Belle pulled him forward. "I know that boy, Dad," she said. "He goes to my school. He's Camille's cousin."

The yellow lab bounded toward them, growling in its throat. Belle clung to his hand in fear.

The woman looked up, and their eyes met across the wide expanse of lawn. Damon couldn't tell the color of her eyes, but remembered them from the previous night as being blue. Not like Brionney's sky-blue eyes, but more the darker blue of a stormy day. She had an adorable smudge of dirt on her cheek.

"Come here, Sasha," she commanded the dog, but Damon sensed a reluctance in her voice. The dog turned and went back to the two boys, wagging her tail, her canine eyes still alert.

"Hello," he said quickly, detecting no welcome in the stormy eyes. "I've come to say I'm sorry."

CHAPTER 21

Mickelle met Mr. Wolfe's bold stare with surprise, barely noticing the two children accompanying him. Slowly, she separated herself from the boys and stood, self-consciously brushing dirt from her black jeans.

Mr. Wolfe wore a tailored dark suit with a matching patterned dress shirt. His shoulders were broader than she remembered, tapering to a narrow waist. His amber eyes gleamed, but held none of the hardness she had glimpsed the night before.

He actually looks sorry, she thought. Well, this was a much better start than at their previous meeting. She waited for him to continue.

"Bri didn't call you?" he asked. "She knew I was coming."

Mickelle shook her head, wondering what Brionney had to do with this man. Had her sister taken it upon herself to call him? She was about to ask when she glanced at the little girl who held onto the man's hand. She looked so familiar! But where . . .?

Then it hit her. She *had* seen this little brown-haired beauty before. She had seen her in a dream.

No! It couldn't be!

"Is this your daughter?" she asked through the tightening of her throat. *A coincidence,* she told herself. *That's all it is. She just looks like the girl in my dream. It was so long ago, maybe I've forgotten.*

Mr. Wolfe chuckled. "Yes. This is Belle."

Belle? Where had she heard that name before? Mickelle's heart raced, and she prayed silently, *Not a panic attack now. Please, dear Father. Not now. She's not the girl in my dreams.* She took a deep breath. "Hello, Belle," she managed.

The girl smiled, showing a dimple on each cheek. "I know that boy," she said, pointing at Jeremy. "He's Camille's cousin."

Jeremy looked at her. "Oh, yeah. I've seen you before. You go to my school."

Mickelle tore her gaze away from Belle. "And how do you know my sister?" she asked Mr. Wolfe.

He didn't flush, but by the sheepish expression on his face Mickelle would bet he was embarrassed. "I guess we ought to properly introduce ourselves. I'm Damon Wolfe, Jesse's business partner."

"You're the . . . the, um, guy Brionney and Jesse are always talking about?" Mickelle had been going to say the "good-looking guy," but stopped herself just in time. "The one they say turns everything he touches to gold?"

He rubbed his chin. "Yeah, I guess that'd be me."

Mickelle didn't know what to say, so she introduced herself. "I'm Mickelle Hansen."

"Tell her, Dad," Tanner urged, smiling at her tentatively.

Damon Wolfe nodded. "Yes, we'd like to talk to you about fixing your car. I've spoken to my son, and in reviewing the facts, uh—" He cleared his throat. "We've decided that Tanner really was at fault, and we would like to make it right."

"I'm really sorry," Tanner added, his brown eyes soulful.

Mickelle felt emotion well in her breast. How glad she was that she had prayed for this little family instead of throwing rotten eggs at their windows!

"Come on into the house," she said. "I have the estimates inside." She looked at the boys. "Put Sasha back in her run, please." She paused a few seconds to make sure the boys were heading toward the large dog run she had constructed of chicken wire in the back corner of the yard.

Instead of taking them through the kitchen door, where Mr. Wolfe might see the dinner dishes she had left in the sink, Mickelle headed around to the front. She saw Mr. Wolfe's eyes move to the station wagon and guessed at what he was thinking. "I know she's not much, but the Snail is all we have."

His deep and ready chuckle showed genuine amusement. "Snail, huh?"

"Yep. The Snail gets us where we need to go." She kicked the car as she passed.

Parked in front next to the curb, she saw a sleek blue car which looked as new and modern as hers did old and archaic. *Must be his.* She laughed to herself. *He drives a blue streak. Wonder if he talks it, too.* Aloud she said, "Nice car."

"What is it?" Bryan asked as he and Jeremy caught up to them in the front yard.

"Mercedes," Tanner answered. "Can I show it to 'em, Dad?" He looked at Bryan. "It's got a cool stereo setup."

Mr. Wolfe reached into his pocket and threw his son the keys. "Just turn it one click. Don't start the engine."

"I won't."

All three of the boys took off toward the car while Mickelle led Belle and her father into the house, glad that she had been motivated enough after Jim Lowder's visit to clean and dust the living room. The old newspapers were gone, too, and this morning she had canceled the gift subscription to the paper to wean herself from her fascination with the obituaries.

"Please have a seat, Mr. Wolfe."

"Thank you. But call me Damon. I can just see Bri laughing about me letting you call me Mr. Wolfe."

"Then you must call me Mickelle."

"Mickelle," he repeated, seating himself on the sofa. "It's a beautiful name. Unusual."

"Damon is unusual, too." She paused, feeling awkward in her dirty jeans in front of this handsome, well-dressed man. She was about to excuse herself to wash her hands and to find the estimates for the car when he spoke again.

"My son really is sorry." He glanced out the large front window at the boys, who were now inside the car. "He's agreed to spend his savings to repair your car, then wait until he earns more to have his own fixed."

"He seems like a good boy."

"He is—most of the time. And I plan to help him out—with the repairs, I mean. I always give them a generous sum for their birthdays." He turned from the window, and his eyes widened at something behind Mickelle. "Belle! Don't touch!"

Mickelle whirled around and saw that the little girl had thrust her hand into the glassless curio cabinet and was reaching for one of the roses in her collection. "It's okay," she told the startled child. "As long as you are very gentle. Besides, there's not much left to break. As you can see, the glass is already gone." At Mr. Wolfe's surprised expression, Mickelle realized she had let bitterness enter her voice.

She quickly changed her tone. This precious little girl had nothing to do with Riley and his vengeance. "Here, let me show you this one." She took out a carved wooden rose that Bryan had made in scouts. "See how smooth the wood is? And it's tough, too. It wouldn't break if you dropped it." *Or if someone purposely tipped over the cabinet.*

"It's very soft," Belle said. "I'm mean, it's hard, but it feels soft."

"I know exactly what you mean. It's more than smooth. It's almost silky."

Belle smiled up at her, and Mickelle had a strange feeling of déjà vu. How could this child so resemble the little girl in her dream? None of it made sense.

Belle had to hold or gently stroke each rose in the collection, and not for the first time, Mickelle lamented the loss of the roses Riley had destroyed. Belle would have liked them.

Mickelle helped the girl put back the last rose. "I'll just wash my hands now," she said, looking at the particles of dirt imbedded in the small lines and creases on her hands. "And find the papers."

Damon looked up from where he was studying the ugly crack along the side of the cabinet. "Take your time. I should have called first, but I was afraid you'd hang up on me."

"I might have," she answered with a teasing smile.

While washing her hands, Mickelle also brushed her hair and noticed the most embarrassing spot of dirt on her cheek. She rubbed it off impatiently. *Why do these things always happen to me?*

When she returned to the living room with the repair estimates, Belle was sitting on the piano bench, her father standing by her side. Belle played the piano with tiny fingers, not banging as Jeremy did, but softly and with feeling.

"I hope you don't mind," Damon said.

"Not at all. I wish my boys would try to play instead of just banging on it." Of course, since they hadn't been able to afford lessons, they hadn't learned much about playing real songs.

"We have a piano," he said, "but Belle has never shown any interest in it. Tanner did for about six months when he was ten. I didn't push it."

Belle looked up at Mickelle. "We have a bi-i-i-g piano. A grandfather one. And it cost about a million bucks. Rebekka said so." The little girl glanced at her father. "I think that's why she wants to marry my dad. So she can have my mother's piano."

Damon's lips twisted in a grimace—or perhaps a painful attempt at a smile. Mickelle couldn't tell which. To avoid any further awkwardness, she sat at the piano next to Belle.

"I took lessons when I was a kid," she said. "Listen to this." Her fingers found the right keys quickly and surely as she played the first few bars of "The Entertainer." She stumbled near the end, but Belle didn't seem to notice.

"I want to learn to play that song!" the little girl exclaimed eagerly. "Will you teach me?"

Mickelle didn't know what to say. She was a beginner herself, despite the impressive song. "It's the only complicated one I know," she admitted. "I have a book that has more songs, but I don't know if I can teach you. You probably need someone better than me."

Belle looked disappointed. "Well, if I come over, can you at least show me that song, a little at a time?"

"Sure," Mickelle agreed readily, before she remembered that she might never see the girl again.

"Cool! So where's the first key?"

Mickelle showed her, surprised at how fast Belle remembered. Her little fingers stretched almost impossibly to find the right notes.

"Mom!" Jeremy came in the front door, looking disgruntled.

Mickelle turned from the piano. "What?"

"Bryan's being stupid. And I'm bored."

That usually meant Bryan was talking about something Jeremy had no interest in—like gym class or girls. "Well, if you've done your homework and your room is clean, you can play your Game Boy for a while."

"You have a Game Boy?" Belle asked, interested.

Jeremy went to the side table and found his Game Boy under an old copy of the *Ensign*. "Yeah, and I'm gonna play Pokémon. Wanna watch?"

For an answer, Belle slid off the piano bench. "Sure. I've got Pokémon, too—at home. I play it all the time."

"I'm trying to find a Bulbasaur." Jeremy spoke with enthusiasm, as though grateful for an audience.

"I got one." Belle's voice was matter-of-fact, not boasting.

Jeremy gaped. "Yeah? Where?"

"From Professor Oak."

Jeremy nodded. "You must have the blue version then," he said. "On yellow, a Bulbasaur is hard to find. At least it is for me."

"I didn't know that. Show me." Without a backward glance at her father, Belle followed Jeremy out onto the porch.

Damon grinned at Mickelle. "You catch any of that?" he asked.

"Some—not much," Mickelle replied with a laugh. "I know Professor Oak is a Pokémon expert in the game. That's all. Frankly, I just don't get the whole video game idea. It seems like a waste of time."

"It's a way to relax, to get away from real life." Damon walked to the couch and settled onto it. "And some of the games improve children's cognitive abilities—or so I'm told. I used to play a lot when I was a kid."

"And look where you are now."

There was a long silence while they stared at each other. Then Mickelle shook her head and sighed, breaking their eye contact.

"What?" he asked. She could feel him looking at her intently, as though trying to read her inner thoughts.

Mickelle sat in Riley's chair. "Nothing."

"Tell me."

Mickelle felt herself blush. She couldn't tell him what she was thinking, could she? He was, after all, a stranger. "Well, it's just that if you're so ri—successful, why would you balk at paying a measly five hundred dollars?" The words escaped before she could stop them. *Oops.*

He shifted his position on the couch, looking uncomfortable. "I guess it's the principle of the thing. At first accounting, I really thought you were as much to blame for the accident as Tan was. And I thought you were taking advantage of my son's age to get work done on your car." His eyes met hers. "Now I know that's not true, and I'm very sorry for all the trouble we put you through."

"That's understandable. I mean, we all want to protect our kids." He frowned. "Sometimes too much."

"It's hard being a single parent," Mickelle said sympathetically. "I care deeply about my children, but sometimes it's a big task being the only one responsible for them." *Even Riley was some help,* she added to herself.

"That's exactly it," he agreed. "And whether you fail or succeed, you have no one to share it with—at least no one who loves the kids in the same way you do."

But she had never had that, not even with Riley. She had always cared more about the children than he had. "How long . . . have you been alone?" she asked. "Tanner told me your wife was . . . gone. I'll bet it's been difficult for him and Belle."

He let out a long sigh. "My wife died of cancer two years ago. Tan did take it kind of hard at the time, but he bounced right back. It's amazing how resilient kids are. As for Belle, she never really knew her mother. Char—Charlotte—had been sick and bedridden almost since Belle was born. Sometimes I would take both Belle and Tan with me on business trips—with the nanny—because many times Char was too ill to even have the children near her. Having to make a simple parental decision would make her gravely ill."

"No wonder you're so close to your children." Again Mickelle spoke without meaning to, but when she saw Damon's gratified expression, she was glad she had. "An honest observation," she added. *Not like the compliments I gave Riley so he wouldn't be angry or depressed.*

Why did she have to think about Riley now? One thing was certain: it was good being able to speak her mind without fearing an angry outburst. If she angered this man, who cared? It would make no difference in her life.

Damon leaned forward. "Thank you for saying so. I've tried really hard with them. And that's really why I'm here tonight. I mean, I want to help you, but more than anything, I wanted my son to take responsibility for his actions."

"That makes sense to me." Mickelle retrieved the repair estimates from the top of the piano and handed them to Damon.

He glanced briefly through the pages, then met her gaze, looking somewhat embarrassed. "You know, the part they fix is going to look better than the rest of the car."

Mickelle laughed. "Don't I know it!" She sobered. "Look, Mr.—Damon—the only thing I need is for the fender to be straightened and the door fixed so it doesn't stick and I can open it from the outside. You needn't pay for sanding or paint or anything; that's pretty useless. The car will go to the junkyard just as soon as I can afford something else."

Damon rubbed his chin thoughtfully. "Well, in that case, I'm getting an idea here. What if I take your car home tonight, and I get Tan working on it? He might possibly be able to straighten it all himself. If not, I know a mechanic who can help. At the very least, Tan can order the door parts, touch-up paint, and whatever else is needed. That way, he's actually taking responsibility for what he's done." His eyes never left hers as he spoke, and Mickelle felt an odd warmth permeate her body.

It's because he wants so much to help his son, she told herself. "That's fine with me," she said aloud.

"Of course, I'll still want you to have the money the estimates are asking for—just in case you change your mind about the paint."

Mickelle shook her head vigorously. "Oh, you don't need to do that! Fixing the car will be enough."

"No, I insist," Damon said. "I won't make Tan cover it all—he'll just pay for the parts—but you ought to be compensated for your trouble. If you don't use it on the car, I'm sure you can find some other use for it." His glance rested briefly on the damaged curio cabinet.

Mickelle followed his gaze. She could certainly use the funds. In fact, she needed the money more than she wanted to admit to this stranger. Though her pride begged her to reject his offer, she accepted it graciously. "Well, all right, if you feel that you must. Thank you."

"I do." Damon stood "Now, there's just the matter of getting your car back to my house." He laughed and rubbed his chin again, an action that was quickly becoming endearing to Mickelle. "Too bad Tan doesn't have his license—he could drive it home!"

Mickelle smiled, knowing that for a boy of Tanner's age and economic situation, driving the Snail might be worse punishment than having to repair it. "I could drive it over," she offered. "If you'll bring me home. Or I could get my sister to drive me."

"No, I'll take you home. But this job won't be done in a day. What will you do without a car?"

She shrugged. "I don't really need one. I've been shopping already." *For all that I can afford,* she amended silently. "And the boys can walk to school."

Damon frowned. "You might have an emergency. I don't feel good about leaving you without a car. Tanner might not be able to get it done before Saturday."

"My sister lives nearby. I can always use her van if I need to."

"Hmm." His frown turned to a smile. "What if you use my car? Hey, that's it! I'll take your car, and you keep mine."

Mickelle glanced out the window at the dark blue car that looked brand-new. "I don't think so. What if I damage it?"

"It's easy to drive."

"Yes, but another boy without insurance might run into me." Mickelle's voice was filled with irony.

He laughed as though she had told him the best joke he had ever heard. A laugh that seeped right through her bones and made her heart ache with longing for the life she had lost. "It's fully insured, no matter what," he said. "Even the deductible has been paid because of a ding I had repaired earlier in the year. So what do you say?"

He was earnest, and so nice! Besides, she'd love to drive a decent car, if only for a few days. "But what will you drive to work?" her conscience made her ask.

"Oh, I've got a dealer friend who's been wanting me to try out a new car for a few days. He says I'll like it better than the Mercedes. I wasn't going to do it, but who knows? Maybe I really will like it better and decide to trade up." He smiled and held out his hand. "I'll need your keys."

Feeling stunned, Mickelle went to the kitchen where she kept the car keys. When she returned to the living room, Damon was already outside with all the children. He had obviously told them his idea, because Bryan and Jeremy were nearly bursting with excitement.

"Mom!" yelled Jeremy. "We're keeping their car!"

"Just till they fix ours," Bryan corrected.

Belle skipped down the sidewalk toward the station wagon. "Does it have seat belts?"

Tanner didn't seem as upset at driving in the Snail as Mickelle had envisioned. He smiled confidently at her. "I'll fix her up as good as new," he told her. "Well, as good as she was before, anyway. Don't worry about it at all."

"Yeah, he's grounded from his friends anyway," Bryan added. There was a note of admiration in his voice. Mickelle hoped the admiration was for Tanner's ability to fix the car, not the fact that he had done something to deserve a punishment.

Tanner shrugged with embarrassment. "I'd do it even if I wasn't."

"Of course you would." Mickelle walked with the family to the Snail, hardly daring to look at Damon. It was difficult to believe that a multimillionaire was going to drive off in her battered station wagon. He wasn't sending a mechanic, he wasn't letting her drive it over, he was taking it home himself. It was beyond belief.

Belle bounced into the backseat of the Snail, finding the safety belt with Jeremy's help. "I'll be back," she said to Mickelle. "And then we can play the piano."

Damon removed a few keys from a set in his pocket and tossed the rest to her, which she was almost too stunned to catch. "I'll give you a call when I know what's going on. Oh, and here's my card with my work and cell numbers if you need to contact me."

She nodded dumbly and watched him climb into the Snail—from the passenger side, of course. As crotchety as ever, the old car wouldn't start until the third try. Damon gave her a jaunty smile and waved. Mickelle lifted her own hand in reply, continuing to stare after the car until it disappeared from sight.

Bryan and Jeremy whooped and hollered. "Come on, Mom!" Jeremy said. "Let's take his car for a spin! I'll bet it goes fast—like that rabbit in the race against the turtle." He smirked. "I mean against the Snail."

"Can you take me to school tomorrow?" asked Bryan.

"Me too!" shouted Jeremy.

"We'll see," Mickelle said. "But we're not driving it now. It's time for bed."

Jeremy's face fell. "Aw, Mom! It's not even dark yet. Come on! Damon said you could drive it whenever you wanted—even tonight. I asked him." It sounded like something Jeremy would do.

Bryan nodded—whether in agreement or encouragement, she couldn't tell. Both boys looked so hopeful. "All right," she said finally. "Just around the block."

The boys ran to the car, arguing over who would get the front seat. In a magnanimous gesture, Bryan let Jeremy sit in front. "I'll ride there in the morning on the way to school." Then he added, "I hope my friends see the car tomorrow," which explained the generosity.

Mickelle was too excited and nervous to call him on it. Besides, Jeremy was content with the arrangement. She started the car hesitantly and pulled out from the curb. As Damon had promised, the Mercedes was easy to drive, and a pure luxury after the Snail.

"It's much better than a rabbit," Jeremy announced.

Mickelle couldn't have put it better. She took in a deep breath through her nose, noticing a strange but pleasant aroma emanating from the interior of the car. It wasn't only the rich leather seats, but a mix of decidedly masculine scents she identified as belonging to the owner. The fragrance gave her a warm, secure feeling. How would it feel to have a man like him take care of her?

With effort, Mickelle shoved the idea aside. First, she had to depend on herself. Never again could she rely on a man for her happiness.

* * * * *

When the boys were in bed and Damon's car was safely parked on the cement slab next to the house, Mickelle called Brionney and told her what had happened.

"Well, I'm glad he came over," Brionney said. "I knew he would eventually, but I'm glad he didn't put it off. He's a pretty busy guy."

"Hmm." Mickelle wasn't really listening.

"Aren't you glad it's over? Or almost?" her sister pressed.

"Yes. I am. It's just . . . something . . . well, his daughter."

"Belle? Isn't she beautiful? But sometimes she can be a real stinker. Didn't I tell you about how she came home last Friday with my girls and hid in their room—all so their father wouldn't be able to go out on his date?"

Mickelle did remember Brionney saying something about the incident, but she hadn't connected the name with the child she had met today. "So that's where I heard her name before. I thought it was familiar. Still, it was so strange . . ."

"What?" Brionney asked. "Did something happen?"

"Well, she just reminded me of someone I'd seen before."

"You might have seen her. Probably at the school."

"That's right." Mickelle made a quick decision not to tell her sister about Belle's resemblance to the girl in her dream. *It was only a coincidence.*

CHAPTER 22

Rebekka was glad when Samuel Bjornenburg returned from Cincinnati with a small team of experts from his own company consisting of translators, programmers, and the vice-president of foreign marketing. Her weekend had been bleak without his presence. She had seen little of Damon, and wondered if he was trying to avoid her until she moved out. Since neither he nor Brionney had found someone to replace her, Rebekka continued to work at the office during the day and play sitter in the afternoon until Damon returned at six-thirty. There was a strange feeling about the situation, as though she was on the verge of an important discovery that somehow eluded her grasp. Tanner continued to worship her, though he was occupied more now with school, girls, and cars, and Belle still used every means to avoid her. Rebekka frequently felt like she was an intruder in their home.

Samuel didn't make her feel that way at all. Unlike the rest of his employees, who slept in a hotel, he was again staying at the Wolfe mansion. They had spent the past two evenings together, talking, laughing, swimming, and strolling around the estate. He complimented her often, went out of his way to be with her, and asked her opinion on numerous occasions. With him, she felt needed and wanted and content. She tried not to imagine what life would be like when he left for good.

"You know, we'll have to go to France to set up a test hospital or two," he told her on Friday morning, the last day he would be in Utah. "I think you would be great to go as part of the team." They were in the conference room, which had been turned into several office cubicles for Samuel's team and Rebekka.

She glanced around at the others, who were working intently. "I don't know." If she went to France, she would have to visit home . . . and that would also mean seeing Marc.

"At least come back to Cincinnati with me." Samuel's voice was low and intense. "I'll put you in charge of the whole foreign project. You've got what it takes, Rebekka. You're an amazing woman." By the admiration in his eyes, she knew he meant what he said.

"But the company . . . Damon and Jesse—"

"You'd still be working with Damon and Jesse," he said. "For as long as the partnership lasts. Think about it. We leave tonight, and then we'll be doing most of the translating work in Cincinnati. I'm sure there'll be things on this end for you to do, but nothing so challenging as with our team."

She knew he was telling the truth. In Cincinnati, she could move quickly up in the company, develop new skills. But was that what she wanted? What about Damon?

What about him? a mocking voice inside her asked. There wasn't anything between them, really. Not yet.

But there could be.

As though reading her thoughts, Samuel grabbed her hand and gently pulled her toward the door and out into the hall. Rebekka felt several of his employees watch them leave.

"It's not only that, Rebekka," he said earnestly. "I like you. I've been a bachelor a long time, but that's because I've never fallen in love before. But I think I might be falling in love with you." The intensity of his gaze deepened. "Rebekka, I don't want to give you up. I want to find out if there is something between us. I want to learn who you are and show you what kind of a man I am. But I can't stay here." His green eyes pleaded with hers. "Please come with me. I promise I won't force a relationship on you. Just give us six months. We'll work together, go out and see the sights, get to know each other and see where it leads."

His closeness made her pulse race. This successful, handsome, sincere man wanted a relationship with her! And she knew him well enough to know that although he wasn't a member of the Church, he was a good man. He might be able to make her happy, the way her father had made her mother happy. But would that happiness last for a lifetime? And what about eternity?

These thoughts filtered through her mind as Samuel waited for her response. He had opened himself to her, and she couldn't hurt him—didn't want to hurt him. "It sounds like a promising idea," she answered softly. "I like the work, and I like you, too." Now she made her voice firm. "But there are some unresolved issues I have to deal with here. I need to think about it a little more."

He grinned, causing her heart to dance. "Well, at least it's not a no."

"It's definitely not a no."

"Is it Damon?" he asked.

"Partly." But her possible relationship with Damon was only beginning. More important was the issue of her religion and her relationship with the Lord. She liked Samuel; she felt sure she could even grow to love him. But did she want to put herself in a position where she had to choose between him and God?

Samuel leaned toward her, and she could feel his warm breath on her face. She thought he might try to kiss her, and a part of her wanted to let him, but he simply stared into her eyes, as if drinking her in. The details of his tanned, good-looking face burned into her mind. Their breaths mingled, and the delicious tension between them deepened until she almost couldn't stand the pressure. Just when she thought she couldn't bear it any longer, he spoke.

"There are good things in store for us, Rebekka with two Ks. Wait and see."

He kissed her then, but it was light and brief like something she would give her brother. When his lips left hers, she felt empty, unsatisfied. "That wasn't a kiss," she challenged, wondering how he would answer. It wasn't exactly that she *wanted* him to kiss her more fervently, especially since she was going out with Damon that evening. But his reserve confused her, contrasting so completely as it did with what he had been saying.

He smiled faintly, his eyes never leaving her face. "It's hard to control myself when I'm around you." His soft voice sent shivers down her spine. "Once, even last week, it might not have mattered. But if I give you a kiss now, I give you my heart. And I don't want to do that until I know you want it."

She nodded in perfect understanding. He wasn't a member of the Church, and yet he saw the physical aspect of their relationship as something not to be toyed with. Kissing was a commitment not to be taken lightly.

Placing a finger lightly on his lower lip, she whispered, "Thank you."

He smiled again before making an attempt to nibble her finger. "When will I have your answer?"

He would make a great missionary, she thought. *He knows how to invite and commit. How many times had she asked a similar question on her mission? She still remembered the words: What day will you commit to following the Lord's example by entering into the waters of baptism?*

"Next week," she said.

His eyebrows drew together as though he was worried. "After I'm gone."

"Yes." She gave him her best smile. "Undue influence, you know."

"I see." He touched her cheek with his hand, letting it slide down to her chin, and finally back to his side. The tension between them was palpable, both enticing and promising. "I'll be waiting."

Opening the door, Samuel disappeared inside the conference room. Rebekka slumped against the wall, suddenly feeling weak in the knees. What was she supposed to do now? Silently, she prayed for an answer.

She looked up to see Damon emerging from his office. "Hi, Bekka." Gathering her wits, she smiled and nodded in greeting.

"Going to get Belle from school?"

She glanced at her watch. "Yes. I guess I am."

"Tan called; he needs to go pick up those parts for Mrs. Hansen's car. Do you think you could take him to the dealership after you get Belle?"

"No problem."

"I'm sure proud of that kid. You saw how he straightened out that fender, didn't you? Pounded it out—I never knew he was so strong."

She laughed. "I could barely *lift* the hammer he showed me."

Damon practically beamed. "Yeah, that was something, wasn't it?" He hesitated and then added, "So are we still on for tonight?"

"Yes. We're going to a little restaurant in Provo. They serve escargots."

As she expected, he made a sour face. "Wait a minute. Isn't that snails?"

"It's about time you tried them. They're really good." She knew this would be a night he would never forget.

"Can I try one of yours and then have a steak?"

"Nope." She drew her lips into a pout.

He held up his hands. "Okay, okay. I guess if I can clean up after the kids when they're sick, I can eat snails."

She punched his shoulder. "Damon! Gross! They're delicious."

"We'll see."

Shaking her head in amusement, Rebekka left Damon and went to her car. She drove through the streets as fast as she dared, wanting to make sure that this time she arrived at the school before Belle had a chance to run away again. Tonight, nothing was going to get in the way of her date. Once and for all, she needed to know where she and Damon stood.

* * * * *

Damon grinned to himself as he returned to his office. *Snails. What a marvelous idea.* He thought it best not to let on to Rebekka that he had not only eaten escargots before, but had enjoyed them. Not yet, at any rate. He would surprise her later. It had been a few years, of course, since he had eaten the dish, so maybe he wouldn't like it as much as he had during his younger and more adventurous days.

Snails . . . the Snail. Unbidden, thoughts of Mickelle Hansen and her golden Snail came to his mind. What was she doing now? Was she enjoying his car?

Similar thoughts had plagued him all week. At first he thought it was guilt because of the way he had treated her before, but now he wondered if it could be something else. She was an attractive woman, but so were many others he had met. What was it about her that preyed on his mind? Was it her helplessness? He recalled the angry woman with flashing eyes who had confronted him on his porch . . . no, she was far from helpless. And yet . . .

One thing was certain: her car was a complete disaster. Not only was the damage from the accident as bad as she claimed, but the engine didn't sound right and the tread on her tires was almost gone. In his opinion it wasn't safe to drive, but he didn't yet know what he was going to do about it. At least the damage Tanner had caused would be fixed. He should let her know.

Her phone rang three times before she answered. "Hello," she said a bit breathlessly.

"Hello. It's Damon Wolfe," he said. "You remember me." It was a statement. How could she not remember him?

"I'm sorry. You must have the wrong number." But her voice was teasing. "And I can't talk now because I have to go pick up my son from school in my new Mercedes."

He threw back his head and laughed. She was funny! "I hope you've been enjoying the car."

"Oh, yes." Now her voice was wistful, and Damon wanted more than anything else in the world to say, "Keep it, then. It's yours." But he knew she wouldn't hear of it, and he would be embarrassing them both by the offer, sincere as it might be. Brionney had told him of Mickelle's refusal to accept financial help from her family, and he, a virtual stranger, could hardly expect to accomplish what they could not. Still, he admired her tenacity.

"I'm calling to let you know about your car," he told her.

"Oh, your son fixed it already?"

"Well, almost. He had to order the door parts from the dealer, but they came in today. The car should be ready tonight, or tomorrow at the latest."

"That's great!" she said, actually sounding like she meant it. Her next words told him why. "I'll bet you're missing your car."

"A little," he admitted. "But driving this other car hasn't been too difficult." He was glad when she didn't ask what kind of a car it was. "I'll give you a call as soon as I know more."

"Thank you," she replied. "Oh, wait a minute. I might not be home tonight."

"Out joyriding in your new Mercedes?" He made his tone as light and teasing as hers had been earlier.

"Uh, no . . . I have plans with a friend."

She didn't explain further, and he couldn't exactly force it from her. What did he care, anyway? It wasn't his business who she went out with.

He cleared his throat. "I actually have plans for tonight myself. So I'll call you tomorrow."

"Sounds good."

There was nothing more to add, so Damon said good-bye, replaced the receiver, and leaned back in his leather chair. Almost immediately, he leaned forward again and placed a call to his dealer friend who had loaned him a Lexus for the week. "Hey Kirk, it's Damon."

"Hello, buddy. So, are you enjoying that car, or what?"

"Actually, I am," Damon admitted.

"You buying it?"

"Probably. Only one problem. I can't get used to the color. Red just doesn't do it for me. How about something in a dark green?"

"No prob. You can take your pick. In fact, I've been thinking of keeping the red one for myself. It's good advertising."

Damon chuckled. "I'll bet." Kirk would probably continue to lend out the car to hook someone else with its undeniable comfort and luxury. "But I'm calling about something else. The thing is, I know this lady who needs a car really bad. It's got to be something cheap, and I was wondering if you had any trade-ins that would fit the bill. She's not looking for help, even though she needs it, if you get my meaning. And she doesn't have much money. I'd like to help her out."

"How much she got?"

"Five hundred, six tops. She really needs this car. You know I wouldn't ask if she didn't. But I wouldn't mind tossing in a bit more if we keep it between us."

"Well, we don't carry things that cheap here."

"You've already sold me on the Lexus," Damon reminded him. "Come on. You have to know somebody who can find what she needs."

"My brother may have some on his lot. Let me see what I can come up with. I'll get back to you as soon as I can."

"Terrific. I'll be waiting for your call."

Damon hung up, feeling pleased with himself. He wondered what her response would be when he told her about the nice little car she could get for the six hundred he would give her. Would her stormy eyes flash with excitement and gratitude as they once had in anger? He could hardly wait to find out.

* * * * *

Barely half an hour had passed since Damon had talked to Mickelle. When his office line rang, he picked it up quickly, expecting Kirk to be calling about the car. He knew the man would be anxious to find Mickelle a car so that Damon would hurry in to purchase the Lexus.

To his surprise, it was Rebekka. He could tell she was upset because her usually faint accent had become noticeable.

"Belle's gone again!" she announced.

"Oh, you're kidding!" But he knew she wouldn't tease about something like this.

"We've searched the school and the grounds. Should I call the police again?"

"Let me check with Bri first. I wouldn't put it past Belle to try that hiding stunt again. And this time, I swear, she won't escape a spanking!"

He disconnected and called Brionney, hastily explaining the situation. "She didn't come home with the girls," Brionney said. "Savannah had a project that was too big to carry all the way home, so I picked the girls up today. Belle wasn't with them. Of course, she knows the way and could have come by herself. Hold on a minute, and I'll look for her. But if she's here, my girls are in big trouble."

While he was waiting for Brionney to return, a call came through on his cell phone. This time it was Kirk. "What's the news?" Damon's voice was strained, but Kirk didn't appear to notice.

"Well, I didn't expect to find anything so soon, but my brother has a nice little car on his lot. A Geo Metro. Old by your standards, but in surprisingly good condition. My brother gave 'em three thousand for it in a trade-in, so we can't go any lower than that."

"No? I'm sure you can do something," Damon prodded.

"You trading in the Mercedes?"

"Uh, no. I guess not. I like it, too."

"Well then, since you're buying the Lexus, I could probably manage to get you the Geo for twenty-five hundred."

Damon tapped his fingers on the other receiver he held to his ear. *What is taking Bri so long?* Maybe the delay meant she had found Belle. "I'll think about it," he told Kirk.

"What?" Brionney's voice said on his office line.

"I might go as low as two thou," Kirk said. "But that's the bottom line."

Damon spoke into his office phone. "Hold on a sec, Bri. I'm on the cell, too." Then he spoke to Kirk. "Look, I apologize, Kirk, but I'm a little busy here. My daughter has disappeared, and I need to find her. I'll get back with you as soon as I can." Without waiting for a reply, he hung up and said to Brionney, "I'm back. Sorry about that. I answered my cell because I thought it might be about Belle. What did you find out?"

"She's definitely not here, and she didn't tell the girls anything. But I'm sure she's okay. Belle's a smart little girl."

"She's going to be a smart little girl with a burning butt," Damon said, letting his anger cover the fear that was eating at him. Belle was a beautiful child and trusting of strangers; she could have been kidnapped. "I think I'd better call the police."

"I'll start calling the other girls in her class," Brionney said. "Maybe they know something."

"Thanks."

Damon dialed the American Fork police, and was explaining his dilemma when his cell rang again. Kirk! "Please excuse me just a second," he told the police officer.

"What!" he barked into the cell phone.

"Uh, hi," replied a hesitant voice. "Is this Damon Wolfe? This is Mickelle Hansen."

"Oh, sorry," he said. "I thought you were someone else. My daughter's missing, and I'm a little impatient right now."

"That's what I'm calling about. Your daughter."

"You know where she is?"

"She's here. She followed my son home."

Damon's relief was so intense that he nearly dropped the phone. "Can you hold on a minute?" he asked. "I've got the police on another line."

With more than a little embarrassment, Damon told the woman on the phone that his daughter had been found, then apologized for taking her time. "Better safe than sorry," she quipped.

"Okay, I'm back," he said to Mickelle. "Now, how did Belle get there?"

"Well, it seems she followed Jeremy and his friends home from school. He claims he didn't see her until they were almost home, and then they walked the rest of the way together. I tried to call you as soon as they arrived, but you didn't answer. I left a voice-mail."

"I'll be right there to get her," Damon said. "Don't let her leave."

"Don't worry. She's at the piano now. I think that's the reason she came—she wanted me to teach her some more of the song. And you know, I really think she's got talent. You might want to consider giving her lessons." She paused, as though considering her words carefully. "It might relieve her boredom."

Damon was amazed. "Her boredom? She's only five years old! How can she be bored?"

"I'm sorry if I've offended you." Mickelle's voice had grown stiff and polite.

"You haven't," he answered quickly. "I'm sorry. I'm just feeling really inadequate as a parent right now." He took a deep, calming breath. "I'd love to hear what you have to say when I get there. But I hope it includes a good spanking!"

She laughed, and the warm sound seemed to offset his inadequacies, or at least forgive him for them. "We'll be right here waiting."

On the way to Mickelle's home, Damon rehearsed what he would say to Belle. She had to stop this nonsense. But why was she acting out? Was she still worried about Rebekka leaving her? Did she hate Rebekka so much that she couldn't stand the idea of his going out with her? Or was it all just a ploy to gain his attention?

She's only five years old, he kept thinking. *She's too young for this kind of thing. What'll she put me through when she's a teenager?*

CHAPTER 23

Mickelle had fun teaching Belle another few bars of "The Entertainer." Her tiny fingers seemed to remember the correct place on the keys of their own accord.

"Wow, it's like magic!" Jeremy said. "I can't believe she can play that. She's so little."

"Am not." Belle's lower lip poked out. "I can do anything you can do."

Jeremy didn't take up the challenge. "Maybe you're like that girl in *Ella Enchanted*. It's a book my teacher's reading to us at school. When someone tells her something, she has to obey 'cause she has a curse on her. So it's like you're her, and Mom told you to play, so you can. Cool."

"I read that book," Belle said. "I have it at home. It was great!"

Jeremy's brow wrinkled. "But you're only in first grade. You can't read that big of a book."

"Can too." Belle lifted her chin stubbornly in the air. "And even bigger books. Want me to show you?"

"Hey, maybe someone ordered you to read big books, so you have to!" Jeremy said, looking pleased. "Just like Ella."

Belle giggled. "I just hope someone doesn't tell me to like Rebekka."

"Well, I could always order you to hate her again," Jeremy declared. The two laughed until their eyes watered.

Mickelle smiled, but she was curious about Belle's apparent aversion to Rebekka. "Why don't you like Rebekka?" she asked.

Belle shrugged. "Just don't." Her eyes darted to the piano. "But

Rebekka can play the piano really well. Sometimes Bear and I sit on the stairs and listen. She never sees me at all."

"From what I hear from Brionney, Rebekka is a very nice person," Mickelle offered.

"Yeah, I guess. I just don't want her to live with us. I don't want her to go out with my dad." Belle's eyes were troubled, but Mickelle didn't know how to fix the worry there. Maybe she should talk to Damon. *Like it's any of your business,* she thought. But she had heard so much about the family from Brionney that Mickelle did care. And besides, the resemblance between Belle and that girl in her dream was uncanny.

"How about some soccer?" she asked, opting for distraction. "Do you know how to play, Belle?"

"I could just order her to play well," Jeremy said, bursting into another fit of giggles.

Mickelle tickled him, and he laughed even harder. "How about me against both of you?"

"No fair!" Jeremy shouted. "I'll get Bryan to help."

"Sorry, he's at a friend's."

"We can beat her!" Belle exclaimed.

They ran through the kitchen and out to the backyard, where Jeremy insisted on a two-goal lead to begin the game. "And we get the ball first." He set the ball on the ground and looked at Belle, a bright smile dancing on his thin face. "I order you to score a goal. Go!"

It was all Mickelle could do not to collapse on the ground and laugh herself silly at their efforts. Belle might be a piano prodigy, but she wasn't wired for soccer. She fell down more times than Jeremy, who had never been very coordinated like his older brother. Mickelle had to try hard not to win by too many goals.

In her pen, Sasha barked loudly, as though wanting to join the game. Normally, Mickelle would have let her out to join the game, but didn't think it was a good idea until the dog became more accustomed to Belle.

Damon arrived as they began a second game, this time with the children starting with five goals. His face was flushed and his mouth tense, and his eyes were hard as he focused on his daughter. Belle's smile vanished, and she stared at the ground. Jeremy watched them warily, his mouth slightly open. Mickelle recognized the expression, although she hadn't seen it on his face since Riley's death. He was worried about Damon's reaction, and was getting ready to make himself scarce.

"Hi." Mickelle smiled at Damon. He glanced her way, and she saw the frustration beneath his anger. "We're just going to play another game, but these kids are too much for me alone. Want to play?"

He stared at her. "Excuse me?"

"Got a moment to kick a ball?" She looked at his suit. "I know you're not dressed for it, but kicking a ball always clears my mind." She knew he would refuse. That's what Riley would have done. Riley would have erupted and told her to stop being childish, but at least his anger would have been redirected toward her and not at the children.

"I—I . . ." Damon trailed off. His eyes shifted toward the ball, almost in longing. "Okay," he said suddenly. "The Wolfes against the Hansens."

"Yay!" Jeremy shouted. "That's your goal over there." He pointed to the far fence. "Between those little trees." Damon ran for the ball, but in a moment of never-before-seen dexterity, Jeremy kicked it out from under Damon's foot and shot it toward Mickelle. "Go, Mom!"

* * * * *

Damon watched as Mickelle dribbled the ball across the lawn. He recovered from his miss and ran in front of her, but she darted around him and scored. Wow! That woman could really play. Of course, it didn't help that he had been spending so much time at work behind a desk.

"You are good," Damon said in admiration. "But now it's my turn." He took off down the lawn with the ball, but Mickelle stole it away. She passed it to Jeremy, who lost it to Belle. He stole it back, then passed it to Mickelle again. She made another score.

Damon took off his jacket. "Come on, Daddy," urged Belle. "We have to get at least one score!"

They did, but it was their only one for the entire game. In the last play, Damon and Belle both kicked the ball at the same time and lost it to Jeremy, who made his first goal of the game.

"We won!" the boy shouted with such glee that Damon was glad he and Belle had lost.

Damon fell to the grass with Belle. "We give up!"

Belle laughed and hugged him. "You were good, Daddy, but Mickelle is much better. Maybe she can teach you."

His eyebrows drew together as he remembered abruptly why he was there. He made his voice stern. "I'm still upset with you, young lady."

She gazed up at him earnestly. "I'm sorry, Daddy."

"I don't think you are. This is the second time you've done it. If you had been truly sorry, you wouldn't have done it again."

"But I didn't hide. I just wanted to play with Mickelle again. And Jeremy."

"Then why didn't you ask? Don't you know what it does to me when they call and tell me you're missing? And to Bekka? She was so upset."

Belle's lower lip protruded. "She doesn't care."

"She does care. And if you'd only give her a chance, she'd show you that she does."

"I hate her!"

Damon regarded his daughter silently for a long moment. He noticed that Mickelle and Jeremy had disappeared into the house, allowing them privacy. "Isn't it time we tell each other the truth?" he said. "We both know why you really came over here, don't we?"

Belle hesitated, then nodded once, quickly.

"You know, I was so mad at what you did that I was ready to spank you so hard that you wouldn't be able to sit down for a week!"

"You wouldn't do that!"

"No, but I wanted to. But thanks to Mickelle and Jeremy, I've calmed down. I no longer want to spank you, but I do need to be sure you won't do this again without permission. There has to be a punishment, and it's going to be a hard one."

"What?" she asked in a timorous voice.

"You tell me. What do you think fits the crime?"

"I'm grounded from my friends?" She sounded almost hopeful.

"Nope. Too easy. Besides, you were grounded last weekend, and that didn't work. You need something more."

"I can't go swimming?"

He shook his head. "Try again."

A tear rolled down her cheek as she mumbled, "I can't have the horse I want."

Damon felt his heart constrict. Since they had moved to the big house in Alpine, Belle had been begging to fill the adjoining pasture with a horse. He had purchased the land at the end of the summer and had promised her a horse by Christmas. Of anything she could give up, he knew this meant the most.

And he had so wanted to give it to her!

"Ah, ma Belle." He stroked her hair tenderly. How he wished he could give her another punishment. He had so looked forward to seeing her eyes light up when he showed her the horse, imagined the way she would giggle in delight.

He fought down the desire to refuse her offer, but he knew he had to put an end to her disobedience now—even if it was painful for both of them. He had learned the same lesson with Tanner; it was better to teach a child on a relatively unimportant matter than wait until it was serious and perhaps too late.

"I think that is a fitting punishment—at least for now." More tears slipped from her eyes as he spoke, filling him with compassion. "But not forever, Belle. Once you can show me that you are to be trusted and that you can be obedient, you will regain your privileges." He hugged her. "I know it's a hard thing, but I think you can do it. I *know* you can."

Her arms went around his neck. She felt small in his arms, unprotected, and he was grateful that Mickelle had distracted him from his anger so he could react rationally and with wisdom. This time, he had no regrets about his reaction to her disobedience as he had in the past. There had been no screaming or harsh words that would later plague him until he begged her forgiveness. "I love you, Belle," he whispered.

"I know, Daddy. I just wish I could have my horse."

"You will."

"I'll try real hard."

He smoothed her hair. "Look, Belle, if you really don't want me to go out with Bekka, I won't. But before you tell me that's what you want, you should know that I'm already trying to find you a new nanny—someone you can get along with better."

"Bekka's leaving?" Her eyes were wide, and not nearly as happy as he had expected.

"No. She's going to stay with Jess and Bri, and she's still going to be our friend. But I've been very concerned about how you're getting along with her. You'll see Bekka as often as you want, but meanwhile, I want you to be with someone you can be happy with every day. Wouldn't that be great?"

"How about Mrs. Hansen?" Belle asked, her sadness vanishing. "She doesn't have to go to work, and she likes to play with kids."

"I'm sure she's got enough on her hands."

"But you can ask her. Please, Daddy." She looked at him earnestly, batting her eyelashes a few times as if that would help her cause.

Damon couldn't help a grin. "I'll think about it."

"Thank you, Daddy!" Once more, her arms encircled his neck.

"Come on. I have to get back to work." He climbed to his feet, still carrying Belle. When he bent to get his suit jacket from the grass where he had thrown it, she clung to him like a monkey.

As they rounded the house, Mickelle and Jeremy emerged from the side door. "Care for a drink?" she asked.

Damon was about to say no, but he suddenly felt very parched. Resisting the urge to glance at his watch, he nodded. "Actually, I would. Thank you."

"We have lemonade or root beer," Jeremy announced.

"Root beer, root beer," chanted Belle.

Damon stepped up the two cement stairs and into the kitchen, where Mickelle had already laid out the beverages and four tall glasses on the small eating bar. Seeing that, he was glad he hadn't refused her offer.

"You gotta be careful you don't drop these glasses," Jeremy said to Belle as they seated themselves on the tall stools. "They'll break into about a million pieces."

"Or two million," Belle agreed.

Mickelle smiled at Damon, making him feel warm inside. "Root beer or lemonade?"

"Lemonade."

He and Mickelle had lemonade while the kids drank root beer. Damon was glad for the children's chatter, because he suddenly didn't know what to say to Mickelle. He felt that he was staring at her altogether too much, but she didn't appear to notice.

Then he remembered the Geo Metro. "I've been talking to this car dealer guy I know, and he's got a nice little car I think you might be interested in."

Mickelle looked down at the Formica countertop, her lashes leaving delicate shadows under her eyes. "I don't like my station wagon," she said, "but right now it's all I can afford."

"Well, that's just it. It's a really good price." He almost tripped over his words in his hurry to tell her the great news. "You can get it with the six hundred dollars I'll be paying you."

Her blue eyes met his in surprise. "It can't be much of a car, then. And I don't want to trade one problem car for another. The Snail is old, but at least she's solid."

"But that's why this is so great for you. My friend assures me that it's in good condition. He's only willing to part with it for such a low price because he knows me. It's practically a steal." He continued, describing everything he could remember that Kirk had told him about the Geo Metro, leaving out only the price.

Anger sprang to Mickelle's eyes—not exactly the reaction he had anticipated. "Look," she said coldly, "I didn't fall off the turnip truck yesterday. Brionney and I have been looking at car advertisements this past week, and a car like you describe is an easy two thousand—and that's only if it's nine years old."

"It's not that old."

Sparks seemed to shoot out of her eyes as she continued to glare at him. "My point exactly."

"Oh, yeah." He wanted to look away, but her turbulent eyes held him. "Well, I am buying a Lexus from him."

"Okay, now we're getting to the bottom of this . . . this *steal.*"

"I was going to pay for the rest." Damon tried to be angry, but he couldn't feel anything but admiration for this woman. "I just wanted to help you."

Her expression softened. "I know that. I really do. And I appreciate it." She gave him a slight smile. "Brionney said you were nice, and you are. But I want to pay my own way. I need to."

Damon wanted to insist, but backed off in the face of her quiet dignity. He frowned. "It's a shame. The guy was willing to go as low as two thousand. You might never find something that good."

"Well, I'll have to wait." She grimaced. "At least the Snail will be fixed."

"I know how you could get money for the car," Belle piped up. She had been watching their exchange with interest.

"How?" Jeremy asked quickly.

Belle looked at Mickelle. "You could baby-sit me—and Tanner, too."

Mickelle's eyebrows rose in surprise. "But I thought you had a nanny."

"We're looking for another one," Belle answered. Damon was surprised at how mature she sounded. "Daddy promised me one I would like, and I like you."

Jeremy nodded. "She hates Rebekka." At Mickelle's sharp look, he shrugged and added innocently, "I don't know why."

"And Daddy pays a lot of money."

"I'm sure he does." Mickelle turned to Damon and he held his breath, wondering what she would say. The more he thought about it, the more perfect the solution seemed. She could get the money and the car she needed, and he could have someone he trusted for the children. He wondered why Brionney hadn't thought of it before.

Instead of speaking to him, Mickelle addressed the children. "Why don't you two go outside and play for a few minutes?"

"That means they want to talk," Belle said.

Jeremy rolled his eyes. "Yeah, about us."

Belle touched Mickelle's hand. "Please be my baby-sitter. I'll come over every day and do my homework, and you can teach me to play the piano."

"And Tanner has a Game Shark!" Jeremy added. "I could get my own Mew using that."

"Mew?" Damon asked.

"A Pokémon."

That, of course, explained everything.

When the children had left, Damon refilled his glass of lemonade, though he was no longer thirsty. "Well?"

"You really want me to watch your children?" Mickelle asked. "You don't even know me."

Damon felt that he did. "You're Bri's sister," he said. "I'll get references from her."

She smiled. "Well . . ."

"Of course, if it's not something you want to do . . ."

"Now that you mention it, I had thought about getting a job. I'm going back to school again, though, and I didn't know how I could work and go to school without leaving the children." Her forehead creased. "I don't like being away from them too much."

Damon knew exactly how she felt. "Then you'll consider it?"

"Yes, actually. I think I would like to. But there is one thing."

"What?"

The tip of her tongue slid along her lower lip. "I'm worried about Belle and Rebekka."

"Belle doesn't want to be with her. That's been a big part of the problem."

"So you'll just remove Rebekka from her life? What about finding out why Belle dislikes her so much?"

Damon sighed. Mickelle was perceptive, and he tried to be grateful for her concern over Belle's welfare. He picked up his glass and swirled the ice around in the lemonade. "I know why. At least I think I do."

She said nothing, but her silence urged him to continue.

"She's afraid of losing Bekka. Oh, I know that might not make much sense, but she was very attached to our former nanny, who had been with us since my wife died."

Mickelle leaned back in her chair, nodding. "So she's afraid Rebekka is going to leave, and she didn't want to get too attached. But won't that be a bad thing, taking Rebekka away from her now?"

"I won't, not completely. I thought if I could just give them some space—you know, invite Rebekka over socially. Maybe then Belle would see that Rebekka can be her friend, no matter where she lives."

"It might work," Mickelle said. "Provided that Rebekka agrees. I wouldn't want to kick her out of a job or anything."

Damon laughed. "Oh, no. Bekka wants me to find a replacement. We both agreed from the start that our arrangement was temporary.

In fact, maybe that's why Belle hasn't let her crusade against Bekka die. That must be it; I hadn't thought of it until now. She knew all along that it wasn't permanent."

"The benefit of hindsight," Mickelle murmured. "But are you sure Rebekka wouldn't mind?"

"Not in the least. Bekka is really good at languages, and I've already put her to work at our company. I'll have to be careful that no one steals her out from under me."

"She sounds like a wonderful woman." Mickelle picked up her glass and took a sip of her drink. Damon noticed that she wore a plain gold band on her left ring finger.

"I'm sure you'll have a chance to meet her. She's going to be staying with your sister." For some reason Damon didn't care to identify, he steered clear of mentioning his romantic leanings toward Rebekka. "You know, several people have suggested to me that Tanner watch Belle every day until I get home, and he's usually responsible enough. But I worry about giving him so much responsibility. He needs time to be a child, and Belle needs to be around a woman. Besides, there will be times occasionally when I'll have to go out of town for a day or so, and then they'll need to stay overnight. That's one reason I've always had in-home nannies before. But I think they're old enough that a night or two away from home every now and again might just be a good change."

"Overnight. Hmm." Mickelle considered for a moment longer. "Okay, Damon. You've got yourself a deal."

They worked out the details carefully. Damon would see that Tanner was awake before dropping Belle off at Mickelle's. Then he would call from work to make sure Tanner was leaving for his school bus. "He won't be completely alone," Damon said. "We have a live-in maid who came with us from Alaska."

Belle would walk to school with Jeremy, unless it was too rainy or snowy, and at those times Mickelle would drive them. In the afternoon, Mickelle would pick up Tanner from school in Alpine and bring him back to her house in American Fork. "Only until he gets his license," Damon added.

Mickelle would be home from picking Tanner up in plenty of time to wait for Belle and Jeremy, who would walk home with the neighbor children. Occasionally, Bryan might be home alone for a few minutes after school while she was in Alpine collecting Tanner, but not long enough to make a difference to him. Damon would pick up Belle and Tanner on his way home from work at about six-thirty.

"Of course, if you're going to pick up Tan from school, you're going to need a decent car." Damon smiled as he spoke.

She smirked at him. "Can't have him getting embarrassed, can we? He could ride the bus to your house, and I could pick him up there."

"Or a new car could come with the job."

"A Geo Metro?" There was amusement in her voice.

"Would you mind too much?"

She thought for a moment. "What color is it?"

His mouth opened, but nothing came out. "I don't know," he said. "I forgot to ask. Does it make a difference?"

"Well, lime green looks good on ice cream."

"Oh, I see." He had been so busy trying to be a hero that he had overlooked a few things.

"After we look at it, we can discuss payments," she said.

Damon's protest was drowned out by a blood-curdling scream.

"Belle!" Mickelle was on her feet and running to the door in an instant. Damon was right behind her.

CHAPTER 24

Mickelle found Belle in a heap by the fence, and her heart immediately went out to the child. She was sobbing uncontrollably and gingerly holding her right arm with her left hand. "It hurts, it hurts, it hurts," she cried.

Jeremy hovered around her, his thin face tight with concern. "I told her not to do it, Mom. But she wouldn't listen."

"What did you do?" Damon rushed past Mickelle and gathered his daughter onto his lap.

"Ow, Dad! You're hurting me."

"I'm sorry, but I need to take a look at it."

"No! Don't touch it—please!" Belle's voice ended in a wail as he examined her arm.

"She was on the fence," Jeremy reported. "Walking on it. She's a pretty good balancer."

"Belle," groaned Damon. "You ought to know better than that." But his voice held only regret, not reprimand, for which Mickelle was grateful. In her mind, Belle had already been punished enough.

"It hurts! Oh, Daddy, it hurts so bad!"

"Put your good arm against your stomach," Mickelle said. "And then put this one on top—give it some support. That should make it feel a little better. No, don't push hard. Here, I'll show you. Slowly, now." With much care, Mickelle helped Belle position her arm. The child still cried, but the sobs were no longer so desperate.

"I think you'd better take her to the doctor," she told Damon. "Her arm could be broken. See how it bends here?" She pointed to a spot just above Belle's wrist.

"It could be swelling," Damon said.

"Yes, but from the way she's crying, it sounds serious. Does she cry easily?"

He shook his head. "Think I'd better take her to the emergency room?"

"Actually, a doctor would be better, not to mention cheaper. They'll probably x-ray it and put a temporary cast on, then have her come back when the swelling goes down. They can't cast it if it's too swollen. Who's your doctor?"

"Uh, I don't have a doctor here yet—haven't gotten around to it. We visited one guy before school started, but it was just a checkup, and Bekka took them."

"We can take her to mine. He's wonderful with children."

Damon looked at her gratefully. "I really appreciate it."

Mickelle loved the warm feel of his eyes on hers. She forced herself to look away. "Jeremy, go call Bryan at the Adamsons' and tell him to come home. He'll keep an eye on you until we get back."

"Aw, can't I go? I want to see the x-ray."

Mickelle glanced at Damon. "I don't mind," he said.

"Okay, then at least call him and let him know where we'll be. He knows where we leave the extra key. Hurry! We'll wait for you in the car."

Damon carried Belle to the Lexus. Her cries had now relaxed into whimpers, but each time her arm moved, the whimper was louder. "Don't let me go, Daddy," she said as he carried her toward the car.

"I can drive while you sit with her," Mickelle said, motioning him instead to the blue Mercedes. Watching father and daughter brought a lump to her throat and a tenderness to her chest. She hadn't felt that way about a man since she had watched Riley hold Bryan for the first time.

Without speaking, Damon nodded and moved toward the Mercedes. He waited for her to unlock the door to the backseat, then slid inside with Belle. As Mickelle started the engine, Jeremy flew out of the house.

"Aren't we supposed to call ahead or something?" Damon asked.

Mickelle frowned. "Oh, yeah." There was something about him that made her forget all the details. "Just a minute. I'm sure they'll see us, though. They always leave a few open appointments for emergencies." She hurried into the house and dialed quickly.

In moments, she returned. "They said they'll work us in. At least they know we're coming."

"Maybe they'll have a good video," Jeremy said hopefully. He sat in the back next to Belle, who was on the seat with her head against her father's chest.

Mickelle drove cautiously to her doctor's office, which was situated near the American Fork Hospital. She had the urge to drive faster, but knew they'd only have to wait once they arrived. Besides, she wanted to show Damon how well she had been driving his car.

"Uh, I don't mean any offense," he said tersely, "but could you go a little faster?"

Jeremy leaned forward in his seat as far as the safety restraints would allow. "Yeah, Mom. Grandma drives faster than you!"

Feeling herself color, Mickelle stepped on the gas—a little too hard. Belle moaned from the back. "Sorry," Mickelle apologized.

While they waited at the doctor's office, the kids kept occupied with the latest Disney release, and Damon and Mickelle talked about their children. Belle now seemed remarkably calm, though her face was pinched with pain.

"Oh, I almost forgot to check in at work." Damon pulled out his cell phone. "I need to let them know what's happening, and that I won't be there for a meeting we're having. I can't believe it's after five already."

Finally, a young nurse Mickelle didn't know called Belle's name and led them to a small room. "I'm sorry you've had to wait so long. We seem to have had a rush of accidents today."

"It's okay," Damon murmured.

"You have beautiful children." The nurse helped Belle sit on the examining table.

Mickelle hesitated, then smiled and replied, "Thank you." Feeling Damon's gaze, she shrugged her shoulders. His amber eyes glinted.

Abruptly, Mickelle wanted to weep. If Riley had lived, she could have had a daughter like Belle. This really could have been her family.

But if Riley had lived, he would never have come to the doctor with her. He wouldn't have spared the time, not even on a weekend. He hadn't come with her either of the times Bryan had broken his arm, when Jeremy had stitches, or for their checkups. He always had more important things to do.

From beneath partially closed eyelids, she observed how tenderly Damon held his daughter. *What could be more important than this?*

After asking them a few questions, the nurse left the room. They waited ten more minutes for the doctor, then another fifteen for someone to take the x-rays.

Belle's arm was broken, and as Mickelle had predicted, the doctor gave her a temporary cast and asked them to bring her back on Monday morning.

Jeremy checked out Belle's sling. "Can I try it on after you get your cast?" he asked on the way to the car.

"If you'll carry my books home from school."

"Okay."

"Better be careful," Damon warned. "She'll have you doing her homework."

Belle stuck out her lower lip. "I will not. My homework's too easy. I don't need anyone to do it."

"All the same, you'd better be careful, Jeremy." Damon winked at the boy, who gave him a smile so filled with admiration that Mickelle felt a lump form in her throat.

As they drove back to the house, Belle asked, "Daddy, can I have a shake? Please, Daddy?"

"Me too, Mom!" Jeremy bounced on the seat excitedly, making Mickelle check to be sure he was still using his seat belt.

Damon glanced at his watch. "Do you have time?" he asked.

"If we make it fast." Mickelle wasn't worried about leaving Bryan a while longer, but she did have her date with Officer Lowder that evening.

They stopped at Parker's Drive-In on the corner of State and 500 North for the shakes. Belle decided she wanted a hamburger, too. "I'm hungry," she said. So Damon ended up buying hamburgers, shakes, and fries for everyone, including Bryan. Mickelle didn't know how to tell him she already had a dinner date, so she let him buy her a hamburger, too.

"We'll have to eat them on the way," Damon said. "We're running late."

"For your date?" asked Belle.

Damon cleared his throat. "Yes. Does that bother you?"

Belle's brow furrowed. "I guess not. You can go."

"Well, I'm not sure about leaving you, anyway."

Mickelle wondered if his date was with Rebekka, and she found herself disliking this woman she had never met. "Are you sure you want the kids to eat in the car?" she asked.

He shrugged. "They'll be careful. And it can always be cleaned."

But when they left the drive-in, they noticed that the front passenger side tire was nearly flat. "Oh, no! I must have driven over a nail or something. I'm so sorry!" Mickelle stiffened, wondering at his reaction. Would the muscles in his neck tense with anger as Riley's had always done? Would his face darken, and would mean, disrespectful words erupt from his mouth before he could gain control?

"Don't worry about it. I've got a spare." Damon smiled wryly, and Mickelle felt herself slowly relax. He peeled off his jacket, revealing a torso that was strong but not fleshy. He caught her steady gaze, and she felt herself color. He regarded her silently for a full minute, smiling, and her blush deepened, but she didn't turn away from his stare. She could certainly hold her own against any man.

At last, he opened the trunk. "This shouldn't take too long."

The children sat at an outdoor table to eat while Damon worked on the car. Another half hour elapsed before he succeeded in freeing an obstinate bolt and replacing the tire. Mickelle was amazed that he could do it all without destroying his suit pants and light yellow shirt.

"Sorry it took so long," Damon said.

She smiled. "Couldn't be helped."

"You should have eaten your hamburger with the kids."

"Well, I . . . it's okay."

"You can eat with Bryan," he suggested. Mickelle was touched that he remembered her oldest son's name.

He threw her the keys, but this time she blanched. "You can drive. After all, it's your car."

"Not until I give you back the Snail."

She laughed. "All right. Let's go, kids." She walked to the car and opened the door.

Belle yawned sleepily as she stumbled to the car. Once inside, she removed her shoes and cradled her broken arm against her chest. To Mickelle, she looked like a miniature angel.

"Is something wrong?" Damon asked, following her gaze. "Belle, do you need help with the seat belt?"

"No. Jeremy did it."

Damon looked at Mickelle over the top of the car, a question in his eyes. "What's up?"

Mickelle leaned forward and said softly, so the children wouldn't hear, "Are you sure you want me to watch her? I mean, look what happened . . . her arm."

"Hey, I was there, too. It couldn't have been prevented."

She sighed. "Only by knowing the rules. The children aren't allowed on the fence."

He raised his hands helplessly. "I guess a few accidents will happen until she gets the hang of the rules."

"Nothing so severe as this, I hope," Mickelle said dryly.

"With Belle, one never knows. We just have to take her as she comes."

Mickelle was grateful for his attitude. The man she once thought so hateful and unpleasant was actually a very nice person. More than nice. She wished . . .

Neither spoke, and the tension between them grew thick. What was it exactly? Mickelle didn't have an answer. She only knew that when she looked into his amber eyes, she didn't feel like a widow, but an available woman whose heart had a life of its own. What would it be like to feel his lips against hers?

Damon didn't take his eyes from her face, and Mickelle could hardly breathe. She prayed that her thoughts weren't visible in her eyes. Thankfully, Belle called out, and Damon ducked back inside the car without further comment. Mickelle took a deep breath and slipped into the driver's seat.

"Belle, why are your socks on inside out?" Damon asked as he adjusted the Velcro strap on her sling.

"So they don't hurt, Dad. I *always* put them on that way."

Damon glanced at Mickelle and rolled his eyes. She laughed, and the tension between them vanished. Or perhaps it had existed only in her mind. "I remember those days," she said. "Boy, do I ever."

She drove home slowly, oddly wishing that her time with Damon wouldn't end. "I'll let you know about the car," he said as she pulled up the drive.

"Which car?" she asked with a laugh.

"Oh, that's right. Both cars." There was amusement in his voice. "I'll call you tomorrow."

"All right." That sounded good. Really good.

She shut off the engine, and Jeremy was out of the car in a shot. "I'm going to tell Bryan what happened—if he's home!"

Belle was asleep in the backseat, and Damon had barely lifted her out when Jeremy barreled back outside. "Mom! That cop is inside with Bryan. He's waiting for you!"

Mickelle paled. "Oh, is it seven already?"

"Is something wrong?" Damon looked at her reassuringly. "Maybe I can help."

She didn't want to tell him, though it should make no difference. It wasn't as if they had any sort of relationship—not even remotely. And he had a date for tonight, as well. At least she would not look desperate in front of him.

Lifting her chin firmly, she said, "Thank you, but there's no trouble. He's here for me. We're going out tonight."

"For dinner," Jeremy added.

Damon eyed the bag of burgers in her hand, and Mickelle felt her face redden. What was it about this man that made her feel so sensitive?

"I'll just give these to Bryan. I guess I won't need . . ." Mickelle trailed off, feeling more idiotic by the moment.

"Well, have a good time," Damon said lightly. He smiled at her over the child asleep in his arms, and Mickelle felt her stomach flip-flop as though she were a young girl having her first crush on a member of the opposite sex. "Would you open the door to my car?" he asked. "So I can put Belle inside?"

Mickelle nodded and took the keys from his hand.

There was a noise, and Mickelle glanced up to see Jim Lowder come out on the porch with Bryan. She waved at him. To her relief, he didn't come down to the sidewalk as she opened the door of the Lexus.

Damon paused before placing Belle in the car. "Thanks for sharing your doctor. And for going with us. I enjoyed your company."

"You're welcome. It *was* rather fun for a broken arm." Mickelle didn't know what to say next, but she couldn't keep staring into the amber eyes that almost seemed to see into her soul. She finally managed to focus her gaze on Belle, cuddled in his arms. "Sleeping beauty." She smoothed Belle's hair and gently kissed the child's forehead with all the longing she held in her heart. How she wished she could keep Belle with her! What if she woke in the night and needed someone?

Damon will be there. He's a good father.

She felt his eyes on her and risked looking at him. There was an emotion on his face she couldn't identify. For long seconds, they said nothing. The tension she had felt between them earlier had returned—not an awkward tension, but a delicious one she never wanted to end.

Aware that Jim and the boys were waiting, Mickelle spoke. "I hope she doesn't have too much pain tonight."

"Well, she seems to be all right now." He settled Belle flat on the seat, fastening the seat belt despite her awkward position. "I'll be in touch with you tomorrow about the cars."

Mickelle watched him drive away, feeling oddly deserted. His presence had filled all her senses—filled and entranced them until she almost forgot that only five days earlier she had practically wanted to kill the man.

"Uh, Mickelle, is everything okay? Is this not a good night after all?"

She turned to see Jim Lowder watching her, a puzzled expression on his good-looking face. He wore tan slacks and a matching polo shirt—casual, but not sloppy.

"Oh, no," she said with a smile. "I'm sorry. You see, Belle broke her arm, and—why don't I tell you about it on the way? Just let me give these hamburgers to Bryan and tell my sons good-bye." She'd also take a moment to slip into the bathroom to put on a little lipstick and check her hair. At least her dark-gray pantsuit didn't seem to be out of place.

Mickelle walked with him back to the house, but she could not resist a final glance after the red Lexus. She wondered how Damon's date would go that evening. Did he really like the children's nanny?

Not that it was any of her business.

Silently she sighed, forcing her attention away from Damon Wolfe. She was going to have a good time tonight if it killed her.

* * * * *

Damon drove away from the Hansens' feeling rather deflated. He had known Mickelle had plans for the evening, so why did it bother him that she was going out on a date? And what of it? He himself had a date with Rebekka.

Oh, no! He glanced at the clock on the dash. He was already half an hour late, and he hadn't remembered to call. He'd been so wrapped up in the accident . . . and Mickelle. But how could he leave Belle now, with her arm in this condition? She had said it was all right for him to go out, but he knew it wasn't. The doctor had warned that she would probably be in pain and awaken several times during the night. She would need him to hold and comfort her.

He glanced in the backseat where Belle slept soundly, and realized that he didn't want to leave his daughter. Rebekka wouldn't be happy about his decision, and he could understand that. But he'd try to make her understand the need he felt to be with his injured child.

"I wonder what she sees in him, anyway." When he spoke the words aloud, Damon realized that his mind really hadn't left Mickelle or her policeman date. The man was younger than Mickelle. *Immature,* Damon thought. Of course, her date was still pleasant-looking by any standards. *Baby-faced.* And if Mickelle liked him, the policeman was probably a nice guy. *Saccharine.*

Why can't he stick to dating women his own age?

He thought of Rebekka and himself, seeing the same situation in reverse. But that was different, wasn't it?

Maybe Mickelle and the police officer were just friends.

His cell rang, and Damon tore his thoughts away from Mickelle, hoping it was Rebekka so he could explain. "Hello?"

"Hi, Dad. It's Tanner. Where are you?"

"I'm in the car. I'll be home in a minute."

"Rebekka's in there, playing on the piano. She's steamed. Gosh, Dad, why didn't you get home for your date? Even I know not to keep a lady waiting."

Damon groaned. Rebekka was angry, and justifiably so. He should have called her. "Belle fell off a fence and broke her arm. We were at the doctor's."

"Is Belle all right?"

"Yeah, she's asleep now. But she'll have a cast for about six weeks."

"Well, that's a good excuse, anyway. Maybe Rebekka'll forgive you."

"I hope so."

Damon said good-bye to his son and ended the call, noticing an angry glare from the passenger of a passing car. Yes, he had read the statistics and knew that using a cell phone while driving increased the chance of accidents by four times, and he usually tried to pull to the side of the road. But tonight, there hadn't been time.

He sighed. Sometimes he wished there were more hours in the day. Next week, he would have to work overtime to make up for the time he'd lost today.

But Belle was worth it.

And being with Mickelle had been very enjoyable.

The way she had kissed his daughter came to his mind—gently, caressingly, longingly. At that moment, he had wanted nothing more than to take Mickelle in *his* arms and kiss *her*. Just to take a brief taste of her soft lips. The attraction between them had been like an invisible elastic band, pulling them together, and the intensity of the emotion had shocked him.

If it hadn't been for the cop . . .

Rebekka is very beautiful, he reminded himself. *And smart. She actually likes me. And she has no children, either.*

But he had liked Jeremy very much, and what he had seen of Bryan. And Mickelle obviously got along with Belle. She was beautiful, too—not in the same dramatic way as Rebekka, but in a rather classic sense.

Damon pulled into his driveway, wishing he could drive back to the Hansens'.

The cell rang again.

"Hello?"

"Damon? Hi it's me, Brionney. I'm sorry to call you when I know you're probably on your date with Rebekka—she told me you were going out—but I just had the best idea. Well, actually, I had it a few days ago, but I've been so busy that I kept forgetting to tell you. What about my sister watching your kids? She's intelligent, patient, very nice, and I know she could use a job. What do you think of that?"

"I think," Damon said with a smile, "that it might be the best idea you've had yet."

CHAPTER 25

Rebekka suspected the moment Belle was missing that she and Damon wouldn't be able to keep their date. Even when Damon had called to say that he had found his daughter, she had understood that events would somehow conspire against them.

Though prepared, she became angry when he didn't show up at six-thirty. It wasn't that she was upset with Damon or Belle so much as she was at the situation. The little girl was only trying to protect herself from what she saw as an infringement upon her property, and Damon was simply doing the best he could as a single father.

Understanding didn't make Rebekka feel any better. She was angry at Damon and Belle anyway, and even at Tanner for being so solicitous of her feelings as he waited with her for them to return home.

She was also angry at Samuel for not being around to take up Damon's slack.

And while she was being angry, she was upset at her mother for marrying a nonmember and at her father for being one. If she hadn't seen the great pain in their lives because of their religious differences, she might well have taken Samuel up on his invitation. She still might.

But most of all, she was furious at Marc.

She played out her frustrations on the Steinway. The music boomed throughout the house, an echo of her restlessness. She played every piece of music she could find in the piano bench, and then the ones she knew by heart. Perspiration dotted her brow, and her arms began to ache with the effort. She purposely avoided playing the as yet nameless song she had composed for Marc. In her present mood, she might cry, and that was unthinkable. She was young, healthy, educated, and at least passably good-looking. She had everything going for her. Why couldn't she find happiness?

At last she heard Damon in the hallway, though how she managed it above the waltz she was playing, she couldn't say. Perhaps it was more the movement she had seen from the corner of her eye than an actual sound. Though waltzes were her favorite, she stopped playing and rose to meet him.

Belle was in his arms, looking considerably worse for the wear. There was blood on the edge of her T-shirt and tear stains on her cheeks.

Rebekka's eyes flew to Damon's weary face. "What happened?"

"Didn't Tanner tell you?"

"No. He's in the garage. He came in once, but he must not have wanted to interrupt my playing."

"She was climbing on a fence and fell. Broke her arm."

"Was the break bad?"

He saw her looking at the blood on her shirt. "Fairly. It didn't break through the skin or anything like that—the blood's from the scrape she got on the arm."

"Poor Belle."

The girl opened her eyes groggily at the sound of her name. She moaned softly.

"Does it hurt, Belle?" Damon asked.

She nodded and took a shuddering breath.

"Is there anything I can do for you?" Rebekka asked, already feeling guilty for the anger she had felt toward the child.

"I broke my arm," Belle said mournfully. "It hurt real bad . . . And I'm not getting a horse." There were tears in her eyes.

Damon rocked her. "It'll be okay, Belle. Why don't we give you something for the pain? It might help a little."

"Are you leaving? Is Tanner going to tend me?" Belle's voice wavered slightly as she asked.

"Your daddy's not going anywhere, Belle," Rebekka answered. "No one is. We're going to stay right here." She risked a glance at Damon, who smiled at her gratefully. "Would you like me to do something for you?"

Belle regarded her seriously. Rebekka half expected the little girl to ask her to leave, and was surprised when a request actually came. "I want you to play that song. It's my favorite."

"What song is that?" Rebekka asked almost eagerly.

"The one—I don't know its name. It goes like this—" Belle hummed a few bars, and Rebekka recognized it immediately.

Her heart sank. "Are you sure that's the one, Belle? What about a Primary song?"

"No, that one's the best."

"Okay, then."

"Don't you want your medicine first?" Damon interjected.

"No, the song."

Damon sat with Belle on the couch while Rebekka went to the piano. With a heavy heart, she began to play the song she had written for Marc, wondering how Belle even knew the music well enough to hum the opening bars. As she played, Rebekka found herself caught up in the music, and her anger and frustrations melted away. Perhaps she had been wrong to avoid the music that had come directly from her soul.

"Thank you, Rebekka," Belle said when she was finished.

Damon nodded in agreement. "That was beautiful."

"Thank you for listening," she returned.

"I guess I don't care if you go out with Daddy," Belle said abruptly. "But now that you aren't our baby-sitter, are you still going to come over?"

Rebekka looked at Damon. "You found someone?"

"Yes; Brionney's sister. I think she'll be great."

"Are you sure? Isn't she the one whose husband . . ." Rebekka trailed off as she noted Belle's interested stare.

"You'll have to meet her," Damon interjected. "She's a lot like Brionney."

"She's great!" Belle put in. "And she plays the piano, too."

"Oh. She sounds nice." Rebekka was relieved, or at least mostly relieved. Now she wouldn't feel so guilty at work, knowing that Belle had someone she liked looking after her.

She listened quietly as Damon and Belle talked about Mickelle and her boys. Was that a light she saw in Damon's eyes? She couldn't be sure of the light—or of her feelings if Damon had actually seen something special in the other woman.

"Daddy, my arm's hurting again." Belle touched the top of the temporary cast. "It feels like it's pounding inside."

"Let's get you fixed up and ready for bed," Damon said. "I'll read you a story until you fall asleep." He met Rebekka's gaze. "We'll take another rain check, okay?"

She smiled. "All right."

Rebekka held her smile in place until she was safely in her own room. Then she let it drop and sighed. Her room seemed empty and cold, devoid of the life and memories that had filled her room in France. She had left most of her pictures and other memorabilia there. Today was the first time she had missed any of it.

At the laptop, she checked her e-mail and found nothing of interest. Raoul had written yesterday and so had her mother, but she had hoped Marc would write. The tears that hadn't come during the song gathered in her eyes. *I won't cry for him!* she told herself for what seemed like the millionth time.

Staring at her empty inbox, she knew that for all her running away, she had still hoped that Marc would come after her. But he wasn't coming. Not now, not ever. Too much time had passed. And what if he had come after her? How could she ever be sure that he loved her for herself, and not because she reminded him of her mother? She would have spent a lifetime of being second-best. No; it was better that she never saw Marc again.

The tears came, and this time she let them. Yes, she would cry, but not for Marc. Never for Marc. She would cry for the little girl who had lost her dream. She would cry for the little girl she had been.

When at last the tears had subsided, Rebekka felt curiously free.

* * * * *

On Saturday morning, Marc checked his computer. Rebekka usually answered his e-mail after she received it, and he had written her last night. Although her replies were usually short and unsatisfying, he looked forward to hearing from her more than he would readily admit to anyone.

But she hadn't answered, and the depth of his disappointment shocked him. Why hadn't she written? Was she off dancing again with some nameless suitor?

Another thought came: *Maybe she was offended by something I wrote.* It wouldn't be the first time he'd said something idiotic. But she had always boldly pointed out his missteps, and he had done the same with her. Could it be that she no longer cared even that much?

Quickly, he went to the computer folder where a copy of each of his sent e-mails was automatically filed. There was no recent message to Rebekka.

"But I know I wrote it," he muttered. It hadn't been much, mostly full of trivialities about the people they both knew. He had written it sometime near midnight.

He found it then, in the outbox, waiting to be sent. A sickening feeling grew in his stomach. Rebekka didn't get his letter because he hadn't sent it. So of course she hadn't replied. Angrily, he clicked on the send key. Now he would have to wait hours for her reply. With the time difference, she would still be sleeping.

Marc rubbed his hand through his hair, which was long overdue for a cut. Suddenly, he stopped. What was wrong with him? First he had dreams about Rebekka, and now he was going crazy wanting to hear *anything* at all about her life. They were only friends . . . this was ridiculous! When had all this happened?

His eyes fell on a journal near his monitor, where he had set it the previous night after writing to Rebekka. Since his teen years, he had written in the journal religiously . . . well, at least once a month, although since Rebekka had left, he seemed to be writing more.

He looked at the last line of what he had written the previous evening:

Wonder what Rebekka's doing. If she were home, I'd call her and see.

Nothing odd there. After all, he *had* just been writing to her. Naturally, she would have been on his mind. It wasn't as if he wrote about her all the time.

The week before, he had written:

I remember when Rebekka and I used to go down to the river during lunch breaks.

Rebekka again?

He began thumbing through the pages more rapidly. On every page there was mention of Rebekka—in fact, she was in almost every paragraph. Snatches of text came to him seemingly all at once: *Rebekka would have laughed at this . . . Rebekka used to say . . . loved to listen to her play . . . she could set Raoul straight . . . the way her eyes seem to stare straight into my soul . . . blading was always an adventure with Rebekka . . . hated me calling her a pest, but it was just a joke . . . odd not having her at church . . . that if my kidney was going bad, I'd die and not be able to tell her good-bye . . . I miss her . . . talk me out of this weird mood I'm in . . . her laugh . . . those gorgeous gray eyes . . . probably marry and have a dozen kids . . . she'd make a beautiful bride . . . I miss her . . .*

He stopped reading and put his head in his hands. For all his strange American ways, it appeared that his brother-in-law Zack was right. Even though Marc would never admit it to him or to his wife, Josette, the answer to Marc's malaise was indeed in his journal. His twin sister would laugh him out of the country if she knew.

Knew what? That he cared about Rebekka? That he was completely and utterly obsessed with her?

Josette's laughter would be heard all the way to America.

To America . . . where Rebekka was falling in love with her boss. As she had every right to do. More than anything, he wanted her to be happy.

He snapped his fingers. *That's it!* Maybe it was time he checked this guy out. He had a right, didn't he? As Rebekka's friend.

Friend?

Could she ever possibly see him as anything else?

An idea came swiftly, as though it had been lurking in a far corner of his mind, waiting for the slightest attention. He had a passport and also a visa ready for the engineering convention he and André planned to attend next month in New York. What was to stop him from going earlier? And taking a detour to Utah?

Yes! He would find a plane to America if it was the last thing he did. Marc bolted from his chair and ran to the phone.

CHAPTER 26

Damon spent a rough night with Belle. He read her stories until she fell asleep, then lay near her, listening to her soft breaths. She awoke often, and he held her while she moaned at the throbbing in her arm. The doctor had said she would feel better after the first night, and the arm shouldn't hurt at all once the real cast was on, as the bone would be immobile.

He had a lot of time to think, but instead of solving business problems or contemplating his children, he let his thoughts stray to Mickelle. She was a beautiful woman, and he was very much attracted to her. His admiration for her seemed to increase each time he saw her.

Having lost his own wife, Damon knew how much effort it took to cope with even the smallest everyday things. Sometimes he still felt very much alone. He missed Charlotte terribly, but worse, he found it hard to remember a time when she had not been sick. Their early years together had now faded into a dreamlike quality, and if not for the children, which were proof of their intimacy, he thought he might have only imagined that part of their life.

Mickelle would understand, he thought.

At last he dozed, only to be awakened as daylight came into the room. Belle was still sleeping, less restlessly now, and Damon felt he could leave her.

Despite the lack of sleep, Damon didn't feel tired. He went down to the garage and found Tanner already there, working on Mickelle's station wagon.

"Hi, Dad. I've almost got it done."

Damon surveyed the work. The bent fender had been straightened, sanded, patched with car putty, sanded again, primed, and then spray-painted. While it wasn't a professional job, it looked considerably better than the rest of the car.

"The door was the biggest problem," Tanner said. "You think she'll mind this little folded-over part?" He ran his finger over the place where the edge of the door met the fender. "There was nothing I could do about that without replacing the whole fender. But with the little bend and the new handle, she can open the door just fine. Watch." Tanner demonstrated.

"That's really great!" Damon was impressed. He had supervised Tanner for a few nights, but the boy had done most of the work on his own. "I'm really proud of the way you dug right in and got this done," he said, clapping the boy on his shoulder. "I am very impressed."

"Can we take her for a ride?" Tanner asked. "I'm still a little worried that it'll scrape against the wheel. I mean, I know we drove it up and down the driveway to test it, but that's not the same thing as going around the block."

"All right, let's do it. But I'll have to see if Rebekka's up to watching Belle for a minute."

"She's up. We ate breakfast together. Last I saw, she was heading for her room."

Damon used the intercom to ask Rebekka to listen for Belle. "I'll go peek in on her, too," she offered. Damon smiled at the answer. Despite Belle's aversion to her, Rebekka obviously cared about both of his children. Eventually she might make a good mother—although, after seeing her expertise at the office, he had a hard time imagining her staying at home with children.

Damon and Tanner drove around the block in the old station wagon. The Snail was ugly, but everything seemed to work. Back in the driveway, he helped Tanner wash the car, and that was when he discovered the windshield wipers were in far less than working condition.

"We'd better check the blinkers and the headlights, too," he told Tanner. He expected the boy to protest, to say that he hadn't caused that damage, but Tanner seemed to be happy about making sure the whole car was in good shape.

"Is this like going the extra mile?" Tanner asked.

Damon wished he had brought up the analogy himself. "Exactly."

They found one blinker light burned out, but a quick trip to the auto parts store remedied that. The wipers turned out to be more difficult, as Damon broke the plastic while trying to replace the rubber part and had to return to the store for the complete assembly.

"I don't think you were doing it right," Tanner said.

Damon laughed. "Probably not. I haven't changed my own wiper blades since I was a little older than you are."

With his hands on his hips, Tanner looked over the car. "I guess it's done. We can take it back now."

"We'd better call first." He put his arm around Tanner's shoulder. "There's one thing you need to remember about women, Tan. Always give them plenty of time before you come over."

Tanner's brow furrowed. "Why?"

"They like to be prepared. Something about makeup."

"Oh, that makes sense."

"I'm glad it makes sense to you, because when you're my age, little about women does."

Tanner chuckled uncertainly. "Rebekka seems to like you. Are you going to marry her?"

"Would that bother you?"

Tanner shrugged uncomfortably. "She's not really the mom type. I mean, she's so young. Practically my age."

Damon thought it prudent to change the subject. "What would you think about staying at the Hansens' every day after school? Just until I'm done with work?"

"What about Rebekka?"

"She'll be staying with Jess and Bri, but we'll see her as much as we want. In fact, they live within walking distance of the Hansens. But how do you feel about hanging out there until I get home? I mean, I know you're too old for a baby-sitter, but I don't like the idea of you here all by yourself. And Belle needs some womanly influence instead of being with us all the time, don't you think? She'll feel more comfortable if you're there, too. At least at first. Could you just humor me for a while and hang out there until I get home from work? Once you're driving, you could come down to the office instead, maybe earn some money, if it doesn't interfere with your schoolwork."

Tanner scratched at a dab of dried paint on his arm. "Sure, I won't mind. Mrs. Hansen's a cool lady. She plays soccer better than anyone I know."

"She does, doesn't she?"

"So how will I get there? The bus from my high school doesn't go to American Fork."

"She'll pick you up."

Tanner's face blanched. "In that?" He thumbed at the Snail.

Damon stifled his amusement. "Well, I thought it'd be important for her to have another car—you know, for when this one cuts out on her. So I found her a little Geo Metro."

Relief showed clearly on his son's face. "Good idea, Dad. Thanks. I think you just saved my social life."

"Like I said, it's only until you get your license. I don't know how long that will take. Remember, we have to see the juvenile court judge next week. Maybe when I tell him what you've done here, he'll go more lightly."

Tanner frowned. "I wish it had never happened."

"Yeah . . . but then I wouldn't have found Belle a sitter."

"You really like her, don't you?"

"Who?"

"Mrs. Hansen."

"She's a nice lady."

"Yeah. I think so, too."

* * * * *

Mickelle worked in her garden Saturday morning, noting that the pumpkins were shaping up nicely. Next month they would carve wonderful jack-o'-lanterns and have pumpkin cookies with rich chocolate chips. The memories of past Halloweens were so vivid that she could almost feel the pulp of the pumpkin oozing between her fingers, and the hard feel of the thin seeds.

Of course, Riley wouldn't be there to help carve the pumpkins. But he wouldn't be around to disapprove of their annual seed fight, either.

Mickelle sighed. She missed Riley, the good with the bad. Eventually, they would have worked things out. He might even have learned to enjoy the sticky seed fights in the backyard.

Purposefully, she turned her mind to other topics. Her date with Jim last night had gone well. He had taken her to Wallaby's in Lindon, and they were soon chatting like old friends. He was comfortable to be with, and she had found herself laughing. The only awkward moment was when he had brought her home. She hoped he wouldn't try to kiss her; she wasn't ready for that, though there was a part of her that longed to be kissed and to feel like an attractive woman again. When he didn't try, she was relieved.

We're just friends.

That morning Jim had called, surprising her. "I just wanted to tell you how much I enjoyed being with you last night," he said.

"It was fun."

"I'd like to go out with you again."

"All right," she agreed readily.

"I'm not sure of my schedule next week, but I'll call, okay?"

"Sounds good."

Perhaps there could be more between them than friendship, she mused, tugging at a tender weed. He was at least six years her junior, but that didn't mean anything in this day and age. He was a good listener; in fact, she had probably talked more than she should have, but he seemed genuinely interested in what she had to say. He didn't know the first thing about children, but he could learn. She was almost positive he would never degrade them or her. Jim was also attractive in a boyish sort of way . . . nothing like Damon's strong magnetism. But that direction of thought was dangerous. She had loved a man once with her whole heart, and if she ever decided to have another relationship, she didn't want the love to control her.

Her disturbing thoughts stopped as Jeremy came running from the side of the house. "Mom, Mom! The Snail's back! Belle came too, and Tanner. He's brought his Game Shark! So can I play Game Boy? I finished my chores."

"Even under the bed and inside the closet?" Mickelle straightened and brushed her hands together to remove the dirt.

His face fell. "I'll go check."

"It won't take you more than two minutes. But what about your bed? Did you take the sheets downstairs—and the blanket if it got wet?" She had been trying to make him take responsibility for his nightly accidents, hoping the inconvenience would cure him of wetting the bed, or at least give her some reprieve.

"It's not wet."

"The blanket?"

"None of it." He glanced over his shoulder to be sure no one heard. "I didn't wet."

"That's wonderful, Jeremy! I'm so glad!"

He beamed with pleasure. "So after I check the closet, can I play?"

"Yes."

"Thanks, Mom!" He tore around to the side door just as Damon came into the yard. Mickelle thought he looked particularly handsome in new jeans and a blue T-shirt. His shoulders appeared broader and his face more relaxed.

He smiled. "Good morning."

"I thought you were going to call," she said, feeling frumpy in Riley's huge black T-shirt and her worn gray jeans, cut off at the knees. Her feet were bare and dirty, and she wore no makeup.

"We did. Jeremy said you were outside, and that we should come on over."

"Oh. He didn't tell me."

"I'm sorry." He stood watching her for a full minute without speaking. Mickelle began to feel more uncomfortable. Why was he studying her so carefully? Did she have dirt on her face again? If only he weren't so good-looking!

"Would you like to see the car?" he asked.

"Sure."

They walked to the driveway, and Mickelle studied the Snail. "Looks wonderful." She opened the door. "Nice."

"Tan practically did the whole thing himself." For a moment, Damon was the perfect picture of a proud father. He leaned conspiratorially toward Mickelle. "In fact, I've been a little worried about you getting the new car, because I didn't want Tan to feel he'd done it all for nothing."

"It wasn't for nothing. He learned something, I'll bet. But all the same, I'm in no hurry to get another car. It can wait."

"Oh, but you have to have a new car in order to pick him up," Damon said quickly. To her delight, his face flushed. "I know it might sound rather snobbish, but he is only fifteen, and appearances are important to him. Besides, he's worked really hard to make amends."

"So what do you suggest?" Mickelle was impressed that he cared about his son's feelings enough to analyze them.

"I still want you to get the other car, but I just wanted to know if you'd consider keeping this one for a few months, even if you don't use it much. You don't have to if you feel it's a problem."

"It's no problem. Really." Mickelle slammed the door and bent to examine the fender. "He did a great job."

"Yeah, too bad I can't frame it." They both laughed.

"It's clean, too. He didn't have to wash it."

"We wanted to."

"Thank you." Mickelle stood, blinking away sudden tears. "So when do I go look at the Geo?" She began to walk toward the front porch, keeping her face averted.

Damon followed her. "Well, I'd hoped today, but apparently Kirk's brother is out of town somewhere. How about Monday evening? I know that's normally family night, but we can make it quick."

"Hey, throw in an ice cream and a soccer game, and that *is* family night," Mickelle answered with a laugh, glad that her voice was normal.

Damon laughed with her. "Then we'll go when I come to pick up the kids. I'll see if I can get off early, although we do have an important potential client coming in from New York. I shouldn't be any later than six." His step faltered. "Oh, I forgot I was supposed to take Belle in for her cast."

"I can do it," Mickelle offered.

"But the extra stuff wasn't really part of our . . ."

She faced him. "Am I going to be her sitter or not? There's no reason I can't take her to the doctor for her cast. One thing's certain: she can't go to school until the real cast is on. She could hurt that arm again. And she'll be at my house anyway, right?"

"I hadn't thought of that."

"You could meet us at the doctor's office, if you want. But if you can't get away, she'll be fine. And when you come home, she'll have all sorts of things to tell you."

"Thank you, Mickelle," he said seriously. Then his face cracked into a wide grin. "Looks like my son ran into you just in time."

Mickelle laughed. "Nonsense. Rebekka would have taken her."

"Yeah, but right now she's needed at work even more than I am."

"Then Brionney would have helped you out. There's also the fact that if Tanner hadn't run into me, Belle would never have climbed on my fence."

He shrugged. "Yours, the neighbor's. She'd find a way. Are you sure you don't mind?"

"Not if Belle doesn't."

"I think she'd prefer you to Rebekka."

They climbed the steps and entered the house. All the children were in the kitchen, gathered around Tanner, who held a Game Boy in his hands.

"How are you, Belle?" Mickelle asked.

The girl turned from the game. "My arm hurt all night, but Daddy stayed with me and told me stories."

"How's it feeling now?"

"Better. Except when someone hits it." Her eyes drifted back to the game.

Mickelle glanced at Damon with sympathy. "Tough night, huh?"

"I didn't mind. It actually gave me time to be with her."

Mickelle wished her attitude was more like his. When she had to change Jeremy's bed in the night, as she often did when he awoke wet, she sometimes had many less charitable thoughts.

But last night, there had been no accidents according to Jeremy. She stifled the urge to go into his room and check, just to be sure.

"Well, kids," Damon declared, "we've delivered the car. Hadn't we better get going? Don't you have chores or homework or something?"

"Aw," the children chorused.

Jeremy looked at Damon. "Do you really have an inside pool *and* an outside one?"

"We do."

"Cool. Could we come over and swim?"

"Jeremy," Mickelle warned.

"I know how to swim like a fish," Jeremy went on, ignoring her.

"Daddy doesn't let us swim alone," Belle said. "He has to watch us."

"And Belle can't swim with her arm," Mickelle added. She already knew where this conversation was leading. Perhaps Riley's death had made her more cautious, but there was no way she would let either of her children go swimming without her.

"I don't mind," Belle said. "I can just put my feet in."

Damon looked at Mickelle for a long moment without speaking. Then he said to Bryan and Jeremy, "You know, I'd love to have you boys over to swim sometime, but today I promised to help Rebekka move her things." He placed a hand on Jeremy's shoulder. "How about next week? If your mother says it's all right."

"Well, I . . ." Mickelle hesitated. How could she say no? This man was trusting her with Belle every day. But she couldn't say yes, either. What if he didn't watch them closely enough? What if she lost Bryan or Jeremy?

Again Damon's eyes met Mickelle's, where he seemed to read her unspoken fear. "And your mom could come, too," he said, speaking to Jeremy but still looking at her.

"Cool," Jeremy said. "Mom's a good swimmer." He sighed. "But I wish we could go today."

Damon glanced at his watch. "Well, I do have time for a short game of basketball. Isn't that a hoop you have out there?"

"Yeah, but I don't know how to play. My dad and Bryan played sometimes. Dad was really good." Jeremy suddenly frowned and looked at his hands. "He said I was too little to play."

Mickelle's heart ached at the sadness in Jeremy's voice. Riley had told him that he was too small to play, but only because he didn't want to take the time to teach him. He had played with Bryan because he had learned the rules at school.

"Well, you must have grown up in the past few months," Damon said, "because you look exactly the right size to me. And I may not know much about soccer like your mom, but I do know basketball."

"There's a ball in the shed!" Jeremy was out the door in an instant.

"I'll move the car," Mickelle said.

Not even Pokémon could compete with basketball, and soon the three boys and Damon were playing basketball in the driveway, while Mickelle kept Belle company on the sidelines.

"Do you mind if I take you back to the doctor on Monday?" Mickelle asked her. "While your dad's at work, I mean."

The little girl shrugged. "I don't mind. But can I go to school afterwards? I want everyone to sign my cast."

"Sure. In fact, tonight I'll buy a special pen just for you to take."

"Can I have a whole bunch of colors?"

Mickelle gave her shoulders a squeeze, careful of her arm. "I think I can manage that."

"Cool." Belle echoed Jeremy's favorite word.

She noticed that Belle's hair didn't look as though it had been combed that morning. "Would you like me to put a braid in your hair?" she asked.

"Sure," Belle agreed. "I combed it when Daddy told me to, but it was hard with only one hand."

"Let's go into the house for a moment. I'll bet I can find an elastic."

The boys played a full hour before Damon finally announced that he had to leave. Jeremy ran up to Mickelle, who was back outside with Belle. "Did you see me play, Mom? Did you see me? I'm *not* too little. Damon was right!" He didn't wait for an answer, but ran back to where Bryan was still shooting baskets.

"Rebekka's probably wondering what happened to us," Damon told Mickelle. "We left her at Jess and Bri's hours ago."

"So that's how you got my car here . . . and the Lexus. I was wondering."

"Bekka drove the Lexus here, and I drove your station wagon. Then we took her to your sister's, unloaded some of her boxes, and returned here. I told her I'd pick her up as soon as you saw the car and we talked about Monday night."

"You could use my station wagon if you need more space for moving Rebekka," she volunteered.

"That's okay. Jesse's coming over with his truck."

Mickelle walked Damon to his car, wishing she could ask how his date with Rebekka had gone last night. Did he love her? Why should she even care?

Because I want to take care of Belle, she told herself.

"Thank you," she said quietly when they reached the curb. Tanner and Belle were inside the Lexus, out of earshot. "For playing basketball, I mean."

"You've got two great boys there," he replied.

Mickelle smiled her response. She wanted to tell him how much the game had meant to Jeremy, and probably to Bryan as well. Their grandfather and uncles had tried to make time for them, but she still worried that they would grow up feeling the lack of a father in the home. And now she had agreed to watch Belle, without thinking how having Damon around, even for just a few minutes each day, might benefit her boys. Perhaps the Lord had been responsible for their meeting, however unusual the circumstances. Jeremy especially seemed taken with the man.

She found this impossible to explain without seeming too forward, or appearing as though she expected more than Damon might be willing to give.

Again he seemed to read her thoughts. "Belle needs someone like you," he said. "And I'm glad to play ball with your boys."

A clear exchange. They both had something the other needed, and both were willing to accept the responsibility. She could live with that.

"It'll be good having a girl around," she said with a smile.

"See you Monday morning then, when I drop off Belle." His grin sent a chill down her spine, and a sweet yearning began in her stomach. She nodded and waved as they drove away.

In the driveway, Bryan and Jeremy were still playing basketball. Mickelle stole the ball away from Bryan and sent it into the hoop.

"Wow, Mom, you're good," Jeremy said.

She shrugged. "A lucky shot."

"How come you never played with Dad?" Bryan asked suddenly, his eyebrows drawn.

"We used to play when you were small. But . . ." She trailed off, not wanting to admit that she hadn't enjoyed playing with Riley. "Damon's a pretty nice guy, isn't he?" she said instead.

"He's great!" Jeremy exclaimed.

"He's okay," Bryan admitted. He let the basketball drop onto the cement. "I don't feel like playing anymore."

* * * * *

Later that evening, Mickelle decided to go to Wal-Mart with Jeremy. Bryan refused to accompany them, not understanding why she insisted on driving the Snail instead of the Mercedes. "That's only to pick up Tanner," she explained. "Now that our car is fixed, we need to use that for our business."

"Damon wouldn't mind," Jeremy said.

He probably wouldn't, but Mickelle wasn't willing to face the embarrassment if she ran into him unexpectedly. She wondered if multimillionaires even shopped at Wal-Mart.

Once outside, she saw that dark clouds had blown in, threatening rain. She hated driving in the rain, but she wanted to keep her promise about the colored pens to Belle.

Fortunately, the rain held off. At Wal-Mart, she found a pack of thin colored markers she felt would do the job. She balked a little at the price, but reminded herself that she was now employed. Damon was paying her a monthly salary that amounted to nearly ten dollars an hour for the time she would actually be watching the children. She had felt it was almost too good to be true, and her conscience made her protest the wage, but he had assured her that he had paid much more than that for a full-time nanny. Since she would be on call much of the day, he felt it was only fair that she receive an appropriate wage.

On the way home, it started to rain. Mickelle flipped on the windshield wipers and instinctively leaned forward. To her surprise, the windshield cleared. She leaned back against the seat, marveling at being able to see the road in spite of the rain.

"He changed the wipers," she said.

"Who?"

Mickelle had nearly forgotten that Jeremy was with her. "Damon. He must have changed the wipers. See? They work."

When they drove up to the house, Mickelle didn't turn off the engine, but stared at the wipers swishing back and forth against the window. He had changed them for her! And without her having to ask!

"Mom, aren't we going in?" asked Jeremy. "You're wasting gas."

But Damon had filled the tank, too. Mickelle could barely see past the tears in her eyes. *Too bad I don't have wipers for my eyes.*

She was so touched at Damon's thoughtfulness that her heart swelled with the desire to do something for him. She thought of his broad chest, his striking amber eyes, his kind face. Such a wonderful man! If this incredible feeling came from being cared for by him, how would it feel to be loved by him?

Desperately, she tried to squelch her enthusiasm. There was danger in getting too close to Damon. After all, how well did she really know him? What if his outward show of kindness was a farce, as Riley's had been?

Damon was a powerful man with undeniable magnetism—someone who would demand complete devotion. Once in love with such a man, it wouldn't be easy for Mickelle to maintain the sense of herself that she had regained since Riley's death. Surely her freedom, her self-worth, and her children were more important than having a man around to change the wiper blades. She must not let her emotions carry her away. She simply couldn't put her future into the hands of another man—no matter what.

Of course, that didn't mean they couldn't be friends. Perhaps even good friends. She would do something nice for him, but that was as far as it would go.

She began to smile at her own foolishness. Damon had simply done her a favor. He had no hidden agenda where she was concerned. She was going to watch his children, nothing more. Besides, he was obviously in love with Rebekka.

"Mom, are you okay?" Jeremy asked.

She turned off the car, seeing that the rain had already let up. "Yes, Jeremy. I'm just fine."

CHAPTER 27

Sunday afternoon, Mickelle made pumpkin cookies. The pumpkins from the garden weren't ripe, so she used some she had frozen from last year. She was in a great mood. The day was beautiful and warm, church had been moving, and best of all, Jeremy hadn't wet the bed again. Two days in a row that she hadn't washed his sheets! Until now, she hadn't realized how much his wetting had bothered her, and how much work it had been.

"Why are you making so many cookies?" Jeremy asked.

"We're going to take some to the Wolfes."

Bryan looked up from the table, where he was devouring a sandwich. "Why?"

"Because they're nice people," Mickelle said. "Look at what they did to our car."

"Tanner's the one who bashed into it," Bryan reminded her.

"Yes, but they didn't have to change the wiper blades, fill it with gas, or wash it, did they?"

"And the blinker works, too," Jeremy added.

Bryan frowned. "Well, after the way he treated you . . ."

Mickelle put her hands on her hips. "Bryan, that was all a misunderstanding, and I'm not going to hold it against them forever. Goodness, wouldn't we hate it if our Heavenly Father held our mistakes up to us for the rest of our lives? The Wolfes are nice people, and I'd say it's about time we started reaching out to others. Don't you agree? We are supposed to serve others. That's how we can be happy."

Bryan looked at her, amazed. "Yeah, I guess. We haven't taken cookies to anyone since before Dad . . . can I put in the chocolate chips?"

"Oh, no, we're out!" Jeremy wailed. He knelt on the counter, searching the cupboard. "And it's Sunday. We can't go to the store on Sunday."

"That's okay," Mickelle said. "Your aunt will have some. Why don't you two run on over there while I finish the dough? I'll call and let her know you're coming. We'll need two bags because I'm making a double batch. Tell her we'll bring some over to them, too."

An hour and a half later found them in the Snail, driving to Alpine. Mickelle almost wished it would rain so she could use the wipers again and relive the feelings the discovery had given her.

She didn't feel nervous until she turned into the long driveway leading to the Wolfe place. The immensity of the house seemed to mock her purpose. What was she thinking, bringing homemade cookies to a multimillionaire who certainly could hire someone to make his cookies?

The way the porch wrapped around the circular portion of the house still reminded her of a castle. *Right . . . and Damon's a knight.* She smiled at the thought.

"I get to ring the bell!" Jeremy shouted. He bounded up the porch stairs and pushed the button. The low bongs Mickelle remembered from her previous visit echoed through the house. Her heart thumped loudly and her hands, holding the plate of cookies, grew moist.

The door opened, and one of the most beautiful women Mickelle had ever seen came into view, regarding them with large gray eyes. Her oval face and high cheekbones were framed perfectly by dark auburn hair. Her skin was smooth and unflawed. She was completely and totally feminine, except in the slightly squared jaw that showed a streak of stubbornness.

Rebekka, I'll bet, Mickelle thought, her stomach sinking. This woman was perfect for Damon, and she would obviously resent their visit.

Rebekka wore a close-fitting teal skirt that skimmed the floor and a matching light-weave sweater. She looked elegant and ethereal. Mickelle was grateful she had remained dressed in her black broom-stick dress; it might wash out her face, but it still set off her figure. Even so, she wished she had chosen another color. How long had it been since she had worn anything but black or dark gray? Once the black had seemed to go with the desperate, longing feelings inside, but now the color made her uncomfortable. She was the same black blob she'd been on the night she had met Damon. *Well,* she thought, *at least I'm not wet.*

The gray eyes flicked over Mickelle and then to the boys. "You must be the Hansens." Her voice was soft and velvety, and her French accent so slight as to be almost unnoticeable. She turned back to Mickelle. "You look like your sister."

Mickelle was flattered. She had always thought her sister was beautiful. Did Rebekka see her that way? She finally found her voice. "Are you Rebekka?"

"Yes, I am."

"I thought you moved out," Jeremy said. Normally, Mickelle would have censured him for saying it aloud, but she had wanted to ask the same question herself.

Rebekka gazed at him with amusement. "I did. But I'm still going to the same ward, and after church Damon invited me over for the afternoon." She paused, then added pointedly, "May I help you?"

"We brought some cookies!" Jeremy said, hopping from one foot to the other excitedly.

"Could we speak with Damon?" Mickelle asked.

The gray eyes regarded her coolly. "Sure. I'll go get him. Please, come in."

Mickelle and the boys entered, and Rebekka closed the door behind them before gliding across the entryway. When the other woman had safely disappeared around a corner, Mickelle looked about her. The entryway was nothing short of huge, with shiny wood floors and elaborate moldings. A wide, curving staircase with a carved railing led to an upper floor. They could also see into a beautiful living room that filled the curving turret and looked more like a picture than anything else.

"Did you ever see a piano so big?" Bryan whispered.

Mickelle saw him pointing toward a room that adjoined the exquisite living room. Sure enough, a concert grand piano filled half the room. Surely it was very expensive, and she wondered what it sounded like. Could it actually be a coveted Steinway? Of course, at that size, any brand of piano would be far beyond her budget.

The entryway was open to the high ceiling—at least two full floors, with a beautiful crystal chandelier reflecting the sun from the stained-glass windows above the door. She had seen places like this on television, and was amazed at how open it was. Almost like being outside.

Before she had taken it all in, Damon appeared, wearing dress slacks and a shirt, as though he had been to church and had removed his suit jacket. To her relief, Rebekka was not with him, only Belle, who ran eagerly toward Jeremy and Bryan.

"Come on!" she shouted. "I'll show you our pool."

"No swimming on Sunday," Damon warned.

"'Course not, Daddy. Besides, my arm, remember?" Belle looked at the boys' feet. "Take off your shoes first," she commanded imperiously. "We always take off our shoes in the house. Put them by the door."

Mickelle noticed that Damon wore slippers over his socks, and that beneath her dress, Belle was bare-footed.

The next moment the children were gone, and Mickelle was left alone with Damon, feeling more than awkward. He looked so familiar to her, so handsome, and yet he was basically a stranger.

"What's this?" he asked, pointing to the plate in her hands.

"Last night I went to the store," she began. "It rained. And my wipers worked." Tears threatened to form in her eyes, and she blinked them away impatiently. "So I made you some cookies to say thanks. Pumpkin and chocolate chip."

Just then, Tanner appeared from around the corner. "Dad, the cookies are ready, I think."

Damon flashed Mickelle a smile. "Seems like today is a day for cookies," he said. "Come on."

"Wait . . . my shoes."

"You don't have to take them off. That's only for the kids."

But Mickelle slipped out of her black pumps anyway, and with one foot pushed them beside the door. To her embarrassment, there was a wide hole in her thick black tights, and two of her middle toes stuck out. Only clear fingernail polish around the edges of the hole had prevented it from growing any wider.

She flushed and looked up to see Damon smiling. "Don't worry about it." He shook off his slippers and lifted his left foot for her inspection. On the heel was a large hole. "It happened when I pulled them on this morning, but I was too lazy to change. By the time I got home from church, they were holey and hopeless."

Mickelle grinned at him. "Don't you mean hopelessly holy? They must have listened hard at church."

He laughed, a whole-hearted sound that filled Mickelle with warmth. "You can put your shoes back on if you want," he said.

She refused to be embarrassed. "Hey, what's a little free air conditioning?"

So in her holey tights, Mickelle followed Damon to a spacious kitchen, where he picked up a padded oven mitt and removed a batch of cookies from one of two ovens. Mickelle watched him for a moment, but then was distracted by the size of the kitchen and the adjoining family room. The entire top floor of her house could fit into this space! The numerous cupboards and cabinets were made of carved oak, glistening with fresh lacquer; the floor was a fine blue ceramic tile; the long banquet table and padded chairs looked like something from an expensive showroom; and she had never seen so many counters. The ceiling was so high that she wondered how anyone cleaned the cobwebs. Would cobwebs even be allowed in this mansion?

The family room was equally attractive, with plush blue leather furniture and elegantly carved wooden table accents. Huge curtainless floor-to-ceiling windows let in ample amounts of light and over-looked the outdoor pool, the pool house, and a green lawn carefully sculptured with flower beds and pink dogwood trees. This was a room to be lived in! A room where family could gather. She could almost see her whole extended family here, talking and laughing while the children darted in and out, playing tag.

Mickelle stopped short. What on earth was she thinking? No one in her family besides Brionney would ever see this house. She refocused her attention on the people in the room. Tanner had joined Rebekka at the bar, watching as she poured tall glasses of milk. Mickelle's nervousness returned as she again noticed the beauty and grace of the other woman.

"I guess you've met Bekka," Damon said.

"Yes, we've met."

"Damon likes to use nicknames," Rebekka explained with an engaging smile.

"It's easier." Damon set the hot baking pan on top of the gas stove and began to remove the cookies. "They're chocolate chip," he announced unnecessarily. He raised his voice an octave. "Belle, the cookies are out!"

Within seconds Belle raced into the kitchen, sliding to a stop on the slick tile. "Cookies, cookies! I want the biggest!"

"Would you like some cookies, boys?" Damon asked as he gave Belle a plate with a large cookie on it.

"Daddy makes them with us every Sunday," Belle explained. "They're the best cookies in the whole wide world! But you have to eat them very hot." She took a big, gooey bite and followed it with a swallow of milk.

The boys accepted cookies from Damon, and Rebekka passed them each a glass of milk.

"Sunday's the only day our cook's not working," Damon said. "She doesn't like me messing about in the kitchen when she's here."

"That's an excuse," Tanner informed Mickelle. "He's done this on Sundays even when we don't have a cook."

Damon pretended to ignore his son. "Would you like a cookie?" he asked Mickelle, his amber eyes full of amusement.

Suddenly, the absurdity of the situation overcame Mickelle's nervousness. "I would," she said, seating herself on a barstool. "That is, if you'll taste one of mine. I won't poison you if you won't poison me."

"Agreed!" Damon replied with a laugh. He set a plate with a hot cookie before her, then removed the foil from the plate she had brought. "They're still warm," he said, as though impressed.

Mickelle bit into her chocolate chip cookie and chewed in amazement. "Why, Damon, these *are* great!"

"I told you!" Belle exclaimed. "But I like them the best super hot. When's the next batch coming out, Dad?"

"Patience, Belle," Tanner muttered.

"Would you like some milk?" Rebekka asked Mickelle politely.

Mickelle felt her confidence drain away. Why did she so resent this younger woman? It was certainly none of her business whom

Damon dated. Mickelle was going to be Belle's sitter, after all. Nothing more. She didn't *want* anything more.

Still, she couldn't help noticing with a tiny bit of satisfaction that Belle sat as far away from Rebekka as possible—unlike Tanner, who could barely wrench his gaze from her face.

"Yes, thank you. I'd like some milk." Mickelle waited until Rebekka handed her the glass before looking toward Damon, who was busy devouring his second pumpkin cookie.

"These are wonderful!" he said after swallowing. "You should go into business."

"Well, I like cooking, but not *that* much," Mickelle replied. "Besides, Mrs. Fields has pretty much cornered the cookie market. Although after tasting yours, I think you could give her a run for her money."

Rebekka laughed. "And what do you bet Damon would make a million from it?"

"You just hate me 'cause I'm so good-looking," Damon jested.

"Daddy, I hate it when you say that!" Belle groaned. "Now can I taste some of those pumpkin things before you eat them all?" Damon passed her the plate, and Belle took a tentative bite. "I like them," she announced. "They're much better than Rebekka's cookies. Hers always taste strange."

"Hey, you can't be good at everything," Rebekka said, smiling at Belle.

Belle didn't look at Rebekka, but added, "Mickelle is good at soccer, too."

Rebekka frowned for an instant. "How nice."

"I like Rebekka's cookies," Tanner said. "She can't help it if the French eat a different kind than we're used to."

From bad to worse, thought Mickelle, feeling an unexpected sympathy for Rebekka. "Uh, Tanner, where do you want me to pick you up at school? In the front?"

"Yeah, I'll just wait outside." He looked at her hopefully. "You'll be in Dad's car, right? Until you get your new one, I mean."

She threw Damon an amused glance. "Yes. Although I have to tell you that the Snail is working really well. You must have a great knack with cars. At least with Bugs and Snails."

Everyone laughed, and Tanner's grin grew so wide that it threatened to break his face. "I like cars," he said.

Mickelle pushed the plate of pumpkin cookies toward him. "These are for you, too. A thank-you for doing such a great job."

Tanner bit into a cookie. "Mmm," he murmured.

Rebekka rose from her stool. "Well, as much as I'm going to miss you all, I'd better get going." She looked at Mickelle, as though waiting.

Mickelle read her thoughts as clearly as if she had spoken: Rebekka wanted her to leave. *If he were my boyfriend, I wouldn't want him alone with me either. Or any woman.*

Mickelle stood. "We should be going, too."

"If you'll wait, I'll walk you out," Damon said, peering into the oven.

"I'll show her," Rebekka volunteered.

"At least take some cookies." Damon piled some on two paper plates and handed one to each of them.

Mickelle said good-bye to Tanner and Belle, who were busy eating cookies. Damon walked with them as far as the front door, where they put on their shoes. Rebekka retrieved flat teal sandals from the closet behind the door.

Bryan and Jeremy took the plate of chocolate chip cookies from Mickelle and ran to the Snail. As delicious as they were, Mickelle knew they would eat them all before they arrived home.

"Thank you for the cookies," Damon said.

Mickelle inclined her head, aware of Rebekka's eyes upon her. "And you, too."

"See you tomorrow," Rebekka said in her silky voice. She leaned forward and gave Damon a kiss on the cheek. Mickelle wondered whether that was her French upbringing or a show of proprietorship. Not that it mattered, since Mickelle had no designs on Damon in the first place.

"Dad, the cookies!" Belle's voice came from the kitchen.

Damon hurried away, and Mickelle found herself on the wraparound porch with Rebekka. A few gray clouds had covered the sun, but the air was still warm and inviting.

"Nice meeting you," Mickelle said, starting for the stairs.

"You too." Rebekka hesitated. "Uh, Mrs. Hansen . . ."

"Mickelle."

Rebekka acknowledged the correction with a nod of her head. "Thank you for agreeing to watch Belle. She's a special child, and I love her a lot. But we need a little time apart. What I mean is, sometimes she's a handful, but she seems to really like you. With two boys of your own, I think you'll be good for her."

The sincerity of the other woman was evident, and for the first time, Mickelle saw a little of what Brionney must respect in this French woman. While she didn't want to remain their nanny, Rebekka obviously cared about Belle. About the whole family.

"I'm looking forward to watching Belle," Mickelle answered. "It'll be nice having a little girl around, after having just the boys."

"I thought so, too." Rebekka's velvety voice was barely a whisper, but Mickelle heard.

"About Belle," Mickelle began, almost against her own volition, wanting to help but not knowing if it was her place.

Rebekka's eyes narrowed. "It's okay, I know she doesn't like me. That's one reason Damon is trying a new sitter."

"He's a great father."

"I know that." Rebekka said it somewhat defensively, as though she felt challenged by Mickelle's comment.

"Of course you do." But how could Rebekka really know or appreciate Damon's relationship with his children? She had nothing with which to compare it. At least nothing close to her, if what Brionney had told Mickelle about Rebekka's life held true.

"You're a lucky woman," Mickelle continued, forcing her voice to be light. "I hope things work out between you two." Before she changed her mind, she rushed on. "But what I was trying to say . . . I mean, about Belle. I've been thinking a lot about her relationship with you these past few days. And I may have hit on something that might make a difference." She paused, seeing that Rebekka was listening. "You play the piano, right? Did you know that Belle would like to play?"

The anger that had been growing in Rebekka's expression faded with the last sentence. "Belle?" she asked thoughtfully.

"She told me she listens to you play. She sits on the stairs where she can't be seen."

Rebekka looked at Mickelle, but seemed to see right through her. "The other day when she broke her arm, she asked me to play for her. And sometimes . . . I've felt someone listening."

"She seems to have a knack for playing. I only know a little, and I've showed her some things. She picks out the notes easily. I told Damon that she should have lessons when her arm heals. Maybe you could be the one to give them."

Rebekka's smile was warm. "There's a lot she could learn, even with a broken arm." Her hand briefly touched Mickelle's arm. "Thank you. When Damon told me about you, I was really worried. Brionney said you were great, but I thought . . . a widow, you know, with children . . ."

"You thought I'd want him for myself."

Rebekka flushed, but the color only made her more beautiful. "I don't know what I thought. Please forgive me."

Mickelle smiled. "Don't give it a second thought." She glanced toward the Snail. "Well, good-bye."

"Good-bye," Rebekka repeated.

Mickelle watched Rebekka duck inside her car, then walked to her gold station wagon, where the boys were eating heartily.

"These are really good, Mom," Jeremy said. "Aren't they, Bryan?"

"They're all right." While the reply wasn't enthusiastic, Mickelle noticed that Bryan ate as many cookies as Jeremy.

Mickelle drove home, thinking of her conversation with Rebekka and feeling melancholy. Damon was a good father. And if he weren't so rich and involved with Rebekka, and if she weren't still grieving for Riley, maybe . . .

A light rain began. Smiling, Mickelle turned on her new wipers.

CHAPTER 28

Early Monday morning, Marc gave his mother a hug at the airport in Paris. André watched them with a slight smirk on his face. Marc ignored him.

"Try not to be gone long," Ariana said. "Remember that Louis-Géralde gets home next week. He'll only be here two weeks before he's off again. You'll want to see him before he goes."

Marc was glad his mother had reminded him. Thoughts of Rebekka had blotted out all else. Louis-Géralde was returning from serving a year in the French army, and shortly thereafter would be leaving on his mission. "Mom, I'll be back in time. I just need a little vacation. It'll be good seeing Brionney again after all this time. And a few of my old missionary companions."

"And Rebekka," Ariana said. A smile graced her lips, but Marc pretended not to notice. He hadn't told them he was going to see Rebekka, couldn't bring himself to admit aloud how much he missed her, and how he had tortured himself for the past forty-eight hours since his decision to go to America. Tortured himself by imagining her in the arms of her employer. What would she say if she knew how he felt about her? And how *did* he feel, anyway? He didn't dwell on that aspect. It would be too painful to admit his feelings if she didn't return them.

André slapped him on the back. "Have fun."

"You can take care of the company all right, can't you?"

André grinned and shook his head in mock disgust. "Been doing it since May anyway." His brown eyes gleamed.

"What?"

"Never mind. I'll keep Perrault and Massoni Engineering and Architecture running. Take as long as you need."

"Thank you." Marc shouldered his flight bag. He had already checked the rest of his luggage, and now needed to continue through the international gate checkpoint alone.

Ariana's gentle touch on his arm stopped him. She looked into his eyes. "Marc, you're a very smart man. You've obtained an education, you and André have started a successful architecture and engineering firm, and you've made me and your father proud by the way you've lived your life." Her hand moved to his chest. "But now I want you to listen to your heart. Sometimes—just sometimes—the mind can be too logical."

She kissed him twice on each cheek and gave him another hug before walking away, followed by André. Marc stared after them for a long moment, pondering the meaning of her words.

The flight to America was tedious. Marc spent half the time angry at Rebekka and the other half wondering what he was doing. He hadn't told anyone in America that he was coming, and unlike his twin Josette, who was fluent in both English and Portuguese, French was the only language he felt comfortable using. How was he going to find a place to sleep? He had learned a lot of English in school and from the missionaries, but it was quite another thing to put his few words to a real test like this. He began to have misgivings about his brash decision. Should he have called Rebekka first?

She might have said no.

It's a free country, he countered, *or so they're always saying. I can visit if I please.*

And what if Rebekka was happy with the life she had chosen? He would not interfere with that—no, her happiness came before his crazy emotions. If she was happy with her choice, he would return to France alone.

Alone.

He knew that leaving her would be the hardest thing he had ever done.

CHAPTER 29

Mickelle enjoyed her time with Belle as they waited to leave for her doctor's appointment. They read together, practiced notes on the piano, and talked about the roses in the curio cabinet. Mickelle was amazed at the little girl's vocabulary and the extent of her knowledge. She never stopped talking and asking questions, which sometimes Mickelle couldn't answer.

When it was time to drive to the doctor's office, Mickelle was actually relieved. Obviously, she would have to get a few project books from the library to keep Belle occupied after school. And while she was at it, she would include some reading books on unusual subjects, as Belle's mind seemed to hunger for knowledge far above her typical age level.

"Daddy says he might come if he has time," Belle said as they exited the Mercedes. "But he said he might not make it. Can we call him if he doesn't come?" She turned a hopeful face toward Mickelle.

"I have an idea you might like." Mickelle held the glass door open for Belle. "After we're finished, we can stop by his office. That way, he can be the first to sign your cast."

"But I don't have a marker."

Mickelle pulled a small package out of her purse. "Yes, you do."

Belle hugged her. "You're the best, you know? You have great ideas."

In less than an hour, they were on their way to Orem to see Damon. Belle had chosen a pink cast that went from the base of her fingers to an inch past her elbow.

"So how do you like it?" Mickelle asked.

"It's nice." She frowned and added, "But my arm hurts some."

"That's because they moved it around when they put the cast on. It should feel better again by tomorrow."

"Good, because I don't think I can go to school with it hurting so much."

"Don't worry. Let's give it a few hours while we see your dad and eat lunch. Then if you don't feel better, maybe we can stop by the school and get your homework and take it home."

Belle's face brightened. "Could we really? And can I show them my cast?"

"Sure. But that's only if it's still hurting, okay? Otherwise, you can stay with your class." Mickelle felt a little odd as she made the promise. After all, whether Belle went to school or not that day was really up to Damon. *But if she's in pain, there's no use sending her.*

As they drove into the parking lot, Mickelle's stomach began to churn. She told herself they were here so Belle could see Damon, but a part of her wondered if they couldn't have waited. Who really wanted to see him more—Belle or Mickelle?

A young, dark-haired receptionist with pale brown eyes was in the small lobby behind a modest desk. "May I help you?" she greeted them. Then she noticed Belle. "Oh, Belle, it's you."

"Hi, Juliet."

"Hey, you got your cast. Your dad told me you broke your arm. Can I sign it?"

"Yes, but only after Daddy does. That's why we're here. Mickelle says it's probably dry enough now. Can we see Daddy, or is he in a meeting?"

"Actually, I think he just got out. Let me check." Juliet's gaze flickered over Mickelle. "I can tell you're Brionney's sister," she said. "You look a lot like her. Of course, you're thinner and your hair's a darker blonde, but your eyes are big and beautiful, just like hers. I always envied her eyes." Juliet stood as she talked. "I'll just be a moment. Have a seat while I get Damon. My phone system's on the blink this morning. Only the outside lines seem to be working."

In a breath, she was gone. Belle wandered to a couch against the wall. "I like Juliet," she commented. "She's going to get married soon, I think."

Mickelle had no sooner sat on the couch than Damon appeared. "Hi," he said brightly.

Belle jumped off the couch. "Finally!"

"How'd it go?"

Mickelle had the feeling that his cheerfulness covered underlying worry. "Everything's fine," she assured him. "Well, Belle is having a little pain in her arm, but we're here because you get to be the first to sign the cast."

The creases in Damon's forehead eased. He knelt down to look Belle in the eye. "What an honor! I'd love to be the first to sign your cast, ma Belle."

The little girl held out her package of marking pens. "You can pick whatever color you like." She hesitated before adding, "The blue is my favorite."

"Then I'll use that one." Damon scrawled his name boldly on the pink fiberglass. "There, that ought to do it." He put his arms around Belle. "Now, what's this about your arm hurting?"

"Mickelle says it's because they moved it around so much. But she says if I don't feel good, we can just go get my homework. Isn't that neat, Daddy? I can still show my cast, but I won't have to go to school."

"It sounds like Mickelle knows what she's doing," Damon said. Mickelle was relieved that he agreed with her decision. "Thank you for coming." He smiled, and her knees felt suddenly weak.

I came for Belle, she thought, but her heart belied the words.

"That red looks nice on you," he said.

Mickelle had worn blue jeans and a crimson thermal shirt that had matched her happy mood this morning. She wondered if Damon noticed that it was the first time he had ever seen her in anything but black or gray.

Without warning, Rebekka appeared in the lobby. "Hello, everybody. Juliet told me you were all here."

"I got my cast." Belle held up her arm. "See?"

Rebekka approached to take a closer look. She looked both professional and beautiful in her dark green suit jacket and skirt. Next to the auburn-haired beauty, Mickelle felt grubby.

Rebekka sat down on the couch, near where Belle was standing. "Cool color. Hot pink. I like it. So does your arm ache?"

"A little," Belle confessed. "And if it doesn't stop, I might not go to school."

"Well, I think they might survive one day without you," Rebekka answered. "And you're certainly ahead on your assignments, anyway."

Belle shrugged. "It's baby stuff."

"How would you like to learn something really cool?" Rebekka asked, as though she had been waiting for the opening.

"What?" Belle's voice was cautious.

Rebekka's eyes briefly met Mickelle's. "Mrs. Hansen and I've been talking, and she seems to think that you have quite a talent for the piano. So today I talked with your dad, and we thought that if you agreed, I could come over to the house a couple of times a week and we could learn a few songs together. Would you like that?"

Belle's eyes had grown continuously wider as Rebekka had spoken. "Oh, yes! Yes! I want to a lot! Thanks, Rebekka!" Belle hugged her, wrapping her good arm around Rebekka's neck. "I'm so excited. I'm going to learn to play just like you!"

Rebekka cast Mickelle a grateful glance. "Well, it might take some time, but I believe you really will."

Belle smiled. "Do you want to be the second person to sign my cast?"

"I certainly do." Rebekka signed with a green marker as Mickelle watched with more than a little envy.

"You know," Belle said quietly, "I've been thinking a lot, and it's okay with me if you and dad . . . you know, go out together."

Rebekka glanced at Damon, flushing prettily. Damon didn't meet her gaze, but was watching Belle, a pleased grin on his face. Mickelle felt her own smile fade as confusion entered her heart. She had wanted Belle to like Rebekka, if only for her own sake. Then why did she feel so glum now that it seemed Belle was at last accepting Rebekka?

"Well, we'd better be getting Belle some lunch," Mickelle said into the awkward silence.

"And then we're going to the school," Belle added.

Before they could take a step toward the door, the receptionist reappeared in the lobby, bringing with her Jesse Hergarter, another woman, and several other men. "We came to sign the cast," Jesse said as they converged around Belle.

"Wait!" The little girl turned to Mickelle. "I want you to sign it next. Will you?"

Mickelle felt decidedly better at Belle's plea. "I certainly will." With a red marker, she signed her name and drew a small heart.

"You can draw hearts good," Belle said, examining it. Then she held out her arm to the crowd. "Okay, sign it. But not too big, so the kids at school will have some room."

Mickelle felt eyes on her, and glanced up to see Damon looking her way. He smiled and sidled closer. "Thank you for bringing her. It meant a lot to me."

"You're welcome."

"Are we still on for tonight?"

"I take it that means the guy with the car is back in town?"

"Yes. He'll be waiting with your car at the same lot as the guy with my Lexus."

She shook her head. "What are you going to do with all those cars?"

"I don't know, actually." Damon grimaced. "Maybe I'll sell the Mercedes."

"I used it to take Belle to the doctor. I hope you don't mind."

"I want you to. I'm not sure how safe your Snail is."

She smiled. "At the pace it can manage, it's pretty safe." He laughed with her, and Mickelle felt good. She looked again toward Belle, and found Rebekka watching them with her liquid gray eyes.

Mickelle stepped purposely away from Damon, hoping to reassure Rebekka. As likeable as Damon was, she would not stand in the other woman's way.

* * * * *

Rebekka's mood alternated between exhilaration and frustration. She had spent an enjoyable day with Damon and the children on Sunday—at least until Mickelle Hansen had shown up. She couldn't feel angry at the woman, though, because she had shown the way to Belle's heart.

Truth was, Rebekka liked what she had seen of Mickelle. What she didn't like was the way Damon seemed to watch her every move, as he did now while Jesse and the others signed Belle's cast. Could Damon be falling in love with Mickelle? Or were they simply friends, bonded by the fact that both had lost spouses and were raising their children alone?

Rebekka left the group in the foyer, not knowing where she fit in. She enjoyed being with Damon, and the enticing memories of their one kiss hinted that they could be compatible physically. And yet, if she did marry him, would he expect her to stay at home and be a mother to his children? She had thought that was what she wanted, but now she was not so sure. She loved her job and the way it made her feel needed.

I could work part-time. Or he could. We would find a way. She suspected that once she had her own baby, her feelings might change completely. Brionney was content with her role as a mother. Apparently so was her sister, Mickelle Hansen, and both women struck her as being very intelligent. They were also very good with children, and Belle certainly enjoyed their company—especially Mickelle's.

Belle asked me to sign her cast before Mickelle. Rebekka felt petty even as the thought came. She wanted Belle's happiness more than she craved the child's approval.

The phone rang as she approached her work station, situated in one of the small cubicles portioned off from the rest of the conference room. The cubicles, erected during Samuel's second visit, had stayed for the new employees that were being hired. Soon Hospital's Choice would need to move to a larger building.

Rebekka grabbed the receiver. "Hello?" she knew her voice was grumpy, but she didn't care.

"Hello, Rebekka with two Ks. Did I call at a bad time?"

"Samuel." The pleasure at hearing his voice blocked out all her former frustration. "It's good to hear from you. What's up?"

"Nothing. Absolutely nothing. I mean, our part over here is doing well—although it would go better if you were here—and I really don't have any reason to call except that . . . you've been on my mind. I miss you."

She could hear the sincerity and the longing in his voice. At this moment, she could imagine his green eyes half closed, watching, waiting hopefully for her reaction.

"I miss you, too." She did, more than she cared to admit.

"So, have you given any thought to my offer?"

She hesitated. "Yes. It's very tempting. But I still don't know yet." She made her voice light. "Hey, I told you I'd tell you this week. I didn't say which day."

"If I call you every day, do you think it'll help?"

"It might." Just hearing his voice made her happy.

"Well, then, I will do just that. And I also promise that if you come, I won't make you eat five-way chili—at least not every day."

She laughed. "That's a load off my mind." She was rewarded for the comment by his warm chuckle. It did strange things to her heart.

They talked for a few moments more about inconsequential matters, and when Rebekka hung up the phone, she was smiling.

* * * * *

Mickelle glanced down at her casual dress that flowed to her sandaled feet. She knew the blue color matched her eyes, and hoped Damon would notice it as he had the red shirt earlier. He would be here any moment now.

Something on her leg caught her eye and Mickelle looked closer, appalled to see that she hadn't remembered to shave her legs for at least a month, probably more. In the long dress no one should notice, but what if someone—okay, Damon—did? Maybe he already had.

Quickly, Mickelle retrieved her razor and a can of shaving cream from the windowsill in the bathroom. Sitting on the edge of the tub, she turned on the water. A second later, she was soaked.

"Rats!" She had forgotten to check to see if the lever that made the water go to the showerhead was up. Bryan always left it that way. Now her hair was wet, and all the curl from the steam rollers gone!

She groaned and towel-dried her head quickly. Her hair wasn't as wet as she had feared, though she'd have to blow it dry. And what about her legs? Leaving her hair, she returned to the tub and, carefully pooling the skirt of her dress in her lap, she wet her legs from the knees down and lathered them. She began shaving, one long stroke after the next as the scent of the lime shaving cream blended with the steamy water.

At once she was transported back in time. Riley was shaving, and she watched him in the doorway, breathing in the smell of the shaving cream and watching him squint into the steam-covered mirror. Riley looked up and saw her. Throwing his razor into the sink, he wiped off the last of the cream and came toward her. He took her in his arms, kissed her . . .

Tears sprang to Mickelle's eyes, but they weren't tears of pain or anger, but of tenderness. And oh, how she needed those memories to remind her that her relationship with Riley hadn't been so terrible! There had been many moments when they had honestly loved each other. Though Mickelle had been too consumed by bitterness these last few months to admit it, Brionney had been right after all—parts of her marriage were well worth repeating.

She finished the last strokes and rinsed her legs. In the drawer, she found a tube of lotion and rubbed it into her skin. Now to fix the hair before Damon arrived. As if reading her thoughts, Belle and Jeremy, who had been waiting on the front porch, came inside. "Mom! He's here!"

Mickelle groaned at the sight of her wet hair. She raked through it with her fingers, trying to maintain a few of the curls that had survived underneath. Finally, throwing herself a disgusted look in the mirror, she left the bathroom and went to the door. Damon was just entering the house.

"Did you take a shower, Mom?" Jeremy asked, a puzzled expression on his face.

Mickelle glanced at Damon, then away. "No, I just had an accident with the water. Now, why don't you kids go out in the backyard and let Bryan and Tanner know we're leaving? They're playing soccer."

"But I'm hungry, Mom," Jeremy complained. "We didn't have dinner yet." He looked hopefully at Damon. "After we see the car, could we go and get hamburgers again . . . and ice cream? And could we play basketball again? Please?" He said the words calmly, but Mickelle recognized the need in his eyes. It cut into her deeply. She had to remember to take him more often to see her father.

"I bought ice cream already," she said. "Belle and I did before we took her to school."

Belle tugged on her father. "We got chocolate. Then I went to school the rest of the day, and my arm didn't even hurt one bit."

Damon looked properly impressed. He put a hand on Jeremy's shoulder. "We'd better watch out when she gets that cast off. She'll beat both of us at basketball. So we should probably practice a bit tonight, if your mom doesn't mind. I've got a spare T-shirt in my car."

"Yay!" Jeremy shouted. Without waiting for Mickelle's response, he ran into the kitchen, heading for the side door. Belle went with him.

Mickelle blinked away the sudden moisture in her eyes. "You shouldn't encourage him," she said, keeping her voice light. "He'll make you play every day."

"And what's so wrong with that?" Damon laughed. "I work ten to twelve hours a day, with little exercise. Jeremy just might save me from a heart attack."

"He hasn't wet his bed since last Friday."

Damon looked confused.

Mickelle explained. "He's been doing it since Riley . . . since his dad died. And now he's stopped." She snapped her fingers. "Just like that. I think it's because of you."

"That's good, isn't it?" His words were sincere.

"Yes." More tears threatened, and Mickelle walked into the kitchen and pretended to look out the window. Why had she felt the need to confide in him?

Damon followed her. "Hey, I brought you something."

Before facing him, she ran her fingertips rapidly under her eyes to make sure they were dry. "What's this?" she asked, taking a small package wrapped in white tissue.

"Oh, just something I picked up at Mervyn's. I went to the mall to grab a quick bite for lunch."

Mickelle could think of many faster and quieter places to eat, but she was too curious to ask further questions. She tore off the tissue to reveal a dark pair of thick wool socks. "You bought me a pair of socks?" she asked incredulously.

He shrugged. "Well, winter's coming, and I didn't think you'd need the free air conditioning anymore. I would have gotten some of those long things, but there were just too many kinds and sizes. I don't know how women find what they need."

The picture of Damon shopping for women's socks was just too much to bear, and she began to laugh. "Thank you," she sputtered through her mirth.

"You're welcome." He grinned with her, and she caught sight of his gold tooth, glinting like his amber eyes. "It's good to hear you laugh."

How easy it would be to fall in love with him!

Neither spoke for a long moment, though Mickelle's thoughts raced wildly with no sense of purpose. She could never remember feeling so vitally alive.

"What are you thinking?" he asked softly.

In confusion, she put her hand to her damp hair. "Do you mind if I take a moment . . . I don't know why, but you always seem to come when I'm working in the garden or playing soccer or . . ."

"Having accidents with water," he suggested helpfully.

"Yes." She couldn't tear her eyes from his.

"I'll round up the kids and put them in the car. Take your time." He started for the kitchen door.

"Uh, Damon . . ."

"Yes?"

She held up the socks. "I love them. Thank you."

He grinned and went out the door.

Mickelle hurried to the bathroom and dried her hair, using a round brush to form a few loose curls. "Not too bad," she said, surveying the repairs. She added a touch of lipstick.

Jeremy and Belle had to share a seat belt on the way, but neither minded the arrangement. With Tanner and Bryan leading the conversation in the backseat, the children more than filled the car with sound. Mickelle was comfortable to sit in silence.

The Geo Metro at the dealer's was exactly what Mickelle needed. "The blue matches your eyes, Kelle," Damon said. "Like your dress."

"It's *Mi*ckelle, Dad," Belle said.

"But Kelle sounds good, don't you think?" he asked. "Kind of like Belle."

Belle began to smile. "Kelle, Belle." She looked up at Mickelle. "I like it, don't you?"

Mickelle nodded. "Yes, I do." In fact, she was very touched that Damon had given her a nickname as he had everyone else close to him.

Tanner rolled his eyes. "He's always doing that. I'm going to go through my life as something everyone else is trying to do to their skin." That provoked more laughter, even from Bryan, who had been unusually silent since they had arrived at the lot.

An hour later, Mickelle and Damon both left the lot in their respective cars. "Are they coming over for ice cream?" Jeremy asked, watching the Wolfes drive away in their new dark-green Lexus.

"I don't know." Mickelle had been so caught up in buying the new car that she had forgotten to confirm anything.

"He said he'd play basketball with me," Jeremy said.

"Well, maybe he forgot." Bryan's face was grim. "Or maybe he's too tired."

Mickelle's heart ached for her children. How could she have allowed this to happen? If Damon didn't appear, maybe she would dispense with a proper bedtime and take them to her parents' house to see her dad. On the way they could grab a hamburger, if she could scrape together enough money.

Mickelle drove straight home, and once there began to stack the dried plates and cups in the cupboard. Not for the first time, she wished for a dishwasher where she could leave the dishes out of sight until she needed to reload.

The boys were outside with the basketball, just in case, but Damon and his children didn't appear. She was reaching for the phone to call her parents when she heard a shout from outside. The kitchen door burst open and the boys, followed by Belle, Damon, and Tanner, filed inside.

"They got us hamburgers," Jeremy said, his thin face beaming. "That's why they took so long."

"We got ice cream, too," Belle announced. "Shakes. With chocolate cookies in them."

Mickelle was almost speechless, but the tight feeling that gripped her heart began to relax. She looked at Damon gratefully.

"I hope you don't mind," he said. "I know you already had ice cream. But a hamburger just isn't as good without an Oreo shake."

"Hey, fewer plates to wash." Mickelle smiled at him, and a tingly feeling spread throughout her body. "So do I get one of those shakes?"

After a blessing, the children devoured the food and ran outside to play basketball. Mickelle and a newly T-shirted Damon soon joined them. Mickelle noticed that Bryan's resentment had seemed to fade, and she was grateful that Damon had remembered his promise. Her sons had already experienced enough disappointment in their short lives.

Darkness crept over them before she realized how much time had passed. Damon glanced at his watch. "Okay kids, in the car. We have to go."

"What about your other car?" asked Bryan.

Damon frowned in the direction of the Mercedes. "I'll have to get that another day."

"I can drive it to your house sometime," Mickelle offered. "It's only fair, since I've been using it. Although that means you'd have to bring me back."

"I don't mind. When do you want to do it?"

Mickelle laughed. "How about right now? It's kind of looking like a used car lot around here."

"Can we go too?" Jeremy asked.

"No," Mickelle decided. "You guys get ready for bed. When I get home, we'll have prayer." She propelled him gently to the door. "Get going now. Bryan, you're in charge."

Mickelle followed Damon to his house, regretting the loss of the Mercedes. She would miss driving it. The leather interior and smell reminded her of Damon—comforting and exciting at the same time. While the new Geo was nice, it didn't give her anywhere near the same feeling.

In Alpine, Damon sent his children to get ready for bed, promising to return quickly. Belle hugged Mickelle good-bye. "This was the best family night ever," she whispered before obeying her father's request.

Damon opened the passenger door of the new Lexus and helped Mickelle inside. They drove silently through the sleeping town until they arrived at her house. Damon killed the engine, then went around to open her door. "I hope the boys aren't watching TV," she mused as they strolled up the cement walk.

He laughed. "Or playing Game Boy."

Mickelle's hand went to the door, but she didn't open it. "Thank you for tonight, Damon," she said softly. "I appreciate it." She took a deep breath and plunged on. "I want you to know that we won't keep you every night when you come to pick up the kids." She gave a short laugh, silently wishing she could do just that. They had almost seemed like a real family.

"Kelle, I—" He broke off, as though unsure of what he would say. He stepped closer, and she could smell the musky scent of his cologne.

Though she was tall, he was taller still, and she felt odd looking up into his face when it was so close. Her breath came more rapidly, and her heart threatened to jump out of her chest. Her face flushed, and her vision blurred until she could barely make out his face.

I'm having a panic attack, she thought desperately. *I thought I was through with those!*

His arms slipped round her as he pressed his lips against hers, achingly tender at first and then with more intensity. She realized then that her reaction wasn't a panic attack at all, but a response to Damon's nearness. Closing her eyes, she kissed him back, admitting to herself that she had been waiting for this moment for days. He murmured her name. She could feel his moustache as his mouth glided from her lips to her cheek and down to her throat. Then he kissed every inch of skin back up to her lips, leaving a trail that set fire to her heart. She sighed, wanting nothing more than to surrender herself to the bliss of the moment, his touch, the feeling of family they had shared this evening.

"Kelle," he murmured, the name a hot whisper against her cheek. She could taste the salt on his skin, smell the maleness of him. "You are so beautiful tonight. That blue dress . . . It's better than all that black."

"Damon," she whispered, but the name came out with difficulty as she recalled her intimate moments with Riley.

What on earth was she doing? She knew better than to toy with such fire. She pulled abruptly away.

He kept his arms loosely about her, gazing into her eyes with a forcefulness that frightened her. "Kelle, I think I'm falling in love with you." His voice was hoarse with emotion. "I think I've been falling in love with you ever since I saw you on my porch, soaked to the skin, glaring at me like you wanted to kill me."

"Damon, I . . ." She wanted to say how much she enjoyed being with him, how she had longed for his kiss, how she suspected that she was also falling in love with him. But she couldn't do it. Something inside her rebelled at giving her heart away again. After all, how well did she really know him after only a week? She thought she had known Riley.

"What about Rebekka?" she managed.

Damon sighed. "I think that as hard as we try, Bekka and I will only be friends. Don't you think that after living under the same roof for five months, we should have progressed past the first date? Belle had a lot to do with the delay, certainly; but if we had truly been meant for each other, we would have made time to be together. At work, for instance." He cupped her chin with his hand, softly stroking her skin with his thumb. "Bekka is a beautiful and intelligent person, but you are the woman I've dreamed of meeting."

"Damon," she protested, pulling her face away from his touch. "I—I'm not ready for this. Please, let me go."

He dropped his hands immediately. "I don't understand. When I kissed you . . ." He bent his head as though to kiss her again, but Mickelle backed up against the door, fighting both panic and the contradictory urge to fall into his arms. She pushed her fists against his chest.

He stepped back, raising his hands in surrender. "All right. Don't worry. I won't force you. I'm sorry if I upset you."

His face was so defenseless that Mickelle wanted to throw herself against him, to hold him like he wanted to hold her. Instead, she stared at the cement porch beneath their feet. "My husband . . . it hasn't been even five months . . . I'm just not ready. I can't—" *I can't lose myself again. I worked too hard to find me.*

She couldn't say any of that aloud, but felt instinctively that Damon was too dangerous to love. He would demand her whole heart, and she simply couldn't give it. She had done so once already, and had nearly lost her will to live.

"Kelle." His gentle tone encouraged her to look up at him. "It's all right. You just let me know when you're ready, okay? I value your judgment." He reached out and briefly squeezed her shoulder. "I'll see you in the morning."

She wanted to yell after him that she would never be ready, that he should marry Rebekka and move to France where she could never see him again. But the memory of his kiss and the fire in her veins stopped her. For a moment, she had found heaven in his arms. Could any of that be maintained on a daily basis? When she was fixing his dinners and washing his clothes, would she resent it as she had with Riley, or would she treasure the service as other women seemed to do?

Her fingers went to her still-burning lips, and her heart ached with longing. What did she really want?

* * * * *

Damon drove home slowly, pondering Mickelle's reaction. She had responded to his kisses, yet only moments later, her eyes had shown fear. He felt helpless. What should he do next? Certainly that moment had been pivotal for him. He knew they had something good and right, something they shouldn't let slip through their fingers.

She was so beautiful, like a butterfly that had cast off its dull black shell and emerged into the light. Her presence filled him with a sense of well-being. Of rightness. His gut reaction told him they belonged together. Forever.

Somehow he had to find a way to convince her. Couldn't she see that they had been destined to meet? He felt it now as strongly as he had ever felt anything. They got along well—more than well. They were both members of the Church. He was attracted to her, and he knew she felt a similar attraction. He enjoyed her children; they needed a father. She loved Belle; Belle needed a mother. Tanner did, too. He had plenty of money to take care of both families. Above all, he really cared for Mickelle. So why weren't they together, discussing possibilities for the future?

Her husband . . .

Had she been so in love with him that to love another would desecrate his memory?

He rubbed his chin thoughtfully. When Charlotte had first taken ill, he had vowed never to remarry, though Charlotte hadn't asked for his promise. She had told him that he needed a companion almost as much as the children needed a mother. For most of their married life, Charlotte had been too sick to be either of those things.

And now, most unexpectedly, there was Mickelle, whose bright eyes and kind heart had found a place in his life. His soul swelled with love and tenderness, and he blessed the day Tanner had smashed into her car. That ugly old Snail. But what if she couldn't return his love?

I can't give her up.

He had waited a long time to find Mickelle, but while he wouldn't give her up easily, he wouldn't rush her, either. He would put a strong rein on the heady emotions she had unleashed within him, and show her that he was a man she could depend on. A man who would eventually take her to the temple. A man with patience.

He sighed, envisioning her stormy blue eyes. It wouldn't be easy.

CHAPTER 30

Marc spent Monday night in a hotel in Salt Lake City. It had taken over five minutes to find the right phrases in his guidebook to let the taxi driver know his wishes, and another ten to settle things with the clerk at the hotel, but overall Marc was pleased with himself. Getting along in a foreign country wasn't as impossible as it had appeared.

He wanted to call Rebekka immediately, but had no idea where she was staying. They had always communicated by e-mail; he'd asked her for her phone number a few times, but she had never given it to him. Brionney would know where she was, and he did have that number because she kept in contact with her brother in France, but he hesitated to call her so late. The next morning would be soon enough.

So he called France instead, where it was early morning, to let his family know he had arrived in Utah safely. Then he went to bed and dreamed all night of Rebekka walking down the aisle, and of himself arriving too late to stop the wedding.

* * * * *

"I'm sorry for the awkwardness of the situation," Damon said, looking uncomfortable. He adjusted his tie, though it was already straight. "I really didn't expect to feel this way about her, and I thought it only fair to tell you."

Rebekka sighed and sat in the chair opposite Damon's desk. She had seen it coming, seen the way Damon had looked at Mickelle, but

still the blow left her reeling. "It's okay," she muttered. "I understand."

"Even so, I'm sorry. I never meant to lead you on."

She met his eyes then. "You didn't, Damon." She forced a smile.
"We've had fun anyway, haven't we?"

"Yeah. I just worry about Belle, now that she's finally coming around."

"There's the piano, and even if you do get another teacher, I'll stay
in touch. Besides, with Mickelle, she probably won't need me for long."

"Thank you, Rebekka." Damon's words were sincere. "You are a
wonderful woman. I mean that."

Then why am I alone? But Rebekka stifled the retort. She knew in
her heart that Damon had chosen wisely. Mickelle was the sort of
motherly woman he needed for his children. A woman who enjoyed
making a home and caring for others. Rebekka, on the other hand,
didn't know what she wanted.

Damon leaned back in his chair and rubbed his chin. "You know,
for a moment last night I wanted to ask her to marry me."

"So soon?" Rebekka raised her eyebrows. "Not a good idea."

"I know, it *sounds* fast, but everything just fell into place. Like the
answer was in front of me the whole time." He frowned. "But she . . .
I think she's scared."

"Of course she's scared. You've known her for less than a week!"

Damon leaned forward, his amber eyes intense. "But I feel like
I've known her much longer. I know she feels the same way, but when
I tried to discuss it with her, she said she wasn't ready. I need to find
out how to help her be ready."

"This is not one of your business deals, Damon," Rebekka said,
allowing a hint of anger to show in her voice. "You can't *make*
someone feel something." Heaven knew she had tried. "Look, just
give her some time. She already knows what a wonderful father you
are. Give her a chance to see that it's real, not just an act."

Damon sighed. "I know. It's just that I'm afraid of losing her.
She's been dating someone else. A cop—younger than she is. Too
young, if you ask me."

Rebekka had heard enough. She didn't need to sit here and have
her youth wielded against her like a sword. "Look, I have work to do.
That's what you're paying me for."

He grinned. "Thanks for listening."

"You're welcome." And then, because she really was happy for Damon despite her own pain, she added, "Why don't you find out what kind of a relationship she had with her husband? Maybe that will shed some light on why she reacted the way she did last night."

Raising a hand in farewell, she ignored her impulse to have a good cry in the rest room, and went instead to her cubicle and buried herself in her work. When the phone rang an hour later, she almost didn't hear it.

"Hello, Rebekka with two Ks," said a familiar voice.

"Samuel." She was glad to hear from him.

"Hey, I've been thinking. Why don't you just come out here and take a look at our setup? That way you can make an informed decision. If you work for Corban International, you'll have your own private office—a nice one with a great view of the city—a nearby park for lunch, great restaurants. Come and check it out. You could fly out here for a day or two, and be back there by the weekend."

Before Damon's announcement, Rebekka would not have considered picking up and leaving so abruptly, if only for a few days. But now she found herself wanting to leave Utah. "I don't know," she stalled.

"You can work here just as well as there," Samuel urged. "I even bought you a plane ticket."

"Excuse me?"

"It's for tomorrow. But don't worry, it's exchangeable."

"I can't just pick up and leave with no warning."

He must have sensed that her voice lacked conviction. "Why not? The project needs you here." His voice deepened almost imperceptibly. "*I* need you here. I can talk to Damon if you'd like."

"No." Rebekka knew that Damon would say yes, if only to soothe his conscience. But Rebekka didn't trust herself around Samuel. There was a spark between them that threatened to burst into flame, but would it be enough? Despite her continued disappointments with men, she didn't want her parents' relationship.

"Just think about it." Samuel's voice was persuasive.

"Okay. I'll let you know." Rebekka hung up and went back to work. Of course she wouldn't go to Cincinnati tomorrow, even if she decided to accept Samuel's job offer. It was too soon, and she needed time to think.

An hour later, Juliet came in with a large bouquet of fresh flowers. "A company just delivered them," she said, setting the vase on the desk.

"Who would send me flowers?" Rebekka touched the petals of a daisy.

"There's a card," Juliet pointed out.

Rebekka slipped a short fingernail under the flap and read the note: *Did you decide yet?* She smiled.

"Well?" asked Juliet.

"They're from Samuel."

Juliet grinned. "Oh, I knew he liked you. I knew it! That is one good-looking man." She frowned. "Too bad he's not a member." Juliet knew how important that was to Rebekka. "But maybe he could take the discussions."

"His parents are very active in another religion, and I think Samuel is happy where he's at. He told me as much himself."

Juliet looked away from Rebekka and at the flowers. She sighed enviously. "Well, he sure is romantic."

Rebekka gazed at the flowers, seeing instead Samuel's handsome face. "Yes, he is."

She tried to return to work, but couldn't seem to concentrate. She kept thinking about Samuel's offer and Damon's attraction for Mickelle. The more she thought about it, the angrier she became. Why couldn't Samuel be a member, when he seemed so perfect in every other way? Why couldn't Damon have fallen in love with her, and she with him? Confusion reigned in Rebekka's heart, and she didn't know where to turn. She slammed her fist against the padded armrest of her chair. Darn it all! Acting on her anger wouldn't solve anything, but it made her feel better.

Her phone rang again and she picked it up, sure it was Samuel. "Rebekka?" It was Juliet. "There's someone out here to see you. Are you free?" The way the receptionist's voice quivered, Rebekka knew it was probably a man.

"Who is it?"

Juliet hesitated. "He wants to surprise you . . . I think."

Samuel! Why wouldn't he give her time? And how did he get here so quickly? *He must have been in Salt Lake when he called the first time.*

"Okay. Send him back."

Rebekka looked around and saw that the other people who had cubicles in the conference room had gone to lunch. The words on her computer screen danced before her eyes as she tried to focus on them. She couldn't decide if she was angry or excited that Samuel had come to visit.

She heard someone enter, but her back was to the door and she refused to look up. Hands closed over her eyes. "Samuel?" she asked.

"Wrong." The voice spoke in French.

Rebekka jerked her head around in surprise. His dark hair was longer than she remembered, but each curve of his face was the same. His deep brown eyes locked onto hers as she greedily drank in his presence, his smell, his very being. Joy sang in her veins until she squelched it. *Those feelings are gone.* "You!" The anger she had been holding in all day flared. She welcomed the emotion, allowed it to roll over her and through all her senses. Better to feel the anger than the terrible, hurtful gladness at seeing him. "Why are you here, Marc?" she demanded.

He looked puzzled. "I came to visit. I thought you'd be glad."

Glad to have my wounds ripped open? Glad to want nothing more than to follow you around like a puppy?

He raked his hand through his hair. "I've come to check out this man of yours."

Rebekka stood stiffly. She desperately wanted to throw her arms around Marc, but instead she offered her cheeks almost gingerly to be kissed in the French custom. "It's good to see you," she managed.

"My parents send their love. And André."

"What about my family? How are they?" The small talk was difficult for Rebekka, but she forced herself to act as though it was nothing out of the ordinary to have Marc fly thousands of miles to stop by. Once she would have been thrilled, but she was over that feeling. There was no more room for him in her broken heart.

Marc's handsome face looked sheepish. "They were fine the last I saw them. I didn't visit them before I left. I didn't really tell anyone I was going, just my family."

"Oh, so are you here on business?"

"I just needed to get away. You seem like you're having such a good time here. I thought maybe I'd come and . . ." His face grew worried. "Rebekka, is something wrong? You don't seem very happy to see me."

"I am happy to see you. Just a bit shocked, that's all." She glanced at her computer—anything not to look into his eyes. "I have a lot of work to do. I can't take time off." Actually, she could, but she didn't *want* to be alone with Marc any more than necessary.

There was a sound at the door, and Rebekka saw Damon standing there. "Rebekka, can I talk to you for a minute?" he asked. "It can wait if you're busy."

Rebekka took Marc's arm and propelled him to the door. "Damon, you must meet my old friend, Marc Perrault. He's visiting from France and stopped by to see me. Marc, this is Damon. He's the boss around here. Or one of them. The children I used to watch are his."

Damon shook Marc's hand. "Good to meet you. Did you just get in today?"

"No, I come last night," Marc replied. Rebekka winced at the terrible accent, but Damon didn't seem to notice. Marc's language skills in French grammar were better than most, but he had never spoken English very well. "I stay at the hotel last night, and today I rent a car and come here."

"Well, that's quite a long flight. How long will you be staying?"

"I am not sure."

Damon smiled again, then touched Rebekka's arm lightly. "Everything's okay, right?" he said softly, but not privately.

She knew that Damon was referring to their chat that morning, but Rebekka was all too aware of Marc's presence. There was no way she wanted Marc to know that she and her employer were no longer "dating." She slipped her arm around Damon's waist and gave him a half-hug. "Yes, Damon. Thanks." He put his arm around her shoulders and squeezed briefly, then they both dropped their arms to their sides.

"I'll come back a little later." Damon looked at Marc. "Nice to meet you, Marc."

Marc watched Damon's retreating figure. Rebekka studied his expression, but couldn't see even a hint of his emotions. "I thought you said in one of your e-mails that he was tall," Marc finally said in French. "He's only got an inch on me."

"That was Samuel."

Marc's dark eyes turned on hers. "Samuel? How many men are you dating?"

"Just one." She tried to laugh. "Is that why you're here, to check up on me?"

Marc frowned. "Actually, yes. I wanted to make sure he's a nice guy."

"Well, he is, as you can see." She smiled blandly, feeling ice in her heart. She knew Marc hadn't come to profess his love; he had none in his heart for her. At least not the kind of love she had once craved from him. In spite of his protestations to the contrary, she bet her parents had put him up to this little "visit." A cold numbness enveloped her.

Suddenly Marc reached out and took both of her arms in his hands. Electricity seemed to flow between them. "Are you happy here?" His question was urgent.

She looked him squarely in the face, her pride and his hands the only things sustaining her. "Yes."

He seemed to deflate somehow, as though he had expected another answer. "I'm glad then." His voice was almost a whisper.

He stepped away from her, and she teetered on weak knees. "I'll let you get back to work. And we'll see you later."

"Where are you staying?"

He hesitated in the doorway. "I don't know yet. I'll call you. I talked to Brionney on the phone, and she said you were staying with her. If you're not home, I'll leave a message."

She watched him go, grateful that she felt nothing in her heart. *Love does die,* she thought. *I don't love him anymore.*

As the numbness gradually wore off, anger took its place. *How dare he come here! How dare he check up on me!* There were other emotions, too, but she didn't care to examine them. What she needed was to get away from everyone who knew her. She needed to start again, without memories from the past getting in the way and people checking up on her.

Cincinnati. Of course! That was the answer.

But Cincinnati meant Samuel. Could she go to Cincinnati and work with Samuel without dating him? She thought of his green eyes and his unveiled desire for her. No; if she went to Cincinnati something would develop between them, that much was certain. He would treat her like a queen. Would it be enough? She could fall in love with him easily—maybe not with the wholehearted emotion she had once experienced for Marc, yet it would be love all the same. But once she was committed to him, would she regret the fact that they didn't share the gospel? Could she live with the possibility that he might never accept what she believed to be an irrevocable truth?

"Better than being alone," she whispered. "We could be happy. He's a good man." Her hand stole to the phone and dialed the cell number she had never called but had long since memorized. "Hi, Samuel?"

"Rebekka!" His voice sounded happy.

"I've decided to take you up on your offer. If it's still open."

"It is."

"But what about an earlier flight?"

"Funny you should mention that. We had a few problems crop up here, and I just talked to Damon about half an hour ago. He said he'd send someone today if we could find a flight. I didn't mention you because . . . well, you know why. But I'd love it if you were the one he sent." He paused. "I'm glad you decided to come, Rebekka. I don't think you'll regret it."

"Neither do I."

Feeling like she had finally started down the right path, Rebekka hung up the phone. Now she would zip home during lunch and pack a suitcase or two, then return to work until she left for the airport. Tonight she would be in Cincinnati with Samuel.

* * * * *

Marc stalked out to his rental car, feeling angry and alone. Seeing Rebekka had only added to his misery. She hadn't been happy to see him at all. In fact, she had seemed angry at his intrusion. Watching her and Damon interact had been pure torture. Did the other man hold even a trace of the emotion Marc harbored for Rebekka in his heart? He didn't think so.

Yet he couldn't bring himself to confess his feelings for Rebekka now—not when she seemed so content with her life. He had no right, no right at all. She deserved happiness, and even though it hurt unbearably to let her go, he wouldn't stop her from making a life with Damon.

He hung his head and wept.

CHAPTER 31

Mickelle had just finished weeding in the garden on Tuesday and was emerging from her shower when the doorbell rang. "Brionney," she said, opening the door in her robe. "Come in."

"I just dropped the kids' lunch off at school, and I thought I'd stop by." Brionney carried a twin on each hip, and four-year-old Rosalie stood next to her.

Mickelle took Gabriel from his mother. "My, you and Forest are sure getting big," she said to him.

"Can you believe they're almost a year now?"

"I'm four and a half," Rosalie put in. "I'm bigger than them."

Brionney rumpled her hair. "Yes, indeed. That's why you're such a great baby-tender."

As Brionney settled the children on the kitchen floor with a pile of toys, Mickelle went to change from her bathrobe and to brush her hair. Then she applied her makeup in the kitchen while she chatted with her sister.

"So are you registered for school?" Brionney asked.

"Not yet, but I know exactly what I'm going to take." Mickelle grimaced. "I was a little too late to make the deadline this fall." Silently she added, *Because of my depression.* "But it's just as well," she continued aloud, "since I started watching Belle and Tanner. I need to get into a routine with them before I can figure what time to take my classes. But at least I won't have to worry so much about money. Damon does pay well."

"I noticed the new car out there."

Mickelle sat down at the table, frowning slightly. "You know that man was just going to give it to me?"

"Sounds like Damon." Brionney bent to take a toy away from Forest and return it to Gabriel. "He's very shrewd in business, but he's also very generous."

"He's also very forceful," Mickelle noted. "I guess he gets everything he wants." She tried to speak lightly, but her voice trembled.

Brionney sat on the edge of a kitchen chair, still keeping a sharp eye on the twins. "Well, he goes after what he wants, but he doesn't always get it. I mean, his wife died. I know that he was pretty devastated. And then last year, I think he started falling in love with a friend of ours. When she decided to make a last try with her husband, he supported that decision. He could have fought for her harder, but he wanted what was best for her, so he backed off. For a long time, he was very sad."

Mickelle mulled this new information in her mind. The action sounded like the man she was coming to know, but her heart doubted his apparent selflessness. It was all entirely too good to be true.

"So why all these questions?" Brionney asked, meeting Mickelle's gaze. "You're starting to like him, aren't you?"

"Of course I like him, don't you?"

"You know what I mean. As a man."

"No," Mickelle lied. "I can't live in any man's shadow. Not again. And Damon's got a pretty big shadow."

Brionney regarded her for a moment without speaking. "I guess so. But apparently he's dating Rebekka anyway."

"No, he's not. At least I don't think so."

Brionney looked as though she would question her further, but Mickelle was saved by the doorbell. She answered it to find Jim on her small porch, dressed in his police uniform.

"Hello, Officer Lowder," she said with a teasing grin.

"Hi, Mickelle. You look wonderful this morning."

Mickelle glanced down at her tan jumpsuit. "Thank you. Won't you come in?"

"Actually, I'm on my lunch hour, and I have to be getting back to work, but I called you yesterday and there was no answer, so I thought I'd stop and see when we could go out again."

She hesitated, recalling Damon and the way he had made her feel—wild, exuberant, happy. But also apprehensive and scared. She couldn't let herself fall for such a dynamic man. On the other hand, Jim seemed safe, secure. Nice.

"If this week's not good, I understand," Jim said quickly.

His eagerness made Mickelle feel guilty. "I started a new job."

"That's great!" He smiled, then added quickly, "Isn't it?"

She laughed. "Yes, it is. And life has suddenly gotten much busier. But I would like to go out with you sometime. Last time was fun." *No pressure,* she thought silently.

He seemed to relax. "Whenever you're ready. That's great." He moved toward the steps. "I'll give you a call."

Mickelle watched him drive away. "Nice kid," Brionney said dryly from the kitchen doorway.

Mickelle bristled. "Kid? He's your age."

"My point exactly. Last I checked, you were about six years older than me."

Mickelle shut the door and returned to the kitchen. "So? It's the new Millennium. Age isn't important."

"It is when one minute you're acting like you don't want to go out with him or anyone else, and the next you're leading him on."

Mickelle gaped at her incredulously. "I'm not leading him on! He's a nice guy. I *want* to go out with him."

"Damon's a nice guy, too. And obviously there must be some reason he's not going out with Rebekka anymore. Care to share how you knew that?"

Mickelle ignored the comment. "And you heard for yourself that he doesn't mind waiting. Whatever I want to do, Jim won't push."

"Neither would Damon."

"But what if I *wanted* him to push?"

"What?" Then understanding dawned. "So you *are* attracted to Damon. And not at all to Jim. In other words, he's safe."

The words ate into Mickelle's heart. She had been thinking the exact same thing. No pressure, safe. She was in control. No heartstrings attached. If he asked her to do something she didn't want to do, it would be nothing to say good-bye.

Saying good-bye was the one thing that she was afraid she

couldn't do if she pursued a relationship with Damon. She was too darn attracted to him. Already if she went a moment without him in her thoughts, it was a miracle.

Her throat felt like cotton and she swallowed hard, then purposely made her voice light. "He's a cop. Of course he's safe." She turned to the kids. "Now would you guys like something to eat here? Or maybe we could talk your mom into going to McDonald's for lunch."

"The boys don't eat much food," Rosalie said solemnly. "They mostly still nurse and eat applesauce." The little girl's face brightened. "Oh, but I bet they'd like to chew on some french fries."

"I'll bet they would," Mickelle agreed. "And I'll bet you'd like a hamburger, wouldn't you, Rosalie?"

"Yes!" The little girl hugged her.

Mickelle picked her up. She felt her sister's penetrating stare at her back, but worse were the contradicting feelings in her own heart. She could barely wait until six-thirty, when Damon would come to pick up his children.

* * * * *

No one was home at Brionney's when Rebekka stopped off for her luggage. She breathed a sigh of relief. She had half expected Marc to be there waiting for her, and the last thing she wanted was to face him again. She packed a suitcase quickly, taking much more than she needed for the few days she planned to be gone. *Maybe I'll never be back.*

There, she had finally admitted it to herself. This new job, Samuel . . .these were her future. She wrote a note to Brionney and laid it on the bed where it stood out, a rectangle of stark white again the burgundy-colored bedspread.

Feeling suddenly depressed, she left the house and drove back to work.

* * * * *

Damon left the office early to stop by Brionney's house on the way to get Tanner and Belle. She was surprised to see him. "Boy, this is my day for visitors," she said, motioning him inside the house. "First an old friend from France shows up, and now you."

"Oh, is he here? I'm sorry for interrupting."

Brionney waved the words aside. "He's actually taking a nap—jet lag, you know. He had stopped by earlier, but I was at Mickelle's, and I guess he went to the Timpanogos Temple grounds to hang out until I returned. He was pretty beat when he showed up here. Said he'd been to see Rebekka, too. I wonder how that went."

"I don't know. I met him, though, when he was there. Seems like a nice guy."

"So what brings you here?"

"I have a few questions. About . . . about Kelle."

Brionney's eyebrows rose. "Kelle? Oh, you mean, Mickelle. Okay. But do you mind if I clean up in the kitchen while we talk? The boys are taking a late nap, and the girls are playing next door. It's my only time to get dinner started and things organized before the terror twins are back to playing demolition derby."

Damon chuckled. "That'd be fine." He followed her into the spacious kitchen, marveling at how the light and airy feeling of the room made his spirits rise. He sat at the bar, and a moment later Brionney set a healthy serving of leftover spaghetti casserole in front of him.

"I know you probably haven't eaten much today," she said with a smile. "I swear since you and Jesse started Hospital's Choice, he's lost ten pounds." She smiled indulgently. "Not that he couldn't afford to lose them."

"Thanks." He dug into the food eagerly with a fork. Brionney was an excellent cook.

She picked up a dishrag and began wiping the counter. "So what's up?"

"Well, I—I just wanted to know what kind of a relationship Kelle had with her husband." The words came out awkwardly.

Brionney threw the dishrag in the sink and came around the bar. "Wait a minute. This doesn't sound like a baby-sitter checkup to me." Her bright blue eyes seemed to pierce his heart.

He shook his head slowly. "I really like your sister, Bri. In fact, I think I love her." He stood, his food forgotten, and began to pace the tiled floor. "Oh, I know it sounds so stupid. We've only just met, and yet I feel something. It's so strong." He walked back to the bar and laid both hands on it. "Have you ever felt anything like that?"

Her eyes looked at him, but seemed to see something else. "With Jesse," she said softly. "I was in Arizona to sign divorce papers from my first husband when I met him. Less than a week, no dates, but there was this . . . connection."

Damon slapped the bar. "That's it! A connection!"

"Well, Jesse still had to prove himself to me," Brionney said. "After the way my first husband had treated me, I wasn't ready to trust him right away. But he was so good with Savannah, and so . . . well, so Jesse. I couldn't help falling in love with him."

"What was Kelle's husband like?" Damon re-seated himself on the stool.

Brionney's pleasant expression darkened. "We thought he was great, but there was a lot going on that we didn't see. He was abusive."

"Abusive?" Damon was horrified. He fought a sudden anger in his heart. How could anyone want to hurt Mickelle?

"Not physically. But he didn't treat Mickelle right. Or the children. He had a lot of problems mentally. When he was a child he had some sort of an accident, and for many years he had seizures. He was really shy and withdrawn. Then he had an operation, and he apparently regressed into his missed teenage years or something. He became selfish and mean, and all of his worst tendencies came to the forefront of his personality. It was all for him and nothing for her or the children, except when he was feeling magnanimous."

"I had no idea," Damon murmured.

"Of course, I learned all this in retrospect, from stuff Mickelle or my parents have said since his death. I do know that Mickelle threatened to divorce him just before he killed himself. For a long time she felt guilty about that, like she had driven him to it."

Damon shook his head. "I didn't realize she'd been through so much." He clenched his jaw, trying to control his anger at the man he had never known. *If he wasn't already dead . . .* He made his hands into fists, but didn't finish the thought. *What she must have endured!* An overwhelming desire to comfort her filled him. He could make her happy—he would spend his life making up for all she had suffered—if only she would let him.

"No one knew about it," Brionney continued. "She always kept quiet. She really loved him." She paused before adding quietly, "Between you and me, I think their relationship would have eventually worked out. She was that determined. And I think that in his own way, Riley really loved her, too. Certainly he didn't want to lose her."

Damon rubbed his chin, forcing his feelings of anger and helplessness to a far corner of his mind. "Well, this at least partly explains why she reacted the way she did last night."

"What happened?" Brionney looked at him curiously, a smile hovering on her lips

Suddenly embarrassed, Damon stalled for time by picking up his fork and shoveling in a mouthful of casserole. He chewed and swallowed before speaking. "I kissed her," he admitted finally. "And she kissed me back. But then . . . I don't know. I think she got scared."

Brionney's brow wrinkled. "I'm not surprised. Just two weeks ago, she was telling me that if she were ever to have another relationship, it would have to come into her life with a bang, because she certainly wasn't going looking for it."

"Well, Tan did hit her with his car." Damon took another bite of food. "That was a bang if anything was."

"Yeah, you could say that." Brionney laughed, but sobered almost immediately. "I think Mickelle doesn't want to have to watch everything she says or does. I can relate with that a little. My first husband was very hard to please, and I nearly went crazy trying to reach some goal that was always too high. I know my sister; she's a wonderful, loving person, and she needs someone. But of course she's afraid. I think her exact words were something like, 'I don't want to be a slave.'" Brionney shivered.

Damon blinked in amazement. "She would never be that to me. I want to take care of her."

"I know that and you know that, and she probably even knows that. But it's hard to believe anyone when you've made wrong choices before. Not that she believes Riley was a wrong choice, but there were definitely problems."

"So what do I do?" Damon set his fork on the counter and looked intently at Brionney. "I think we have something great here. I know it. And I don't want either of us to miss out."

Brionney frowned. "I don't know. I just don't know. Let me think about it, okay? Maybe it's only a matter of giving her time."

"You may lose her that way," said a heavily accented voice from the door. Damon looked over to see Marc standing there, watching them.

Damon stared at him without speaking for a full minute, wondering what his romantic life had to do with this French man.

"Does she know how you feel?" Marc asked.

Damon nodded, hoping he understood the man's heavily accented question. "Yes. And I think she feels the same way. But she's scared." He glanced at Brionney. "She's been hurt before."

Marc dragged his hand through his hair. "She told me that before she left France. I did not know she and this French man were so serious."

Brionney's head swiveled from one man to the other. "What are you talking about?" she asked Marc finally. "Because I'm really lost. I don't think we're talking about the same thing."

* * * * *

Marc hadn't meant to eavesdrop on Damon and Brionney's conversation, but even so had lingered a little too long in the hall. He heard the passion in Damon's voice, and all the hurt and anguish that had fallen over him since seeing Rebekka that morning returned without mercy.

"I am talking of Rebekka," Marc said now in answer to Brionney's question. He didn't want to help Damon, but his loyalty to Rebekka forced him to continue. He wanted her to find happiness. "She told me when she leave France that she leave because of a man." He met Damon's gaze. "I am glad she found you. Do not let what is wrong get in the way of love. She deserves . . ." he searched for the words. ". . . to be happy."

Damon's face grew more puzzled. "Rebekka? We were talking about Brionney's sister, Kelle."

Marc felt anger leap to life in his heart. "Does Rebekka know you love another?"

"I told her this morning. She was a little disappointed, but didn't seem that upset. We haven't even been out on a date yet."

The information was coming in all wrong. Marc wondered if he needed to go back to his room and sleep a few more hours. "I thought Rebekka was in love with you. She told me she . . ." Marc was genuinely confused. "She let me think . . ."

"You need to talk to Rebekka," Brionney said gently. "There must be some kind of a misunderstanding."

A misunderstanding! Marc had never been more happy to be so confused. Rebekka didn't love Damon!—or at least so he said. That meant there was still a chance.

"When she come home?" he asked Brionney.

Brionney glanced at the clock. "Any minute now."

"Uh, no, she won't." Damon appeared decidedly uncomfortable.

"What do you say?" Marc demanded.

"She left when I did, but she was on her way to the airport. To Cincinnati. She was driving herself, and going to leave her car in parking at the airport."

Marc glared at him.

"For work," Damon added, but he said it as though there was something more.

Brionney heard it, too. "Damon, what aren't you telling us?"

"The company we work with there . . .well, the owner really likes Rebekka. We had quite a talk this morning, and then again this afternoon after Rebekka agreed to go to Cincinnati. He was relieved to know that Rebekka and I aren't involved. He has a pretty romantic few days planned for her—showing her the countryside, taking her to meet his parents, that sort of thing. I don't know if we'll even be able to get in contact with her." Damon hesitated, as though trying to read Marc's soul. "And what's more, I think Rebekka's attracted to him, but since we had planned to go out, it sort of stifled her feelings. I was a bit upset with Samuel at the time, but now that she's free, I don't have the right . . ." His eyes met Marc's in sudden understanding. "She is free, isn't she?"

Marc felt as though he had been punched in the stomach. For a moment, he wanted to smash his fist into Damon's earnest face.

Samuel. He had heard the name earlier today. Rebekka had mentioned him, hadn't she? He struggled to breathe evenly, to remain calm.

"Well, good luck," Damon said. "I have to get my kids . . . and talk to Kelle."

Brionney waited until Damon had left, and then she said in French, "I don't believe Rebekka would go without saying good-bye to me. And she'd have to pack some things."

But Marc could believe it. She had left before without saying good-bye. Or tried to. Did she hate him so much that she had to leave before he could tell her how he felt?

Brionney had disappeared down the stairs leading to the basement, and now returned with an envelope, her face pale. "She's gone. She really is. She must have come for her clothes while I was out this afternoon. There's a note. It's in French." Brionney read it before handing it to Marc.

Brionney,

Sorry for leaving without saying good-bye. I got called away suddenly for work. But to tell you the truth, I've been thinking about accepting Samuel's offer—in more ways than one. I need a new start, and he's a good man. Perhaps one day he'll even come to know the gospel. I'll let you know what happens. Please tell Marc I'm sorry I had to leave. You'll understand why, Brionney, but he won't. He hasn't all these years.

  Rebekka

What did she mean? The message tore into Marc more than anything that had gone before, but it didn't make sense. Why couldn't she make sense? Were all women so confusing, or was it only Rebekka? They had been friends for many years, perhaps best friends, and he had come all this way to make sure she was happy. Yet she didn't have the courtesy or the guts to tell him the truth about anything.

"You've got to go after her," Brionney said abruptly. "You've come this far, and she has to know how you feel. Before she goes to Samuel. Before it's too late."

Marc forced his gaze away from Rebekka's handwriting, wondering what Brionney had seen in his heart when he wasn't even sure what he felt. "I can't. I want her to be happy. If this is what she wants—"

Brionney looked as though she would explode. "She wants to be with you! That's all she's ever wanted since she was five years old! But you're the one who's been too blind to see that the crush she had on you as a kid is much more than that now. She loves you! I know she does. *You're* the reason she left France, not some other guy. And you're going to lose her forever if you don't go after her."

Marc's head ached and tears gathered in his eyes, stinging like salt from the ocean. "As I lost you."

Brionney inclined her head. "I wanted you to come after me when I left France. I really did—at least for a time. But we didn't love each other like that, not really. Rebekka's different; she loves you with the kind of love I have for Jesse." Brionney placed her hands on her hips, and now there was a hint of anger in her blue eyes. "The question is, what do you feel for her? And before you answer that, maybe you ought to ask yourself why you've come to see her. Why are you here, Marc? You didn't love me enough to come after me, but you are here because of Rebekka. Something about your feelings for her has finally got you moving. What is it?"

Stunned, Marc sank onto a stool by the bar. "It's been her all this time, hasn't it?" Tears squeezed out of the corners of his eyes. "These feelings aren't new. She's the reason I've never married all these years. Why didn't I see it?" He hit his chest. "I love her like I've never loved anyone . . . not even Danielle." There, he had finally said the words aloud. He moaned and dropped his head into his hands. "Oh, what am I going to do?" Panic filled his heart. He had to get to Rebekka. He had to tell her the truth about why he had come to America. He had to tell her . . .

Marc leapt to his feet. "How do I get to the airport? Your friend said she was just leaving. Maybe I can get there in time. Maybe it's not too late. I have to at least try."

Tears shimmered in Brionney's eyes. "It's easy if you know the way, but if you don't you could get off on the wrong exit. I could take you if—Jesse should have been home by now. He's already fifteen minutes—" She broke off as she heard a rumbling noise. "Yes! That's the garage door. Jesse's home." She grabbed her purse from the counter and ran toward the door. Marc was only a few steps behind.

They passed Jesse in the garage, climbing out of his truck. "We have an emergency," Brionney said quickly. "We have to get to the airport. The girls are next door, and the boys should be waking up any minute. For dinner we'll have to eat leftovers—it's been a rather busy day." She gave her husband a quick kiss on the mouth. "I'll be home as soon as I can."

"Be careful." Jesse dug into his pocket and removed his cell phone, handing it to her. "Call me if you need anything."

Brionney drove her van while Marc stared anxiously at the road in front of them. He wished he could drive to alleviate his nervous tension, but he recognized the need of having a driver who knew the road. Every second counted. He was accustomed to delegation—he had founded a whole corporation by delegating—but this was different. This was his life—his eternity. He found it hard to delegate his future to a friend, even one as trusted as Brionney.

His need for Rebekka was so profound, so alive and absolute. How had he not understood how much she meant to him until it was almost too late?

Dear God, he prayed, *don't let it be too late.*

Brionney tossed him the cell phone and asked him to dial a number. "I need to find out what flight she's on," she explained. "Juliet will know. She works at our company. She should be home now, but I know the number. She sometimes stays with the kids for me."

Marc dialed the number and returned the phone to Brionney. "Hi, Juliet, it's Brionney. Thank heaven you answered! Look, I need to know Rebekka's flight information."

Marc knew it might already be too late, but he also knew she could have stopped somewhere after work. It was possible her plane didn't leave until . . .

"Six forty-five? Okay, give me the airline and gate number. You don't? Okay, then just the airline. We can find the gate number when we get there."

Marc's watch read three minutes after six. They had forty-two minutes. He looked at Brionney anxiously as she disconnected the call.

"We have enough time—barely," she said. "If the traffic's not too bad."

Marc began to pray with his entire being.

That was when he noticed the child sitting in a mud puddle that reached to the right edge of the road in front of them. Because of the distance, he couldn't tell if the toddler was a boy or a girl, but it couldn't be older than a year or two. The traffic wasn't going fast, but there were enough cars to pose a real danger to such a small child. Where was its mother?

As they approached, he saw that the child had very pale skin and wore only a long T-shirt that had once been white, but was now speckled with mud. Marc craned his head, looking all around, hoping to see someone coming for the mud-caked toddler. He saw nothing but a row of faceless houses. The child began to crawl around in the mud, splashing with innocent delight. Any moment now, he expected Brionney to see the child and stop, but she was concentrating on the car in front of her, as though contemplating an opportunity to pass.

They sped past the mud puddle, with Marc still searching for the mother. His conscience protested leaving the child behind, each moment crawling closer to the pavement on the street. *It's not my problem. I have to get to Rebekka.* But he couldn't live with that. What if the child ended up in the street? Or what if some young hot-blooded teen tried to pass illegally on the right side? The child wouldn't been seen until it was too late.

"Brionney, stop," he choked out in hoarse French. "There's a baby back there, and it's nearly in the road. We have to stop."

Her eyes flicked to the mirror and grew wide. "Oh, my gosh!" She pulled over at once. Together they left the van and ran back toward the child.

As Marc fished the smiling little boy out of the messy puddle, his heart filled with an agonizing emotion he could not name. *I'm sorry, Rebekka. I'm so sorry.*

CHAPTER 32

After leaving work, Rebekka stopped briefly at the Hansen residence. She had gotten the address from Damon earlier when they had discussed her trip to Cincinnati, saying that she wanted to tell Belle good-bye. That was part of it, to be sure. But she also wanted to see Mickelle.

Belle herself opened the door. "Rebekka!" she said with a wide smile.

"Hi, Belle. Wow! Look at all those signatures on your cast. I bet your whole class signed it."

"All except Tristian. He's gone on vacation to Disneyland."

"He'll just have to sign it later, I suppose. I'm sure he won't stay in California for six weeks." Rebekka took a deep breath and hurried on. "Hey, you know what? I came by to tell you that I have to go out of town for a little while."

Belle's forehead scrunched, and her amber eyes, so like her father's, were suddenly cool. "You're going back to France?"

Rebekka's heart ached as she knelt in front of the child. "No honey, honest. I'm going to Cincinnati to work on your dad's program."

"Will you call me?" Belle's eyes became calculating.

"Yes. I promise." Rebekka put her hand on Belle's arm. "Don't worry. We are friends for life."

Belle smiled, her eyes once again warm. "Kelle—that's what Daddy calls her—isn't that cool? It rhymes with my name. Kelle, Belle. Anyway, Kelle made a cake for our after-school snack. Want to come and have a piece? We still have some left. We couldn't eat it all, or we'd ruin our dinner."

"Who is it?" Mickelle came from the kitchen, her eyes widening in surprise as she saw Rebekka. "Hello. Why . . . uh, what brings you here?"

"I have to go out of town for a few days," Rebekka replied, straightening to meet the taller woman's eyes. *Or maybe forever.* "I wanted to say good-bye to Belle."

"That's nice, isn't it, Belle?" Mickelle said warmly.

Rebekka didn't wonder that Mickelle was so friendly. She would be, too, if her competition stepped out of the way. *But then I never was her competition,* she told herself bitterly. *Damon and I were never anything but friends. It was just wishful thinking on my part, but neither of us tried, not really.*

"I also came to talk with you." Rebekka glanced meaningfully at Belle.

Mickelle touched Belle's shoulder. "Will you go see what the boys are doing outside? If they want to play soccer, tell them I'll be out in a minute so the teams will be even."

"Okay." Belle left immediately, holding her cast to her chest. Rebekka had never seen her so docile.

"Come on in and sit down," Mickelle invited, walking into the living room.

"Well, just for a minute." Rebekka took a peek at her watch for emphasis, although she didn't really see the time. "I have to catch a plane soon."

Mickelle seated herself in an easy chair and indicated the couch for Rebekka, who sat nervously on the edge. "Where are you going?"

"Cincinnati."

"I've never been there." There was no envy in Mickelle's voice. "I must tell you that I'm so glad you came by to see Belle. I think she really needs contact with you. You're the closest thing to a mother she's had for the past five months."

Rebekka swallowed hard, realizing that she had misjudged Mickelle's earlier warmth. The woman had been happy to see her for Belle's sake, not because Rebekka was leaving town. "She hated me the whole time—until now."

"She was afraid of losing you."

"But now she has you," Rebekka said quickly. "She won't need me."

"Perhaps eventually." Mickelle's voice was guarded, her blue eyes intense. "But I thought you and Damon . . ."

"That's why I came." Rebekka shifted her position uncomfortably. "Damon and I talked this morning, and I wanted to let you know that I wish you well with him."

Mickelle's face colored at the words. "I'm not trying to take—"

"He likes you," Rebekka interrupted. "And I'm okay with that, really. There was never anything between us. I thought there could be, and for a while I was attracted to him, but if it was meant to be, it would have happened months ago. It's not only that we're from different generations, but we just . . . I don't know. At any rate, I like what I've seen with you and Belle, and I just wanted to let you know that Damon's a great guy. I've lived with the family for five months, and what you see is real. He's everything he shows himself to be. Not fake, if you know what I mean." She sighed. "If things had clicked between us, I would have married him in a heartbeat."

"I don't know what to say." Mickelle looked thoughtful and then spoke, as though finally coming to a decision. "I haven't known him very long, you know. And my husband . . . well, I don't know if I'm ready for another relationship."

Rebekka swallowed hard. "Maybe you should think about giving him a chance." She gazed seriously into the other woman's eyes. "I know this may not mean anything to you, but if you have a chance to love someone, don't pass it up. Some people never get a chance to be with the man they love. I mean, it's not like you have to marry him tomorrow or anything. Just get to know him."

"Well, thank you for your advice," Mickelle said politely, expressionlessly. "I'll think about it."

There was an awkward silence, and Rebekka wondered if she had gone too far. She stood. "I really must go."

"When are you coming back?"

"I don't know." She looked into the other woman's eyes, and felt a need to confess. "I might not be coming back at all."

"Why?"

"There's a man in Cincinnati. He's offered me a job."

"You like him, don't you?"

Rebekka's voice must have given her away. "I do. I don't know how it's going to work out, but I think . . ." She shrugged. "I guess I'm taking my own chance now. I can't pass it up."

"What about Belle? About her piano lessons?"

"I don't know," Rebekka said miserably. "I'll somehow make it up to her."

Mickelle's eyes were sad, but she didn't voice her disapproval.

"I'll call her," Rebekka felt obliged to say. She meant it, but her words didn't erase the sadness in Mickelle's eyes or the sudden worry line in her forehead. "Belle will be all right. She has you . . . and Damon." But Rebekka felt like a jerk.

"Thank you for coming," Mickelle said graciously, without reproach.

Rebekka blinked back the tears springing to her eyes. She inclined her head briefly in farewell, then ran for her car.

I can learn to like five-way chili, she thought desperately, irrationally.

Only after she had pulled away from the curb did she let the tears fall.

* * * * *

Mickelle watched Rebekka leave, feeling oddly sorry for the younger woman. There had been a sort of desperation in her eyes. What could she have done to help? She bowed her head and offered a silent prayer.

"You're praying for Rebekka, aren't you?" asked a soft voice.

Mickelle lifted her head and saw Belle coming around the side of the house. "Yes, I am." She sat down on the top step of the narrow porch, and Belle sat with her. Reaching out, Mickelle adjusted her sock—one of the pair Damon had given her. It didn't need adjusting, but she enjoyed the soft, rich feel of the wool between her fingers. Just touching the fabric brought a warmth to her heart that she could not deny.

"Her face looked funny." Belle frowned. "Like she was running away. I think she does that a lot."

"She really loves you."

Belle thought for a moment, tracing Rebekka's signature on her cast with a small finger. "Yeah, I think you're right. And she's coming back. She's going to give me piano lessons."

Mickelle tried to pave the way for an alternative, just in case. "Well, I was thinking maybe you and I could take lessons together—until Rebekka gets back. There's a high school girl next door who's begun to teach, and she could help us learn a song or two. What do you think?"

Belle grinned. "We could surprise Rebekka!"

"That's right!"

"Only it's going to have to be a one-handed song." Belle tapped her cast with her good hand. "I can't even play 'The Entertainer' now with my right arm broken. Do you think you can show me something else?"

"Sure. I'll show you some scales. You can do those with either hand."

Mickelle went inside with Belle, feeling happy. She enjoyed being with this little girl more than she could say. But the joy flooding her heart now had come not only come from Belle, but from Rebekka's confirmation of Damon's words of last night. She had also vouched for him as a person. Could loving him bring happiness after all? Was what she saw real?

* * * * *

"Thank you so much," the young mother said profusely. "I've been looking everywhere for him! I was downstairs doing the wash, and I turned around and he wasn't there. I can't imagine how he got outside. If you hadn't happened by when you did . . ." She buried her face in her little boy's neck, squeezing him tightly, unmindful of the mud that now covered her jeans and pink T-shirt. "If I lost him, I don't know what I'd do!" Tears glistened in her eyes. "Thank you again so much. It's not everyone who would stop to help."

"We're glad to do it," Brionney said, touching the young mother comfortingly on the arm.

Marc nodded in agreement, trying not to let his anguish show. He was grateful the toddler was all right—more than grateful. But in a few moments, Rebekka would be getting on a plane and flying out of his life again—perhaps this time forever. This had been the third house they had tried when looking for the child's mother, and with every passing second his agony had increased. Of course, he had no one to blame but himself. All these years, she had been right in front of him. If only he hadn't been so blind and stubborn and stupid!

He hurried down the three short steps on the woman's front porch, looking anxiously toward the van. Brionney followed. "Thank you again so much," the woman called out from behind her screen door.

"You're welcome," Brionney returned as they sprinted toward the van. Both knew they could never make it to the airport in time, but once in the car, Brionney sped toward the freeway anyway.

"We can pray for a miracle," she said softly in French.

He nodded, not admitting that he was doing just that.

Their drive to the Salt Lake airport was the longest of his life. They made good time, however, and the traffic wasn't as terrible as he had expected. But would it be enough?

Marc had faith; he believed in the Lord and in His ability to somehow prevent Rebekka from leaving Utah. But he didn't know the Lord's will in this matter. Did Marc deserve Rebekka? Was she meant to go to Cincinnati and to Samuel? Had his blindness over these past years been the Lord's way of protecting her?

I love her! he said prayerfully. *I'll do anything to make her happy. Please give me that chance.*

What if that chance only lasts a short time?

Marc didn't understand where the thought came from, but he knew the answer. *There is always eternity.* Because that was how long he wanted to be with Rebekka. He had already lived nearly half the span of an average life without her; one moment more was too long. *I will take whatever time I am given with her. And gratefully.*

Brionney let him off outside the airport. "I can find it," he assured her, not wanting to wait for her to park. He prayed as he sprinted into the building, running the length of the airport until he found the correct airline and a video monitor listing the flights to Cincinnati. The plane leaving at six forty-five was still boarding. The line of flight information blinked rapidly, as though urging him on.

He *ran.* Just like in Paris, when he had been so desperate to find Rebekka before she left. Oh, that he had known his feelings then! He would have begged her to stay, pleaded with her to give him a chance, to love him.

He ignored the quizzical gazes of those he ran past. Once he went down the wrong corridor, berating himself for the delay. *I have to get there in time,* he told himself. *I have to. Rebekka, please wait!* He knew exactly what he would do when he found her. He would fall to his knees and beg her to forgive him. Beg her to marry him. Would she say yes? His heart ached to find out.

Out of breath, he finally arrived at the gate, only to see the door closed and another flight number being posted at the desk. "The plane—is it gone?" he asked the young blonde woman at the computer.

"What flight number?" she asked kindly. He told her, and she shook her head. "I'm sorry. That plane is out on the runway. Already on its way. It's that one there." She took a few steps with him to the window and pointed. Marc saw a distant plane rise into the air, as though lifted by an invisible hand.

"I could get you on the next flight," she said. Her gaze strayed to his pants, and then up again to his face. Marc glanced down and saw that his slacks were spattered with mud, and his shirt had a large smear where he had carried the toddler. He remembered the gratitude on the young mother's face as she cuddled her son. Even though his good deed had cost him Rebekka, he knew he would do it again. There had been no other moral choice. Rebekka would have understood . . . if she had known.

Fighting tears, he thanked the lady and walked away, slumping into one of the chairs at the gate. *I'm too late.*

Of course he would go after her. Knowing how he felt about Rebekka, he couldn't do anything else. But would he be too late? After everything Damon and Brionney had told him about Samuel, he suspected that Rebekka would be committed to him before Marc caught up to her. She might even be married.

Marc couldn't blame her. If what Brionney had told him was true, Rebekka had already waited too long for him to wake up. Why should she expect him to suddenly change?

Still, he had to try. If she was already committed to this Samuel and happy, he would back off and hide his secret love rather than cause her more pain. But at least he would try.

He stumbled to the gate, where the blonde lady was typing something into a computer. "I would like the next flight to Cincinnati," he said in his halting English.

"May I see your ID?"

He pulled out his wallet and his passport.

"If you have any luggage, you'll have to check it in at the front desk."

Again, Marc glanced down at his soiled clothing. There was no time to return to American Fork to retrieve his luggage. Instead, he would have to buy what he needed along the way. Each moment he delayed meant a greater chance of never seeing Rebekka again. "No luggage," he said.

"The next flight I can get you will be in two hours, but not from this gate. You're lucky. At least there's an opening."

After putting the flight on his credit card, Marc returned to his chair, agony stealing over his heart. Brionney would catch up with him soon; he would do best to wait for her here. They would have plenty of time to search out the boarding gate to his flight when she arrived.

He sat miserably, head in his hands and elbows on his knees, praying that he would be in time.

A gentle hand touched his shoulder. Marc looked up, ready to explain his decision to Brionney. In his heart, he continued to pray.

CHAPTER 33

Mickelle opened the door to see Damon standing there. The moment she saw him, her fear from last night returned. His presence was too forceful; she was too aware of him; she would drown in her own love. No, better to keep a distance. To stay cool.

"Uh, there's something on your pants."

Her eyes strayed to the mud and grass stains coating her right leg and the seat of her blue jeans. She had being playing with the kids in the backyard, and had slipped on the edge of her freshly watered garden and fallen in the mud.

He looked amused. "Did I come too soon?"

"Right on time, as usual," she said dryly.

His grin became a laugh. "Kelle, it's good to see you. I always feel like laughing when—" He suddenly became serious. "Well, not always."

Mickelle knew he was thinking of last night; she was, too. And for just a second, she wanted more than anything for him to take her in his arms and proclaim his love again. What would she say? Would she push him away?

Her heart started pounding erratically and she turned away quickly, moving toward the kitchen. "I'll call the children."

He followed her. "Kelle, wait. I brought you something."

She glanced down at the socks on her shoeless feet, and then away again. He followed the movement and smiled at her warmly. Mickelle felt her face flush, and prayed he didn't notice. "More socks?" she said with a hopeful expression. "Please, oh, please. Because these are just wonderful." She looked at her feet again, wiggling her toes for emphasis.

He laughed, then looked chagrined. "Actually, it's not socks. Sorry."

She snorted. "Damon, you don't have to be bringing me gifts all the time. If you do, I'll feel guilty about charging you for watching your children."

"Hey, anyone who's as good with Belle as you are is worth her weight in gold."

"Then I'd better start eating more."

He laughed, reaching for a box that was under his arm. She knew it said a lot about her frame of mind that she hadn't noticed it before.

The box was a dark red, about three inches wide and a foot long. He handled it carefully, as though it held the finest crystal. "I saw it yesterday at the mall, just after I found the socks. I bought it because it seemed like something you should have, something you would enjoy. But I didn't . . . I wanted to give it to you, but I thought you might think me too forward. And then after last night . . ." He paused, then hurried on. "I know what you said last night, and I respect your feelings, so please don't read anything into this. It's just something I know you'll like, and if you accept it, I swear I'll give you only socks from now on. Sale socks." They both grinned at this, and she didn't fight the tenderness swelling in her breast.

She was also dying of curiosity. What was in the box?

Finally, he offered it to her. Through the plastic window that covered a portion of the box lid, she saw what looked like a once-living gold rose plucked from King Midas's garden. She felt her eyes widen. Below the window was a black oval sticker with a thick gold border and gold lettering that read:

Real Rose
Dipped in 24 kt Gold

With Damon close behind, she turned into the living room and sat on the couch, then carefully removed the lid. Inside, the gilded rose gleamed, reflecting the light. She had never seen such a bright, beautiful gold color. The rose itself was perfectly formed, from its petals and leaves to the thorns on its stem, frozen forever in its encasement of precious metal. In awe, she removed the flower, felt its weight. This was no garage-sale rose.

"Damon, you shouldn't—" Mickelle tore her eyes away from the rose and looked at him.

"But you had a collection, and all those rose bushes outside. I thought it belonged with you."

He sat beside her, his amber eyes more earnest than she had ever seen them. And at that moment, staring at him over the gold rose, she knew that she loved him. Not just because he had noticed her passion for roses, or because he had bought her an expensive present, and not even because of the vision she had seen of herself as Belle's mother. She loved him because he was good and kind and caring. She loved him because their souls had touched, and in that instant she knew— *knew*—that she had to give him a chance. Or spend the rest of her life wondering what might have been.

"Kelle." His voice was a whisper, almost a question, filled with yearning and uncertainty. "I know you're afraid to trust me, but I swear you won't have to do anything you don't want to. I want you to be happy, please believe that. All I ask is a chance. You can have as much time as you—"

"Shut up," she said, her voice hoarse. Before his eyes could register surprise, she added, "Shut up and kiss me before the kids find out you're here."

She set the rose on her lap as he reached for her. His kiss was tender and full of promise, and Mickelle felt her heart soar. Yes, Damon would demand complete devotion, but he would give it as well. And he would love her enough to give her space, cherish her enough to let her go free in the end, if that was what she wanted.

At the moment, she wanted nothing more than to feel his lips trace the contours of her face, eyes, lips. A delicious tingling rippled up her spine. Maybe getting to know Damon wouldn't be as frightening as she had expected.

She moved into his kiss, and without warning the golden rose slid down her leg and tumbled to the floor. Mickelle pulled away from Damon, trying to save it. For a brief moment, she envisioned the long-stemmed Capodimonte rose that Riley had given her and later crushed into the carpet that terrible day in May.

Damon quickly scooped up the rose from the carpet. "No damage," he said, examining it. He laid it carefully in her waiting hands.

Mickelle stood and moved to the curio cabinet. She still hadn't replaced the glass, but decided that her collection looked fine without it, especially with this new addition. She caressed the smooth metal once again before facing Damon.

"I love it," she said, suddenly shy. "Thank you." How should she act around him now? She might be in love with him, she didn't know him very well. And she was still more than a little afraid of the tempestuous emotions in her heart.

He held out his hand, as though reading her thoughts. "Come on, let's go play ball with the kids. You are so beautiful, and I think right now I'm in desperate need of four loud and obnoxious chaperones."

Mickelle smiled and placed her hand in his.

CHAPTER 34

The moment Rebekka entered the plane, she started crying and couldn't stop. She told herself at first that the liquid seeping from her eyes wasn't tears, but that her allergies were acting up as they had when she was a child. *It's just something in the air.*

Her heart felt as heavy as lead. Ever since she had left Mickelle's, the heaviness had grown. And grown. Was it because she felt so guilty about leaving Belle?

She tried to concentrate on imagining how joyful Samuel's face would be when he met her at the airport, but all she could see was Marc as he had been that morning—so alive and . . . so Marc.

Sighing, she took her scriptures from her carry-on bag. Reading the sacred words always had a calming effect on her, but lately she hadn't been giving them the attention they deserved. Lovingly, she fingered the leather cover. These battered scriptures were special to her for more than one reason. They had accompanied three Perrault missionaries: first Marc, then Josette, and finally André, who had given them to her when she had received her call. There were teeth marks in them where Marc had once fended off a mad dog, and the pages were well-marked and worn, but she treasured them more than any other set she possessed.

As she opened the scriptures, a bookmark fell out. It was from Marc. She picked it up, remembering the day he had given it to her at church almost a year ago. As president of the Sunday School, he'd prepared one for each teen in their ward—well, she suspected he had enlisted his sisters' help for the actual production—and he had given her one because she was a teacher in the Sunday School. Bubble letters across the front read: *Did you think to pray?*

A new rush of tears blurred her vision, and she wiped at her eyes impatiently, hating her weakness. She had always been taught to make a decision and then to pray about it, but she hadn't done that since leaving France. Once she even had prayed for Marc to love her. He never had.

Tears continued to fall, despite her efforts to stop them. She felt the stares of the other passengers. An older lady leaned over the aisle. "Are you all right, dear?" she inquired kindly.

Rebekka nodded and looked down at the bookmark in her hand, purposely allowing her long hair to hide her face. *Stop it,* she ordered herself. *You'll be a mess when you land. What will Samuel think?*

Dear God, she prayed. *What's wrong with me?*

"You don't have to go, you know," the woman said in a firm voice. "If you're that upset, why don't you stay? Is it really worth it? There's always tomorrow. God's time, you know, is different from ours."

Rebekka lifted her eyes and stared at the woman, whose white hair was cut short and immaculately styled. Wrinkles gathered closely around her eyes, which twinkled with kind understanding. Next to her was an equally aged man who was reading a magazine, one hand clasping his wife's.

Many thoughts went through Rebekka's head as she stared at this loving woman who had so much concern for a complete stranger. Rebekka realized that she wanted the kind of relationship that the woman seemed to share with her companion.

Now that she thought about it, love and companionship were so much more than learning to like five-way chili. Could she develop such a deep and lasting bond with Samuel? Perhaps in everything save religion. But was she willing to forsake her God even that much?

Never.

Her heart felt like it would burst with the pain. No! She could not abandon her God, her Father in Heaven. He meant too much to her.

Then why was she so willing to settle for a relationship that did not fit her eternal plans? She didn't love Samuel, not yet. Given her lingering feelings for Marc, she probably wasn't ready to love anyone else, and pursuing a relationship with Samuel wouldn't be fair to either of them, even if he shared her religious beliefs.

I thought I was free from my obsession with Marc, but I'm not. I still love him, and all this time I've been trying to replace him. She could see it so clearly now: first she had gone after Damon as a substitute because of his similar age, and when that hadn't worked, she had practically fallen into Samuel's arms. Anything not to be alone.

And all because of Marc.

So what now?

I'm a woman, she thought, lifting her chin, still staring at the elderly couple. *Millions of women have dealt with broken hearts. I am strong. I will survive, and I will be happy. I'm not wasting a second more of my life questioning my worth simply because I don't have a man at my side. I am a daughter of God, and I will get down on my knees and pray to be happy. And I will be.*

A strange euphoria filled her, and Rebekka felt light and free. Happy. *The Father does reward those who follow Him,* she thought, acknowledging the source of her happiness. *Forgive me, Father, for not understanding until now.*

She stood abruptly, dragging her flight bag with her. "Thank you," she whispered to the lady. "Thank you so much."

She ran down the aisle and off the plane, stopping to tell the gate attendant that she would not be on the flight. Passengers were still boarding, but Rebekka walked away, not looking back. Taking a deep breath, she went into the rest room to fix her face. She had some honest talking to do with Marc that evening. *I'm through with hinting. I'm going to tell him how I feel and get it out of my system once and for all. Maybe then we can be friends again.* Tears started behind her eyes once again, but this time the melancholy was tempered by a sweet feeling of relief.

She spent a long time in the rest room, collecting her wits and repairing her makeup. When she was almost ready to leave, a blonde woman in an airline uniform came into the room. "Excuse me," she said, "but do you speak French?" At Rebekka's nod, she continued. "Then I really need your help."

* * * * *

Marc looked up not into Brionney's eyes, but Rebekka's. Her thick auburn locks perfectly framed her oval face and did absolutely nothing to hide the red-rimmed eyes. He jumped to his feet in surprise. "But you're—" He glanced out the window where he had seen her plane leave.

"The lady at the desk told me you were here," she said. He couldn't believe how soft and wonderful her voice was, although her French sounded slightly Americanized.

"I was in the ladies' room," Rebekka continued. "She came in a minute ago and said she needed someone who spoke French. Then she pointed me to you."

Marc sent a look of pure gratitude to the lady behind the desk near the gate, who was more observant than he had given her credit for. She smiled at him and turned back to a conversation with a fellow employee.

"Marc, I—" Rebekka began.

But Marc had planned what he would do from the minute he had lost her. He fell to his knees on the worn carpet, taking her hand in his. "Dearest Rebekka, I love you. I didn't know it before, but I do now. That's why I'm here. I've been a darn fool—I know that. Please, please forgive me! I love you, and I want nothing more in this whole world than to marry you!"

Her mouth opened in surprise, and her face suddenly paled. For a moment, Marc thought she would faint. Instead, she eased into the seat he had vacated. She blinked twice, but still didn't speak. Her hand was limp in his grasp.

"I know you might love this Samuel guy, but you love me, too, don't you? Rebekka, I'll spend the rest of my life making you happy, if you'll just give me a chance. I miss you so much!"

"What about my mother?" she asked slowly, pointedly.

Marc knew then that he had lost. If she knew about Danielle, she would never believe that he loved her and not her mother. Yet he had to try. He gripped her hand more tightly. "No, it's always been you, Rebekka. What I felt for Danielle was a young boy's crush, but it was replaced years ago by my feelings for you. And I didn't even know it until you were gone. I swear that's the truth. Everyone knew it—my mom, André, Raoul. And you. Only I was too blind, too scared, too much of an idiot—"

She put her fingers over his lips to silence the words, tears streaming down her face. Leaning forward, she pressed her cheek against his. *Oh, no. Here it comes,* he thought, and knew he deserved every bit of the letdown she would give him.

"Part of me wants to hit you," she said softly, hoarsely, "for all the years I've waited to hear you say those words. Part of me would like to string you up by your toes and leave you there for at least a month . . . without food or water . . ." She pulled away from him slightly, and he could see her grimace. "Or air, for that matter."

He held his breath, waiting for what would come next.

"But I'm not going to waste one more second of our life together." She met his gaze without wavering. "I will marry you, Marc Perrault, and I'll make you the best wife you ever dreamed of." Her bottom lip quivered ever so slightly, and her voice deepened and sounded odd, as though she was fighting tears. "And you'd just better make me the best husband, 'cause you're getting old and you won't have another chance."

Marc couldn't believe his ears. He whooped and caught Rebekka up in his arms, bringing them both to their feet. He hugged her tightly, his happiness suddenly so large and all-encompassing that it threatened to take flight.

She laughed at him, her gray eyes full of love. Why hadn't he seen it before? He held her more tightly, this precious gift. He would love her for as long as they had left in this life, and then forever after.

"Rebekka," he murmured into her hair. Their lips met for a long, searching moment, their first real kiss in the almost twenty years they had known each other. Her skin was incredibly soft, her sweet scent intoxicating. Emotions flooded his entire being, penetrating him to the core. For a brief instant, he felt an aching for the years he had wasted, for the years they had not held each other . . . until the memories of their long friendship washed the pain away. Today wasn't a day for regrets, but a day for looking toward the future. And, like Rebekka, he wasn't going to waste another second of it.

"I see you found her."

Marc reluctantly looked up and saw Brionney watching them, a satisfied smile on her face.

"Yes, and I'm never going to let her go." Marc held Rebekka's hand and gazed at her lovingly. He became aware of other eyes upon them. In fact, everyone around them was staring and smiling their approval.

"Uh, excuse me." It was the gate attendant from the airline desk. "Will you still be needing that flight?"

Marc took his eyes only briefly from Rebekka's face. "No. I guess not."

The blonde lady laughed. "I didn't think so. I already canceled it."

"Boy, you're good," Brionney said admiringly.

The attendant laughed and lowered her voice. "Just don't tell the airline. I'm supposed to sell flights, not cancel them. I'm just sorry I didn't put two and two together until after I sold him the flight in the first place."

"You'll never know how much it means to us," Rebekka said.

"No, but maybe someday I will."

Rebekka touched the attendant's shoulder fleetingly. "It's certainly worth the wait." She looked at Marc again, and he felt himself melt into her gray eyes. His knees were uncharacteristically weak. How long would it take them to get married? Thank heaven they were in Utah, where they had ready access to a temple.

Rebekka must have been thinking the same thing. "Did you bring your recommend?"

He smiled. "I did."

"We'll have to tell our parents. They'll want to be here." She frowned. "My dad won't like not being able to give me away. But I guess he'll have to get used to the idea."

"He's had a long time to get used to it," Marc said gently. "You've been a member a long time."

Brionney clapped her hands together, her short white hair dancing around her like a halo. "Does this mean what I think it does?" When they nodded, she continued exuberantly, "Finally! All the match-making I've been doing has paid off! I can't believe it! Come on, let's get out of here so we can start making plans."

With one arm still possessively about Rebekka, Marc followed Brionney down the wide corridor. He had never felt so content in his entire life.

CHAPTER 35

In the end, Rebekka and Marc discarded the idea of eloping and decided to travel to France to personally announce their pending wedding to their families. Rebekka had especially worried about her mother's reaction if they did elope. "I'm the only daughter she has, and she won't get another chance to plan a wedding." She was relieved when Marc agreed without too much reluctance. Of course, she knew that he found it hard to deny her anything at the moment, and she reveled in his love. She had dreamed of it for so long, and now he was finally hers.

She couldn't stand to be separated from Marc for a moment, and seeing this, Jesse and Damon hired a replacement and gave her a month off, telling the disappointed Samuel that he would have to do without her for a while. Rebekka was grateful for the time, not knowing exactly what her future held, or where she would be in a month . . . except, of course, with Marc. It had always been him. She wondered if any woman in the world had ever been happier.

Rebekka felt her decision to return home to plan their wedding was even more inspired when she received an e-mail from Raoul on Friday morning, the day before their flight to Paris.

Dearest Rebekka,

I'm afraid you will not be content when you learn that Desirée and I have eloped. While her decision not to become a member of the Church or attend meetings with me has broken my heart, I cannot live without her. Please find it in your heart to understand and forgive. Father and Mother have made a fairly happy life together, and I will do the same. André says that I have done wrong, that I am giving up my chance of an eternal family for immediate pleasures. Could it be so? Could I be giving up someone I could love more than Desirée? I cannot believe so, and yet . . .

Rebekka, dear sister, I'm so confused, but I MUST be with her. We eloped to evade her parents as well as our mother. Desirée was afraid this was our only chance, and I had to agree. I am determined to keep up my church attendance, and will pray that she eventually sees the light of the gospel for what it is. I love her. I really do.

Love from your brother,

The Happy Fool

Rebekka mourned Raoul's decision to marry outside the Church, but she didn't blame him. Hadn't she been about to turn to Samuel in the face of Marc's rejection? Yes, she had decided in the end not to pursue the relationship, but she could have so easily boarded that plane and gone to him. Samuel would have loved her and treated her well; of that she was certain. But how long would that have been enough? How long would Raoul and Desirée be happy? Would their differing views split them apart? Would she finally embrace the truth, or would he desert his faith and his family for his wife?

Later that evening, Rebekka was sitting on the couch in Brionney's living room, thinking of Raoul and his dilemma. Her heart was heavy, despite her own happiness. Marc came from the kitchen, where he had been stirring the contents of a boiling pot for Brionney, and settled beside her. "Why so glum?" he asked, encircling her with his arms. Before she could reply, he added, "It's Raoul, isn't it?"

Tears smarted in her eyes, not only because of her worry for her brother, but because of Marc's intuitiveness. They knew each other so well! How could she ever have thought of living without him at her side? His friendship was every bit as important as his newly awakened passion for her.

"It'll be all right," Marc murmured in her ear. "We'll be there to help him. We'll love him no matter what."

She rested her cheek against his shoulder, grateful for his strength, wondering how she had survived these months without his ready grin and constant support. He kissed her cheek and leaned against the back of the couch, pulling her tightly against him. Rebekka felt safe and loved.

Brionney burst into the room with a camera. "I got the film. What a cute picture!" She snapped a few shots. "Great! I'll send you a copy for your album." Taking another quick picture, she darted into the kitchen, where the oven timer had begun shrilling loudly.

"You'd think this was a wedding reception, for all the fuss Brionney's going through." Marc reached out to grab a handful of nuts from a dish on the corner lamp table.

Brionney was having a going-away-engagement party for them; she had invited everyone Rebekka knew, as well as a dozen of their old missionary companions and their families. Except for stopping to nurse the twins, Brionney had done nothing but plan, shop, and bake for the past three days. Jesse laughingly complained that he was having to change altogether too many diapers, and since he never used less than six baby wipes with each diaper—all at the same time—he had stopped at the store to buy five large containers.

Rebekka reached for the nuts, but Marc brought a few to her lips. She licked his fingers, and he kissed her lingeringly. "I wish this *was* our wedding day," he said in a husky voice.

She kissed him back. "Soon." For the first time in her own life, she understood how comforting it was to have a relationship for eternity. Despite their anxiousness to be married, there was no real hurry.

They forgot about the nuts, the party, and even Raoul as they sat blissfully in each other's arms.

* * * * *

Mickelle stopped at the cemetery before going to the party for Marc and Rebekka. Bryan and Jeremy had walked to Brionney's earlier with Tanner and Belle, and she planned to meet them there. Darkness seemed to fall earlier each night, and already the sun had set behind the mountain, obscuring most of its light. She paused for a moment to watch the brilliant reds and purples fade into the darkening sky.

Each day that week she had spent the evening with Damon and his children, and each day she was more and more certain that she was falling in love with him. There had been little opportunity to think, and at times she was so happy that she was afraid it wouldn't last.

And she felt guilty.

That was why she had come to talk to Riley. Since she had been dating Damon, she hadn't been able to talk to Riley at the house, as though the ghost of his presence had fled. But at his grave, she could feel him—an intangible essence, a whisper of his former self, but there all the same.

"I know you might not be happy about this," she explained in the utter stillness of the cemetery, "but it's what I want. I know you loved me once . . .wanted my happiness. Can you understand?"

The small headstone on his grave was covered in shadow. There were flowers there, too—roses like the ones almost dead on her bushes. Had someone visited recently? It was likely Bryan, who had been unusually pensive this week. He hadn't spoken against her growing relationship with Damon as she had feared, but he certainly wasn't as happy about it as Jeremy.

Despite Bryan's apparent reservations, it was good for the boys to have a man around again. Jeremy no longer wet the bed, and both boys adored playing basketball with someone who genuinely enjoyed spending time with them. Damon was so good for them all. If only Riley could understand . . .

Mickelle was the only living person in sight, although she could hear a few birds in the trees, now decked in their bright fall colors. A car or two passed on the road far behind her.

She took a steadying breath. "So, I guess I've come to say I'm sorry about the way your life ended. I loved you so much." She wiped away a stray tear. "I think maybe you are learning just how much I did love you . . . do love you. And I wish more than I can say that things could be different—I really, really do—but since they can't, I need to go on. The boys need to go on." She blinked back a few more tears. "Will you give us your blessing?"

Until that moment, she hadn't understood how deafening silence could be. She felt a wild urge to laugh at herself, at her earnestness in talking to the dead.

Where was her answer? There was no sudden breeze to stir the trees, no light dancing on the headstone or apparition walking on the bright carpet of fallen leaves. But her heart filled with a warm sense of approval. And with love.

Her husband wished her well.

Then his presence was gone, if it had ever been there, and Mickelle walked slowly back to her car. She was startled to find Damon waiting there for her. "I saw the children at Bri's," he said. "I came to give you a lift, but you were pulling away as I drove up to your house. I followed you here." His voice was apologetic, as though to say that he had not meant to intrude upon her privacy.

"Is everything okay?" he added, glancing behind her at the rows of stones on the leaf-covered grass. Now he sounded anxious, and the handsome face that had become so dear to her crinkled in worry.

She smiled and offered her hand. "Everything's fine," she responded quietly. "I just came to say good-bye."

He nodded in understanding, and she was grateful that he didn't demand further explanation. Someday she would share the feelings she had experienced here, but not today. No, she would store these feelings as a buoy against the trials to come. Blending two families certainly wasn't going to be easy, even with a man as wonderful as Damon.

"I know that you loved your husband," he said softly. "I can live with that. And I know you were sealed to him. But I'm not going anywhere, and we have a lot of time to work all that out. I want us to be together forever; I feel that we will."

The warmth in her heart increased, and she hugged him. "What's important now is that we've finally found each other."

"I love you," he answered simply. He returned her embrace with a fervency that said more than words ever could how much he cared for her.

The joy of new love filled Mickelle's heart. Feeling warm and secure, she lifted her head to look at the single star winking in the twilit sky above, and smiled.

ABOUT THE AUTHOR

Rachel Ann Nunes (pronounced *noon-esh*) knew she was going to be a writer when she was 13 years old. She now writes five days a week in a home office with constant interruptions from her five young children. One of her favorite things to do is to take a break from the computer and build a block tower with her two youngest. Several of her children have begun their own novels, and they have fun writing and plotting together.

Rachel enjoys traveling, camping, spending time with her family and reading. She served an LDS mission to Portugal. She and her husband, TJ, and their children live in Utah Valley, where she is a popular speaker for religious and writing groups. *This Time Forever* is her tenth novel to be published by Covenant. Her *Ariana* series is a best-seller in the LDS market.

Rachel enjoys hearing from her readers. You can write to her at P.O. Box 353, American Fork, UT 84003-0353, send e-mail to rachel@ranunes.com, or visit her website at http://www.ranunes.com.